THE OPPORTUNIST

by

Bill Rogers

CATON

ALSO BY BILL ROGERS

DCI TOM CATON
MANCHESTER MURDER MYSTERIES

The Cleansing
The Head Case
The Tiger's Cave
A Fatal Intervention
Bluebell Hollow
A Trace of Blood
The Frozen Contract
Backwash
A Venetian Moon
Angel Meadow
The Girl and the Shadowman

JOANNE STUART
NATIONAL CRIME AGENCY SERIES

The Pick, The Spade and the Crow
The Falcon Tattoo
The Tangled Lock
The Blow Out

INDIVIDUAL WORKS

Teenage and Young Adult Fiction
The Cave

Short Crime Stories
Breakfast at Katsouris

Eight walks based on the
Manchester Murder Mysteries
Caton's Manchester

A CIP record for this book is available
from the British Library.

Published by Caton Books

Paperback ISBN: 978-1-909856-22-6

Cover Design: @blacksheep-uk.com
Design and Layout: Commercial Campaigns
Editor: Monica Byles

First published January 2020
Copyright © Bill Rogers
First Edition

Dedication

This book is dedicated to the memory of Martin Flatman, OBE, who passed away on 2 April 2020.

Martin, who was a friend and former colleague of myself and my wife, was one of the first people to die of Covid-19 in Manchester. He graciously allowed me to use his name for the eponymous Home Office pathologist Professor Flatman in the DCI Caton series. Martin was nothing like the character I created. His personal faith shaped his life and fuelled his passion for education, and especially for vulnerable children. Long after he had retired from a distinguished career, he continued to set up support systems for excluded and struggling pupils, and gave his own time as a volunteer providing one-to-one support and mentoring in schools. Martin was one of the kindest, most inspirational people we have ever had the privilege to know or to work with. We will all miss his unfailing optimism, humour and kindness.

Martin would have wished me to acknowledge NHS staff, carers in homes and the community, as well as members of the teaching profession who worked tirelessly to develop new ways of bringing the gift of learning to their pupils, while at the same time providing a lifeline to families in dire need. Recognition is due to all key workers and volunteers whose selfless service is supporting us through this pandemic. May we keep in our thoughts and prayers those whom the virus took, and those who mourn them.

'There is thy gold, worse poison to men's souls,
Doing more murder in this loathsome world,
Than these poor compounds that thou
mayst not sell.'

William Shakespeare – Romeo and Juliet

Chapter 1
Sunday 5th April 2020

The Observer lay on the mat in the hall. Caton slid a pair of nitrile gloves from the radiator shelf, slipped them on, and stooped to pick it up. He glanced at the headlines.

> *Queen to address the Nation*
> *Police 'Stay at home' plea*
> *Labour leader criticises Government's virus response*
> *Parts of the nation enjoy hottest weekend in six months*

A different kind of killer stalked the streets of Manchester. Silent, invisible and indiscriminate. Victims chosen at random. With every pub and club closed down, serious assaults resulting in manslaughter or murder had almost dried up. But the domestic abuse team were working flat out, and there was no telling what might be happening behind closed doors. Caton sighed, folded the paper in half and headed for the kitchen.

There was laughter in the lounge where Kate, Emily and Larissa, in their third week of lockdown, were attempting another online workout for kids. With the university closed, Kate was providing online support for her postgrad students and assessing work. She was also on call in her role as a Home Office profiler, but even that seemed to have dried up. As for Caton, although he was still at work, his syndicate hadn't had a single new investigation for over two weeks, and it was beginning to feel as though they were treading water.

He placed the newspaper on the draining board, opened the cupboard under the sink, and withdrew a tub of alcohol wipes. Then he shrugged his gloves into the sink, and turned his attention to breakfast.

He tipped his usual quantity of oats into a pan, took a handful of nuts, blitzed them until they resembled a fine flour, and added those too, along with a thinly sliced banana. He poured in some milk, and set the pan on the stove over a low gas. Then he slipped his gloves back on, picked up the paper and the wipes, and went out into the garden.

He was struck, as he had been every morning since lockdown began, by the uplifting chorus of birdsong. That, and the absence of any other sound at all, not least the irritating hum of traffic on the M60 and the A34. Traffic was down by over sixty per cent – the lowest it had been since 1955, when Ruth Ellis had been hanged and Anthony Eden had replaced Winston Churchill as prime minister. The result had been a dramatic improvement in air quality, so much so that Caton, just for the hell of it, had been driving to work with the car windows down.

Placing the paper on the wrought-iron table on the patio, he wiped along the four edges and across the centre, then flipped the paper over to repeat the process. The pair of resident wood pigeons were nowhere in view, so he left the newspaper to dry and headed back into the kitchen, where he placed the gloves in the sink, washed his hands while singing 'Happy Birthday' twice, and then checked the pan. He added a dollop of yogurt, poured his breakfast into a dish, and sat at the table.

His laptop lay ready for the Zoom call he had promised his son. Only two weeks in, and already lockdown was proving hard for Harry. Emily, on the other hand, was revelling in all the extra time with Kate and Larissa, and even seeing a little more of her dad than usual, but poor old Harry had only his mum, Helen, for company.

Caton had been feeling increasingly bad about not being there enough for his boy. The enforced separation of lockdown hadn't helped. He knew these feelings of guilt were unwarranted. After all, Helen had made the decision to keep Harry's existence secret for over seven years. Had it not been for that chance meeting in Albert Square, Caton would still have been none the wiser. And he'd had to fight tooth and nail to persuade her to allow him contact with his son. Now, six years on, Harry was well and truly a part of his family, albeit that they lived twenty miles apart. It was inevitable that Caton was going to feel guilty, and there was nothing he could do about it. The phone in the hall rang.

'I'll get it!' shouted Kate.

He guessed from her expression as she entered the kitchen, the drop of her shoulders, the phone thrust out like an accusation.

'It's Assistant Chief Constable Gates,' she said. 'Apparently, it's urgent.'

Caton took the phone. He mouthed 'Sorry,' but she had already turned her back, and was heading for the lounge.

Chapter 2

'Ma'am?' he said.

'I'm sorry, Tom,' she replied, 'I know it's Sunday, but your syndicate's on call, and this isn't something I can leave Division to deal with. And I think I'm right in saying that you have two completed investigations awaiting due process that are currently stalled until the Crown Courts come out of lockdown?'

'Unless they decide to dispense with trial by jury, that is.'

'Well, that's not going to happen any time soon. And you have that cut and dried manslaughter case that just needs the i's dotting and t's crossing?'

'Yes, Ma'am.'

'Good. In that case you'll be pleased to learn that there's been a report of a suspicious death. A woman living on her own, in Stretford . . .'

Pleased to learn? Caton hoped she wasn't serious. He still found a great deal of satisfaction in his work, but seizing a challenge wasn't the same thing as wishing someone dead. Never had been, never would be.

'. . . because,' she continued, 'Syndicate Two has that young man found floating in the canal, three rapes, and two Section 18s to contend with. Syndicate Three is tied up with a murder-slash-manslaughter case, on top of a domestic murder slash murder. Syndicate Four has that horrific infant homicide ongoing, three rapes, and one manslaughter. And Syndicate Five has one domestic murder, and one domestic attempted murder. Ergo, this one is definitely yours.'

There was no arguing with that.

'Yes, Ma'am,' he said.

'Good, then can you get over there ASAP? By the way, I've got some actual good news for you.'

It would be the first in a long time, Caton reflected.

'Given the scale of depletion in the force due to the number of officers in self-isolation or quarantine, the Chief Constable has been recalling all officers on secondment to the College of Policing and other forces. Consequently, the Chief Constable has informed the National Crime Agency that he'd like Detective Inspector Stuart's secondment to end so she can return to her role with FMIT.'

Now that *was* good news.

'And DI Stuart's happy with that?' he asked.

'As it happens,' Gates said, 'I've spoken with her myself and she's delighted. Not that she had a choice. She'll be joining DCI Holmes' syndicate as from today.'

That was not what Caton had been expecting, or hoping.

She picked up on his hesitation. 'What's the matter, Tom? You don't approve?'

'It's not that,' he replied, 'it's just that I was assuming she'd be rejoining my team, and it might be an opportunity for DI Carter to step up as part of Gordon's team. They've always worked well together,' he added, although he knew that it sounded lame.

'Not a problem.' She sounded uncharacteristically smug. 'Carter's promotion has just been made permanent, on my recommendation, so he can continue as your deputy senior investigating officer. Gordon is a detective chief inspector down and really up against it. As for the two of them working together, while you were away at the College of Policing, they cooperated closely on two operations, her at the NCA, him here with GMP.

As I remember, they got on like a house on fire. Besides, as good as DCI Holmes is, it won't do any harm for him to have her on his team.' She chuckled. 'The Government doesn't have a monopoly on nudge theory, you know.'

Caton sensed her smirking on the other end of the line. She was really enjoying this. He was silent as he digested the news. He had missed working with Joanne Stuart and would have relished doing so again, but was pleased for Nick Carter. He had a feeling this was just a stepping stone for Jo to get her own syndicate before too long. She deserved it and was more than ready. He was disappointed that Helen hadn't run it past him first, but these were anything but normal times.

'You do approve?' she said, in that uncanny way she had of reading his mind.

'Of course I do, Ma'am,' he told her. 'Carter's well capable and he's waited long enough. And DI Stuart and DCI Holmes will make a great team.'

'Good. In that case, there's no more to be said. You'd best get over there. I've sent you the address. Good luck.'

'Excuse me, Ma'am,' he said, 'what exactly is this shout?'

But she had gone.

'Thank you, Ma'am,' he said. He closed the laptop and pushed his plate away.

Chapter 3

Caton had never known the motorway this quiet, not even in the middle of the night in the heart of winter.

Those vehicles still in evidence were of a type. Almost exclusively courier vans, wholesale lorries restocking supermarkets, and ambulances. He closed in on a taxi crawling along the inside lane. As they drew level, the driver looked across. The eyes, above a pale blue mask, seemed wary, almost fearful, and not just because of the strobing blue lights he'd have seen in his rear-view mirror.

Two ambulances sped past, one on either side of the carriageway. In the four miles between home and the crime scene, he counted several more, plus three marked police cars. He hadn't seen this many emergency services on the streets in years. Perhaps, he reasoned, they just stood out more now that the only other vehicles were those of essential workers.

He drove down the slipway onto Chester Road. An officer in uniform, along with a PCSO, both on mountain bikes, were remonstrating with a group of youths kicking a ball around on Crossford Bridge playing fields. He recalled hearing that there had been over one thousand breaches of the Covid-19 regulations in the force area since Friday alone, and that sixty-six house parties had been broken up over the weekend. How many more deaths would it take, he wondered, before they got the message? Bitter experience had taught him that there would always be those who thought the rules didn't apply to them, or simply didn't care. Gordon Holmes had reminded him on more than one occasion that if they did suddenly start caring, there'd be no need for the police and they'd both be out of a job. A silver lining, according to Gordon, but then he was looking forward to retirement.

Caton drove under the motorway and up to the roundabout, where he doubled back and turned left into the estate.

Here was an eclectic assortment of well-proportioned Edwardian houses, former council houses built either side of the Second World War, and a handful of newer flats and maisonettes. No sign of life. Overgrown verges bleached by the unseasonable drought. He would not have been at all surprised to see tumbleweed come drifting down the street towards him.

His satnav directed him to a tree-lined cul-de-sac at the back of the estate. White-rendered, attached bungalows with red roofs were arranged in rows of four, each pair separated by a large wooden gated archway. The last time he had seen something resembling this had been stone-built almshouses in a Cotswold village. One of the gates was open. Through it he glimpsed a garden, and beyond the fence mature woodland.

Two uniformed officers were standing two metres apart in the middle of the road. They flagged him down, and indicated that he should pull into the kerb beside a cordon tape strung between two trees.

The elder of the two policemen lifted a mask from below his chin, and secured it over his mouth and nose. Caton took a fresh mask of his own from a pack in the glove box, put it on and secured it behind each ear. This had become an inconvenient ritual, one he had quickly come to hate. It wasn't so much the discomfort, nor even the added layer of difficulty it meant for face-to-face communication, but rather the constant reminder that accompanied it. The invisible menace behind every human contact.

The officer stood well back on the verge, tablet in hand.

Caton held up his ID. 'Detective Chief Inspector Caton,' he said. 'I'm the SIO.'

'Thank you, Sir,' the officer said, entering the details. 'If you could keep to the path, please. You'll find sets of coveralls by the front gate. I've been asked to remind everyone to dispose of them in the box provided when you leave.'

He didn't wait for a reply, but moved smartly away. Just another reminder that infection was a two-way street.

Chapter 4

There were four people standing by the doorway. He recognised them all, in spite of the protective Tyvek suits, hoods and masks.

DI Carter and DS Carly Whittle were standing with appropriate social distancing to one side of the garden path, with Jack Benson, the crime scene manager, and Mark Patterson, the newly appointed young medical examiner for the force, on the other. Caton adjusted his hood and went to meet them.

'What's all this?' he said. 'Are you waiting for me or are you too frightened to go inside?'

'Both,' said Carter. He sounded serious.

Caton instantly regretted his levity. 'Sorry,' he said. 'What are we looking at?'

'The deceased is a Millie Dyer,' Carter began. 'Seventy years of age, widowed, living on her own. Been in self-isolation from before the lockdown began. Keeps herself to herself, according to neighbours. She has one child – a son living in Cape Town. Generally in good health, apart from needing reading glasses and hearing aids, and well capable of independent living. Her neighbours on this side' – he pointed to his right – 'are a youngish family. They offered, early doors, before the start of lockdown, to run errands for her, collect her prescriptions, etcetera. She said thanks, but she was fine for the moment. They gave her their phone number and said to call if she needed anything. Her son's been calling her every other day. She was one of the old school – no computer, and insisted on paying for everything by cash or cheque. Her only concession to the twenty-first century was council tax, gas and electricity paid by direct debit. When the son called yesterday, and she didn't pick up, he assumed she'd fallen asleep or forgotten to put her hearing aids in. He rang again this morning at . . .'

'Eight p.m. our time,' Carly Whittle supplied.

Carter nodded. 'Eight p.m. And when she still didn't respond, he rang the neighbours. They couldn't raise her, so they rang 999. A local patrol officer forced entry, and found life extinct. There was no sign of forced entry or disturbance of any kind, and no evidence of assault. He called 111; they called her GP. She came straight over, and after examining the deceased stated that she wasn't willing to provide a medical certificate as to the cause of death, and advised the constable that she was concerned it might be suspicious. That's when we got the call.'

He pointed to a figure sat on the neighbours' garden wall. 'The GP's over there if you want to speak with her.'

Caton did. Carter caught her eye and waved her over.

'How long have you been here, Nick?' Caton asked, while they waited for her to arrive.

Carter pulled back the cuff of his Tyvek, and checked his watch.

'I arrived at nine-thirty.' He looked at DS Whittle. 'You were what, Carly? Ten minutes after that?'

She nodded her agreement. 'Nine forty-one,' she said.

Caton checked his own watch. 'And you got all that information in less than fifteen minutes? I'm impressed.'

The GP stopped halfway up the path.

'This is Doctor Karcher,' Carter said. 'Doctor, this Detective Chief Inspector Caton. He's the Senior Investigating Officer on this case. I've just been explaining

17

that you were Mrs Dyer's GP, and you're the reason we're here.'

She was under five foot tall and what Kate would describe as petite, although it was difficult to tell under a protective coverall two sizes too big for her. All that was visible of her face was a stray wisp of black hair that had escaped the hood, and a pair of serious eyes the colour of ochre. It wasn't much to go on but Caton suspected that she was close to thirty years of age and therefore relatively new to her role. Not that he was judging. Sometimes new blood in any profession brought up-to-date ideas and protocols, and a necessarily disciplined and cautious approach.

'Doctor Karcher,' he said, 'thank you for waiting. I've been told you were unwilling to provide a medical certificate as to cause of death. Why was that?'

Despite the distance between them and the mask, her voice was strong and confident.

'When I took the call from your officer,' she said, 'I was immediately concerned. Mrs Dyer came to the surgery for regular checks. Her last such appointment was back in November. She had no underlying health problems, other than early signs of osteoporosis. Not even diabetes or high blood pressure, which was unusual given her age. Your officer mentioned coronavirus, but in that case, I'd have expected some early symptoms that might have led her to contact us. When I checked, there was no record of her having recently rung 111 or the surgery. That led me to believe it was unlikely to be Covid-related, but I knew that even so, it would take a post-mortem to confirm it. Such is the current pressure on mortuaries, however, there was no certainty when, if ever, that would take place. That was why I told him I'd come out straight away.'

'And when you examined the deceased, what was it that made you think her death might be suspicious?'

'My initial suspicion,' she said, 'was that Mrs Dyer might have had suffered a cardiovascular arrest. However, when I looked more closely, I noticed that her colouring was way off.'

'In what way?' Dr Patterson asked.

'There were traces of cherry red in her cheeks, indicative of high levels of oxygen in her blood at the time of death – the exact opposite of what you'd expect of a Covid-19 patient. And she'd been sick.'

'You're thinking poison?' the FME said.

'Possibly. My first thought was carbon monoxide, but the boiler was off. There were no appliances on at all. And she has one of those CO_2 detectors on the mantle that the fire service provides for senior citizens. I checked and the reading was normal. Then I looked more closely and noticed that where the blood had settled on the underside of her arms, the lividity had a brick-red cast.'

'Potassium cyanide?' Patterson suggested.

Karcher shrugged. 'That did occur to me,' she said, 'although I've never seen a case myself.'

'I have,' Patterson said, 'two years ago. Dr Tompkins was assisting Professor Flatman. I was observing as part of my training. The deceased was a silversmith. He'd been using cyanide in an electroplating bath. The inquest found that the deceased had failed to use adequate ventilation, a respirator or protective clothing. He inhaled cyanide in mist form and it was also absorbed through his skin.'

'That's not what happened here though,' said the GP. 'I'd say that whatever it is, she ingested it.'

'It'll take a post-mortem to confirm or rule it out,' said Patterson, 'but as it's now part of a police investigation, there's unlikely to be any hold-up.'

'How long do you think she's been dead, Doctor?' Caton asked.

'At least twenty-four hours,' she replied, 'but probably two or three days.'

Caton nodded.

'What are you thinking, Boss?' Carter asked.

By way of answer, Caton turned to Jack Benson. 'I assume you've done a risk assessment?' he said. 'Is it safe for us to do a walk-through and let Dr Patterson here take a look?'

'It had better be,' said Dr Karcher, 'or I'm doomed.'

Patterson mistook her attempt at a joke for an appeal for reassurance.

'You *were* wearing PPE when you examined her?' he said.

'Of course,' she replied sharply, 'it is standard practice for home visits of any kind during the pandemic.'

Benson jumped in. 'It won't be a problem, Sir,' he said, 'so long as everyone keeps their hands away from their face at all times, bins their gloves, mask and coveralls, washes their hands, and uses the sanitiser on the table beside the bin before they leave. Much the same as for Covid-19. But could you give me a few minutes for my team to finish gathering the photographic and video evidence?'

He started to enter the house, and then turned back.

'Don't forget,' he said, 'only two at a time, and observe strict social distancing.'

Chapter 5

It was hot and oppressive in the small conservatory. The nauseating stench of vomit didn't help.

The deceased wore a pink short-sleeved blouse over navy blue cotton trousers. On her feet were a pair of plain grey slippers. She was lying on the floor on her right side, beside a chair, her left arm extended in front of her, as though pointing. Three feet away lay a phone, that Caton guessed must have been knocked from her grasp as she fell. Her glasses had slipped forwards, and were barely hanging on. The righthand lens was broken.

The FME crouched down, obscuring the upper half of her body. When he had finished, he stepped back and sideways to allow Caton to take his place.

Millie Dyer's hands and face had a slight sheen, and the cherry-red colour the GP had mentioned was evident on her cheeks, and in blotches on her forearms. Her mouth was open, and he could see a pink-tinged scum on her teeth. The carpet to the left of the body was soiled with a large dry patch of regurgitated stomach contents.

Caton stood up and looked around. A book lay open on a small table beside the chair. Beside it was a half-empty glass of water, and a plate on which sat a toasted teacake, untouched, unless you counted the blowflies.

Caton left the FME with the body and went through to the kitchen.

Millie Dyer had been house-proud. The surfaces gleamed; the windows sparkled. Other than a few crumbs around the toaster, everywhere was neat and tidy. Pots of herbs and houseplants on the window ledge had dried out and were beginning to wilt.

Caton opened the dishwasher. It was empty. The fridge was adequately stocked with the sort of products he would have expected. The two-litre container of milk was labelled long-life, so he didn't bother with checking to see if the milk was off.

He turned his attention now to the cupboards. Three contained pots and pans and cake tins. One held packets of cereal and pasta. The one that held his attention was a medicine cabinet. On the top shelf were spray-on suntan lotions and aftersun moisturiser. The next one down had plasters, bandages and an old-fashioned mercury thermometer. On the remaining shelves sat a bottle of mouthwash, and a variety of boxes of pills, including a low dose child's analgesic and two packets of a popular generic painkiller. The only one with a prescription label was a large bottle of Vitamin D tablets. Caton closed the cupboard, and went to check the two bedrooms and the bathroom.

Both bedrooms were as orderly and spotless as the rest of the house. The wallpaper, curtains and ornaments were too fussy for his taste, but exactly right for a widow of her generation. He had a moment of déjà vu, and then realised it was because they reminded him so much of his aunt's house during her later years.

On the bedside cabinet in the larger of the two bedrooms was another book, *Still Alice* by Lisa Genova. Beside it lay a box of prescription medicines. Caton crouched down and read the label. They were *statin 10mg tablets*. He stood up and went back through to the conservatory, and then waited in the doorway for the FME to finish his examination.

Patterson closed his bag and turned to face him.

'So what have you got for me?' Caton asked.

'I concur with the GP's assessment,' he replied. 'It's definitely suspicious. The fact that she's been violently sick. That pink tinge you can see. And the remaining areas of post-mortem lividity – or hypostasis – are brick red, which is indicative of cyanide. Poisoning is a distinct possibility.'

'What about the time of death?'

'The heating thermostat on the wall in the hall is set to manual, and it's on twenty degrees. The temperature in here will never have fallen below twenty, and given the hot spell we've had for the past week it will have reached maybe twenty-two to twenty-three during the day. Given the deceased's internal temperature, the fact that such maggots as I've found are between the first and second instar developmental stage, and that she's just about to enter the bloat state of decomposition, I would say that she's been dead close to three days. So, seventy-two hours or thereabouts.'

Caton led the way outside. Nick Carter and Carly Whittle were waiting for their turn to go in. It wasn't strictly necessary that they see the body in situ, especially given all the photographic and video evidence Benson had collected, but Caton knew there was nothing like first-hand experience, up close and personal. He addressed the GP.

'You said she had no underlying health problems, but she appears to have been on statins?'

'That is correct. Our practice took the decision, as a preventative measure, to prescribe those automatically to anyone over sixty-five.'

'And you also prescribed Vitamin D tablets?'

'For age-related osteoarthritis, but that doesn't count as a health problem with significance for a raised risk with Covid-19.'

'Why would she have a low dose NSAID?'

Dr Karcher shook her head. 'I have no idea. I can only assume she decided to self-medicate.'

'I expect you can't wait to get back to the surgery?' Caton said.

'Actually, I do have a backlog of video appointments and telephone consultations,' she told him, 'so, yes, I'd appreciate it if could get back, unless there's anything else?'

'No, that's fine,' he said. 'You've been really helpful, Doctor. If you'd not agreed to come out, this could have slipped through the net, so thank you very much.'

'It's my job,' she said, 'and I'm not going to let this bloody virus stop me from doing it.'

Caton was impressed. He had to stop himself from saying something she might read as patronising. Fortunately, she had turned away and was already beginning to unzip her Tyvek as she headed towards the gate.

'I'm sorry about your patient,' he called after her.

She stopped, pulled the hood down, carefully slipped the mask from around her ears and turned back to look at him. She was of Mediterranean appearance. IC2 – Spanish, Italian, maybe Greek.

'Me too,' she said.

'Mr Caton?' Jack Benson was standing under the archway between the adjoining houses. 'Are we okay to go back in?'

'As soon as Nick and Carly come out,' Caton replied. 'I'll hurry them up. When you do go in, continue to treat it as a crime scene, pending the results of the post-mortem. And you'd better preserve all evidence as potentially contaminated until proven otherwise. Oh yes, and make sure you bag up all of her meds. We're going to leave the deceased in situ until I've spoken with the duty Home Office pathologist.'

'That'll be Dr Tompkins,' Patterson told him, from the opposite side of the garden. 'Do you want me to give her a call?'

'Please,' Caton replied. 'Ask if she needs to see the body in situ? If not, can she get the coroner's permission to move the body, and if so where to. Oh, and given the circumstances, what precautions need to be taken. Then finally, ask her how soon she can perform the post-mortem.'

The crime scene manager went to his van to make the call.

'Boss!'

Carter was standing in the hallway, gesticulating for Caton to move further away so that he and his DS could come outside. Caton walked towards the bottom righthand corner of the garden, and waited for them to join him at a safe distance.

'What do you reckon?' Caton said.

'Difficult to tell,' Carter said, 'but if the medics are saying poison, who are we to disagree?'

'Well, if it was poison, I don't see anything to suggest that it was suicide, do you?'

Carter and Carly Whittle shook their heads in unison.

'In which case,' Caton said, 'we do a door to door and see what passive media we can get, and if any of the neighbours have spotted anyone calling on her in recent days. Start with those neighbours who offered to pick up her prescriptions. We also need to know the details of every vehicle owned by residents so we can eliminate them from our enquiries. And let's get a record of all calls to and from her landline and her mobile over the past three months, plus, details of all of her contacts.'

They were dropping their Tyvek coveralls in the bin when Patterson approached.

'It's Dr Tompkins,' he said. 'She'd like a word.' He held out his phone.

Caton stared at it as if it were a burning coal.

'Don't worry,' Patterson said, 'I've given it a once-over with an alcohol wipe and put it on speakerphone. Just hold it away from your face.'

None of this filled Caton with confidence.

'Are you there, Detective Chief Inspector?' said Carol Tompkins.

'Sorry, yes I am,' said Caton, holding the phone at arm's length.

'Confirmed and suspected Covid-19 deaths are being fast-tracked by the coroner,' she told him, 'and, ironically, there are fewer non-Covid-related suspicious deaths than normal. I can therefore perform a post-mortem for you first thing tomorrow morning. Will that do?'

'Thank you, Doctor,' he said. 'It would be helpful to know what we're dealing with as soon as possible.'

'How long has she been dead?' the pathologist asked.

'Did Dr Patterson not tell you?'

'I wouldn't be asking if he had, would I?'

Some detective I am, thought Caton. 'FME says seventy-two hours, give or take,' he said.

'Then your golden hour is long gone,' she said. Before he could protest, she added, 'Fear not, I'll do what I can. The sooner you get her here though, the better. Tell Dr Patterson to speak with the coroner and arrange for the body to be taken straight to the morgue.'

'Thank you,' he said. But she had already ended the call. A lot of people seemed to be doing that these days. He handed back the phone and went in search of the sanitiser.

Chapter 6

On the way to Nexus House, Caton decided to call Helen Malone, the mother of his son.

'Tom . . . it's you,' she said.

She sounded jumpy, as though she'd been expecting an unwelcome call from someone else.

'Can I have a word with Harry?' he said. 'I wanted to explain, and apologise for missing our video call.'

'No need,' she replied. 'Kate told me, so I've already explained. Besides, he's used to it.'

Caton's fingers tightened around the steering wheel. 'It?' he said.

'Your job. The frequent disappointments. It goes with the territory. He knows that.'

Frequent? Caton nearly fell into the trap, but he knew where this was going. Him accusing her of gross exaggeration, her quoting chapter and verse. The more he countered her examples, the angrier she would become. One or other of them would end the call mid-skirmish. And where would that leave Harry? Who quite possibly was listening in on the extension upstairs?

'I would still like to tell him myself, Helen,' he said.

'Well, you can't,' she told him. 'He's in the middle of an online maths lesson.'

'On a Sunday?'

'It's the only way that Mr Rigby can fit them all in. It's good that his teachers are going above and beyond.'

But not me, thought Caton. 'How are you both coping?' he asked.

'I've been furloughed,' she told him. 'They say there won't be any football for at least three months. Even then it might have to be behind closed doors. I'm just doing the odd press release, and I can do that from home.'

'And Harry?'

'It's not easy,' she said, 'just him and me, twenty-four seven.'

'He has his online lessons though. Have you tried doing online exercise classes together? He'd love that.'

'I'll check it out,' she said.

Caton was not convinced.'Tell Harry I'll call him later,' he said.

'Don't, Tom' she said.

'Don't what?'

'Don't make promises you can't keep.'

It was a fair point, much as he hated acknowledging the fact.

'Tell him I called,' he said.

'I will.'

'Stay safe,' he told her.

'Bye,' she said.

Caton now had another reason to feel guilty. That he was actually counting his blessings that Helen had kept her pregnancy secret. Being Caton, he would have felt impelled to ask her to marry him, and persisted until she agreed. What a disaster that would have been. He still liked Helen, and he understood why he had been attracted to her in the first place, but it had become increasingly evident that she was a glass half-empty person, and fragile. They were only a couple of weeks into lockdown and she was already on the way to meltdown. He didn't want to contemplate how it might have ended if they'd been trapped in that house together for months on end. Like Harry was. Dammit!

Chapter 7

Caton had to do a double take. He had forgotten that this was the Nexus House 'new normal'.

Every third workstation had gone into storage. The remaining ones were spaced at two-metre intervals, or had head-height partitions separating them into carrels. Hand sanitiser pumps had replaced the shared kettle, toaster and microwave. Each workstation had a tub of alcohol wipes to clean the desk, phone, keyboard, mouse, screen and chairs at the end of every period of sustained use. A large National Police Chiefs' Council wallchart set out the different regulations regarding PPE for inside duties and outside/public-facing duties. A poster declared that sharing desks was strictly forbidden, and the same went for sharing cars, except in designated bubbles and in extremis, and even then, with surgical masks and gloves. There was even a one-way system in operation around the room. Everyone had their own pack of disposable masks and gloves that they had to carry at all times.

Handwashing on entering and leaving was strictly enforced by Ged, the syndicate's formidable office manager. Her title was Administration Officer, but everyone knew she was so much more than that. All of this was down to her. How she had managed to source all of the PPE, wipes and gels, Caton had no idea. He hadn't dared ask. He was scrupulously washing his hands when she approached.

'DS Hulme informed me about Operation Pendle Hill,' she said. 'I've begun setting up all of the standard administration procedures. I can see only one obvious challenge thus far.'

That was something else he loved about Ged – always challenges, never problems.

'Go on,' he said, shaking his hands and drying them on a paper towel.

'As of this morning,' she told him, 'two of the team are off self-isolating following confirmation of close contact with confirmed cases. Nothing to do with us. Family members apparently. I've arranged for them both to be tested, just in case.'

Caton dropped the towel in the waste bin.

'Are either of them showing any symptoms?'

'Not at the moment, thank heavens, or else we might all have to go into quarantine and work from home.'

That would be a first, he mused. *A murder investigation carried out entirely on Zoom.*

'Well done with all this,' he said. 'It looks about as safe as it could possibly be.'

She smiled. 'Let's hope so.'

Caton went over to Detective Sergeant Jimmy Hulme's workstation. Jimmy pushed his chair back and grinned up at him.

'Pendle Hill,' he said. 'I told you that computer had a sense of humour.'

'How so?' said Caton.

'The Pendle Witches? This case has magic written all over it. Death by poison? Doors locked? No sign of illegal entry?' He raised his eyebrows. 'Definitely mysterious and supernatural forces at work.'

'I hope not.' Caton pointed to Hulme's monitor screen. 'Is this the Enquiry Management flow chart?'

'Yes, Boss, I'm halfway through it.'

'In that case,' said Caton, 'Make a note that we need someone to find out everything there is to know about cyanide poisoning, and allocate two of the team to deal with the passive media analysis as soon as it starts to come in. I'm going to talk to the deceased's son and let him know that his mother has passed away. I need him to tell me all about her, and any friends, acquaintances, or other contacts she may have had. Let's hope she was chattier with him than she seems to have been with her neighbours.'

Several of the team were standing up and had started to applaud. Caton followed their eyes to the door, where Joanne Stuart stood, pretending to be embarrassed.

'Settle down, settle down,' Caton said. 'It's not exactly Beyoncé, is it?'

He pointed towards the sink, and beckoned for his former DI to meet him there.

'This is different, Boss.' She turned on the tap with her elbow, and began to wash her hands. 'You were never this particular before.'

'Good to see you too, Jo,' Caton replied. 'Welcome back, by the way.'

He waited until she'd finished, and then led her through to his office. They had to pause by every other workstation because all the old-timers had wanted to say hello. Caton took this opportunity to see how she had changed.

Her hair was longer. He guessed that was because the virus had closed down all of the hairdressers some weeks ago. She had put on a little weight, although it suited her, probably because it was almost certainly muscle rather than fat. He remembered Gordon telling him that she'd taken up Krav Maga, and become a skilled exponent of the Israeli Defence Forces' martial art. He made a mental note not to offer to join her in a workout once the gyms were open again. But then, who was he

31

kidding? She had a good ten years or more on him.

'You take the seat by the coffee table,' he told her, 'and I'll sit at my desk. You'd better leave the door open too. That way we won't need to wear our masks.'

'I hate all this,' she said. 'They should have called it *anti*social distancing.'

'How does it feel to be back?' he asked.

'Strange,' she told him. 'Although that's as much to do with this Covid-19 business, as the fact that I'll be working with Gordon and not with you.'

'That won't be a problem, will it?'

'Not at all,' she said. 'Gordon and I have worked on a few cases since I began my secondment to the NCA, not to mention all those years together in your syndicate. He's a good boss. He learned a lot from you.' She smiled. 'As did I.'

'And me from both of you,' Caton said. 'I'm sorry you're not going to be on my team, Jo, but I've no doubt our paths will cross. How did you find it working for the NCA?'

She pursed her lips. 'Let's just say it was . . . interesting. In some ways it was a lot less formal, and the team I was with had a lot more autonomy. It was a real odd mix of characters too – more like the way I imagine the FBI profilers to be.'

'I heard they sent you to the Killing House at Sterling Lines?'

She nodded vigorously and her eyes lit up. 'Now that was something else! Like GMP's firearms course on steroids.'

'I don't suppose you missed the politics?'

'They have plenty of their own,' she told him. 'And they're into reorganisation just as much as GMP. My team, the BSU, is being closed down on the Quays and sent to join their Behavioural Investigative Support team in London. That's another reason I was pleased when I heard my secondment had been cut short.'

'You're looking good,' he said. 'Keeping up the Krav Maga?'

'You heard about that?'

He grinned. 'Everybody's heard about it. Possibly something to do with that photo of you with your black belt in the force magazine?'

She looked surprised. 'There was a photo in *Brief*? First I've heard of it. Someone at the gym must have put it out there without my knowing. That's really embarrassing. I suppose I'm going to have put up with a load of jokes from the knuckleheads.'

'Nothing you can't handle,' he said. 'Is your gym still open?'

She shook her head. 'It closed last week. That photo was taken a couple of months back. How about you, are you still going to the Y Club?'

'I was having trouble finding the time even before it shut,' he told her ruefully.

'That'll be why you're piling the weight on.'

'Piling the weight on, *Boss*,' he said.

She grinned. 'Only you're not my Boss now, are you, Sir?'

Caton laughed. 'I see you haven't changed, Jo.'

'Tell me about GMP under lockdown?' she said. 'Has it made much difference?'

Caton sighed. 'Where do I start? It's like the landscape shifted beneath us as soon as the lockdown started. Deaths due to drunkenness are down, simply because the pubs are closed. Rapes and burglary are both forty per cent down. On the other hand, domestic violence incidents doubled in the first two weeks, including murder and attempted murder – that's why you've been recalled. But it's been even worse for uniformed officers. There's been a surge in antisocial behaviour, mostly to do with younger people ignoring the restrictions. People have even started lockdown-shaming neighbours and rivals as a form of revenge.'

Jo grimaced. 'I saw the reports of NHS staff being mugged for their lanyards so people could get preferential access to supermarkets,' she said. 'And idiots leaving lit barbecues on the moors. Not to mention those youths in a car spitting at officers, and shouting "Corona! Corona!"'

'How has it affected the NCA?' he asked.

'They've had to step up their support for regional serious crime units. The drug dealers have been facing supply shortages and county lines were badly hit by the travel restrictions, so instead they've started using kids on mountain bikes to distribute benzodiazepines and Fentanyl. The worst of it is, there's been a massive rise in "cuckooing", because it's harder to detect with so many people self-isolating. And then there's the rise in right-wing hate crime targeting Muslims and ultra-orthodox Jews.'

DS Whittle appeared in the doorway. She and Jo exchanged a smile and a nod that told him they'd met before.

'Sorry to disturb you, Boss,' Carly said, 'but I've got the deceased's son on video link.'

'I'm on my way,' he told her.

Jo Stuart stood up. 'It's been great to see you again, Boss,' she said. 'Give my love to Kate and give Emily a hug from me. And good luck with this one, whatever it is.'

'You too,' Caton said. 'Just one thing though.'

'Go on?'

'Don't go giving Gordon Holmes a hug from me.'

She grinned, then lapsed into a heavy Manc accent. 'Wouldn't dream of it, cock. Social distancing, yeah?

Chapter 8

Caton sat slightly to the right of the twenty-one-inch monitor, to enable Carly Whittle, sitting two metres back, to see and be seen.

Harold Dyer, forty-nine years old, had a far more impressive backdrop. He appeared to be seated in a luxuriously furnished, lofty and generously proportioned lounge. Caton's eyes were drawn to the floor-to-ceiling wall of glass, behind which was a balcony with views across Cape Town, all the way to Table Mountain.

'I'm Detective Chief Inspector Caton,' he said. 'Behind me is Detective Sergeant Whittle.'

'This is about my mother,' Dyers said. 'She's dead, isn't she?'

'I am so sorry, Mr Dyer,' Caton replied, 'but yes, I'm afraid she is.'

Dyer's face was in shadow, making his expression hard to read. 'How did she die?' he asked. 'I take it that it wasn't natural causes?'

'What makes you think that?' Caton asked.

'Is it normal practice for an officer of your rank to break such news if it's not suspicious?'

It was a fair point, but not the reaction Caton had been expecting. 'At the moment,' he said, 'we're treating your mother's death as unexplained.'

Dyer leaned towards the screen, as though trying to read the expression on Caton's face. 'What exactly does that mean?' he asked.

'Well,' Caton began, 'the probable cause of death was a heart attack. However, according to your mother's GP, she had no history of cardiac problems and no other underlying health issues. And there are other circumstances that lead us to suspect that something else may have brought on a heart attack.'

'Other circumstances?'

'Your mother may have eaten or imbibed something that may have triggered a cardiac event.'

Caton hated this. He knew he must sound like a slippery politician, but there was only so much he could divulge at this stage. Come to that, there was only so much he knew.

'You're not suggesting my mother committed suicide?'

'No, Mr Dyer,' Caton responded, 'there is absolutely nothing to suggest that.'

Dyer was a silent for a moment. When he spoke it was slow and deliberate. 'So either it was food poisoning or someone else poisoned her?'

'It's far too early to tell,' Caton told him, 'but the post-mortem has been arranged for tomorrow, so we should have a better idea when we receive the pathologist's report.'

Dyer sat back. 'Don't you need my permission to carry out a post-mortem?' he said.

'Actually, no, we don't,' Caton told him. 'Not if the coroner has agreed that there should be one. Why, would you object?'

'No,' Dyer replied, 'it's just that I assumed you'd need me to make a formal identification first.'

'Your mother's GP and one of her neighbours have both formally identified her,' Caton said, 'but if you're imminently intending to come back to England, you can of course see your mother, and your confirmation as to her identity would be most helpful.'

'Even after the post-mortem?'

'I assure you, Mr Dyer,' Caton said, 'that your mother will be exactly as you would wish to remember her. More so after the post-mortem.'

Dyer sat in silence. Caton decided to wait.

'So it wasn't this bloody awful virus then?' Dyer said.

'No, we don't think it was.'

'How did she die? I mean . . . was it peaceful?'

Caton wasn't going to lie, but there was no need to tell the truth either. 'The doctor thinks it would have been both sudden and quick.'

More silence.

'Do you mind if I ask you some questions, Mr Dyer?' Caton continued. 'It's just that I'm conscious that it might not be easy for you to get a flight back here at short notice, given the disruption to foreign travel due to the pandemic.'

'Of course,' Dyer said. 'Please, go ahead.'

'Thank you,' Caton responded. 'So what is it that you do exactly?'

'I'm the senior management accountant for a multinational pharma company with its headquarters here in Cape Town.'

'Pharma – that would be pharmaceuticals?'

'That's correct. We're licensed to research, patent, develop, market and distribute both branded and generic drugs and healthcare medical devices throughout the world. Our company is currently one of those engaged in developing a potential vaccine for Covid-19.'

'And your role is . . .?'

'I'm the senior accountant responsible for the internal company accounts, and as such, I have a seat on the board, where I advise on managerial planning and commercial decision-making.'

That explained the apartment.

'When were you last in England?'

'Christmas. I flew back just before the New Year. I had intended to come over for the weekend to see my mother a fortnight ago, but all of the flights were cancelled. I've been calling her every couple of days instead.'

'Was that by phone or video link?'

'By phone. Mother wasn't into digital technology. I bought her an iPad, an iPhone and a Kindle. I also told her all about Facetime and how to sign up to Skype, and then to Zoom. Whatever I tried, she wasn't having any of it.' He grimaced. 'She could be very stubborn, my mother, just like my grandmother.'

'How long has your mother lived on her own?' Caton asked.

'When I was nine years old, my father was killed in a freak accident at the brewery where he worked. It was just her and me until I left home twenty-three years ago. Five years later, my grandma moved in. She suffered from rheumatoid arthritis, and agoraphobia supposedly.'

'Supposedly?'

'I've always believed that was just a convenient excuse to get her daughter to wait on her hand and foot.' He sounded bitter.

'What was your mother's occupation?' Caton asked.

'She was a school catering supervisor at one of the local high schools. She was good by all accounts – introduced healthy options before they became de rigueur. But then my grandmother deteriorated, and she had to leave work and become her full-time carer.'

'When did your grandmother die?'

'Six years ago. She had a stroke, followed by a heart attack. My mother struggled for the first year or so. She'd never had time to develop friendships or hobbies of her own. I got the impression she didn't know what to do with herself, but she finally settled into a sort of routine.'

This was more like it.

'What kind of routine?' Caton asked.

'She'd get up at seven a.m. on the dot, have a bowl of cornflakes for her breakfast, then she'd clean a room from top to bottom, with the radio on in the background. A different room every day, so that come Sunday they'd all have had a good clean, and she could spend the Lord's Day in peace.'

'She was religious then?'

Dyer laughed. 'Not a bit of it. It was just a thing she used to say. She lost her faith in God the day my father died.'

'Go on,' said Caton.

'She'd have a cup of tea and some fruit for lunch, then potter around in the garden. A round of toast and another cup of tea at three p.m., then read a book. Tea at five, that was her main meal of the day. Given the job she'd had, she tended to cook things from fresh – shepherd's pie, lasagne, casseroles, that sort of thing; salads in the summer. She'd usually make enough for two meals and freeze some for later, leaving her more time with her precious books. And then she'd watch *Coronation Street* and the news, before reading a few more pages, with the radio on. She'd always be in bed by nine-thirty p.m.'

'Did she have anything to eat or drink before she went to bed?' Caton asked.

Dyer shook his head. 'I did try to persuade her, but she'd got in her head not to drink anything after six p.m. or she'd be back and forth to the toilet all night. I told her that was a recipe for bladder infections, but she wasn't having any of it.'

'Was your mother staying in during lockdown, do you know?'

'Definitely. I persuaded her to stay in, back at the beginning of March. I could see what was coming your way, even if your government couldn't.'

'Who was doing her shopping for her, Mr Dyer? Some of her neighbours offered to help back then, but they claim that she told them she was fine for the moment?'

'That's right. As I understand it, because she'd worked for the city council catering department, they'd approached her, and offered to do a weekly drop-off of basic supplies. Her milk was delivered three times a week and she could always add on eggs. And I believe they'd started doing a fruit and veg too. Oh, and I arranged some deliveries from Amazon – a few treats: chocolate, cake, that sort of thing.'

Caton glanced at Carly to check she was busy taking notes. 'Did your mother talk about any other people visiting her? Friends, for instance?' he asked.

Dyer looked up at the ceiling, and thought about it for a moment or two, then he sighed, and looked back at the screen. 'No, I don't think she did. She was never a big socialiser, not that she had much time with her own mother and her work. The only close friend she had died a few years back. Why do you ask?'

Caton ignored the question. 'Any idea what her intentions were with regard to her will?' he said.

'Her will?'

'Her will. Did she have one, do you know?'

'Well, yes, I think so,' Dyer replied. 'I persuaded her to get one done after my father died. She said she didn't need one because it would all go to me, and she trusted me to do right by the grandchildren. I told her that probate would be really difficult if there was no will, especially with me being out here. She promised me that she would. Now you come to mention it, I never actually followed up on it.'

Caton glanced at the list of questions he had scribbled down. 'Did your mother ever talk about disagreements, with anyone. Neighbours, for example? Things that may have upset her?'

Dyer shook his head vigorously. 'No, definitely not. She was old school, if you know what I mean. Very polite, very proper. And she always kept her opinions about others to herself. She was a good woman.' He leaned towards the screen again.

'If you're asking me whether I think anyone might have had reason to murder her, Detective Chief Inspector, I can tell you categorically that the answer is absolutely not.'

Chapter 9

'Well, somebody had a reason to kill her,' said Carly Whittle.

They had rearranged their chairs, placing themselves at opposite ends of the table.

'We'll only that know for certain after the PM,' Caton reminded her. 'So, what do you think about the son?'

'He sounds genuine enough,' she said. 'He wasn't exactly distraught, but then his mother didn't really sound the affectionate sort. He can't have poisoned her himself though, can he? Not if he's been out there all this time, and the flights were cancelled like he said?'

'If he did enter the country, there'll be a record of it,' Caton said. 'Of course, he could easily have paid someone else to kill her.'

'But if he was in line to inherit, what would he stand to gain?' she said. 'And he'd have everything to lose.'

'That's a lot of ifs,' Caton observed. 'Before you write up your notes, I'd like you to ask DS Hulme to action the following: UK entry and exit checks on Mr Dyer in the past three months; tracking down Mrs Dyer's will, assuming she did go through with it – it'll either be in the house, with her bank or with a solicitor; contacting the council catering department to find out who was making those deliveries; ditto, whoever delivered her milk. When he's got names for the latter two, I need them interviewed. Got all that?'

'Yes, Boss,' she said. 'Plus, have you thought about checking on Harold Dyer's financial situation? I mean, he clearly lives in a very classy pad, but it could be rented. And we only have his word for it that he's on the board of a multinational company.'

She reminded Caton so much of Jo Stuart when she'd stepped up to detective sergeant – sharp as a pin, brimming with confidence and eager to learn. Except that Carly Whittle was blonde and a full head taller.

'Quite right,' he said. 'Add that to the list.'

They went back to the Incident Room. Jack Benson was talking to Jimmy Hulme. Caton went over to the sink to wash his hands, and then joined them. They formed a neat three-metre-sided equilateral triangle.

'What have you got for us so far?' Caton asked.

'We've lifted quite a few fingerprints,' Benson replied, 'from all the usual surfaces: door handles, door jambs and the like. Also from her glass, the book, the box of painkillers and so on. Other than that, there are just a few items we've bagged.'

'Does that include an iPhone and an iPad?' Caton asked.

Benson raised his eyebrows. 'Are you a mind-reader, Boss?'

'Just answer the question,' Caton said.

'Both,' Benson told him. 'We found them in the bottom of the wardrobe in the second bedroom. They were both in their original boxes – hadn't even been unwrapped by the look of it. I've also asked the team to bag up the contents of all of her bins. What do you want me to do with all this, Boss?'

'Let me give Dr Hopkins a call,' he said, 'then I'll have a better idea.'

Chapter 10

'You're lucky, DCI Caton,' the pathologist said. 'I have a ten-minute window.'

As was increasingly the case now they were doing this by video link, Caton was surprised by how much she seemed to have aged in the decade since their first case together, she as a force medical examiner and he as a detective inspector.

Her hair was now a distinguished grey that matched those world-weary blue-grey eyes. Every wrinkle told of countless bodies meticulously examined, probed and puzzled over, each one a victim of one kind or another, of fate or fury. Yet she was one of the most level-headed and untroubled people he had ever met. Rather like her predecessor Professor Flatman, who had first explained to Caton how best to view a corpse: 'Not as a person with family and friends and a life interrupted, but as a problem to be solved. That way you will be able to remain physically close, yet emotionally distanced.'

'DCI Caton?' she repeated.

'Sorry,' he said, 'I was just thinking about Professor Flatman.'

She pursed her lips. 'I'm missing him too,' she said, 'but I'm afraid you're stuck with me and the clock is ticking.'

'No, it wasn't that,' he began, then realised that it was far too complicated to explain. 'Anyway, the reason I contacted you is that I was wondering if there was any chance you could give me a heads-up in advance of the

PM, as to whether or not we are indeed looking at cyanide? Crime Scene Investigation are champing at the bit to examine the items we took from the house, and if there's a possibility of third-party involvement, the sooner we can start investigating that the better.'

She frowned. 'I can only give you a formal and definitive cause of death following a PM. And at the moment, the requirement is that no PMs may take place until Covid-19 has been ruled out.'

'Isn't that catch-22?' he asked. 'How do you know if she had Covid-19 if you can't do a post-mortem?'

'Exactly.'

'Can't you do a test?'

'Unfortunately, the tests that are currently available, even assuming we could get our hands on one, are far from conclusive.'

'Where does that leave you?'

'Well, since the deceased had not reported any Covid-like symptoms to her GP or the NHS helpline, 111, I am going to proceed on that basis. But it'll have to be under the same extra-sterile conditions as if she had definitely been infected.'

'That doesn't answer my question about an earlier diagnosis?'

'Would you have attempted to badger Professor Flatman like this?'

'We both know the answer to that,' he said.

She shook her head. 'Well, I suppose I could try using a rapid colorimetric paper test strip to look for one of the metabolites that would indicate the presence of cyanide in the body before she died . . .'

'That would be brilliant,' he said.

She sighed. 'Give me five minutes.'

* * *

'What does that tell us?' Caton asked.

Carol Hopkins was holding up what appeared to be a colour chart in one hand and a narrow strip of paper in the other.

'That you're a lucky boy, DCI Caton,' she said. 'The strip in my left hand started out this colour.' She pointed with her thumb to a red bar on the colour chart. 'When I placed a drop of the deceased's blood on the strip, it changed to the colour you now see: the colour purple.'

She was morphing into a female version of her predecessor, Caton decided, revelling in the power of knowledge and the slow reveal.

'And . . .?' he said.

She beamed at him. 'This confirms that there were unusual levels of cyanide in her blood when she died. This test indicates two point one milligrams, which is nought point four milligrams less than the threshold lethal dose. However, given the time that has lapsed since she died, I think it highly likely that the level at the time of death would certainly have been lethal.'

'And there's no question of that having happened by accident?'

'Such as?'

'I don't know. You mentioned smoke inhalation, or exposure to some kind of industrial product?'

'There would have to have been a significant fire consuming most of the furniture and fittings to show anything close to that level. Unless, of course, she spent the last thirty years chewing and sniffing the carpets?'

'Thank you,' he said. 'I really appreciate this.'

She smiled again. 'I'll make a note of that in my special debtors' notebook,' she said. 'What I *won't* be doing though is signing a medical certificate as to the cause of death until I've completed the post-mortem.'

Chapter 11

'Settle down!'

Caton watched as the room came to order. It was the first full briefing he'd called since the start of lockdown. Despite the smaller numbers in the syndicate now, people were still spread out across the entire room. The physical distances between them looked unnatural, and it was obvious that some of them found it uncomfortable too. Several of the male officers had clearly not yet come to grips with social distancing and had to be shooed away by their nearest neighbours. Caton made a note to have a word. If these clowns didn't wake up sharpish and smell the sanitiser, they'd quickly become a threat to the team as a whole.

'Right,' he said, 'Operation Pendle Hill is unofficially a murder investigation.'

He waited for the comments to die down.

'It will become official following the post-mortem tomorrow,' he said, 'but I can confirm that the deceased had cyanide in her system, and that it did not get there by accident.'

More murmurs. A hand went up at the back. Detective Constable Jack Franklin. One of the errant officers whose card Caton had just marked.

'Yes?' Caton said.

'Are we sure it's murder, Boss?' Franklin asked. 'Might it not be suicide? I mean, suicides have been on the up since this pandemic started?'

Caton counted to three. Had it been anybody else

he'd have taken it as a serious question, but Franklin was just trying to be clever, grandstanding for his pals.

'Apart from the fact that there's no evidence to support the likelihood of that, DC Franklin,' he replied. 'There are easier ways for a seventy-year-old widow to take her own life than somehow getting hold of cyanide during a lockdown, manufacturing pills, inserting them in blister packs and then going to the trouble of disguising them in packets of painkillers.'

Anyone else might have taken this as a put-down. Franklin's grin suggested that he was impervious to sarcasm.

'Moving on,' said Caton, 'I am now implementing a fast-track strategy. CSI will go ahead and treat the house and gardens as a murder scene.'

Franklin's hand shot up again. This time he didn't wait to be asked. 'How safe is that?' he said. 'I'm only wondering in case we get a call-out to any other possible victims.'

Keep digging, Caton said to himself, *keep digging.*

'Since it's clear,' he replied, 'that the pills were not manufactured at this address, I'm assured that following standard biochemical hazard procedures, together with continuing the normal additional PPE requirements for Covid-19, will provide CSI with sufficient protection against exposure to such levels of cyanides as may still exist. As for any other sites that may come to our notice, I think it highly unlikely that you will be first on scene, DC Franklin. Although I'll see what can be arranged.'

A ripple of laughter went round the room that wiped the grin from Franklin's face. Caton didn't like making enemies – you never knew when it would come back to bite – and besides, it wasn't his style. But this was preferable to having his authority undermined, especially in front of less experienced members of the team.

'However,' he continued, 'I am going to make sure that every single GMP division, together with paramedics and GP surgeries, are warned to be especially cautious in responding to any similar suspicious death.' He paused for effect. 'Now,' he said, 'I'd appreciate it if you'd all hang on to any questions you may have until I've finished.'

He pointed to the fast-track aide-memoire on one of the posters on the wall behind him.

'We start with *WHY*?' he said. 'There's no evidence of forced entry or of a violent assault. This is a killing motivated by greed, revenge, self-preservation – did she, for example, know something that could have got her killed, or was this the work of a psychopath? If so, what was the particular motivation? Power? Sexual gratification? And why was *she* chosen as the victim? We need a complete profile for our victim. A complete victim history and list of victim associations. Everything about her, her family, her friends and relationships, her former occupations, her leisure pursuits – the lot. Starting with what the son and the neighbours have told us, and moving out from there.'

He took a sip from the flask of water that he carried with him. Everyone had been required to bring their own refillable as soon as the highly infectious and dangerous nature of the virus had become known. He screwed the top back on and continued.

'Next question is *WHERE?*' He pointed to the map DS Hulme had placed on the first of the boards. 'Why was this house, this location, chosen? Was it because she lived there? Because it was accessible to the killer? Because it was known to the killer? Or all three?

'*WHEN* was she killed? We have an estimated window within which she died. But now that we know she was poisoned, when was that poison delivered? At the time of her death, or sometime before? Hours

49

possibly, or days? Worst-case scenario, it could have been weeks or even months before she was found.'

This was the cue for murmured comments and much shaking of heads as the members of the syndicate envisaged the magnitude and complexity of the task before them, and the hours of passive media that would have to be viewed and analysed.

'That brings us on to *HOW*?' Caton said. 'Our working hypothesis is that she was killed by cyanide poisoning, although that has yet to be established with absolute certainty. We believe that the substance that killed her was ingested. For those of you in the iGeneration, that means she swallowed something.'

He waited for the laughter to die down.

'We need to know what that was. The post-mortem will give us a better idea, but we need all the foodstuffs, medicines and drinks in that house tested until we know for sure. Once we've pinned that down, we can look at how they came to be in that house. In the meantime, we'll have to rely on house-to-house enquiries and passive media. To start with, we need to know if she had any regular callers, and who may have visited that house in the past few days. That's going to be quite an extensive list, including postal workers, couriers and volunteers from neighbourhood and social-media self-help groups, as well as individuals. As soon as we know for certain how the poison got into her system, we'll have a think about appeal posters, and targeted mail drops.'

He took another glug of water.

'Once we have answers to these four questions, we'll be well on the way to the all-important one: *WHO* is our unidentified subject, or unsub, as our American cousins would say? Now, does anyone have any questions or observations?'

Carly Whittle raised her hand.

'DS Whittle?'

'If this is the work of a psychopath, Boss, it could be that this isn't the first death of its kind. Oughtn't we to run checks to see if there've been any other suspicious deaths that may be connected?'

'Good point,' he said. 'I hope to God that isn't the case but, Mr Wallace, you will need to check with the registrar. I also need you to find out everything there is out there about cyanide poisoning, and especially anything involving murder and drug-tampering.'

'Yes, Boss,' said his senior analyst.

'Unless there any more questions,' Caton said, 'DI Carter will allocate your roles and manage the policy book. DS Hulme will set up the case management. DS Whittle will brief the door-to-door teams. And before I let you go, I must stress that we do not as yet have a definitive cause of death. There is to be no mention of cyanide or poisoning of any kind outside of these four walls until I give my say-so. Is that clear?'

This elicited a chorus of agreement and much nodding of heads.

'Good,' he said, 'because if I discover that anyone has shared that information, either deliberately or accidentally, I will consider it as gross misconduct. And you know what that means?'

He could tell from their expressions that they did.

'Good,' he said. 'Carry on.'

He turned to Nick Carter, Jimmy Hulme and Carly Whittle, and asked them to join him in the corridor.

'I know this isn't ideal,' he said, closing the door behind him, 'but my office is too small, given the current circumstances, and it'll only be for a moment or two. I just wanted to check you're all happy with everything?'

The three of them nodded.

'I take it you want all sensitive issues passed by

you?' said DS Hulme.

'Absolutely,' Caton replied. 'As well any policy issues relating to linked incidents or investigations, that's a given.'

'I know we need a suspect first,' Carter said, 'but we're going to need a pretty special arrest strategy for this one, Boss.'

'True,' said Caton. 'We'll need a hazardous materials risk assessment in place. Ask Jack Benson to check that out for us, Jimmy.'

'What about a media strategy, Boss?' Carly Whittle asked. 'This could turn into a nightmare, especially if there's more than one victim.'

That was exactly what Caton had been thinking, ever since the word 'cyanide' had cropped up.

'I'll sort that out with the Press Office,' he said. 'Wish me luck.'

Chapter 12

It was just gone eight in the evening when Caton arrived home.

He went straight to the downstairs loo, gave his hands a thorough wash, and stripped down to his underpants. Then he slipped on the tracksuit hanging on the back of the door and put his clothes in the washing machine.

Kate and Larissa were in the lounge watching the television. Kate heard him come in and pressed the pause button.

'Well, this is a nice surprise,' she said. 'Day one of a murder investigation – we didn't expect you this side of midnight.'

'It's Sunday,' he reminded her. 'The labs are closed and the PM 's not till tomorrow, but I'll have to be in early in the morning. What are you two watching?

'The penultimate episode of *Liar* on catch-up,' she told him. 'If you don't want to know who did it, you'd better have your dinner in the kitchen.'

'I already know who did it. It's obvious.'

'Well, keep it to yourself!' She reached over her shoulder and shooed him away. 'There's a Jamie Oliver carbonara in the fridge – just needs four minutes in the microwave. Oh, and there's a message for you on the landline.'

Caton poured himself a glass of Puglia Rosso from a half-empty bottle, took his pasta through to the study, and let it cool while he listened to the message.

'Tom? This is Nick. I've emailed you the link for the Alternatives' inaugural lockdown meeting at eight-fifteen tonight. See you there. And don't be late!'

Seeing the ugly mugs of his book group for the first time since The Old Nags Head had gone into lockdown was just what he needed to take his mind off the case. He switched on his Mac and started on the pasta.

When the software had finished loading, he clicked the link and watched as one after another the four familiar faces popped up on the monitor. Jerome, true to form, was holding a gin and tonic, the others three bottles of beer.

'I had no idea this was fancy dress,' Caton told them.

Jerome, unsurprisingly, had gone all the way with a white diaphanous top trimmed with gold, a gold-tasselled headdress over a long black wig, and a gold necklace with a heavy bronze pendant. The other three all wore a waistcoat and a fez. Craig's fez was black, the other two red.

'Sorry about that,' Nick said, 'only I reckoned if I told you, you'd find an excuse to opt out.'

'Damn right, I would,' Caton muttered.

'Hi, Tom,' said Craig, with a big grin on his face. 'Glad you could make it. By the way, you'd better mute yourself if you're going to keep making asides.'

'I told them you'd join us,' said Jamie. 'What with crime falling off a cliff, courtesy of this bloody virus.'

Jerome leaned into the camera. 'Of all the gin joints in all the towns in all the world, he walks into mine,' he said.

'Wrong country,' said Craig. 'Casablanca's in Morocco. *La Peste* was set in Algeria.'

'A plague on all your houses!' Jerome replied, with his usual exaggerated petulance.

'Right, let's get this underway,' Nick said. 'We've only got thirty-six minutes left.'

'Ever the teacher,' said Jamie.

'Did you manage to get a copy, Tom?' Nick asked. 'Demand's gone through the roof. Even the online bookstores are scrambling to get copies printed.'

Tom held up his well-thumbed copy. 'I've had this since sixth form,' he said. 'I've got it in the original, too. I intended to read them side by side to improve my French.'

'And did you?'

'I managed the first chapter, and then gave in and stuck to the English version.'

'I take it you received my text about our two themes?' Nick said.

With the back of his hand, Caton wiped a smear of creamy sauce from his lips. 'Yep,' he said. 'What is *La Peste* really about, and what parallels does it have with the Covid-19 pandemic?'

'Why don't you kick us off with the first one then,' Nick said, 'given you're the only one who's actually studied it?'

Caton put his fork down and took a sip of wine. 'First off,' he began, 'we know that taken at face value this is about a cholera epidemic in Algeria, when the city of Oran was put in quarantine. But it's really a kind of metaphor for the Nazi occupation of France and her consequent isolation from the rest of the world, and how people dealt with that.'

Jerome put his hand up.

'Yes, Jerry?' said Nick.

Jerome had clearly made a close study of the TV film critic Mark Kermode. He had his voice and gestures down to a T. 'What we have here,' he said, 'is the plague seen through the eyes of the main characters, all of them men, each of them wondering how best to deal with the situation they find themselves in. Do they fall back on their faith? Do they put themselves first, and let the devil take the hindmost? Do they try to profit from people's fear and shortages of essential goods? Or do they do the reverse and find ways of helping those less fortunate than themselves? There are acts of heroism and acts of shameful selfishness: humanity in a nutshell. The life we live as humans is essentially absurd and always precarious.' He smiled and picked up his cocktail. 'In my humble view, that's what this story is all about.'

'That's interesting,' Craig observed. 'It's almost word for word what Camus' daughter said in *The Guardian* last week.'

Jerome pouted. 'Can't blame a girl for trying,' he said. 'What's *your* take on it, clever dick?'

Craig ignored the jibe. 'One of the things Camus highlighted,' he said, 'was the way the authorities were quick to deny or even stifle the truth, drag their feet, hide their mistakes and shift the blame, especially early on in the outbreak. That's what the two doctors in the book, Castel and Bernard Rieux, are trying to challenge.'

Jamie quickly jumped in. 'And Dr Castel is the first to identify the plague and he dies, just like that doctor in Wuhan . . .'

'Dr Li Wenliang,' Nick supplied.

'That's the one. He alerted other medics to the fact that some patients were showing signs of a new illness not unlike SARS, and was detained by the police for "spreading false rumours" and "seriously disrupting social order". He had to contract it himself and die, before mass public outrage in China forced the authorities to officially declare him an "ordinary hero". Giving in to pressure, they ended up having to change that to "martyr".'

'Which is just like Ibsen's nineteenth-century play, *An Enemy of the People*,' Caton said. 'Kate and I went to see it at the Royal Exchange last year. It's about a Dr Stockman, who wrote a paper claiming the town's water supply from their famous health-giving springs was actually polluted. They didn't make *him* a hero though.'

'What happened to him?' asked Nick.

'His brother, the populist mayor of the town, convinced the people that it was more important to protect the economy than to fix the problem and protect their health. The people turned on his brother, the whistle-blower. He was made a scapegoat and an outcast. Sound familiar?'

'Enemy of the people?' Craig mused 'That's what Trump called the news media when they started asking difficult questions about his handling of the pandemic.'

'There you go then,' Nick said.

'I thought this was about *La Peste*?' said Jerome, twirling his pendant.

'We agreed it was also about similarities with what's happening with Covid-19,' Nick reminded him. 'And there is a parallel in *La Peste*. Take the janitor, Monsieur Michel, insisting there are no rats in the building, when everyone can see rats are dying all around him. And the government-controlled newspapers insisting that the plague is under control when it's obvious that it's not. Shades of our own leaders telling us "We have all the PPE we need", when NHS staff and care workers are still pleading for it – not to mention the tweets Trump makes to suit his own narrative, rather than the reality unfolding in front of him.'

'I've got a question,' said Jerome.

Craig and Jamie groaned.

'No, seriously,' said Jerome, 'if Camus had been writing about our epidemic today, what would Covid-19 be a metaphor for?'

'Great question,' Nick acknowledged.

'I think,' Jamie said, 'that he'd home in on all the wars going on right now that are having a similar impact on innocent citizens – Afghanistan, Yemen, Syria, to name but a few. They're all forcing people into a different kind of lockdown, or killing them in droves, or forcing them to flee.'

Craig wasn't sure. 'Maybe,' he said, 'but I think he'd look deeper than that.'

'What d'you mean?'

'Well, in *La Peste*, as in all of his other works, Camus is shining a light on the essential absurdity of the human condition, not least our pointless obsession with materialism. He even talked about the way that morally bankrupt capitalism was destroying the natural world.'

'I don't remember reading that in *The Plague*,' said Nick.

Craig shook his head. 'That bit was in another of his pieces – *Le Désert* – but it's implied in this book too. He was a genius. If he were alive today, I think he'd be drawing parallels between this pandemic and the plague of selfish and unbridled capitalism widening the gap between rich and poor, and mindlessly killing the planet that we rely on for life itself.'

Jamie frowned. 'Trust you to bring politics into it.'

'To be fair,' Caton said, 'that's exactly what Camus himself did. It was at the heart of everything he wrote. Look how he had Cottard questioning what a return to normal life would mean. Cottard didn't think that was possible. He wanted to know if the administration would change direction – if public services would work just as they did before the plague. He foresaw new problems as a result of the epidemic. He argued that a fresh start was required.'

Nick raised his bottle. 'I drink to that,' he said. 'But one thing they did all agree on was that when the gates were finally opened, however much people might want to carry on as though nothing had happened, the plague would leave its traces, if only in people's hearts.'

There was silence while the five of them contemplated this profound observation.

'I wonder,' Caton said, 'when we finally come out of lockdown, will we behave as they did in the book?'

'What do you mean?' Jamie asked.

'Well,' Caton replied, 'take Rambert and his wife. They had this passionate joyful reunion, and then buggered off home, happy that they'd beaten the plague, while completely forgetting those who hadn't – the ones Camus called the 'lonely mourners', whose loved ones lay in pits, under a layer of quicklime, or in an anonymous heap of ash.'

'No doubt there will be some people like that,' Jerome observed. 'I think the majority though will continue to show the same kind of compassion they're doing right now – like all those volunteers collecting prescriptions for the vulnerable and delivering food to the poor. The people donating to Captain Tom's appeal. And the millions out on the streets every week applauding the NHS and the other key workers. We can only hope it results in people being kinder, more empathetic, less selfish.'

'Amen to that!' said Craig, raising his bottle. 'Like Camus says, at the end of the day, when the human condition is so absurd, all that's left is to love and to hope.'

'On that positive note,' said Caton, 'I'll leave you to it. I have a feeling I'm going to need to build up my sleep reserves while I still can.'

Chapter 13
Monday 6th April 2020

'She died of cardiac arrest . . .'

True to her word, Dr Tompkins had got off to an early start. She was sharing her post-mortem findings with them via video link.

'. . . her heart stopped.'

'Doesn't everybody's?' whispered DS Hulme.

'I heard that!' said the pathologist.

'And her heart stopped because?' Caton asked.

'I can't say for certain. There was some furring of the arteries and veins to be expected of someone her age, but no evidence of cardiomyopathy, congenital heart disease, failure of valves or myocarditis. There was substantial pulmonary oedema, but that was almost certainly a result of her heart failing. One of her kidneys had very little function, but the other was fine. The point is that I was unable to find any underlying condition or disease that might otherwise have caused or contributed to her death.'

'Which leaves?'

'Well, I'll need to do more toxicology, but . . .'

'She was poisoned,' said Caton.

'Yes.'

'And that was what killed her?'

'Possibly,' she said.

'Can I nudge you towards probably?' he said.

She smiled. 'Probably. Although a positive result from a test for the presence of any poisonous substance is not on its own sufficient to establish that this substance was the cause of death. Come to that, a negative result is not sufficient to establish that it was not the cause of death.'

'Why is that?'

'Because among the changes that take place post-mortem there are two – enzymatic action and microbial action – that can affect concentrations in the blood of different substances between the point at which death occurs, and the post-mortem. Both of these are likely to lead to the degradation of many toxic substances, including cyanide.'

'But you did find traces of cyanide?'

'Yes. But I can't say definitively that she died of cyanide poisoning, only that it was the likely cause of death. On that basis, I won't be able to sign a medical certificate as to the cause of death. It will have to be referred to the coroner for an inquest.'

Caton cursed inwardly. It was exactly what he'd feared.

'Can you say how the cyanide got there?' he asked.

'It was definitely ingested. No traces of it in her last meal. My guess is that it was taken in a liquid or powder form.'

'Did you find any traces of medication?'

She paused before replying. 'You're wondering about the box of painkillers?'

'Yes, but there are also the other meds she had in the house.'

'The thing with this analgesic,' she said, 'is that less than five per cent is excreted unchanged through the kidneys. And it has such a short half-life that after twenty-four hours from when it's been ingested, ninety-eight per cent of it will have been eliminated. I've not found any trace of the drug thus far, but if you like, I can run some more intensive tests to look for it?'

'More intensive as in more expensive?'

She smiled thinly. 'As in requiring additional resources, including time.'

She was beginning to sound increasingly like her mentor, Professor Flatman.

'Just do it, please, Doctor,' said Caton. 'You email me the forms, and I'll sign them off.'

'Very well,' she said, 'though there may be a quicker way.'

'Go on.'

'If your own tests find the presence of cyanide in any of the exhibits taken from the household, then you'll have a very strong circumstantial link to the likely cause of death.'

Circumstantial . . . likely. Caton had been hoping for something definitive, but he knew she was right.

'Thank you for fast-tracking the PM, Doctor,' he said. 'I think I already said I owed you?'

She smiled. 'I hadn't forgotten.'

Tompkins ended the meeting, and Caton turned to gauge how the others had taken it. Carter was frowning.

'You look worried, Nick,' Caton said. 'Are you thinking what I'm thinking?'

'That this might not be a one-off? That there may be others?'

'That, and the fact that the press are going to have a ruddy field day when they discover cyanide's involved, and they will.'

'That would be a problem under normal circumstances,' DS Hulme reflected, 'but with all these coronavirus deaths and most of the population in lockdown, it'll be a nightmare.'

'Let's not get ahead of ourselves,' Caton told him. 'First, we have to establish when and why she died. If the motive is personal, we won't have to look any further.'

'And if it's not?' said Carly Whittle.

Caton looked around the Incident Room. His gaze took in the socially distanced desks and the skeleton staff. The small stack of boxes of paper masks by the door, the three remaining bottles of hand gel beside the sink.

'Then we'll have our work cut out, won't we?' he said.

Chapter 14

'Boss!'

Wallace hovered in the open doorway of Caton's office.

'What is it, Duggie?' Caton said.

The senior analyst held up a file in his left hand. 'That information you wanted on cyanide?' he said. 'Do you want me to leave it with you?'

Caton eased his chair back. 'Why don't you take me through it?' he said.

'Do you want me to put my mask on?' Wallace said nervously.

'No, we should be alright,' Caton told him. 'Just leave the door open and sit on that chair just inside.'

Wallace sat down, opened the file on his knee and began.

'Cyanide is a naturally occurring chemical found in many plants, and has been used for poisoning for two millennia. It is highly lethal, whether inhaled as a gas, ingested in solid form, or absorbed through topical exposure. It has been used for centuries in conventional warfare: during the Franco-Prussian War, for example, Napoleon the Third made his troops dip their bayonet tips in the poison. It was also used in both world wars. The French and Austrians used it in World War I and, in World War II, the Nazis used the rat control product Zyklon-B to kill millions in the gas chambers. In the 1980s, cyanide in gas form is thought to have been used in the Iran–Iraq War on the Kurds in Iraq and in Syria.'

He looked up.

'Cyanide poses an ongoing threat as a weapon of terrorism, whether delivered in oral form via sodium cyanide and potassium cyanide, or as a gas via hydrogen cyanide and cyanogen chloride.'

Caton was impatient to get to the point. 'What about poisoning by ingestion?' he asked.

Wallace turned over a couple of pages. 'In November 1978, in a cult settlement known as Jonestown, nine hundred and nine men, women and children died from cyanide poisoning in a mass suicide ordered by their leader Jim Jones. Potassium cyanide and potassium chloride were both used.' He looked up to check that Caton was following. 'There was some confusion over whether injection or oral ingestion was the primary method.'

'I remember that,' Caton said. 'What about food-tampering?'

'The Roman Emperor Nero poisoned his enemies using cherry laurel water, which was rich in cyanide.'

Caton was beginning to wish he hadn't asked him to carry out quite such a comprehensive search.

'What about more recently?' he said.

'Chicago, 1982. Seven people died following drug-tampering. The perpetrator laced capsules with potassium cyanide. No one was ever charged or convicted. It led to over one hundred copycat attacks around the US, with at least a further five deaths. Two were identified as targeted murders, one as a suicide, and the other attempts were assumed to be random. There was also a hoax which created panic and led to the withdrawal of the drug from the market.'

This was exactly what Caton had feared. He vaguely recalled the panic it had caused in the States at the time.

'What happened to the brand?'

'Their sales collapsed overnight, but the company's response was brilliant. They immediately issued a withdrawal and were completely honest with their customers. They also cooperated fully with the police, the Food and Drug Administration and the FBI. As a result, their market share bounced back within the year.'

They were dealing with a generic product, Caton reflected. This was going to hit scores of producers and make a single PR response well-nigh impossible.

'You also wanted to know how it works? As a poison that is,' said Wallace.

'I did,' Caton admitted, wondering if he was going to regret it.

'Characteristically,' Wallace said, 'providing it's a lethal dose, cyanide kills fast. Within seconds in gas form, and minutes if it's ingested. It simultaneously affects the central nervous system and the cardiovascular system. We're talking anything from headaches and nausea to low heart rate, seizures and coma. The only external signs are that cherry-red colour that was present on the victim's skin, and sometimes the odour of almonds. That's because . . .'

'Cyanide is present in almonds, along with the pips in apples, apricots, peaches and a lot of the food we eat,' said Caton.

Wallace looked disappointed. 'You've been doing your own research, Boss.'

'*The Adventure of The Veiled Lodger,*' Caton told him. 'You disappoint me. I've always assumed that Sherlock Holmes was essential reading for all detectives. Don't worry, you can make up for it by telling me if anyone ever recovers from cyanide poisoning and, if so, whether there are any long-term effects?'

Duggie frowned and closed the folder. 'Providing it's a sub-lethal dose and they're treated pretty smartish, most survivors are going to have similar symptoms to what people might have following a heart attack or stroke.'

'Such as?'

'Depression, anxiety, attention deficit, uncontrolled anger. Sometimes post-traumatic stress disorder too.'

'Sounds like one of my quarterly syndicate sick leave reports,' Caton responded. 'I suppose I'd better tell Ged to up our personal protective equipment.'

Chapter 15

'This is really hard,' Detective Sergeant Carly Whittle said. 'It's like getting blood from a stone.'

'That's because of the virus,' DC Henry Powell responded. 'They're scared out of their wits already. The last thing they need right now is a murder on their doorstep.'

'No one's said anything about murder,' Carly said. 'At least, not to them.'

'They didn't have to,' he replied. 'Half the road taped off. Multiple police vehicles, one of them with CIS stencilled all over it. Everyone in hazmat suits. A body bag placed in an unmarked van. And then us rocking up with questions about suspicious vehicles. What would you think?'

He did have a point, Carly had to concede. Actually, lots of points. To be fair, the occupants of three of the houses they'd knocked on had tried to be helpful, although in reality none of them had seen, heard or remembered anything worth a jot. It was the ones who'd refused to come to the door that really bugged her. One woman had actually peered through her net curtains for a full ten seconds before disappearing. Not that she'd get away with it. They'd be back. Or somebody else would.

'Let's hope we have more joy here,' she said. 'At least this one's got CCTV.'

She turned to check where they were in relation to the victim's house.

'It's promising too – opposite side of the road, less

than twenty metres away. It should have captured everyone and everything that went anywhere near the target address.'

'Assuming it's switched on,' her colleague said, pressing the bell.

He gave it twenty seconds, then pressed the bell again, while simultaneously rapping on the door. Still nothing.

Carly had a look through the lounge window.

'There's definitely someone home,' she told him. 'Either that, or money's no object. The television's on.'

'Could be dead, of course,' said Powell banging on the door again.

'Don't say that,' she said. 'That's all we need.'

A window opened above her head. The two of them stepped back, and looked up. What looked like a male in his sixties or seventies stared down at them. It was difficult to tell for certain, because he had a scarf tied around the bottom half of his face. His voice was muffled but there was no misinterpreting his intent. He waved his arm towards the street.

'Go away!' he said.

Carly held up her warrant card. 'Police! We need your help, Sir. We'd just like to ask you a few questions.'

'I know nothing and I saw nothing,' he replied. 'Now go away.'

Henry consulted his list. 'Mr Hollister is it?'

'How do you know my name?' the man demanded.

'We checked the electoral register,' Powell told him. 'This'll only take a minute of your time.'

'If it's about the old biddy across the way,' the man replied, 'I can't help you. Like I said, I've seen nothing and know nothing. I keep myself to myself. It's safer that way, especially now.'

'I understand that, Sir,' Carly said. 'However, your

CCTV camera may well have captured information that may be extremely helpful to our investigation. I take it that it is working?'

'There wouldn't be much point in having it if it didn't, would it?' the man responded.

'In which case,' she said, 'we'd like to request a copy of any footage you may have. We have a high-speed memory stick with which to capture the data. You're welcome to do it yourself and there would be no need for us to come inside.'

'I know my rights,' he said. 'Under the provisions of the Data Protection Act, I don't need to give you anything unless you have a warrant *and* you can convince me that this isn't a fishing expedition.'

The two detectives stared at one another. This was the first time anybody had refused to share their CCTV – ever.

'I promise you,' said Carly, 'that we would not be asking for you to release this data unless we had good reason to believe that it could provide information likely to be crucial to our investigation.'

'Well, I've only got your word for that,' he responded sourly. 'Come back with a warrant or you can forget it.'

'We do have the right to seize this data if you refuse to provide it, Mr Hollister,' Henry told him.

'Only if you have a warrant.'

'We'll be back, Mr Hollister,' said Carly, 'and I must caution you that if in the meantime you delete, dispose of, conceal or destroy any of the data recorded on your system, that will constitute offences under the Data Protection Act 2018, as well as obstruction of the police in the execution of our duty.'

'Bye then,' the man responded, as he closed the window.

'Don't you hate people who know their rights?' said Henry as they walked back down the path. 'Think he'll delete the footage?'

Carly opened the gate. 'It's unlikely. The upside of knowing his rights is that he'll know ours too. *And* the consequences of ignoring them. I'm going to ring the boss and ask him to apply for a warrant for our Mr Hollister. Why don't you see what next door has to say?'

It took her longer than she'd anticipated to reach Caton, by which time Henry Powell had managed to visit two houses. He was smiling as she approached.

'How d'you get on?' she asked.

'Better, certainly. Nothing earth-shattering as such. They all agreed that she was a bit of a loner, more so in the past year or so. Before the lockdown, she'd walk to the post office near the Arndale Centre on Chester Road for her pension, and combine that with a weekly shop at Aldi. One of them remembers her mentioning a chiropodist appointment a couple of months ago. The lady at number three said she remembers her being a regular at the library until it closed down, and then she used the mobile library that used to park at the top of the street. That stopped coming two years ago as part of the council cuts. Other than that, she didn't seem to leave the house.'

'What about visitors?' Carly asked.

'Nobody they were aware of, other than the milkman and the postwoman. There was a council van that's started called every Thursday around ten a.m., according to the guy who lives in the house opposite. He's also seen a Tesco van calling a couple of times in the past few weeks.'

'Well, that's more than anyone else has come up with,' Carly said. 'Did any of them recall having received any unsolicited packages?'

'Nope.'

'Right,' she said. 'So, where does that leave us?'

He consulted his list. 'According to this, that's all of them visited by either us or one of the other teams, apart from the one at the end who didn't respond. We could always give that one another try before we go?'

'Come on then,' she said. 'Let's get it done and get out of here. I don't know about you, but I'm exhausted.'

They had been at it non-stop for three hours, and both of their bottles of water were empty. With all of the cafes closed down by the pandemic, they couldn't even call in for a bite somewhere. Carly was beginning to regret having already eaten the cheese and tomato sandwich she'd packed for lunch.

Chapter 16

Their final stop was the kind of property that estate agents call doer-uppers – the worst house on the best street.

The gate hung forlornly from a single hinge. Flaked paintwork was peeling on the door jamb and the windowsills. There wasn't a single plant in the front garden, other than the knee-high lawn, which was full of weeds. A sign in the window made it clear that cold-callers would be savaged by the animal whose image was attached in the form of a fading photo.

'Looks like a banned breed to me,' said Powell.

'The dog or the owner?' Carly said.

He laughed. 'Both.'

He rang the bell and hammered on the door.

A dog began to bark.

They heard someone deep in the bowels of the house swear and then shout a command.

The bark was replaced by a low, deep, visceral growl.

'It's not a pit bull then,' said Powell hopefully. 'They don't bark.'

'Not true,' said Carly. 'They're only silent when they're hunting or fighting.'

'Like our killer then.' He hammered again on the door and leaned on the bell so that it rang continuously.

A sudden loud bang on the lounge window made Carly jump.

The dog had leapt onto the back of a couch set beneath the window. Its slab-like head pressed against the pane, the ears hung forward over a Neanderthal forehead. Broad cheeks and powerful jaws were supported by a thick neck, whose rope-like sinews sprung from a formidable chest. Cold, coal-black eyes were fixed on hers.

She stepped back a pace and bumped into Powell.

'It's stopped barking,' he observed.

A man appeared beside the dog, to whom he bore a marked resemblance, except that he wasn't silent.

'Fuck off!' he shouted.

The two detectives held up their IDs.

The dog growled.

'We need to speak with you, Mr Atkins,' Carly said encouragingly. 'Please come to the door.'

The dog jumped down from the sofa and disappeared.

'Obviously brighter than its owner,' Powell whispered.

As if on cue, the man turned away and followed the beast. Carly and Powell backed another couple of paces down the drive. The door opened. The dog appeared first, straining on a chain attached to its collar. Its teeth were now bared and slobber dripped from its jaws.

'Shit!' muttered Carly. 'I don't remember anything about pit bulls in the self-defence manual.'

'It looks like a pit bull, Staffy cross,' Powell observed.

She didn't find this particularly reassuring.

'What?' snarled its owner. He all but filled the doorway.

'Good afternoon, Mr Atkins,' Carly began. 'We wondered if you could help us by answering a few questions about the comings and goings on the close.'

'Why?' he said, pulling the dog into a seated position.

'You may have heard that there's been a sudden death involving one of your neighbours,' Powell began.

The man spat out his reply. 'I wasn't talking to you!'

'There's no call for that tone,' Carly said. 'Can we please keep this civil?'

'Providing it's you that asks the questions, I'll see what I can do,' he replied.

Carly sensed Powell tense behind her. She could see where this was heading. This was the kind of provocation the man enjoyed. Ordinarily, she would have taken him on, for Henry's sake. But first and foremost, this was a murder enquiry. The last thing they needed was for it to escalate into something else. Not with that bloody dog waiting for an excuse to launch itself at them.

'Did you know Mrs Dyer by any chance?' she asked. 'The woman at number . . .'

'Her they carted away in a body bag yesterday?' he said. 'I know who she was, but not to talk to.'

'We're interested in any visitors she may have had recently. People on foot. Cars or vans coming and going?'

He shook his head. 'Can't help you there even if I wanted to. I don't give a damn what the neighbours get up to, so long as they leave me alone.'

'Do you have a car, Mr Atkins?' she asked.

'Never have, never will.' He grinned, revealing teeth as yellow and stained as those of his dog. 'Is that it then?'

'You're absolutely sure there's nothing you can tell us, Mr Atkins?' said Powell.

There was no reaction from the man, other than addressing himself to Carly.

'You look knackered, love,' he said. 'Can I offer you a cup of tea and a bite to eat?'

Carly gritted her teeth. 'Thank you,' she said, 'but because of the virus, we're not allowed to accept food or drink.'

'That's a shame,' he said. His grin broadened, and his eyes shifted to her colleague. 'Because I've got these.'

His hand snaked from behind his back, and held aloft a bunch of over-ripe bananas.

Carly's left hand found her baton, while her right reached for the pouch with the handcuffs. The dog rose silently from its haunches and strained at the leash. Powell placed his hand on Carly's arm and drew her gently away.

'Leave it,' he said. 'He's not worth it. Besides, we're not wearing body cams, so it would be his word against ours. And,' he whispered, 'I know another way to wipe that grin off his face.'

They walked in silence to their cars, parked one behind the other. The one person per vehicle rule had been brought in even before the lockdown began. Carly felt sorry for their colleagues for whom social distancing was impossible, like the tactical aid teams, crammed into their vans. Right now though, she was more concerned for Henry Powell. He had dealt with more than his fair share of racism while in uniform. He'd confided in her that CID, and then FMIT, had been a walk in the park by comparison. The irony was that had they been in uniform, they'd have been wearing cameras, and the scumbag would have been bang to rights. She bleeped her key to unlock her car and looked over at him.

'What did you mean back there?' she asked.

'What about?'

'Wiping that smirk off his face?'

It was Henry's turn to grin. 'I'm willing to bet,' he said, in an exaggerated Jamaican accent, 'that that animal is a cross-bred pit bull and American Staffordshire terrier.'

Carly smiled. 'The Dangerous Dogs Act 1991.'

He opened his driver's door and leaned on it. 'Exactly,' he said. 'And then there's that warning in the window implying that he'd use the animal as a weapon? I believe we have a duty to inform the Dog Enforcement Team of our concerns, don't you, officer?'

Chapter 17

'I've a face to face with ACC Gates in fifteen minutes,' Caton told them, 'so let's stay focused.'

They were spaced around the table in the conference room. Half of the windows had been opened so that they wouldn't need masks.

'Let's start with what we have from the passive media. DS Hulme?'

'We're beginning to get there, Boss,' Hulme replied. 'It wasn't as difficult as we'd thought. We've covered the two weeks immediately before her death. It all seems to tie in with the information from the door-to-door enquiries. In that time, she's had no visitors – let alone anyone seen going inside the house – and only a postwoman approaching on foot. She seemed to get post at least every other day. Looked like fliers most of the time.'

'Any parcels?' Caton asked.

'Nothing that wouldn't go through the letterbox, although that could have included a packet of painkillers, of course.'

'Vehicles?'

'Milkman three times a week, always the same person. It's a van with a logo on the side, every Thursday round eleven a.m. Always the same male carrying a large box.'

Caton nodded. 'That'll be the groceries, courtesy of the council catering team.'

'Only it wasn't a council van,' the DS said. 'The logo said "MancShare". Other than that, there was a privately registered Volvo estate that called three times with parcels of varying sizes – looked like courier deliveries.'

'Her son said he'd arranged some deliveries,' Carly Whittle reminded them.

'Get back on to the son,' Caton said. 'Get him to email us whatever confirmations the firm sent him. There'll be a record of the tracking and delivery details. Let's see if they match up with the Volvo. I take it you've got the DVLA details for both vehicles, DS Hulme?'

'Yes, Boss.'

'Good. Let's have teams round to the registered addresses, and we'd better have someone visit the Royal Mail sorting office to interview that postwoman. And let's keep looking at the passive media back at least another fortnight. There's no telling when that packet was delivered.'

Carly Whittle raised her hand.

'Go ahead,' he said.

'What if it wasn't delivered?' she said. 'We now know she used to do a weekly shop at the supermarket. And there's a Boots in the Mall.'

It was the last thing he wanted to hear. He didn't relish having to tell Helen Gates that all of the supermarkets and chemists in the city would have to clear their shelves, carry out searches, maybe even do a recall of any packets sold.

'According to the forensics report they weren't bought from either place,' said Jack Benson.

'How can you be so sure?' Caton asked.

'Well, they carry branded products. These were packets with just the manufacturer's name on. I've asked them to email the barcode, batch number and serial number to makers and see if they can tell us who bought them At the very least they'll have a record of the wholesaler, and the wholesaler should be able to tell us who the retailer was.'

'What can you tell us about the tablets themselves?'

'It was evident that they'd been tampered with as soon as they opened the packet. The blister packs look totally professional, except they have no branding on them whatsoever. Regulations require, as a minimum, the name of the medicine to be printed on the foil. As to their make-up, all of the pills contained the relevant analgesic product. However, each of them also contained five milligrams of potassium cyanide. One on its own would have been sufficient to cause death within a minute or two, but given that most people take two at a time, potentially within seconds.'

'We're going to need to strengthen the team,' said Caton.

'No question,' Carter agreed.

'Why? What are you thinking, Boss?' Hulme asked.

'Tell him, Nick,' Caton said.

'Professional blister packs?' Carter responded. 'That's a lot of trouble to go to for one murder.'

'So, we're looking for . . . what? A serial killer?' Hulme said.

'It's impossible to say on the basis of one death,' Caton replied, 'but it is looking more likely. We still have to work on the assumption that Millie Dyer was an intended victim rather than a random one, and that means continuing to look for a motive that is personal to her. That it was sent or delivered by someone she knew, or who knew her. At the same time, we have to keep an open mind, and be alert to other victims.'

'Is it possible,' asked Henry Powell, 'that because she couldn't go out during the lockdown, she could have bought them on the Internet herself from our unsub pretending to be a proper supplier? If so, that would definitely be random, wouldn't it?'

'Anyone who sells pharmaceuticals on the web,'

said Duggie Wallace, 'is supposed to be registered with the Medicines and Healthcare products Regulatory Agency (MHRA). A logo on the site should identify if the seller is registered and approved.'

'All assuming that people know to look for the logo,' Powell pointed out.

'That's true,' Wallace said. 'And even when it's there, you have to scroll down to find it, and it's not that conspicuous.'

'I bet it's easy enough to buy as many as you want on the Dark Web,' Jimmy Hulme suggested.

'The Dark Web?' said Caton. 'Given what we've been told about the victim, do you really see her using the Dark Web? She didn't have a computer, and she hadn't even unpacked the tablet or the iPhone her son sent her.'

That brought them back down to reality.

'Even with the authorised firms,' Carter said, 'surely it's not beyond the realm of the possible that an employee could slip a dodgy pack into an order before it's sent out? Just as anyone, employee or otherwise, could slip one on to the shelves of a supermarket or a chemist, say?'

'Not without having access to the store barcode printer,' said Benson, 'or it wouldn't register as one of theirs at the checkout. They'd have to open a pack and substitute a sheet before sealing it again.'

Caton decided this wasn't going anywhere. 'Right,' he said. 'I need a list of everyone who manufactures or sells portable equipment for making blister-packs into or across the UK, and then get onto them. We need a list of their customers over the past twelve months. At the same time, we will have to let the coroner know,' he continued. 'I'm going to advise the Assistant Chief Constable that we should warn all GPs and all NHS first responder services – ambulance and paramedics – that with any sudden deaths they should consider cyanide poisoning as a possible cause, and check for unbranded blister pack medication.'

'How are they going to do that without creating panic?' Carter wondered out loud. 'We've all been told to use analgesics if we think we have Covid-19 symptoms, and everyone's completely spooked as it is.'

'Look, we don't have a choice,' Caton replied. 'Our duty of care overrides everything else. They will just have to find the right way to go about it. The problem is that as soon as we do put it out there, we'll have alerted the perpetrator that we're onto him or her.'

'If it is personal to this victim,' said Carly Whittle, 'then surely the perpetrator will already know that we're investigating her death. If, on the other hand, she's only one of a number of victims, then we're looking for a perpetrator who probably doesn't give a damn and who, on the contrary, considers themselves too clever to be caught, and at the same time will probably get a secondary wave of excitement and gratification from all the publicity.'

They all stared at her.

'Great point, DS Whittle,' said Caton. 'It's good to know that someone's been doing her homework.'

She blushed.

'While I think about it,' he said, 'I want that analysis of the contents of her bins, the wastepaper recycling bin in particular. There may be clues there relating to postal and other deliveries.'

'We're already on it, Boss,' Benson said.

Caton looked at his watch. 'I'd better go,' he said, 'unless there's anything urgent?'

DS Hulme raised his hand. 'Just a quick one,' he said. 'It's about the revised regulations for social distancing.' He read from the sheet of paper in his hand. '"For any instances involving contact under two metres with a person who claims to have, or may have, Covid-19, officers need to wear one of the fluid-repellent surgical face masks, make sure the metal strap of the mask fits snugly over the bridge of the nose, and don disposable eye protectors."'

'What about it?' Caton said.

'When I circulated them, I got the impression that one or two of those out there still see it as a bit of joke.'

Caton rose to his feet. 'In which case,' he said, 'kindly remind them that this isn't just about their own health, it's for the safety of the whole team. Any failure to comply will result in a fine and a disciplinary warning. And if they do go off sick and I discover they've been playing fast and loose with the regs, the same will apply – if the virus doesn't kill them first. That should wipe the smile off their faces.'

Chapter 18

'It's a mess, Tom,' said the Assistant Chief Constable for Crime.

She wasn't looking too good herself. She'd obviously been due a visit to the hairdresser when lockdown was imposed. Her roots were showing and the ends were beginning to curl. Plus, she looked as though she'd been up all night. It didn't help that she was too close to the camera. But then, if the image at the top of Caton's own screen was anything to go by, he wasn't exactly hot stuff and photoshoot-ready himself.

'As if this bloody virus wasn't enough . . .' she continued. 'So you're now telling me that we have some lunatic adulterating with cyanide the very medicine that people are relying on to see them through it? This is our very own perfect storm!'

'It looks that way, Ma'am,' he replied, 'although with any luck, it'll be a one-off.'

She leaned closer into the camera as though in the hope of better reading his expression. 'You don't believe that, do you?'

'No, Ma'am,' he admitted. 'It just seems a lot of trouble to go to for one victim.'

'Christ!' she said. 'I might just as well tell them it's the end of the world and be done with it!'

'I don't think it's that bad, Ma'am,' he ventured.

'That was hyperbole, Detective Chief Inspector,' she said. 'I'd have thought a person of your calibre would have known that. Besides, I won't be doing it – you will.'

Caton had seen that coming. 'Could I make a suggestion, Ma'am?'

She sat back and folded her arms. 'Go on.'

'Might it be better to put out two quite separate press announcements, rather than one?'

'Why?'

'In order to reduce the likelihood of people putting two and two together.'

'Saying what exactly?'

'The first, a standard statement saying that the body of a woman in her seventies has been discovered at her home. That the exact cause of death has yet to be confirmed, but her death is being treated as suspicious. Investigations are ongoing.'

'And the second?'

'Quite separately, a public health warning from, say, ourselves, jointly with the Chief Public Health Officer for Manchester, advising people to be on the lookout for packets of painkillers that don't have the name of the drug printed on the silver foil blister pack, especially if it's a packet they have not purchased themselves. If they do find such a packet, then they should not under any circumstances take any of the tablets, but immediately contact the local police on the 101 number. It could be accompanied by a warning to only buy drugs online from approved pharmacies.'

She shook her head. 'I don't think that first part'll wash,' she told him. 'Didn't you see that thirty-second piece on *North West Tonight* last night, featuring a video sent in by a helpful member of the public?'

Caton's heart sank. 'No, Ma'am,' he said, 'I was still at Nexus House. What did it show?'

'Marked cars outside the victim's house, including a crime scene investigation van. Officers putting up a cordon.' She frowned. 'The Press Office should have told you. You realise it means the vultures are circling?'

She leaned in again, and her eyes narrowed. 'Was there any mention of pill-tampering during the door-to-door enquiries? Or surprise packages?'

Bugger, thought Caton.

His expression told her everything she needed to know.

'There you go then,' she said. 'The sooner you issue a statement the better. Whichever way we do it, the press are going to be onto it like a hot potato. If they do make the connection, we'll just have to try and play it down. Tell them we're treating it as an isolated incident, but that our duty of care to the public means we have to err on the side of caution and issue the warning. People should not panic, simply exercise common sense and follow the advice they've been given. You concentrate on that. I'll make sure that all the emergency services are alerted to be on the lookout for painkillers that may have been tampered with. If there's another victim and we haven't issued a warning, they'll have our guts for garters.'

Now where have I heard that before? Caton thought. 'Stay alert. Follow the guidance. Stay safe.'

'Yes, Ma'am,' he replied. 'I'll get straight onto it.'

Drafting it was one thing, he told himself. Fronting it would be another matter entirely. Maybe he could persuade the Press Office to do it?

Good luck with that, he thought.

Chapter 19

Carly and Henry Powell had nipped out for a couple of pre-wrapped sandwiches from the Londis convenience store on Stockport Road. As they entered the Incident Room, Nick Carter called out to them.

'You two, don't bother taking your coats off!'

'What about our reports?' said Carly. 'We haven't finished typing them up.'

'Got your tablets, haven't you?' he said.

'Yes,' they chorused obediently.

'Well, you can finish them in the car, and send them to DS Hulme. Anything you haven't managed to finish, you can complete when you get back from this one.'

He handed Carly an A4 plastic display folder with transparent pockets inside containing several typed sheets and a series of photos.

'What's all this?' she asked.

'The postwoman whose round includes the victim's house, she's waiting for you at the South West Delivery Office on Norton Street. Her name and the address are in the front of the file. After that you'll find details and images of a number of envelopes and the outer packaging of parcels retrieved from the victim's recycling bins. We need to know if the postie delivered all of them, and if not, which ones arrived by other means. We also need to know if she recalls having delivered any small packages in the past month, and if so, whether there's a record of where they were posted from. See what she can tell you about any other comings and goings in that close. Posties can be a fount of information. She'll know all the locals, so strangers are going to stand out like a sore thumb. Got that?'

'Yes, Boss,' they chorused.

'And when you're done, see what the milkman has to say. I'll have DS Hulme text you the details.'

'She didn't have her milk delivered though, did she, Boss?' Henry Powell said.

'Glad to see you've been keeping up, DC Powell,' Carter replied, 'but given that milkmen generally start their rounds an hour or two before the sun comes up – right when it's peak performance time for burglars, prowlers and other such devious bastards – it's got to be worth hearing what he has to say, don't you reckon?'

'Yes, Boss,' Powell said. He held up his sandwich. 'Can we eat these first?'

'No, you can't,' Carter replied. 'It'll take too long. You'll have to wash your hands first, use the sanitiser, wash them again afterwards, sanitise again. You could be there and back in that time. Eat them in the car like everyone else.'

* * *

'At least the army let us stop for our scran,' said Henry, brushing crumbs from his jacket.

They were waiting in the delivery office car park for someone to come and fetch them.

'I didn't know you were in the army?' Carly said.

'I joined up when I was eighteen,' he told her. 'My mum told me I was wasting my life, that I should have gone to uni. My dad pretended to agree, but on the quiet he was secretly pleased.'

'What do your parents do?' she asked.

'My mother teaches maths at Manchester Academy.

My dad was a sergeant in the Paras during the first Gulf War. He did a spell with military intelligence shortly before he left. These days, he's a security ops centre manager in Trafford Park. Not bad for the son of a Jamaican goat farmer, as he's always so fond of reminding me.'

'So you followed in your father's footsteps?'

He laughed. 'Not consciously – it was just something I'd always fancied. He was disappointed when I told him I'd chosen the Queen's Dragoons rather than the Parachute Regiment.'

'Why did you?'

'Because of the Jackals?'

'I have no idea what you're talking about.'

There was a gleam in his eyes. 'It's a reconnaissance vehicle like no other – a superfast, highly mobile weapons platform, with a suspension system that's good for any terrain. Imagine a Humvee on steroids.'

'How fast?'

'Eighty miles an hour max.'

'No shit!' she said. 'No wonder you passed the Advanced Driver training first time.'

He shrugged. 'That's time expired. There's not much call for it in CID.'

'I bet you miss it though?'

'The army or the driving?'

'Both.'

He thought about it. 'To be honest? Neither – not really.'

'You just said "to be honest",' she observed. 'We both know what that means.'

Before he had a chance to respond, a woman in blue trousers and a matching jacket called to them from the entrance to the building.

'Detectives!' she said. 'If you'd like to step this way?'

'"Detectives",' Carly muttered. 'She's been watching too many episodes of *Breaking Bad*.'

Chapter 20

'What do you think?' Carly asked.

She and Henry stood at either end of a table with the evidence bags spread out between them.

Beth Richards, a stocky twenty-seven-year-old postwoman, had been bending over the bags, examining each one in turn and rearranging them in two horizontal rows. She pursed her lips and stood up.

'Those on the top row,' she said, 'I must have delivered, because that address is on my round. They're all postmarked within the past week and I haven't missed a day in that time.'

Carly pointed to the two bags on the second row. 'What about these?'

'The white padded piece looks like it's part of the wrapping from a small parcel – that's two kilos max. It's not a Royal Mail counters parcel though. It doesn't have the stamp or the postmark on it so I couldn't say if and when I might have delivered it, but I don't recognise it. The brown one I know I didn't deliver. It's almost certainly an old Amazon parcel someone's reused. I'd have recognised that for certain if I'd delivered it within the last couple of weeks.'

'How can you be so sure?' Carly said.

The postwoman rotated the evidence bag on the table and pointed to the bottom right-hand section.

'That bit down there that looks like a tail is part of the Amazon logo, and that section of faded barcode is where someone's ripped the original label off.'

The two detectives looked at each other.

'I bet we could find a spot for Ms Richards in our forensics lab,' said Henry Powell.

'*Mrs* Richards, actually,' she informed him. 'I have a husband and two school-age children.'

That was a bit unfair, Carly thought. It wasn't as though he'd been trying to proposition her.

'Sorry,' said Henry, looking and sounding distinctly embarrassed, 'I didn't mean to presume.'

'Forget it,' the postwoman replied. 'It's not important – I just thought you should know.'

'How are you managing to juggle this job and your children's home-schooling during the lockdown?' Carly asked, hoping to lighten the atmosphere.

'My husband's on furlough from British Oxygen,' Mrs Richards replied. 'Demand from restaurants and bars and much of industry has plummeted because they've all been forced to close. Of course, demand's gone up for oxygen for all those ventilators in the NHS hospitals, not to mention the Covid Nightingales, so it's a good job that's not what he works on, because to be honest, it's great having him at home.'

'So you definitely remember delivering all these other ones?' said Carly.

'Yes.'

'And did any of them feel as though they might have contained a small cardboard box or packet?'

The postwoman frowned. 'Like what?'

Carly wrestled with how much she could afford to give away.

Henry stepped into the breach. 'About yay big,' he said, using the forefinger and thumb of both hands to indicate the dimensions of the pack of those tablets retrieved from the victim's house.

Mrs Richard's brow wrinkled as she studied the top

row again. 'I can't say I remember for sure,' she said, 'but I think this one' – she indicated what looked like a large letter envelope – 'had something about that size inside. I remember folding it so it would fit through the letterbox.'

Carly noted down the number on the evidence bag.

'When was this?' Henry Powell asked.

'Possibly last Tuesday or Wednesday,' she replied. 'The postmark should tell you.'

'Have you noticed anyone acting suspiciously in or around the close over the past month or so, Mrs Richards?' Henry asked.

She frowned. 'Suspicious . . . in what way?'

'Loitering? Studying houses? Checking for alarms or CCTV? That kind of thing. Especially people you haven't seen before.'

She shook her head. 'The close is near the back end of my round. I'm there between eleven forty-five a.m. and twelve-thirty, regular as clockwork. That's not when I expect to see people sussing out easy targets for a burglary – though this isn't exactly the best of times, is it? The streets are empty and strangers stick out like a sore thumb.'

'And no one has?' Carly said.

'Not unless you count the online delivery drivers. I know most of those by sight, some of them even by name.'

'That's something we might need to come back to you on,' Carly told her. 'In the meantime, thank you for your time. You've been really helpful.'

* * *

'Has she though?' said Henry as they made their way back to the cars.

'Well, we'll only know the answer to that when

we've tested the three she identified for DNA and fingerprints,' Carly said, 'and even then, only if one or more of them comes back with a match.'

Henry stopped by his driver's door. 'Tell you what though,' he said, 'we should recruit her as a Special Constable, or a PCSO. All that local knowledge and eyes and ears stuff? In fact, we could sign up *all* the posties as volunteers to replace our dwindling neighbourhood policing teams.'

'I'll let you suggest that to the Chief Constable,' Carly told him. 'I'm sure he'd be most appreciative.' She opened her car door. 'Come to that, why don't you throw in milkmen and widow cleaners too?'

He grinned. 'Not window cleaners. With them, you'd be talking paid confidential informants, not volunteers.'

'Now you're stereotyping,' she told him.

'Pot, kettle,' he replied.

'Come again?'

'Milk*men*? What's that if it's not stereotyping?'

Carly laughed. 'It didn't take long for the Boss to work his spell on you already. From Army grunt to politically correct detective sergeant. That's some conversion.'

Henry took an exaggerated intake of breath through pursed lips, while shaking his head.

'Army grunt?' he replied. 'Like I said . . . pot, kettle!'

Chapter 21

Detective Constable Josh Nair slowed as he approached the barrier. He glanced to his left where the New Seasons Inn sat empty and forlorn. He wondered how long it would be before its doors opened again? How long before he'd be able to go out for a meal . . . His stomach rumbled in forlorn anticipation.

Immediately ahead, a twelve-foot-high painting of a leaping salmon on a glass and blue steel building welcomed him to the famous Fish Market. DI Carter had told him that members of the public were welcome to come here and buy at trade prices, providing they didn't bring their children with them. He made a mental note to do that as soon as restrictions were lifted.

He stopped at the gatehouse, lowered his window and proffered his ID. The security guard peered through the window and raised the barrier.

Josh parked next to DI Carter's Golf, ensuring there was an empty space left between them. He checked that he had a mask in his breast pocket, retrieved his tablet from the glove box and climbed out.

'What kept you?' Carter said.

'I've been caught out several times by the ridiculous new speed limits on Whitworth Street East, Boss,' Josh replied.

'You just need to keep your wits about you,' Carter told him. 'I can tell you, blindfolded, where all the fixed cameras are on that stretch.'

'What about the mobile ones?'

Carter grinned. 'If you can't spot those, you don't deserve to call yourself a detective. Come on, let's find this unit where our guy hangs out.'

They headed towards the first of the warehouse buildings that flanked the vast expanse of the New Smithfield Market. Thirty-five acres of imposing green-shuttered, dark brick buildings on which not only the city but the entire region depended for its food. On the side facing them, only a handful of shutters were raised.

'It's very quiet,' Nair remarked.

'That's because they start at two a.m., and most of their commercial business is concluded by ten o'clock,' Carter told him. 'Then it's just the walk-in members of the public. You want to be here around four o'clock in the morning – it's like rush hour in Beijing.'

'Really?' said Josh. 'When were you in Beijing, Boss?'

'I wasn't,' Carter replied. 'I was using a metaphor.'

'A simile, actually,' Josh ventured.

Carter stopped in his tracks, forcing his DC to step back. 'You what?'

'What you just said, Boss. It was a simile, not a metaphor.'

'Same difference,' said Carter, setting off again.

'Actually, it isn't,' Josh insisted, hurrying after him. 'She's *as* wicked as a witch,' he said. 'Now that is a simile. Whereas, she *is* a witch, that is a metaphor.'

Carter scowled. 'And you, Nair, are as annoying as a vanload of smackheads.'

Nair was unable to read the expression on Carter's face from two paces back. 'That is excellent,' he exclaimed. 'A vanload of smackheads. I must remember that.'

He was saved by a short, stocky middle-aged man sporting a lockdown goatee beard, who was blocking Carter's path. He wore a grey bobble hat from which curls of sandy hair protruded, along with a white coat and rubber boots.

'Can I help you?' he asked.

'As a matter of fact, you can,' Carter said. 'We're looking for Unit 21b. MancShare?'

The man nodded enthusiastically. His crinkly blue eyes lit up behind his glasses. He had something of the jolly features and ebullient personality of a young Bill Oddie.

'The soup kitchen guys!' the man exclaimed. 'Brilliant, what they're doing. Mind you, they couldn't be in a better place. A lot of the traders are pitching in with donations of their own. Follow me. I'll take you to them. I'll just have to let Mariella know first.'

He led them into the Fish Hall, where they were met by double-height white walls that would not have been out of place in a hospital, a bright blue floor across which black and yellow tape marked out two-metre social distancing, and the unmistakeable smell of fish, fresh from the sea. They passed units where staff were busy hosing down the chiller cabinets, and the floor behind that led through to preparation areas and the loading bays. Their guide came to a halt in front of a unit over which a large red sign proclaimed J&B WILDE: WHOLESALE FISH, MEAT, GAME AND POULTRY.

'This is me!' said the man.

A series of countertop refrigerated display cabinets held a staggering array of poultry and meat. Where they ended, a row of open polystyrene boxes cushioned all manner of fish and seafood, from octopus to whole wild salmon. Pride of place was held by a six-and-a-half kilo turbot.

'I'm Brian Wilde,' he told them proudly. 'Four generations this firm has been in my family. It's in my blood, and my sister's too.' He turned, and set off at pace, exchanging witticisms with his staff as he hurried past.

'Does he want us to follow him, Boss?' said Nair.

Carter shrugged. 'I've no idea.'

Wilde disappeared into what looked like an office that doubled as a counter, open to the floor below. The detectives followed, stopping two metres away. The desks were piled high with bills and receipts. Behind the counter, scribbling notes as the floor staff shouted out orders was a woman a decade or so younger than Wilde, with long sandy blonde hair to her shoulders. Two of the walls were covered with selfies of Brian Wilde with a host of celebrities.

'Wow! That's Fox Mulder,' Nair exclaimed.

Carter appeared bewildered.

'*The X Files*?' said Nair. 'David Duchovny? The actor?'

'No idea who you're talking about,' Carter told him. He pointed. 'But I recognise that one – it's Steven Segal.'

Now it was Nair's turn to shake his head.

'*Hard to Kill*, and *Under Siege*,' said Carter. 'Brilliant martial arts actor, right up there with Jackie Chan.'

'You've lost me, Boss,' Nair said, 'but I must say that it is most appropriate?'

Carter stared at him. 'Appropriate?'

'Steven *Seagull*. And Mr Wilde being a fishmonger?'

Carter glowered, and turned his attention back to the brother and sister in front of them. 'Excuse me,' he said, 'but do you deliver your fish?'

The two stared at him.

'We've always offered free local deliveries throughout Manchester and the surrounding areas,' Brian Wilde replied. 'On the same day, providing the order is placed before eight a.m., otherwise it's the following day. Mind you, a lot of that's dried up since all the restaurants had to close. We've had to compensate by trying to up our service for the public.'

'Do your vans do regular deliveries around the M32 postcode area in Stretford?' Carter asked.

Wilde turned to his sister. 'Mariella?'

'We had those twice-weekly deliveries to an outlet in the Stretford Mall,' she reminded him, 'but they've been closed since the twenty-eighth of March. Same with the restaurants and chippies on Chester Road.'

'What about the residential estates?' Carter asked.

She shook her head. 'Nothing regular. But there might have been the odd order phoned in. People have been stocking up their freezers for the long haul. It's one of the things that's kept us going. I could check if you like?'

'That would be really helpful,' Carter told her. He took out one of his contact cards and wrote the postcode and the name of the victim's close on the back.

'We'd be interested in details of anyone they may have seen acting suspiciously in this vicinity within the last few weeks,' he said, placing the card on the counter.

She waited for him to step back before picking up the card.

'I'll get right on to it,' she said, with a warm smile that was reflected in her voice. 'Anything to help the police.'

Chapter 22

'This may be bigger and better, but it's a far cry from the old market,' Wilde said, as he led them towards the first of the huge halls. 'It was more alive and pulsating then, and full of characters. Half of them were lunatics, always fighting with each other, but you wouldn't believe the sense of comradeship. It was more like a comedy store than a workplace.'

'Not unlike FMIT then,' Carter muttered.

The first thing that struck them was the heady mix of sweet, pungent and citrusy aromas from fruit and vegetables, piled on pallets stacked to just beneath the massive curved ceiling as far as the eye could see,

'This is amazing!' said Nair. 'It reminds me so much of Azadpur Mandi.'

'Come again?' Carter shouted, over the sound of forklift trucks ferrying full and empty pallets around the hall.

'Azadpur Mandi!' Nair repeated. 'In North Delhi. It's the largest fruit and vegetable market in the whole of Asia. We go there sometimes when we're visiting my grandparents.'

'And it's bigger than this?'

'Much bigger. Open air, as well as enclosed. What's more, it never closes or even slows down. The labourers, porters and guys who do the loading and unloading work round the clock in shifts.'

'The unions would never agree to that,' Carter observed, swerving neatly to avoid a pile of purple onions in sacks.

'Those guys didn't,' said Nair. 'The loaders mobilised themselves and went on strike. They were briefly instrumental in obtaining better wages and conditions, but it looks like they could be under threat again.'

'Sounds like the Police Federation could learn a thing or two,' Carter said. 'Perhaps you should have a word?'

'I'm not sure about that, Boss,' Nair said. 'I think we do pretty well as it is – decent shift pattern, good remuneration for overtime, which is in any case optional.'

Carter turned to face him. 'Speak for yourself, Detective Constable,' he said. 'You're forgetting that overtime for Inspectors and above was bought out years ago. Think about that while you're sunning yourself on the Costa Brava and I'm working a double shift for no extra pay.'

Josh was tempted to reply that he never sunned himself anywhere, let alone the Costa Brava. Firstly, because he did not require a tan; secondly, because it was well known to be a cause of cancer; and thirdly, because he much preferred art galleries, museums and restaurants. The look on Carter's face persuaded him otherwise. He followed sheepishly as Carter hurried after Wilde, who was already exiting the hall. He was waiting for them outside.

'There you go,' he said, pointing to a unit two down that was a hive of activity. 'Good luck,' he said. Before Carter could thank him, he disappeared back into the hall.

Carter and Nair turned their attention to Unit 21b. Backed right up to the unit, with its rear doors open, was a white van. On its side was emblazoned the MancShare logo, and the words CHALLENGING FOOD WASTE, COMBATTING HUNGER! A tall, thick-set man in his fifties and a short, chubby woman, younger by a decade or so, were loading boxes of provisions into the back of the vans. Almost in unison, they were singing 'Happy' by Pharrell Williams.

'They seem content in their work,' Nair observed.

'Amazing deduction,' Carter responded. 'Go to the top of the class.' He held up his ID and raised his voice.

'Police!' he said. 'Is the manager around?'

The man put down the box he was carrying and straightened up. 'That would be me,' he said. 'How can I help you?'

'I understand you make weekly deliveries to this address.' Carter held his printed sheet up at arm's length. 'We'd like to talk to the driver – or drivers – concerned.'

The man approached, looked at it and nodded. 'If I remember rightly,' he said, 'that's one of the clients the council passed on to us.' He turned to his companion. 'This is one of Adam's, isn't it?'

She joined him and peered at the note. 'That's right,' she said.

The man turned back to face the two detectives. His face clouded over. 'His name's Adam Novotný. He's not in any trouble, is he?'

'What makes you ask that?' Carter said.

'No reason, except for the fact that you're asking about him. He's a good man – completely trustworthy.'

'That's reassuring to know,' Carter replied, 'because we're hoping that he may be able to assist in an ongoing investigation. Is he here?'

'Adam went to collect a pallet of apples from one of the traders,' the woman said. 'He should be back any moment.'

'While we're waiting,' Carter said, 'perhaps you could tell us your names, and what it is you do here?'

'We're part of a charitable national network that delivers surplus food to over ten thousand frontline charities and community groups,' the manager replied. 'We get funding from the National Lottery which helps us to maintain and fuel our vehicles and train our volunteers.'

'And this Adam Novotný is a volunteer?' Carter guessed.

'That's right.'

'How long has he been volunteering here?'

'Since the start of December. Saturdays, to start with. But since he was furloughed because of the pandemic, he's been coming more often.'

'And what is it he does?'

'The same as all the others.'

'Which is?'

'Sort the produce as it arrives, take orders, pack the supplies, and then deliver them to wherever: homeless shelters, community cafes, senior citizens' lunch clubs, school breakfast clubs. Wherever we've been advised there are vulnerable people basically.'

'Does that include people on the Government's list of those who are clinically vulnerable to Covid-19?' Carter asked.

The man shook his head. 'No, that's not us. The supermarkets deliver direct to them – same with the pharmacies.'

The detectives exchanged a glance.

'I think you might mean the council's list, Boss?' Nair suggested tentatively.

'Oh, right,' said the manager, before Carter had time to respond. 'Yes, we do have a list of people referred by the council – people who wouldn't maybe qualify under the Government's criteria but whom the council consider vulnerable in one way or another.'

'Here's Adam now,' his colleague said, staring past the two detectives.

They turned to look. A man, in his late twenties perhaps, tall with an athletic build and closely cropped black hair, was pushing a trolley loaded with two boxes of bright red apples. He looked up, saw them staring at him and stopped abruptly. A look of panic flitted across his face, and for a moment it looked as though he might turn and run. Then his expression changed to one of resignation. He began to walk slowly towards them.

Chapter 23

'You're police officers?'

He sounded relieved.

'That's right,' Carter said. 'Why, who did you think we were?'

They had moved to a quiet spot outside an empty unit where they could have some privacy and social distance.

'Immigration,' Novotný replied.

'Is that why you looked so worried back there?'

'I was worried there might be some kind of problem.'

'What kind of problem?'

'With my status.'

'What, you're an asylum seeker? Illegal immigrant?'

'No! Nothing like that,' he protested. 'I've just been granted settled status. I was worried they might have changed their minds.'

'What reason would they have to do that, Sir?' Carter asked.

'None? But who knows with your Home Office?'

'Well, it's *your* Home Office too now,' Nair pointed out.

Novotný laughed nervously. 'That's true.'

'Where are you from?' Carter asked.

The man hesitated, as though considering whether to answer *here*. 'Slovakia,' he said in the end.

'How long have you lived in the UK?'

'Five years. I came to be with an English student I

met at university in Bratislava.' He shrugged. 'Our relationship didn't last, but at least I got a good job here in Manchester.'

'And what was that exactly?'

'I'm an accounts manager and sometimes translator with Cybernolia,' he replied.

'What is that, a fizzy drink?'

'One of the biggest companies you have never heard of. It owns many online retail companies, and we also create bespoke technology platforms for any company wishing to sell its products or services online.' He made it sound like a promo.

'I understand you've been furloughed?' Carter said. 'When did that start?'

'Strictly speaking, it hasn't started. Although the scheme has been announced, my company does not begin to receive the money to cover the eighty per cent of my salary until the end of this month. But we were all told to work from home two weeks ago, and we're still being paid.'

'So how come you can find the time to volunteer here?'

'I can work whatever hours suit me so long as I meet my targets.' He patted his breast pocket. 'I have my mobile phone if anyone needs to contact me. I help out here when I can because I enjoy it, and because it's the only legitimate excuse I have to get out of the house, meet other people and get some exercise.'

'Very commendable, I'm sure,' Carter said. 'Now, I understand that you make deliveries for MancShare in the Stretford area of the city. Is that right?'

Novotný looked puzzled. 'Yes?'

'And does that include . . .' He read out Millie Dyer's address.

Novotný's face lit up. 'Mrs Dyer!' he said. 'This

week will be her third.' He saw the expression on their faces. 'Why are you asking? She's alright, isn't she?'

'I'm afraid not,' Carter told him. 'I'm sorry to have to tell you that Mrs Dyer has passed away.'

In the short time that Nair had been with the syndicate he had come to realise that all of his more experienced colleagues deployed their euphemisms for death with great care, and this was one that DI Carter used sparingly. It had the advantage of minimising the shock factor for those close to the victim, and implying a less violent and potentially innocent cause of death for those who might be a potential suspect, thus lulling them into a false sense of security.

'But that is terrible,' Novotný responded. 'She always seemed so strong . . . so healthy.'

He looked at Carter and then at Nair. Their poker faces stared back at him.

'How did she come to die?' he asked.

'That's what we're hoping to ascertain, Mr Novotný,' Carter said. 'What is that you've been delivering to Mrs Dyer?'

'The same as to everyone else. We pack up identical boxes, depending on what has been donated on that day.'

'Such as?'

'Fish, meat, poultry, fruit such as apples and oranges, bananas, pears, vegetables, maybe a tin or two of soup or tuna. The odd treat, such as cake or chocolate.'

'That's it?' said Carter. 'Only food?'

'That's right. Food that would otherwise go to waste. Even the chocolates have passed their best before date. The Government boxes for the vulnerable only contain goods that can be stored at room temperature, but most of ours is fresh, and can be frozen or refrigerated.'

He sounded proud and passionate. Then his expression changed.

'It wasn't food poisoning that killed Mrs Dyer, was it?'

'Not as far as we're aware,' Carter told him. 'You certainly shouldn't trouble yourself on that score, Sir. What we would like to know is if, when you've been making your deliveries, you may have noticed anyone acting suspiciously?'

'In what way?'

'Anyone who looks out of place – loitering outside houses without any apparent purpose, for instance, making a note of where house alarms and CCTV cameras are placed, or simply sitting in their vehicles and maybe trying to hide their face.'

'I'm sorry,' he said. 'I don't remember anyone behaving in these ways.'

'Fair enough,' said Carter. 'If you could just let my colleague have your address and mobile phone number in case we need to contact you again? Thank you for your help, Mr Novotný. And congratulations on your citizenship.'

After an exchange of details, the two detectives left.

'I hope he doesn't come to regret it,' muttered Carter.

'What?' Nair asked.

'His citizenship. Let's face it, right now the UK's not looking that attractive a proposition, is it?'

Nair was no longer listening. He stopped and turned. 'Just one question, Mr Novotný,' he called out. 'Does your company – Cyberate – own, or have an account with, any pharmaceutical companies?'

'Of course,' Novotný replied. 'Pharma is a major online growth area, along with health and beauty products. Why?'

'Thank you,' Nair said. 'Stay safe, Sir. It's a cruel world out there.'

Carter shook his head and kept walking.

'It certainly is,' he said. 'Here am I, stuck with Danny DeVito for a partner!'

Chapter 24

'Puppa Jeezas!'

Henry Powell's voice exploded over the radio.

'That was close.'

Carly glanced in the rear-view mirror as she braked at the lights at the bottom of the slipway. 'That'll teach you not to overtake when approaching a motorway exit,' she said. 'Did they miss that out on the Advanced Driver test?'

'I lost sight of you when you suddenly sped up, and then pulled in front of that tanker.'

'It's called reading the road, Henry.'

The lights changed. At the next roundabout, she took the second exit into the Logistics North industrial estate. Discovering that she had lost him again, she pulled in to the kerb of the approach road. Thirty seconds later, Henry's Nissan pulled up alongside. She wound her window down and signalled for him to do the same.

'Satnav says it's less than two hundred yards away,' she said, grinning. 'Try not to get lost.'

'You wait till this social-distance nonsense is over,' he told her, 'and I'll give you the ride of your life.'

She raised her eyebrows. 'Sexual harassment, Detective Constable?'

Henry felt himself blushing. 'Come on,' he protested, 'you know what I meant.'

Carly laughed, raised the window and drove off. She stopped at the barrier to the vast blue-grey steel Amazon Distribution Centre and pressed the buzzer.

'How can I help?' said the disembodied voice.

She held her warrant card up in front of the CCTV camera.

'Detective Sergeant Whittle and Detective Constable Powell, Greater Manchester Police,' she said. 'My colleague is in the vehicle behind me. We have an appointment to speak with one of your couriers.'

There was a pause before the voice replied.

'Please continue ahead, following the signs for visitor parking. Then follow the signs to Reception, where you will be met.'

On entering the Reception area, they were asked to sanitise their hands and then, because the chairs were all taped off, had to stand while they waited. A video on a flat screen extolled the many benefits of joining the company as a warehouse operative: market-leading pay rates with an extra two pounds per hour until May sixteenth; full-time day or night shifts with four days on and three days off; restful break areas, and a canteen serving hot and cold food, free coffee or tea; all in a friendly team environment.

'Sounds just like Nexus House,' Henry observed. 'What do you reckon on this for our next career move, Carly?'

'I doubt you'd meet the twenty-three kilo lifting requirements,' she said. Her eyes fell on a man in his thirties or early forties heading towards them.

'Officers?' he said as he advanced.

'And I was just getting used to "detectives",' Powell whispered.

'You lead on this one,' she whispered back.

'I'm the deputy operations manager,' the man told them. 'Is this to do with the phone call we received with regard to an incident in Stretford?'

'That's correct,' said Henry. 'We understood that

you'd identified the delivery driver from the details of the time, place and licence plate we supplied, and agreed to arrange for us to speak with her here?'

'That's right,' the man replied. 'Mandy Sellars.' He hesitated. 'Do you mind telling what this is in connection with?'

Henry looked at Carly. She gave a discreet shake of her head.

'All that I am at liberty to disclose,' said Henry, 'is that your driver was in the vicinity of a serious incident which we're currently investigating. We're hoping she may have seen something that might assist us with our enquiries.'

'So she's not in any trouble?'

'Not as far as we're aware, Sir.'

It was evident that the man had been hoping for more than that. He searched their faces. When it was clear that nothing more was forthcoming, he gave up.

'Follow me, please,' he said. 'We ask everyone to make sure they stick to the safe distance indicated by the markings on the floor.'

He led them down a corridor, at the end of which he opened a door into one of the rooms. Henry and Carly followed him in.

The room was forty foot square, with a table, screen and flip chart at the far end, and rows of chairs that had been spaced apart. More chairs were stacked in one corner. A woman stood at the front of the room, one hand on the back of a chair.

'This is Mandy Sellars,' the manager said.

Chapter 25

The woman looked to be in her early forties. She had curly blonde hair framing a round face, and wore a plus-size, white cotton wrap top over jeans. She regarded the two detectives with curiosity, rather than the anxiety or suspicion to which they had become accustomed.

'Thank you, Sir,' said Carly pointedly. 'We'll take it from here.'

The operations manager appeared reluctant to go.

'I'll be fine,' Mandy Sellars told him. She smiled. 'I'm a big girl.'

'Well, if you're sure?' he said.

'I'm sure.'

He turned to the two detectives. 'I'll be in Reception if you need to speak with me. Mandy will take you back there.'

He started to walk towards them, realised that the aisle was too narrow for him to pass at a safe distance, turned down the nearest row and exited at the back of the room.

'How do you want to do this?' Mandy Sellars said.

'Why don't you sit down right there, Ms Sellars,' said Henry Powell, 'and we'll come and join you.'

He and Carly stopped two rows away and plonked themselves down on the nearest chair, but on opposite sides of the aisle.

'So what's this all about?' Sellars asked.

This close, Carly could see the worry lines on her face that put her somewhere closer to fifty-five.

'We're hoping,' Powell began, 'that you can help us in relation to an incident that took place in an area where you've been making deliveries. And before you ask, you're not under suspicion, it's just that you may have noticed something that may have seemed insignificant at the time, but could be relevant to our enquiries.'

'That was some speech,' she observed with a smile. 'Mysterious too. When was this?'

'That's the thing,' he said. 'We've got a window of opportunity that could be as much as a couple of weeks. But we do know that your vehicle was in the vicinity at eight-thirty p.m. last Saturday, the fourth.'

'Where was this?'

He gave her the address.

She nodded. 'That's the Highfield Estate. I had two or three drops there on Saturday – one to the flats, one to a semi, and one to one of the bungalows you're talking about. I can't swear it was that address, but if it was, it'll be on the system.'

'So if there were any deliveries to this address, whether or not you made them, they'll be on the system?' he asked.

'Of course,' she said, 'no matter who the carrier was.'

Carly made a note to get the list from the operations manager before they left.

'Carrier?' said Powell. 'Do you mean driver?'

She shook her head. 'No, carrier. There's loads of different firms who fulfil Amazon orders. There's UPS, Yodel, Hermes, DHL, DPD, FedEx, Royal Mail. Not just Amazon drivers and flexies like me.'

'Flexies?' said Carly.

'Part-timers. We work flexible hours to suit ourselves and them. Generally, we pick up locally and just do the last mile or so of a delivery.'

'And these carriers, they'll all be on the system too?' Powell asked.

'That's right. It'll tell you which carrier fulfilled the order and whether it was delivered, but if you want the tracking information that tells you exactly when it was delivered and who by, you'll need to contact the relevant carrier.'

'That's really helpful to know,' he said. 'But to get back to last Saturday evening, when you were on that street, did you see anything out of the ordinary? Anything at all?'

'That depends on what you call *ordinary*,' she said. 'These days, deserted streets are what counts as normal. If there's anyone out and about, they're likely to be walking in the road to avoid someone coming towards them on the pavement. I've had a couple of near misses because someone stepped out from behind a parked car. I had one recently in Salford where this old guy had a black mask on. For a moment, I thought it was a hold-up.'

'Do you remember seeing anything at all on Saturday?' he pressed.

She shook her head again. 'Sorry, no. Mind you . . .'

'Go on,' he said.

'If you've got a photo of the bungalow you're interested in, I'm sure I'll be able to tell you if I've done any recent deliveries there or thereabouts.'

Carly held her tablet aloft. 'I'll do it,' she said. In less than a minute, she was holding her tablet at arm's length towards Mandy Sellars, who was craning forward in her seat.

'Have you got another one showing the houses on either side?' Sellars asked.

Carly flicked through to find exactly the right shot and showed it to her.

The courier's face lit up. 'There you go,' she said. 'I'd have known straight off if you'd told me it was the next but one to the end. I've been there a few times since I went flex. A couple of times around Christmas, once in January and once about a fortnight ago. Give me a mo and I can probably even come up with her name.'

'No need,' Powell told her, 'just tell us about the most recent deliveries.'

'Well, let's see,' she began. 'January, that was quite a big package. Mind you, that doesn't mean a thing.'

'I know,' said Powell. 'I once got a paint roller and tray in a box big enough for a kitchen table.'

The two of them shared a laugh. Carly gave Powell a withering look. He pretended not to notice.

'Was it heavy or light?' he asked.

'Heavyish,' she replied, 'but I can't tell you anything else about it.' Her smile was playful. 'We're not supposed to give them a shake, you know.'

'What about the other one . . . a fortnight ago?' Carly said.

Mandy Sellars frowned, whether at the interruption or because she needed to think about it, Carly couldn't tell.

'Smaller, I think,' she said. 'The size you'd expect to find a book in, or a box of chocolates.' She smiled at Henry Powell. 'Not that anyone sends me chocolates any more, or flowers come to think of it.'

'Did you ever see the addressee or anyone else when you delivered to the house?' Carly asked.

'As a matter of fact, I did,' Mandy Sellars replied. 'On several occasions. I got the impression that she must have been sitting near the window, waiting for me to arrive.' She turned to Henry Powell. 'A lot of people do that, you know. They use our tracking app on their phones. Some of them even ask if I stopped off for a cuppa in the next street because I seemed to have been stopped there for so long.' She grimaced. 'That really pisses me off. Not that I do have a break, of course, not even before this bloody virus – I've got my targets to meet.' She smiled and leaned towards him as though sharing a confidence. 'Not that I don't get plenty of offers . . .'

'And how did she seem on these occasions?' Carly asked, barely able to disguise her frustration.

'Seem? Oh, very polite, very old school. Not one for conversation though. I did ask her this last time how she was doing – you know, what with the lockdown.'

'Do you remember what she said?' Carly asked.

'She said she was fine, thank you. That she was very lucky that she had people looking out for her.'

'Did she say who?'

Sellars shook her head. 'No,' she said, 'and I didn't think it was my place to ask.'

Carly stood to signal to Henry Powell that the interview was over. Henry thanked the courier for her help, and gave her the standard spiel about her letting them know if she remembered anything else. Carly was just about to open the door at the back of the room when Mandy Sellars called out to them.

'Hang on!' she said. 'I've just remembered.'

'Go on?' said Carly.

'Mrs Dyer,' she said. 'Her name – Millie Dyer. Am I right?'

* * *

'What was that all about, Henry?' Carly said.

He drew to an abrupt halt. 'What?'

'"You're not under any suspicion."'

'I was just putting her at her ease.'

117

'Keep up,' she said. 'You know that everyone's a potential suspect until we've ruled them out. If they're innocent, they're not going to appear guilty, are they? But tell a guilty person that they're *not* under suspicion and they're going to relax just enough that you're never going see that telltale apprehension on their face or hear it in their voice.'

'But then again,' he said, 'if they think they're in the clear, they're also going to drop their guard, be that little bit less careful. That's when you're likely to trip them up.'

'And what about your joke about the paint roller?'

'It wasn't a joke,' he protested. 'I was empathising.'

'And what did that lead to?'

He looked confused. 'I have no idea what you're talking about.'

'Her coming on all coy – she was bloody flirting with you!'

He blinked. 'No, she wasn't.'

'Oh yes, she was. "We're not supposed to give them a shake, you know." Pouting her lips like anything, fluttering her eyelashes? "Not that anyone sends me chocolates any more . . . or flowers."' It was a passable impression.

Henry laughed, and set off again. 'You've either got it or you haven't,' he tossed over his shoulder.

'And *you* haven't,' she retorted, 'unless they're over the hill and looking for a toy boy!'

Carly reached her car first, switched on the engine and held down the button to lower the window. Henry swung open his driver's door.

'You're only jealous,' he said.

'In your dreams,' she said, before raising the window and setting off.

Chapter 26

Caton had one foot inside the Press Office when his mobile rang. It was DI Carter.

'Sorry,' Caton said, 'I have to take this.' He stepped back into the corridor. 'Yes, Nick?' he said.

'I'm afraid it looks as though we've got another one, Boss,' Carter said.

'Where?'

'Chorltonville.'

'That's what, three miles from the first one?'

'Just over.'

'Male or female?'

'Female, seventy-four, living alone.'

Caton swore silently. 'Same victimology then.'

'Looks like it, Boss.'

'Who found the body?'

'Paramedic. GP's been informed. FME's on his way. I'm just about to leave. I've advised the team to let their nearest and dearest know not to expect them home for dinner tonight.'

'Text me the address,' Caton told him. 'I'll be with you as soon as I can.'

He shoved his mobile in his pocket and went back into the Press Office.

'I'm sorry,' he said, 'I've got to go.'

The senior press officer looked startled. 'Where are you off to?' she said.

'I've got a body to investigate,' he told her.

She pushed her chair back and stood up. 'What about this press statement?'

'You'd best get someone else to do it,' he said. 'You might want to hold off for an hour or so, because if this does turn out to be a second victim, you'll want to rethink the statement. It'll be better coming from a member of the Command Team, don't you think?' He didn't wait for a reply.

As soon as he reached his car, he switched on the radio and tuned in to BBC Radio Manchester to see if news of this suspicious death had leaked out. It didn't take much – a nosy neighbour, whoever it was that had dialled 999, a first responder with an unhealthy relationship with a member of the press. It turned out that there was a much more important event grabbing the headlines.

'We have just received this statement,' said the announcer, 'from the Prime Minister's Office at 10 Downing Street.

Since Sunday evening, the Prime Minister has been under the care of doctors at St Thomas's Hospital, in London, after being admitted with persistent symptoms of coronavirus.

Over the course of this afternoon, the condition of the Prime Minister has worsened, and, on the advice of his medical team, he has been moved to the intensive care unit at the hospital.

The PM has asked Foreign Secretary Dominic Raab, who is the First Secretary of State, to deputise for him where necessary.

The PM is receiving excellent care, and thanks all NHS staff for their hard work and dedication.'

Caton shook his head. 'That is well bad,' he said, in his best Liam Gallagher imitation.

But not as bad as what was happening right here in Manchester. Not from where he was sitting. Covid-19 might be the ultimate serial killer on a global scale, but there wasn't a lot he could do about that, whereas it was most definitely his responsibility to nail the sick, cowardly bastard who was killing defenceless women on his doorstep.

He turned the radio off, switched on his blues and twos, and put his foot down.

Chapter 27
Chorltonville. 1900 hours.

Caton paused at a roundabout bristling with heritage signs in this garden village built in 1911 after the style of the Arts and Crafts Movement, just three miles south of the city centre. He was left in no doubt that this was a hallowed place.

Conservation Area. Private Road. Access Only. No Heavy Vehicles. Slow Down. Speed Ramps.

If this had been built today, he reflected, it would be a gated community, with a passcode or a barrier operated by a security guard. He ignored the motorist behind him who was leaning on his horn, and studied the map on the screen of his satnav. He plumped for the third exit and turned his blues and twos back on so he could enjoy the look on the face of the driver in his rear-view mirror.

Ahead of him, a winding road emulated a country lane, with grass verges hosting numerous trees. Pairs of semi-detached houses mirrored each other, yet no two pairs were the same. They sported, in various combinations, bay windows, patterns of tiles on gable ends and under windows, stained glass and exposed beams. He recalled that the last time he'd been here was on a local history field trip from Manchester Grammar. It felt like a lifetime ago.

The destination turned out to be a leafy street just off the Meade, a circular green at the heart of the village.

The sun, sinking slowly in the west, cast the trees as long black foreboding shadows across the grass. Caton parked up behind three chevronned police cars, two unmarked cars he recognised as belonging to DS Whittle and DC Powell, another car with a portable blue light on the roof, two CIS vans, and a green and yellow North West Ambulance rapid response vehicle. Two uniformed officers were stringing tape between the trees and fences to create an inner cordon.

He had a sinking feeling of déjà vu, as he picked up his tablet and his murder bag, signed in with the loggist and went to join his colleagues standing beside a uniformed officer at the gate of one of the semis.

'This is a nice place, Boss,' Carly Whittle observed. 'It's like a little oasis. Straight out of a Miss Marple murder mystery.'

'Or *Midsummer Murders*,' Henry Powell added.

'Let's hope it's as easy to solve,' Caton responded.

Nick Carter arrived, breathing heavily. 'DS Hulme says the press release Central Park has just sent out has caused a stir. Apparently, the NHS helpline has been besieged by people worried their pills might have been tampered with, and CrimeStoppers have had to set up a separate helpline to deal with the calls.'

Caton cursed silently. He was just grateful his name hadn't been on it.

'And have you heard about the Prime Minister?' Carter continued. 'That'll be him shaking hands with those people on that corona ward. I wouldn't be surprised if the entire cabinet have got it.'

'Let's concentrate on the job at hand,' Caton said. He turned to the uniformed officer. 'What can you tell us about the deceased?'

The officer consulted his tablet. 'Erica Edwards, seventy-four years of age, lives alone. Her next-door neighbour has been checking on her at the same time every evening, at six p.m. on the dot. He rang the bell as usual, and when there was no response, peered through the net curtains. Saw her head and shoulders on the floor, sticking out from behind an armchair. He used the key she gave him to enter, checked her pulse and breathing, realised she was dead and rang 999. A senior paramedic was first on the scene. She thought it suspicious, and called it in. The deceased's GP was also informed.'

He looked up from his tablet. 'The paramedic did mention something about tablets and a safety alert.'

Helen Gates had been true to her word, Caton realised, and had acted immediately he left her office. Thank God.

'I take it the paramedic is still here?'

'In her car,' the uniformed officer said.

'And the GP?'

'He didn't come out,' said Carly Whittle, 'but he was happy to confirm her health record with the FME. Dr Patterson is inside with Mr Benson.'

'There's a common approach path?'

'Yes, Boss.'

'Right,' he said, 'let's take a look then.'

'It's one in, one out, Sir, I'm afraid,' the uniform told him. 'Covid regs.'

'In that case, Detective Inspector Carter and I will kit up while you tell us what separates the estate from the rest of Chorlton?'

The officer put his tablet down on the wall to free up his hands.

'Over there, to the west,' he said, pointing over to the opposite side of the green, 'is woodland. Across there, beyond the houses, are the fields of Hardy Farm and the Mersey Valley, comprising the south-west boundary. Behind the house itself is another row of houses lining Brookburn Road, and then a large belt of trees through which Chorlton Brook flows. That's the northern boundary. The southern and eastern boundaries are formed by South Drive, which is just behind those houses over there.'

Caton, one arm in his Tyvek suit, one arm out, took a moment or two to visualise it. 'Tell me about access to the area, and to the green itself,' he said.

The officer nodded. 'Vehicular access into the estate is via Brookburn Road from the north, and Claude Road from the east. Access to the green is via four roads, each of them named after one of the primary points of the compass. The one nearest to the house, for example, is North Meade.'

'What about alternative access on foot?'

'There's a footpath to and from Hardy Farm and the football field, and another to Hurstville Road to the south.'

'Here we go,' said Carter, stepping away from the gate.

They followed his gaze. Two CSIs in full protective gear and carrying evidence bags were walking towards them from the house. Caton and the others moved aside to let them pass.

'Right,' said Caton, 'let's get in there before they come back. You're with me, Nick. Carly, you get a statement from the paramedic. Henry, you do the same with the neighbour that found her.'

He set off up the path to the front door, followed less closely than normal by his DI.

'Let's hope this is a wild goose chase,' Caton shouted back.

'And if it's not?' Nick Carter called after him.

'Start praying that this time the perp has left us something to go on.'

Chapter 28

The common approach path led them through the first door on the right into a front-to-back lounge with a plush cream carpet and floral wallpaper. In this half of the room, a two-seater sofa faced an Edwardian fireplace with a surround of glazed floral tiles. A few feet beyond the sofa, Mark Patterson was kneeling with his back to them beside a matching armchair, angled to face a television in the opposite corner of the room.

'Doc,' Caton said.

The FME sat back on his heels and turned towards them. He looked tired. 'We really must stop meeting like this,' he said.

'Was the paramedic right?' Caton asked. 'Is this another one?'

Patterson raised his eyebrows. 'What, like Miss Dyer?'

Caton didn't have time for this. 'Come on, Mark,' he said, 'is it or isn't it?'

'On the face of it, I'd have to say I'm not sure at this stage.'

'"On the face of it." Meaning what?'

Patterson smiled. 'That it's a good job the paramedic didn't just take the GP at his word. He'd said he wasn't surprised that she'd passed away, because she had a record of poor health. Overweight, type 2 diabetes, high blood pressure, a number of TIAs.'

'Transient ischaemic attacks . . . mini-strokes,' Caton said.

'Exactly. All of which was consistent with how she presents.'

'Which is?'

'A sudden death. No sign of any violence, wounds or external trauma. The assumption would be that her heart had stopped as a result of a stroke, or sudden cardiac arrest from any one of a wide spectrum of cardiovascular diseases that can only be confirmed by a post-mortem.'

'You're saying there are none of the telltale signs of poisoning that Millie Dyer had? The cherry-red cheeks, the vomit?'

The FME shook his head. He got to his feet and then stepped away into the back half of the through room.

'See for yourself,' he said.

Erica Edwards lay in a second doorway, between the lounge and the hall, beyond which Caton could see into the kitchen. She was on her left side behind the armchair, with her head and shoulders protruding into the lounge, just as the neighbour had stated. The most striking thing about her, apart from the fact that she was dead, was her size. The GP, it seemed, was a master of understatement. The deceased was morbidly obese.

The skin on her face and the back of her one visible hand was very pale. There was no sign of the frozen shock and horror they had seen on the face of Millie Dyer. The eyelids were open, and her eyes stared down absently at Caton's shoes. She was still in her pyjamas, although it was fair to say that half the population was choosing to stay in them all day during lockdown.

'Rigor mortis had not yet begun when the paramedic found her,' Patterson told him, 'and it was only just starting when I arrived. Given the ambient temperature, it was probably delayed a little. I estimate that she's been dead less than five hours.'

'Sometime shortly before or after two-thirty p.m. then?'

'Give or take.'

'So, if the GP was assuming natural causes, what was it that made the paramedic suspicious? There was some mention of tablets?'

'She'll tell you herself,' Patterson replied, 'but if you take a look in the kitchen, I'm sure you'll work it out.'

Caton sighed. First Carol Tompkins, now Patterson. Unquestionably, Flatman's legacy lived on. With some difficulty, he stepped over the body onto the stepping plates leading through to the kitchen. They were damned slippery when wearing paper overshoes.

The melamine surfaces were covered in grime. A frying pan lay in a bowl of greasy water in the sink. A bluebottle buzzed around an overflowing pedal bin. In a pot on the window ledge lingered the shrivelled remains of a potted plant. Beside an electric kettle stood a half-empty glass of water and two boxes of tablets.

The larger of the two had a prescription sticker. The packaging told him that it contained fifty-six five hundred milligram tablets of metformin hydrochloride. The second was a proprietary brand of painkillers.

The box was open, and someone had partially removed one of the silver-foil strips that held the pills. Caton didn't need a magnifying glass to tell him that it was devoid of any brand or product markings, or that it was identical to the one they had found at Millie Dyer's house.

'That what I think it is, Boss?' Carter was standing in the doorway.

Caton moved to the other end of the kitchen so his DI could see for himself. Carter bent down to have a look.

'So much for a one-off murder,' he said, straightening up. 'It's a good job the paramedic had the wits to open the box and check the contents.'

'Unless it was already open,' Caton said. 'Either way, if we hadn't got that warning out there, she'd never have known to check in the first place.'

Not exactly the royal 'we', he reflected, but there was nothing to be gained from sharing the fact, other than loss of face. He knew he should have insisted on putting it out there from the outset, but consoled himself with the thought that it was unlikely it would have saved Erica Edwards. At least, he hoped so.

'Are we going to take a look upstairs?' Carter said.

'It's not as though we have any reason to suspect the perpetrator has been inside this house,' Caton replied. 'These are arm's-length killings. I doubt it's going to tell us anything we won't get from the CSI photos and video footage.'

Jack Benson's muffled voice responded right on cue. He was standing halfway down the hall. 'I take it you're happy for us to get on with it then?'

'Unless you've found something you think we should see?' Caton said.

'Sadly, no.'

'In which case, you carry on,' Caton told him. 'Same evidential capture as at the previous crime scene. Let me know if there are any surprises.'

'Will do,' the crime scene manager said.

He backed down the hallway and headed up the stairs so that Caton and Carter could exit safely. On the way out, Caton popped his head around the door to the lounge.

'Mark?' he said. 'Metformin hydrochloride?'

'Routinely prescribed for type 2 diabetes,' the FME replied. 'And before you ask, I've been on to Dr Tompkins. She's on her way, and she's promised as a favour to you to conduct the PM late tomorrow morning, although she says it may get to early afternoon.'

Caton didn't like favours, they generally had to be repaid, and Carol Tompkins already thought he owed her one. He went out into the garden, stripped off his Tyvek and overshoes, and dumped everything in the container by the gate. He thanked the uniformed PC for his succinct report and walked back to his car.

Chapter 29

Carly Whittle and Henry Powell were waiting for him.

'Was the paramedic right, Boss?' Carly asked.

'It looks that way,' he said. 'What did she have to tell you?'

'Nothing we don't know already,' Carly replied. 'She was inclined towards sudden cardiac arrest, especially after she'd spoken to the GP, but then she took a look in the kitchen, saw the tablets, and that's when she told her Control to call 999.'

'Did she touch the packet?'

'She says not. She saw the blister pack, could see it wasn't right and got out of there ASAP.'

'I hope you thanked her?'

'I said she done brilliant, and we'd make sure to tell her bosses that, but in the meantime, we'd appreciate it if she didn't talk to anyone else about it, least of all the press.'

Caton was impressed. It was exactly what he'd have done in her place. He made a mental note to talk to Nick Carter about making sure she had roles that challenged her. Another four or five years, and he'd persuade her to apply for the Inspectors' Board. Her competence in her current role was self-evident, and the way she appeared to be mentoring Henry Powell suggested she'd breeze her way through the rank-specific assessment. All the exam required was focused study of the Blackstone's manuals, and some practice with their online Q&As.

'Well done, Carly,' he said. 'What about you, Henry? How did you get on?'

DC Powell had no need to consult his notes. 'The neighbour,' he began, 'has known her and the family for over forty years. He says she was basically a good person, and for the first twenty years or so they rubbed along together until her husband started to drink heavily. He turned into a violent alcoholic. She divorced him when she turned forty-eight, which was around the same time their youngest child – a daughter – left home, pregnant, at seventeen. The son, Robert, who's an accountant, had already left home some years before. He lives in Lymm, and he and his mother have been estranged ever since the divorce. Apparently, he blamed his mother for kicking his father out. Her daughter, Sally, is now forty-three and lives in Farnworth. He reckons she's got problems of her own, reliving her mother's nightmare with her own partner, a feckless alcoholic gambler called Aaron Buller.'

'Did you get contact details for the son and daughter?'

Powell nodded. 'He's given me phone numbers for both of them. Mrs Edwards gave him them in case of emergency.'

'I hope you've made note of all this?' Caton asked.

Powell looked hurt. 'Of course, Boss. Verbatim.'

'I hope he hasn't already rung them?' said Caton. 'The son and the daughter?'

'No, Boss, and I told him not to. I said we'd handle it.'

'Good, because that's where you two are going next. I want you to talk to the daughter. You know what to ask?'

'Yes, Boss,' Carly and Henry chorused.

'Did you get an address or a contact number for the father?'

'No, Boss,' Powell replied. 'He was the last person she'd want him to contact. But I wouldn't have thought we'd have a problem tracking him down.'

Neither did Caton. The odds were, he'd have form. Failing that, there was always the electoral register.

'I'll tell DS Hulme to expedite it,' he said. 'And there's just an outside chance the daughter will know where he is. As soon as you know, you can pay him a visit too. I'll speak to the son. Text me his number, Henry.'

'Yes, Boss.' DC Powell tapped his tablet, entered the password and swiped away.

Caton checked his screen, looked up and found the two of them still standing there. 'Off you go then,' he said.

He watched the two of them walk away, DS Whittle on the pavement, DC Powell in the road. This social distancing was a bugger, he reflected. It was surprising how much it changed the dynamics of relationships within the team.

'Henry!' he called after them.

DC Powell stopped and turned. 'Yes, Boss?'

'Good work,' Caton told him. 'Well done.'

Powell's face lit up. 'Thanks, Boss,' he said.

The power of praise never failed to surprise Caton, so long as you used it sparingly. He rang the number on his screen. It went to voicemail. He began to leave a message, but no sooner had he mentioned Greater Manchester Police than a voice cut in.

'This is Robert Edwards,' it said. 'What is this in connection with?'

'Mr Edwards,' Caton began, 'I am sorry to have to tell you that your mother was found dead at home earlier this afternoon.'

This was met with silence. Caton imagined him trying to decide exactly how he felt. Surprise? Relief? Guilt? Probably a muddle of all three.

'Mr Edwards?' he prompted.

'Ah yes,' the son responded, 'it's just that it's come as a bit of a surprise.'

'I'm sure,' Caton said. 'When did you last speak to her?'

A pause.

'Oh God, not in a long time. It must be twenty years, maybe more. We've been estranged, I'm afraid.'

'So I gather,' Caton told him.

'It's . . . complicated.'

'You don't need to explain,' Caton said. 'It's just that I need to know if there's any way in which you might know who her most recent contacts were, apart from your sister, of course.'

'I'm sorry, but no. Like I said, we haven't been in touch for decades.' A hint of sadness had now crept into his voice for the first time.

'You didn't ask how your mother had died?'

'No, because I assumed it must have been some kind of heart attack.'

'Why would you assume that, Mr Edwards?'

'Well, her diabetes,' he replied, 'and she was so overweight. I always thought it was . . .' His voice tailed off.

A disaster waiting to happen, Caton guessed.

'You knew about her diabetes?' he said.

'I still speak to my sister, Sally, from time to time. Mainly when she's short of money or there's a crisis.' A pause. 'How *did* she die?'

'It was a heart attack,' Caton said.

'Ah.'

'But we have yet to establish the cause.'

'Hence the questions?'

'That's right, Sir.'

A longer pause.

'Would you like me to come up to Manchester?'

'I don't think that'll be necessary,' Caton told him, 'but I will arrange for someone to come and take a statement from you and to check that you're alright.'

He doubted that Roger Edwards would need the services of a family liaison officer. But then again, you never knew.

'Thank you,' the son said, 'only it's difficult here at the moment. I work from home. I've got three adult children still living with us, two of whom are furloughed, and my mother-in-law is in the annexe. She's got MS and is shielding.'

'I understand,' Caton told him. 'I'm sorry for your loss.' He ended the call.

Nick Carter arrived.

'Where have you been?' Caton asked.

'Talking to one of the neighbourhood police and community support officers,' he replied. 'He's a veritable fount of information, he is. He reckons there's no shortage of CCTV cameras in the village. I asked him to compile a list of all those with eyes on the victim's house. I also told him to start getting the residents ready to hand their footage over when the door-to-door teams arrive.'

'They should be here by now,' Caton said. 'Better get on to DS Hulme and chase them up.'

'Will do,' Carter replied, 'but we're going to need a much bigger supply of SD cards and memory sticks. Duggie Wallace says there's a logjam with procurement at the moment. They've two down with the virus and another two are self-isolating.'

'You'll need to get on to Amazon then.'

'What am I going to pay with?'

Caton opened the door of his car.

'Use your own account or a credit card,' he told him. 'You can add it to your expenses.'

Chapter 30

Sally Buller, née Edwards, lived in a two-up two-down, back-to-back Victorian red-brick terrace, a stone's throw from Farnworth town centre.

The street was tidy, if you ignored the weeds beginning to sprout along the pavements that the cash-strapped council's workers had ceased to spray long before the virus struck. The houses themselves were neat and well-maintained. With the exception of this one.

A rusting child's bike lay across the patch of foot-high weeds and grass that masqueraded as a lawn. Beside it stood three large black bin bags full of rubbish, from one of which spilled empty tins, plastic bottles, and takeaway trays, smeared with congealed rice and sauce the colour of dried blood.

'Nice,' Carly Whittle observed.

'Fits the profile,' said Henry Powell.

On the way, they had both been informed by Duggie Wallace that according to the HOLMES computer, Aaron Buller had a record as long as his arm. It had started with petty shoplifting in his teens, and included breaches of the peace whilst drunk and disorderly even before he was old enough to legally buy alcohol. In the past three years, there had been numerous call-outs relating to domestic disturbances, query, domestic abuse. He was currently on probation, having served six months of a twelve-stretch for burgling a convenience store.

'Convenience store,' said Henry, while Carly rang the doorbell. 'Don't they sell painkillers?'

'Probably, 'she replied, 'but I doubt they sell potassium cyanide.'

Carly rang the bell again and rapped on the glass with her knuckles. A dog began to yap.

'Dogs!' said Henry. 'Who'd be a postman?'

'Or a police officer, come to that,' Carly said.

The door opened a fraction and they both stepped back. A woman's face appeared. The blonde curly perm was way beyond its best before date, giving her the appearance of someone who'd been struck by lightning, an effect that was boosted by the absence of make-up, the dark rings beneath her eyes and her fearful expression.

'Mrs Buller?' Carly said, 'Mrs Sally Buller?'

The woman's eyes crept past Carly to Henry Powell several paces behind her, and then back again. Her nod was barely perceptible, her voice a whisper. 'Yes?'

Carly held up her warrant card. 'Greater Manchester Police,' she said. 'Could we have a word, please? Preferably inside?'

A man's voice erupted in the hallway. 'Woman! What have I told you? Get away from that door!'

The yapping grew louder and faster. The woman's face disappeared as she was jerked backwards, and the door flung wide. A man now took her place in the doorway. He was a foot shorter than Carly but half as wide again, in stark contrast to the stick-thin woman who cowered behind him. His fists were clenched and his face contorted with anger. When he saw Carly's ID, his fists relaxed a little and his look of rage became one of suspicion. When he spoke, his words were slightly slurred.

'What the fuck do you want now?' he said.

Even from a distance, Carly could smell the alcohol on his breath and wished she had put on her mask. She stepped back another pace, forcing Henry to do the same.

'Mr Buller,' she said, 'it's not you we've come to see; it's your wife we need to speak with.'

He looked confused. 'Why? What the hell has she done?'

His expression changed again. Was that panic, Carly wondered?

'Whatever she told you, it's a pack of lies,' he said. 'She's not right in the head, silly cow. It's this c'rona virus messing with her head.'

'Your wife hasn't said a word,' Carly told him. 'I'm afraid we have some bad news to give her.'

'You can tell me,' he said. 'I'll make sure she knows.'

'I understand that you're currently on probation, Mr Buller?' she said. 'Please don't make this harder than it already is. Just step away and ask your wife to come to the door, please. Either that or let us in?'

She watched as he tried to find an alternative to doing as she asked, and finally realised that there wasn't one. He wasn't going to let her get away with it though, not without a moment of triumph of his own.

'You're definitely not coming in! For all I know, you've both got the bloody virus. You go and stand by the gate, and I'll see she comes to the door.'

Carly decided that it wasn't worth arguing. He'd probably take it out on his wife when they left, besides which, he had a point. 'Very well,' she said.

'And shouldn't you two be wearing masks?' he shouted at her back as she retreated.

Henry moved sideways to stand by the hedge adjacent to the neighbours' front yard. Carly stopped by the gate and turned around. The dog began yapping again, but ceased suddenly with a whine. Carly could see Aaron Buller at the far end of the hall, remonstrating with his wife. He stepped aside to let her pass, then followed her to the front door. She was wearing flimsy pyjama bottoms that failed to disguise her skinny legs, and a long-sleeved trackie top that was completely wrong, given it was still twenty degrees in the shade. Her eyes and cheeks were wet.

Christ, thought Carly, *she's already crying, and I've not even told her about her mother yet.*

'Mrs Buller . . . Sally,' Carly said, 'I'm afraid we have some bad news for you. It's about your mother.'

The woman's head jerked up, her eyes widened and she clung to the door jamb. 'Mum?'

'I'm afraid so, Sally,' Carly said. 'Your mother was found dead at home earlier this evening.'

Sally Buller's shoulders slumped. Carly feared she was about to faint.

'Nan? Dead?' said the husband, advancing towards his wife. He hooked his arms around her waist and held her up, as though trying to support her. 'How did she die?'

'Your mother had a heart attack, Sally,' Carly said. 'We're trying to find out what may have caused it.'

'Poor old Nan,' said the husband. 'You alright, love?'

His words said one thing, his voice and manner quite another. It was obvious from the look on Sally Buller's face as she locked eyes with Carly that she wasn't the only one who hadn't been taken in by this pretence of concern.

'When did you last see your mother?' Carly asked.

'About three weeks ago,' Sally Buller replied, 'before the start of the lockdown. She came over on the bus and we had a coffee and a bit of lunch in the Blue Café on Higher Market Street.'

'You didn't tell me that!' said the husband sharply. His hands tightened around her waist, causing her to wince.

'Mr Buller!' said Carly firmly. 'You're hurting your wife.'

'Oh sorry, love!' he responded, moving his hands to her shoulders instead. 'Don't know me own strength.'

'How did your mum seem?' Carly asked.

Sally Buller appeared fazed by the question. 'Seem?'

'Was she well? Was she troubled in any way?'

The jumble of curls swayed from side to side.

'No . . . I don't think so. She seemed alright. Like normal.'

'Normal!?' said her husband. 'Normal? How often have you been seeing her?'

She winced again. 'Now and again, Ron, that's all, now and again.'

'Did your mother talk about any new friends or acquaintances, Sally?' Carly said.

'No, I'm sorry.' She looked desolate, and sounded mortified that she didn't have the answers the detective was hoping for.

'What about you, Mr Buller? When did you last see your mother-in-law?'

'That would be at the wedding,' he said, with a sneer on his face. 'Thirty years ago.'

'Twenty-six,' his wife corrected him.

He laughed. 'Funny,' he said, 'feels a hell of a lot longer.'

Not half as long as it must feel for your wife, Carly thought.

'One last question, Mrs Buller,' she said. 'Do you have any idea of the whereabouts of your father?'

The woman's sadness deepened. 'No, I've not seen since him our mum threw him out.'

'Well, in that case,' Carly said, 'I don't have any more questions.'

'Can I see her?' Sally Buller asked. 'Can I see my mum?'

Carly would have loved to have been able to say yes. It was the least this poor woman deserved.

'I'm not sure that's going to be possible,' she said, 'not in the current circumstances. There'll be a post-mortem, but after that, because our investigation into her death is ongoing, I can't say when your mother's body will be released. At the moment, because of the virus, cremation is preferred, and I'm afraid that no one's allowed to attend funerals currently. It may be that by the time our investigation is complete, the restrictions will have been eased or lifted entirely. All I can promise you is that we will contact you as soon as we know when that will be. A family liaison officer will be in touch with you shortly. And I'm so sorry about your mother, Sally,' she said. She nodded to Henry and began to leave.

'We don't need no family whatsit,' Aaron Buller called after her. 'We'll be fine. I'll look after her.'

Carly stopped and turned to stare at him. She waited until she had eye contact. 'A family liaison officer will be calling on you shortly,' she said. 'Make sure you cooperate with him, Mr Buller. I'm sure I don't need to remind you again that you're still on probation.'

'Nice one,' Henry said, as they walked back to their respective cars. 'I'm not sure I could have held back from lamping him one.'

'That's why I was the one asking the questions,' Carly told him. 'That poor woman. It's bad enough losing her mother like that, without having to live with that monster.'

'She could always leave.'

Carly stopped abruptly and spun round to face him. 'In the first two weeks of lockdown, there've already been eleven domestic violence-related deaths: nine females, one man and one child. God knows how many more there'll be before this nightmare is over. And

141

there's not one vacancy in any domestic violence refuge in the country. Her mother has just been murdered; her father is God knows where; and she and her brother haven't spoken for years. You tell me, Henry, how the hell is she supposed to up sticks and leave there?'

Stunned by the violence of her outburst, he was unable to muster a response. Not that one was called for.

They got in their cars in silence and drove away.

Chapter 31
Nexus House. 2300 hours.

'So what about this Aaron Buller?' Caton asked.

Some of them partially obscured by the desktop screens, the core team were spread out across the front third of the room, perched on the corner of every other desk. It completely changed the dynamics of the meeting, but it was the only way they could keep their distance.

'He rang a whole array of alarm bells re domestic abuse involving coercive control,' Carly said, 'and almost certainly physical abuse.'

'Does he have the intelligence for this though? And even if he does, what possible motive would he have?'

'I'm not sure about intelligence,' she replied. 'Cunning, certainly.'

'And when DS Whittle said his mother-in-law was dead,' Henry Powell said, 'even from where I was standing, I could see the pound signs in his eyes. That house must be worth a pretty penny, and there's only her and the brother.'

'That doesn't give him a motive for the first victim though,' Carter pointed out.

'What about the father?' Caton asked.

'Fred Edwards,' Duggie Wallace answered. 'The last record we have of him is in the 2001 census. He was in a homeless hostel in Liverpool. Nothing after that.'

'Missing Persons?'

Duggie shook his head. 'Negative.'

'I doubt there was anyone who would have missed him,' said Henry Powell. 'Except maybe her son.'

'Keep looking,' Caton said. He turned to Jack Benson. 'Where are we up to on the crime scene?'

'The house is still being searched. The contents of her bins are being analysed. As for trace evidence, all we have so far are the pills themselves which are undergoing toxicology tests, and the foil blister packs and packaging, which are being tested for fingerprints and DNA. Unfortunately, Boss, the results from the first crime scene came back negative, so I'm not holding out too much hope for this one.'

'We have a perpetrator who's forensically aware?'

'Looks that way, Boss.'

'What about passive media?' Caton asked.

DC Franklin raised his hand. 'There are two us working through it. There were over a dozen cameras on the close alone, and scores more on the approach roads. We're still working on footage relating to victim one. We'll keep going through the night, but we could really do with more help, Boss.'

'I'll see what I can do,' Caton told him. 'The fact that there's a second victim should give me some leverage with the Command Team.'

He searched the group for Amit Patel, the civilian analyst newly transferred from Central Park, who was perched on a desk at the back of the group.

'Amit,' he said, 'any progress on the lists of suppliers of blister pack and blister-sealing equipment?'

'I've located thirty thus far,' Patel replied, 'most of them Internet-based. However, ten are from China and six from the US, and getting lists of their UK customers is taking for ever.'

'In that case, I suggest you enlist the support of Europol and get onto the FBI. Do whatever you have to do. We need those names.' Caton glanced at the syndicate clock. 'Now would be a good time because it'll only be three in the afternoon in Langley.'

He turned his attention now to the two murder boards standing side by side. Millie Dyer on the left, Erica Edwards on the right. A single thin thread of red wool linked the boards – the photos of the cyanide-laced pills. No suspect, no motive, no trace evidence. Without at least one of those linking the two dead women, this investigation was going nowhere. He scanned the faces of his team. They looked exhausted and despondent.

'I'm grateful for all of your efforts so far,' he told them 'especially those of you who are going to be working tonight. The rest of you, go home. Make sure you come back bright-eyed and bushy-tailed in the morning. With a little luck, something will have turned up by then.'

It was going to take a lot more than a little luck, he told himself as he packed his bag. A hell of a lot more.

Chapter 32

The house was in darkness, all except for one light in the hall.

Caton stripped off in the downstairs shower room, hung his jacket on the back of the door, bundled his clothes into the basket and had a lukewarm shower. It was a routine he would never get used to, but at least he wasn't the one who had to wash and dry the clothes every day.

He slipped on his bathrobe and went in search of a banana to fill the hole in his stomach and stop him waking in the middle of the night.

Kate was sat up in bed, reading a paperback. She gave him a quizzical look.

'Your text was very cryptic,' she said. 'I take it there's been another victim.'

He slipped his bathrobe off. 'Looks like it.'

'Same MO?'

'Yes.' He sat on his side of the bed and brought up the alarm on his mobile.

'Tampering with meds again?' she asked.

'Yes.'

She put her book down. 'How close to the location of your first victim?'

He pushed back the sheet and slid in beside her. 'Two miles by road.'

'Same victimology?'

He nodded. 'Both elderly women, living alone.'

'Anything else that connects them?'

'Nothing we've discovered so far.'

'I can see why you're worried,' she said.

'There are going to be others, aren't there?' he asked.

She nodded. 'You know there are, Tom. You realise there probably already have been? Whoever's doing this is taking advantage of Covid-19. The lockdown provides thousands of potential victims – vulnerable people isolated even more than usual.'

'Just to complicate matters even further,' he said, 'the absence of effective testing for Covid-19 is creating confusion around the cause of death, especially in the elderly. Hard-pressed GPs without adequate PPE are under pressure to sign medical certificates as to cause of death without an adequate examination, and the usual requirement for a second opinion has been suspended.'

'What about automatic referral to the coroner?' she asked.

He shook his head. 'If a doctor has had contact with the deceased within the past twenty-eight days, in person, by phone or by video consultation, there's no requirement for referral or indeed any examination of the body. Even if the deceased has not been seen by a doctor in the past twenty-eight days, if the coroner agrees, the doctor can complete the cause of death certificate and relatives or even the undertaker can register the death.'

'That's like offering Dr Shipman a free pass,' she said. 'Or Dr Crippen come to that.'

'Is that your first instinct?' he asked. 'That this could be an Angel of Death?'

Kate raised her eyebrows and gave him one of her disappointed looks. 'Neither of those men were acting out of a warped sense of compassion, as you well know. And I also thought you knew me better than this. *You* may deal in hunches and instinct. Give *me* facts and I'll give you possibilities, maybe even probabilities. No more than that.'

Caton sensed an opening. 'Does that mean you'll put a profile together for me?'

She scowled at him. 'That is not what I was saying. You know full well that you can't consult me on a case where you're the SIO. Conflict of interest, etcetera? You'll have to request the involvement of one of the other Home Office profilers.'

'My problem,' he said, 'is that I can't justify approaching one yet. Two deaths don't qualify as a series.'

'Well, only if you're using the FBI definition . . .' she said. '". . . at least three murders over a period longer than a month with an emotional cooling off period in between."' Though you could argue the alternative definition – murders with a psychological motive and sadistic sexual elements.'

Caton frowned. 'It's not obvious that this is what we have here.'

'You only need elements associated with serial killings,' she said. 'In this case, assuming the victims are unconnected, you have apparently random victims, a sadistic way of killing, and a cunning modus operandi.'

He wasn't convinced. 'Persuading the powers that be of the need to engage a profiler won't be easy. I may have to wait for the first case review or even another death to convince them.'

Again, she raised both eyebrows. 'You want me to give you free professional advice to save you having to ask GMP to pay for it?'

'No. I was just hoping that your curiosity was sufficiently piqued to allow you to give me some pointers as to who we may be looking for. Strictly between you and me, no comebacks whatever the outcome.'

He could tell she was close to folding, and pressed his advantage. 'If only to save a life or two?'

'That's not fair,' she said.

She picked up her book and began to read.

He was tempted to point out that neither life nor the perpetrator were playing fair right now, but bitter experience had taught him that point-scoring rarely worked with Kate. He reached for his Kindle and powered it up.

She turned a page in her book.

'I'll let you know in the morning,' she said.

Chapter 33
Tuesday 7th April 2020

Sunlight bled around the edges of the curtains.

Caton turned over to reach for his phone, and stared bleary-eyed at the screen. It was 07.55. He cursed, hauled himself up, and threw back the sheet.

Washed and dressed, he went downstairs. Kate was working her way through a bowl of muesli.

'I'm late,' he said. 'I could have sworn I'd set the alarm on my phone.'

'You did,' she said. 'I switched it off as soon as it started up.'

'What did you do that for?'

'Because you looked exhausted.'

She slid a typed sheet of paper covered in bullet point notes across the table.

'What's this?' he asked.

She looked up. 'Don't pretend you weren't expecting it. That's your starter for ten. Totally deniable. And given that it's based on nothing more than pillow talk, for God's sake, don't quote me on it.'

He picked up the sheet. 'As if I would.'

'I'm serious, Tom,' she said. 'This is for you and you alone. If anyone asks, you did your own research on the net. If you do hire another profiler – and I think you should – you do not share this with them. I don't want you having to defend what are tentative thoughts based on minimal evidence, nor do I want to end up having to explain why I'd set up one of my colleagues.'

'Set up?'

She put her spoon down on the table. 'Would you want to walk into a meeting with the Chief Constable where he's supposedly asking for your professional opinion, then you realise that she's actually comparing what you have to say with an analysis provided by her husband, who just happens to be an equally experienced DCI in another syndicate and is a colleague of yours?'

'When you put it like that . . .'

'There you go then.' She picked up her spoon, and carried on eating.

Caton made himself a bowl of porridge, sprinkled it with blueberries and cranberries, and sat down opposite Kate. He read her notes as he ate. 'This is really good,' he said at last.

She stood up. 'Just as well. It's what you eat four days a week.'

He waved the sheet of notes. 'Not the porridge, this,'

She switched the kettle on and took two mugs from a cupboard. 'Don't patronise me, Tom,' she said. 'This is one of the things I do for a living.'

'Come on, Kate,' he protested. 'You know I didn't mean it like that. What I should have said is that this is so helpful.'

'Try again.'

'Thank you?'

She smiled. 'Much better.'

'You had me going there,' he said. 'I thought for a moment you were being a Covid curmudgeon.'

'And if I was?'

'I wouldn't blame you. Cooped up here for hours on end, day after day. Trying to work from home with Emily wanting your attention every time Larissa gets distracted. I know how I'd feel.'

She lifted the kettle and started pouring water into the mugs.

'I keep telling myself it's the summer holidays,' she said. 'I'm lucky enough to have work to do, and I'm privileged to have Larissa to help out. Besides, the weather's lovely and we have a garden. I get out for a walk every day. I think a lot about people cooped up in high-rise flats with children, living on benefits. Not to mention asylum seekers expected to live on thirty-seven pounds a week. That could so easily have been Larissa.'

She sat down, pushed a mug of coffee across the table, blew on her own and took a sip. He did the same.

'Instant?' he said.

'Is that a complaint?'

'No, I was just wondering.'

'Good. Because we ran out of the capsules on Wednesday, and like most other things at present there's a five-day delivery period.'

He was saved from having to respond by Emily hurtling into the room and throwing her arms around his waist.

'Daddy! Can you play with me today?'

She had loaded her voice with sadness and desperation, in the way that only children can. He reached down, lifted her onto the bench beside him, and gave her a giant hug.

'Daddy has to work today,' he told her.

She pulled a sad face. 'Daddy *always* has to work.'

He brushed her hair behind her ears and stroked her cheek.

'That's what daddies do,' he said. He heard Kate's sharp intake of breath. 'And mummies too.'

'But Mummy does her work at home and still has time to play with me.'

'Your daddy has to catch the bad people,' said Larissa, sitting down beside them. 'We've talked about this, Emily.'

Emily turned to face her. 'Don't the bad people have to do lockdown?' she asked.

Larissa smiled. 'The bad people don't think the rules apply to them. That's why we call them bad people.'

'And that's why Daddy has to lock them up?'

'Exactly.' Larissa reached for her hand. 'Come on, let's go and watch CBeebies while we wait for Joe's workout to come on?'

Emily released her grip on her daddy and pushed herself off the bench.

'One, two, three, let's *go*!' she shouted, tugging Larissa towards the door.

'Sorry, Mr Caton,' Larissa mouthed as she followed her small charge.

'Don't be,' Caton said. 'And it's Tom, remember?' He waited until the two of them had disappeared. 'How many times do I have to tell her?'

Kate laughed. 'That's never going to happen. She's in awe of you. It's what comes of saving her life and giving her a home.'

'It's just as well we did.' Caton pushed back the bench and stood up. 'She was invaluable before the lockdown, but now she's even more of a godsend.'

He walked around the table and bent to kiss the nape of Kate's neck.

'Thank you,' he said, holding up the sheet of A4.

'Don't forget,' she said, 'you owe me.'

Chapter 34
Nexus House. 0820 hours.

'I sent the passive media team home as soon as I got in, Boss,' Carter told him. 'They could hardly keep their eyes open. Frankly, I'm surprised they lasted as long as they did.'

'Did they get any leads?' Caton asked.

His deputy shook his head. 'Sorry, Boss, but it doesn't sound like it. We won't know for sure until all the sightings have been followed up, but there don't seem to be any that are connected with the ones from the first crime scene.'

'Our unsub could have used a different vehicle each time?' Caton mused.

'True,' Carter said, 'but unless at least one of them is registered to him, that's not really going to help us, is it? And given he's this forensically aware, he's hardly likely to let something like a licence plate trip him up.'

Caton knew he was right. And if the unsub was sending the packages by post or getting someone else to deliver them, that would complicate matters further.

Carter pointed to the flip chart. 'What's that you've got there, Boss?'

'Wait and see,' Caton told him. 'I want you to gather everyone in the large conference room. Remind them they still need to keep two metres apart. It may mean everyone sitting on the floor but I won't keep them long.'

* * *

Caton stood beside the flip chart stand.

'What I am about to share with you,' he said, 'is a very sketchy profile of our unsub, based on what we know about the victims and the behavioural traces left at the crime scenes. And before someone decides to pull me up short, in the absence of a usable alternative, I shall be using the male pronoun.'

There was a ripple of laughter around the room.

'That doesn't mean that I'm excluding the possibility that we may be looking for a female perpetrator,' he said, 'because it's equally feasible that we are.' He paused for a moment. 'These sheets will go up in the Incident Room, so there's no need for you to take notes.'

He turned the cover sheet and revealed a mantra familiar to them all: 'Locard's Principle – every contact leaves a trace.'

'In relation to both of our crime scenes,' he said, 'the only contacts identified so far are the pills that we believe killed the victims and the packaging in which they arrived. We need to keep looking for evidence of someone other than the victim having been at that crime scene or, at the very least, some other form of evidence that links these two victims.'

He flipped the sheet back over.

Victimology
- age – elderly
- gender – female
- living in isolation amplified by current 'lockdown' [Is this relevant? Is the unsub an opportunist?]
- compliant
- apparently unconnected to each other, despite neighbourhood proximity
- victims seen as animate objects, rather than human beings

'One of the important facts about this particular victimology,' he said, 'is that both victims appear to share the compliant victim traits common to the victims of serial sexual sadists.'

A hand went up. It was DC Nair.

'Yes?' Caton said.

'But there aren't actually any indications that either of the victims have been interfered with in any way?'

'Apart from them having been poisoned,' observed a wag near the back of the room.

Caton was gratified that none of the others found it funny. Indeed, several of them expressed their disapproval by tutting, frowning or staring at the comedian.

'Quite right, DC Nair,' Caton said, ignoring the interruption. 'But I'm talking about the nature of the victims, not the physical evidence of sexual obsession. Not all offenders motivated by sex get their gratification from an overt sexual act.'

He let that sink in, and then turned to the next sheet.

'From here on,' he said, 'I do not intend to talk my way through these sheets. I'm going to allow time for you to read on your own. If you have any questions, just raise your hand.'

A profound silence fell as his team read the bullet points, and Caton could sense their brains whirring.

Methodology

Use of cyanide poison:

- swift, yet cruel in its execution
- eliminates but does not anonymise the victim
- the metamorphosing nature of the poison after death makes it more difficult to identifycause of death easily mistaken for other morbidities common to these victims

- Unsub has understanding of drugs: manufacture, toxicity and effect, either through his occupation or ability to research them.

Process
- genuine external packaging & genuine pills – from home? shop? Internet? or workplace?
- 'professionally'-made blister packs
- killing remotely – less chance of detection; and it also tells us that the unsub does not need to witness the victim's death throes.

After several minutes had passed, a hand went up.

'Yes, DC Powell?' Caton said.

'That last point about remote killing, and the perp not needing to see them die in order to get a thrill . . .'

'Go on.'

'Could it be, Boss, that it's deliberate? That by sending the pills out randomly, to victims he doesn't actually know, he's making it harder for us, and also deliberately introducing an element of chance? You know, like Russian roulette? I mean, he's no way of knowing if they'll take them. They could just as easily chuck them in the bin, or give them to someone else – especially if they don't know who they're from.'

'You're suggesting it's a game of chance?' Caton responded. 'That he gets his kicks from seeing who does and who doesn't end up dying?'

'It's possible, isn't it, Boss?' the DC replied.

'Possible, certainly,' Caton agreed. 'In fact, when we look at the next category – motivation – you'll see that game-playing is a motive not uncommon among serial killers. But I hope you're wrong, because otherwise we're wasting our time trying to find a connection between our victims, other than the victimology. Had the victims had life-threatening health problems, the use of poison might suggest a so-called *Angel of Death,* or *Angel of Mercy.* Since we've seen no such co-morbidities, that seems unlikely, although we can't discount it entirely. That said, we're left with three prototypes or categories into which these killings may fall.'

He turned the sheet over.

1. Motivation: the need to exercise power and control over the victim, for one or more of the following reasons:
- to demonstrate the unsub's power and intellect
- to ultimately tell his story and achieve notoriety
- to exact revenge for some real or imagined slight
- to play mind games with the police, and accomplish a mission of some kind.

2. For personal gain?
- to hide a scam, an act of forgery or fraud, or to gain directly, as a beneficiary in the victim's will

3. Gerascophobia?
- the unsub has an irrational fear of death and dying, and is unable to accept this as the inevitable consequence of ageing. He transfers this fear into a hatred of those who are a constant reminder of his finite existence.

DS Hulme raised his hand.

'Yes, Jimmy?' Caton said.

'What about gerontophilia, Boss?' Hulme said. 'Like in Operation Minstead.'

Caton nodded. 'The Night Stalker. Not everyone here will remember that. Why don't you enlighten them?'

'It was a Met operation,' Hulme began enthusiastically, 'started in 1998. A succession of rapes of elderly women.

As many as six hundred, they reckoned, although they could only prove a third of that number. Basically, it was a massive cock-up. The IPCC found a string of mistakes including failure to carry out door-to-door enquiries, obtain proper statements from eyewitnesses, or collect details of items stolen from the victims.'

'And worst of all,' Carter interjected, 'even though a witness reported seeing a person in a balaclava climbing into a BMW, and gave them the vehicle's registration number, the owner – who later turned out to be the perpetrator – was never even interviewed, let alone his house searched or his vehicle examined. They even got his name wrong in their written reports.'

'Which is *not* how this investigation is going to be conducted,' Caton told them. 'It took thirteen years and hundreds more rapes before he was brought to justice. It's such a perfect example of how not to conduct an operation that it's become part of the Senior Investigating Officers Development Programme, which is how DS Hulme and DI Carter know so much about it.

'However, gerontophilia is love of the elderly, hence the fact that the crime was rape. And the perpetrator *did* make contact and conversation with his victims, and he even showed some level of consideration towards them afterwards – however contradictory that might seem.'

He looked around the room, playing the audience.

'I know Oscar Wilde wrote "Each man kills the thing he loves", but I doubt he had cyanide poisoning in mind.'

He turned back to the flip chart. 'Right, just two more sheets to go,' he said. 'Hang on in there.'

Gender
The overwhelming majority of violent crime is performed by men. However, poison is a modus operandi favoured by women. The unsub could

159

therefore be either male or female. Because the victims are all women, I incline towards this being a male offender.

Age
Organised serial killers tend to be from the older end of the spectrum for such killers. Late 20s up to late 40s, but beware, this is highly speculative.

Residence
The unsub is comfortable in the locus of these killings. It is therefore likely that he lives, or has lived, or works, or has worked, in the area circumscribed by the murders.

Prior contact
Has knowledge of the victims – at least enough to know that they live alone, rarely have visitors, and would be willing to accept/take unsolicited pills. [N.B. But are they actually unsolicited?]

Occupation
- Skilled or professional – a blue- or white-collar worker
- Unlikely to have achieved the level of success one might expect given his/her intellect and ability

Character
- Highly organised
- Likely to have an IQ of well over 105
- Controlled, not impulsive
- Calculates and mediates risk
- May feel underappreciated
- Has belief that he is omnipotent, and a need to demonstrate that fact
- Is outwardly sane and ordinary, and inwardly remorseless

The final sheet spoke for itself.

> *Things to think about*
> - He is highly organised
> - What is his inner narrative? The story he tells himself that drives him to commit these crimes?
> - What was the trigger to set the unsub off on these crimes?
> - Does he collect trophies? If so, what might that be in relation to each crime? Something taken from the home in advance of the delivery of the pills? A memento after the event – newspaper clippings – photo / video of funeral – obituary?

Caton waited until the room became restless, a sure sign that most of them had finished reading.

'Right,' he said, 'for every interview you undertake, every witness statement that you read, and every piece of data that comes across your desk, I want you to have what I've shared with you this morning at the forefront of your minds. If anything you see or hear sets the old alarm bells ringing, I want you tell or DI Carter, DS Hulme, DS Whittle, or me. Is that clear?'

The response was loud, unanimous and unequivocal.

'Yes, Boss!'

Chapter 35

Carter followed Caton into his office and closed the door.

'That was very impressive, Boss,' he said.

Caton sat down behind his desk, and pretended to examine the contents of his in tray. 'I'm pleased you approve.'

'Almost professional,' Carter smirked. 'If I didn't know better . . .'

'Don't!' said Caton. 'Whatever it is you were about to say, don't. And don't even think about sharing that thought with anyone else. Understand?'

'Yes, Boss,' said a chagrined Carter. 'I'll be getting on then.' He turned towards the door.

'I'm sorry,' Caton said, sitting back in his chair. 'I didn't mean to bite your head off.'

'It's alright, Boss,' Carter said. 'I shouldn't have spoken out of turn.'

'Don't be daft,' Caton told him. 'I should have warned you beforehand. It's just that if it got out, it could cause all sorts of problems for both Kate and me. Professional jealousy. Claims of favouritism. The expectation that Kate should also provide free expertise for the other syndicates. Possibly even suggestions that it involves a conflict of interest on my part and hers.'

'I understand,' his deputy told him. 'I don't blame you. We could have been waiting forever for a profile if you'd gone through official channels.'

Caton wasn't finding Carter's empathy reassuring. It only made him feel more guilty. 'Mum's the word then?'

Carter winked. 'Absolutely.'

He half-opened the door, and then closed it again. 'I tell you what though, Boss – if you'd got someone else to do it and paid through the nose, you wouldn't have got one half as good as that.'

'Do you know where that expression came from?' Caton asked.

Carter looked confused. 'Which one?'

'Paid through the nose.'

'I haven't a clue.'

'Reputedly, in ninth-century Ireland, the Danes split and splayed the nose of any householder who failed to pay their poll tax.'

Carter shook his head. 'And I thought Her Majesty's Revenue and Customs were brutal.'

Once Carter had gone, Caton went through his in tray and emails, and then went out into the Incident Room. He made straight for DC Franklin's carrel. The other two detectives working their way through the CCTV footage sat at neighbouring desks. They all looked shattered. Caton wasn't surprised. He knew only too well exactly how mind-numbing it could be, and that it only took a fraction of a second's lapse of concentration to miss a vital piece of evidence. He pulled up a chair, and placed it where he could keep his distance, yet still see the screen.

'Found anything at all?' he asked.

Franklin eased his own chair back. 'It's been fraught with problems, thanks to the virus,' he said. 'There are so few people out on the streets that we're looking at blank screens most of the time. It also means there are fewer potential witnesses who might have noticed something. Getting footage from private houses has been a problem for the door-to-door teams. People have been reluctant to come to the door, especially the elderly.

Because of the restrictions, when they do, we've had to rely on the occupants downloading the data to a USB stick themselves, and put it in an envelope. Half of them have no idea how to do that.'

Caton didn't want to hear about problems over which he had no control. What he desperately needed was some good news.

'Cut to the chase, Jack,' he said. 'Tell me what you do have.'

The young DC looked chastened. 'Well, we've picked up a number of youths trying door handles of cars and casing properties,' he said. 'DS Hulme said to pass those on to the neighbourhood team. They confirmed they'd already been alerted to this pattern of behaviour by key workers coming off long shifts in the small hours. None of the incidents we spotted related specifically to either of the victims' houses, neither of which incidentally have CCTV cameras covering their properties.'

Was that a coincidence, Caton wondered, or one of the reasons these particular women had been chosen? If so, it meant that the unsub must have cased the area in advance.

'We've checked the registrations of vehicles entering and leaving the street on which victim number one lived,' Franklin continued. 'All but thirteen checked out as belonging to key workers. Five were residents going to the supermarket. One was a couple driving to a park to walk their dog. Two were people claiming to be taking their cars for a run to charge their batteries. One was an ambulance that checked out as taking a suspected Covid-19 victim to Wythenshawe hospital. The remainder look like delivery vehicles of one kind or another. Those are still being followed up.'

'Have any of these same vehicles cropped up in and around victim two's address?' Caton asked.

'Only this one.' Franklin picked up a large pink Post-it note and held it out at arm's length.

Caton read it and stood up. 'Thank you,' he said, 'all three of you. I know how difficult this is, and I really appreciate the overtime you've put in. Make sure you're taking your breaks.' He held up the sticky note. 'And keep these coming, eh?'

He stopped by DS Whittle's desk and placed the Post-it note where she could see it.

'This is a person of interest,' he told her. 'He's a delivery driver for one of the supermarkets. The details are on there. His van has been recorded as visiting homes in the streets where each of the victims lived. It could be sheer coincidence, of course, but you and I are going to check him out. Find out where he is right now, and ask his supervisor to tell him to stay there. I'll meet you in the car park in five minutes.'

Chapter 36

Liam Tinker was white, with the textured medium spiky hair on top, mid fade and beard beloved of footballers. And he looked decidedly nervous. His right knee was bobbing up and down at a rate of knots, and the fingers of his left hand were drumming against the side of his van.

It probably hadn't helped that the two detectives had picked up on that as soon as they got out of their cars, and then deliberately placed themselves at either end of his vehicle, leaving him in the centre. That meant that he had to keep turning his head from one to the other as they fired off questions.

'How old are you, Mr Tinker?' Caton asked.

'Twenty-four,' he said. 'Why?'

'And how long have you been doing this job?' Carly Whittle asked.

'Five years,' he replied. 'But I don't see . . .'

'And what did you do before that?' Caton said.

'This and that.' He turned to the female detective, obviously expecting the next question to come from her. He was wrong.

'Could you be more explicit?' Caton asked.

'Explicit?' Tinker touched his beard with his right hand, as though expecting to find the answer there.

'What were you doing between leaving school and starting this job?' Carly asked.

'I helped out on a window-cleaning round with my uncle for a couple of years,' he said, 'then I worked in a bar in Gorton, and then I got this job.'

'Where was the window-cleaning round, Mr Tinker?' Caton asked.

'Wythenshawe.' Liam's neck was beginning to ache. He ceased drumming and gave it a rub. 'Look,' he said, 'you said you were investigating a suspicious death on one of my rounds. I don't see what all these questions have got to do with that?'

'*Two* deaths,' Caton supplied. 'And your van was seen in the vicinity of *both* of the houses concerned. So, what we would like to know is if during your rounds you've seen anyone acting suspiciously in or around the Highfield Estate in Stretford or near the Meade in Chorltonville?'

Liam didn't even stop to think about it. 'No.'

He looked at Carly Whittle, and then back at Caton, in the hope that at least one of them would realise that he was completely innocent of whatever it was they suspected him of.

'You seem very sure,' Carly said.

'I am,' he told her, 'because I don't have time to see what other people are doing. We're on tight schedules. I've got targets to meet. It's a case of knock on the door, wait for them to unload the bags from my crates, and then on to the next one.'

It was a fair point, Caton decided, but it didn't explain why Tinker looked quite so skittish and sounded so cagey.

'Stretford and Chorltonville aren't exactly side by side,' Caton said. 'Are they normally part of your delivery route?'

Tinker shook his head. His hand went to his beard again. 'No. Before this bloody coronavirus, I was doing Irlam, Urmston and Stretford. But then everybody started ordering online, so they had to take on more drivers and carve up the areas into smaller parcels. I only started doing Chorltonville three weeks ago.'

He was beginning to sweat now and that knee had gone into overdrive. He made a play of checking his watch.

'Look, I'm already twenty minutes down, and I've got chilled and frozen on board. Honestly, I can't help you. Can I get on, please?'

It was the 'honestly' that did it.

'We'd just like a quick look in your van, Mr Tinker,' Caton said, 'and then we'll be on our way.'

He noted the flicker of alarm in the man's eyes just before he managed to pull himself together, and the alacrity with which he started, keys in hand, towards the rear of the van.

'Can you make it quick?' said Tinker. 'Some of this stuff will already be defrosting.'

Caton smiled.

'I think we'll start with the cab,' he said.

Chapter 37

Caton found them hidden in a sandwich box under the passenger seat. Three clear click and seal snack bags, each of them packed with smaller baggies containing pills. In a second box was a mobile phone, and a quantity of banknotes secured with elastic bands.

They had to wait for a sniffer dog to come out and check the rest of the contents of the vehicle, and a custody van to take Tinker back to the nearest station on Talbot Road in Old Trafford. In the meantime, Carly called Tinker's supervisor and told him that if wanted his customers to receive their perishables any time soon, he'd better send a relief driver out p.d.q.

The supervisor arrived in a taxi. Caton took him to one side.

'I'm as surprised as you are,' the man began. 'I can't believe that Liam would do anything like this. Are you sure someone else didn't put them there?'

'That's what we intend to find out,' Caton told him. 'How long have you known Liam?'

'Ever since he started working for us. That's about six years ago.'

'He told us five.'

The man nodded. 'Somewhere in that region would be about right.'

'And you've never had reason to doubt his honesty?'

'Absolutely not. And his customer feedback is brilliant. He's been employee of the month so many times

I couldn't count them on both hands. And his partner's just had a baby. They're planning to get married. I don't believe he'd do anything to jeopardise that.'

That didn't square with Tinker's body language when they'd started to question him. But it did with the hunch that Caton had been nurturing.

'We've searched his vehicle and it's good to go,' Caton told him, 'but I may well need to speak with you again once Mr Tinker has been interviewed.'

* * *

As the arresting officer, Caton conducted the interview, together with a DS from the local CID. Carly Whittle watched on the monitors in the observation suite. The three evidence bags were laid out on the table. Tinker and the duty solicitor were seated behind a second table pushed up against the first to ensure that Covid regulations were being adhered to. Liam Tinker had been crying even before they began the interview.

'Benzodiazepines and methadone,' Caton said. 'We've estimated over two thousand pills in total. I take it these are not for your own personal use?'

The solicitor leaned forward. 'Just to be clear,' he said, 'my client knows nothing about the deaths of those women about whom you have already questioned him. But we have prepared a statement he wishes to make regarding these drugs.'

'We'd like to hear it from Mr Tinker,' Caton told him. 'So, Liam, what is it you wish to tell us?'

The delivery driver's leg was going up and down under the table, and his heel beat a tattoo on the floor as he told his story.

'They're not mine,' he said. 'I don't even take drugs.' He wiped his cheek with the back of his hand. 'I was in the Turing Tap on Oxford Road, celebrating the birth of our daughter with some mates.'

'When was this?'

'The nineteenth of March – the day before they shut all the pubs down.'

'Carry on.'

'I was in the loo when these two blokes came up to me. They asked did I want to earn some money? Good money. I told them I already had a steady job, so thanks, but no.'

'They weren't taking no for an answer,' the CID man guessed.

'They said they already knew about my job, and that it was just a matter of dropping a few things off on my way round my normal route. I'm not stupid, am I? I knew who they were. What they were on about.'

'But you still went ahead?' the DS said.

Caton wanted to reach out and touch his arm, tell him to stop interrupting, but they were too far apart.

'Not at first,' Tinker replied. 'But then they said they knew where I lived. They knew my wife's name, even my daughter's name. They said it would be a tragedy if anything were to happen to them.'

'You could have gone to the police,' said the DS.

'Oh yeah, what with? Hearsay? And then what? You warn them off, and I get a petrol bomb through my letterbox!'

He had a point, Caton conceded. Not that that was going to help him. In fact, it made it more likely he'd be too frightened to grass them up, and end up taking the rap all on his own.

The DS gave an exaggerated sigh. 'So you said yes?'

'Well, what would you have done?' Tinker said.

'Come to us, and we'd have set up a sting operation.

We'd have bagged them and put them away. You would've been in the clear.'

Tinker's expression of incredulity mirrored what was going through Caton's mind.

'And you don't think they're going to get to me and my family from inside? And even if they don't, what d'you think they're gonna do when they get out?'

'Tell us how it worked, Liam,' said Caton, not wanting to be diverted.

'They gave me a mobile phone. Each day, I text them my route and text them when I'm leaving the store. They follow me and flash their headlights when they want me to stop. They get out and bring me the drugs, together with a list of drop-off points along the route. It's always somewhere there aren't any cameras, and I can exchange the drugs for cash by the side of the van, where we can't be seen from the road. I text when I've made my last delivery, and they flash me down before I get back to the store. I give them the cash, any drugs that are left over and the burner phone. They pay me, and give me a new phone to use the following day.'

'I bet it was a relief to get all that off your chest, Liam?' said the DS. 'Now all you have to do is give us some names and descriptions, and I'm sure the court will take that into consideration.'

A disconsolate Liam Tinker looked across at his solicitor and sat back in his chair.

'No comment,' he said.

Chapter 38

It was one o'clock in the afternoon by the time they were back at Nexus House.

'You didn't seem surprised,' said Carly Whittle as they walked across the car park.

'I wasn't,' he told her. 'I bumped into DI Stuart a couple of days back, and she was telling me that the NCA had noticed a massive rise in drug gangs using kids on mountain bikes to do their deliveries. It wasn't much of a stretch to envisage them latching on to the growth in supermarket deliveries. These drug gangs are nothing if not inventive.'

'It does put us back to square one though, Boss,' she said.

Caton offered up his key card to the entry pad. The door swung open. 'We're never back at square one, Sergeant,' he said, 'only we won't know which square we *are* on until we get to the end, and can look back and work out how the hell we got there.'

When they walked into the Incident Room, Ged was tapping a biro on the side of a glass, ready to make an announcement.

'Lunch has arrived!' she said. 'Courtesy of the local gurdwara. Who fancies a curry?'

The cheers were deafening.

'You'll find it in the conference room,' she told them. 'They've come in individual portions so there's no need to rush.'

She was too late. A human tide was already making

its way towards the door. Caton and Carly Whittle had to step back to avoid being crushed.

'Two metres!' Caton bellowed. 'What's wrong with you? Two metres!'

It may have been a rhetorical question, but it finally registered. Those not already through the door began to slow down. Some even stopped and stepped back, until a reasonable sense of order had been restored.

Caton joined the queue, collected a meal and took it back into the Incident Room. The rest of the core team followed him. They colonised the four carrels closest to the wall holding the murder boards.

Caton shovelled a plastic spoonful of butter chicken into his mouth, and studied the stills showing each of the crime scenes.

'The key to all this has to be finding out exactly how those packets of pills ended up in those houses,' he said at last.

'The trouble is,' Carter responded, 'we don't know what timescale we're working to. Those pills could have been delivered months ago.'

'Possibly,' Caton agreed. 'But it's too much of a coincidence that these two victims died within four days of each other. I still think we're looking at them having been in possession of those pills for no more than a couple of weeks. Probably less.'

'What are you eating, Carly?' DC Powell asked.

'The veggie option,' she told him. 'Chana masala.' She grinned. 'Shame about the virus, otherwise you could have tried some.'

'When they find a vaccine that works, I'll see if I can persuade this gurdwara to put on a buffet for us,' Caton told them, 'and we can have a double celebration.'

'Double?' Carter said.

Caton scooped another spoonful. 'Seeing off Covid-19 and catching the killer.'

'Let's hope we don't have to wait too long for either of them,' Carter said.

Jimmy Hulme juggled three foil containers as he walked towards them. 'I may be able to help with the second of those two,' he said. 'DC Franklin has just informed me that they've found another vehicle that's been recorded in the vicinity of both crime scenes.'

Catching an elbow on one of the new dividers between workstations, he was thrown off balance and the topmost container of curry flew into the air. Henry Powell leapt to his feet and caught it in mid-air before it could spill its lurid contents over Caton's desk.

'Howzat?' shouted Carter, applauding loudly.

'Sorry, Boss,' said Hulme. 'That could have been nasty. Leaves a wicked stain does rogan josh.'

'Never mind that,' Caton told him. 'This vehicle – you got a name?'

Jimmy Hulme got his trays down safely on a spare desk. 'Thelma Green,' he said. 'She's a district nurse.'

'That's not unusual,' Carter pointed out. 'Could be she works both patches.'

'One of the crime scenes is in Trafford,' Caton pointed out. 'The other is in Manchester.'

Hulme prised the lid off one of the trays. 'Some of the NHS Trusts do cross borough boundaries,' he said.

'A significant percentage of Angels of Mercy are nurses,' Carly Whittle observed.

'Neither of these women were ill,' Henry Powell pointed out. 'That's hardly mercy killing.'

'DC Powell is right,' Caton said. 'Normally with health professionals, we'd be looking at victims with significant life-limiting conditions – people whose death could be argued as releasing them from suffering, pain or mental anguish. But that isn't always the case. Harold Shipman, for example – that was more a combination of greed and power slash control. Then there was the case back in 2012 that those of us in FMIT hoped we'd never see again in our lifetime.'

Carter stabbed the air with his fork. 'Victorino Chua,' he said. 'Nurse at Steppinghill, connected with seven deaths. Found guilty in relation to two of them, one attempted murder, and twenty-eight others of GBH, poisoning or attempted poisoning. He got twenty-five life sentences and was sent down for thirty-five years minimum.'

'What poison did she use?' Powell asked.

'*He* used overdoses of insulin,' Carter replied. 'Easy for him to access and then he just changed the records to shift the blame onto others.'

'The point is,' said Caton, 'that although his motive was never satisfactorily established, the consensus was that he was a troubled narcissist whose motivations lay somewhere in his frustration with his under-achievement and chaotic life.'

'Frustration?' said Carly Whittle.

'He got rid of patients that annoyed him,' Carter told her. 'Ones he considered troublesome.'

'Although that was never proven,' Caton said. 'It was only implicit in a couple of cases, where he'd had a disagreement with a patient or relative shortly before he administered the insulin. The police found a thirty-one-page letter he claimed to have written after a counselling session and before the poisonings started. In the letter, he described himself as an angel turned into an evil person, and claimed there was a devil inside him. They didn't believe his account of when it was written. They regarded it as a form of confession.'

'Didn't he mention something about making history?' said Nick Carter.

'He did. But nobody believed that was his motivation.

Outwardly, he was kind and compassionate, but inside he was a callous monster. He showed no remorse. He simply dispensed with people.'

'Like a lot of psychopaths,' said Carter.

'Some,' Caton corrected him, 'but by no means all.'

'Do you think that's what we have here, Boss?' Powell asked.

'It's one possibility,' Caton said. 'All I'm saying is that it can't be excluded.'

Conscious that other members of the team had returned and were earwigging, he stood to address the room.

'Everyone!' When he had their full attention, he pointed to the laminated poster on the wall. 'A,B,C,' he said. 'What does that stand for?'

They chorused in unison, the old hacks wearily, the newbies with enthusiasm. 'Assume nothing! Believe no one! Check everything!'

'Make sure you do,' he said. 'Carry on.'

He sat down again.

'Speaking of which, DS Hulme,' he said. 'I want every one of the key workers to be interviewed who are either resident in the same neighbourhoods as the victims, or whose cars travelled to or from either of the victim's streets. And that includes finding out if any of them have access to other vehicles, and if so, whether they were used in the relevant time frame.'

'On it, Boss,' said Hulme.

Caton looked at the two whiteboards and the spiderweb of connections radiating from the photos of the victims.

'What are you thinking, Boss?' asked Carter.

'That back then they had to interview over a thousand doctors, nurses, health workers, patients and families of victims before they nailed Victorino Chua,

177

and that included charging another nurse who turned out to be innocent, before they finally discovered it was him. What if there've been other victims we don't know about? That we'll never know about, because they've already been cremated?'

'Best not to think about it,' said Carter. 'We'll find out soon enough if it turns out that our killer is one for boasting about his exploits. ''Course, we've got to catch him or her first.'

'In which case, eat up,' he said. 'You and I need to pay Ms Green a visit.'

Chapter 39

'This must be her,' said Carter.

They were stood outside a semi-detached house on Nuffield Road in Sharston, one of the ten towns that made up Wythenshawe. Once the largest council estate in Europe, in 2007 the *New York Times* had labelled it 'an extreme pocket of social deprivation and alienation'. An impression that had not been improved by Sarah Ferguson's documentary two years later, entitled 'The Duchess on The Estate'. Caton thought it unlikely she'd be welcome back any time soon.

A woman in her late thirties was standing on the doorstep. Her hair was in a double bun, and she wore a pale blue tunic, dark blue trousers and sensible flat-heeled shoes. A bulky bag hung from her right shoulder. She pulled the door to without closing it, unhooked her surgical mask from one ear and then the other, placed it in one of the side pockets of her bag, and then peeled off her blue nitrile gloves.

'Thelma Green?' said Caton.

She looked up and saw them standing on the pavement. 'Who wants to know?' she said. She clutched her bag protectively, and her eyes scanned the street as though seeking rescue.

Caton held up his ID. 'Detective Chief Inspector Caton and Detective Inspector Carter, Greater Manchester Police. It's nothing to worry about, Mrs Green, we're just hoping you can help us with an investigation.'

179

She put the gloves in the same pocket as her mask and zipped it up.

'*Miss* Green,' she said, walking down the path towards them. 'I'm sorry if I seemed a bit wary. You can't be too careful in this job.' She patted her bag and left her hand resting there. 'It's the drugs they're after.'

She stopped just short of the gate beyond which the two detectives stood.

This close, it was obvious that her uniform was at least a size too big for her, and her face had the gaunt look common to people recovering from a nasty dose of flu. Caton thought she could benefit from a little TLC herself.

'I'm sorry if I startled you, Miss Green,' he said. 'I should have waited until you'd finished putting your PPE away.'

'You mentioned an investigation?' she said.

'That's correct. If I give you a couple of addresses, could you tell me if you happen to have visited either of them as part of your work, or for some other reason?'

'I'll try,' she replied.

He read out the Stretford address. She frowned.

'I've been visiting a patient on the close, but it's definitely not that number. Are you sure you've got the right address?'

'Can you give me the name and address of the patient you *were* visiting?' he said.

She told him and Carter made a note.

'Do you recognise this second address?' Caton said.

This time she did a double take. 'That's odd, that must be three doors down from another of my patients. What's this all about?'

Then it dawned on her.

'Just a minute,' she said. 'You're talking about those women they've just been on about on the radio just now?'

There was no point in denying it.

'That's right,' he said. 'We were wondering if you'd had any contact with them or might have seen others visiting those addresses?'

He could tell from her expression that she knew exactly why they were here – that she was a suspect simply on account of her profession. She folded her left arm across her chest and gripped the shoulder strap so that her bag was now protected by both hands. Her voice was resolute, close to confrontational.

'I have never visited either of those addresses in any capacity,' she said. 'Furthermore, my normal patches are the northern part of Wythenshawe and Chorltonville. The only reason I was on that estate in Stretford is that I was asked to cover for a colleague who's self-isolating. I suggest you check with my boss if you don't believe me.'

'Don't worry,' Caton said, 'we'll do that as a matter of course.'

He watched as a woman in an identical uniform exited the house and closed the door behind her. Thelma Green turned her head to see what he was looking at.

'Better still,' she said, 'you can ask my colleague. She'll tell you.' She called out. 'Angela, will you please tell these policemen . . .'

Caton interrupted her. 'Stop right there, Miss Green!' he said. 'I need you to go and sit in your car while I speak with your colleague.'

There was no way he was going to allow her to alert her colleague to his line of questioning, or taint the truthfulness of her replies. He stepped back to enable her to pass through the gate. She walked to her car with a sullen countenance. Caton turned his attention to the other nurse.

She looked older than Thelma Green by at least a decade and was, he guessed, of South Asian heritage.

Her first reaction had been to check that what Caton presumed was her own car was still there next to that of her colleague. Reassured, she peeled off her gloves and mask, and put them in a polythene bag that was sticking out of her shoulder bag. As she walked down the path towards him, the expression on her face was one of curiosity, rather than concern. When he realised that she wasn't going to stop, he put his arm out to keep her at a distance. She stopped abruptly, and stepped back.

'I'm sorry,' she said. 'It's so easy to forget when you're outside, don't you think?' Her smile was disarming. 'What's this all about then, officer?' she said.

'I didn't catch your name?' he said.

'That's because I didn't give it to you.' Her smile broadened. 'Only kidding. I am Angela Malhotra – Mrs Angela Malhotra.'

'Thank you, Mrs Malhotra,' he said. 'My name is Detective Chief Inspector Caton. I'm with Greater Manchester Police. I was explaining to Miss Green that we're investigating several unexplained deaths in the area involving elderly persons, and we're wondering if you or your colleague may have seen something on your rounds that might help us.'

She raised her eyebrows. 'Elderly person you say? Are you sure these weren't Covid-related? Sometimes it's hard to tell, especially with senior citizens.'

'We think that unlikely,' he told her. 'Now, if I ask you a few questions?'

'Go ahead,' she said. 'I'm all ears.'

'First of all, how long have you been working with Miss Green?'

The question took her by surprise. 'Thelma?'

'How long have you worked together?'

'Just over two years. Though we don't always go out in pairs like this. It depends on the patient's needs. You know, if there's any lifting involved, that sort of thing.'

'I'm going to give you some names and addresses,' Caton said. 'I want you tell me if any of them mean anything to you.'

There was no point in keeping the names of the victims secret now that Thelma Green had put two and two together. He read out Millie Dyer's name and address.

Malhotra shook her head. 'I've never heard of her,' she said. 'She's certainly never been one of my clients.'

'What about the address?' he said. 'It's on the Highfield Estate.'

'Out of my patch,' she said. 'I've never set foot on that estate. In fact, I wouldn't even know where it was.'

Caton gave her Erica Edwards's details. This time there was a glimmer of recognition.

'Now I don't know the name,' she said, 'and I don't believe I've ever visited that particular address, but Thelma and I do take it in turns with a patient on the Meade.'

'When was the last time you were there?' he asked.

She had to think about it. 'Three, four weeks ago?' she said. 'I'd have to check.'

Caton saw little point in pursuing it further. 'Thank you,' he said. 'I'm really grateful for your time. And I, like everyone else, think the work you do is underestimated and really important, especially with this lockdown and everything it means.'

She smiled. 'Thank you,' she said, hitching her bag higher up her shoulder.

'And thank your colleague for me too,' he said. 'I didn't get a chance to tell her.'

They watched as the two nurses had a brief exchange, climbed into their cars and drove away.

'What do you reckon, Nick?' Caton said.

Carter shrugged. 'It doesn't prove anything one way or another. They could easily have found out who their patients' neighbours were. And either one of them could have returned to the area.'

'We need to check with the passive media team if Malhotra's car has appeared at either of the crime scenes,' Caton said. 'It obviously hasn't appeared at both or it would have been flagged up.'

'They could have persuaded someone else to deliver those packages, or even paid them.'

Caton was not convinced. 'I don't see that happening,' he said. 'Would you take tablets given you by someone you'd never met? Both of these victims trusted their killer. If either of these women was involved, they'd have had to make contact with both victims. Nevertheless, I want you to ask DS Hulme to allocate one of the DCs to get over there, speak with their manager and see if their stories stack up. While they're at it, they can find out if there've been any deaths among their patients within the last twelve months. If so, we'll need a comprehensive list of names, addresses, age and cause of death.'

'What if they quote Data Protection and insist on a court order?'

'Then they'll need reminding that the provisions, other than confidentiality, do not apply to the personal data of a deceased patient. And, since we need the information for the purposes of the prevention and detection of crime, they're also exempt from their duty to inform those nurses that we've asked for the information. On the contrary, if they do, they'll be facing charges of obstruction. That should do it.'

Chapter 40
Nexus House. 1600 hours.

Caton stopped by Duggie's desk. The adjacent carrel was occupied by a DC, so he hooked his mask over both ears and pinched the metal nose clip tight.

'Got that data for me on deaths involving the elderly?' he asked.

Duggie wheeled his chair further away. 'It's been a nightmare, Boss,' he said. 'We tried the coroner's office first, but they only had a partial list because there's no requirement at the moment for them to be notified of all deaths, and to make matters worse, all inquests have been adjourned until September 2020.'

Caton was astonished. Not only was it the first he'd heard of it, but it sounded like a killers' charter.

'Okay, great. Well then, what about the Manchester Registration Service?'

'The office is closed to the public currently, and registrations of births and deaths are all being done over the phone, so it took ages to get through. They told me there's a big time lag in registrations of death at the moment, so it's likely there'll be some missing from the list they gave us. I'm still waiting on the Trafford Registrar.'

'What did Manchester give you?' Caton asked.

Duggie consulted his notes. 'Since the first of March, there were nine hundred and fifty-eight deaths in Manchester. Of those, fourteen had Covid-19 on the death certificate. Two died at home, the remainder in hospital. All but two of the deceased were over sixty-five years of age.'

'Told you *we'd* be fine,' said DC Franklin, who was earwigging from the neighbouring desk. Caton ignored him.

'Carry on, Duggie,' he said.

'Of the remaining non-Covid deaths,' the intelligence officer said, 'five hundred and forty-seven were male, four hundred and eleven were female. Of the females, three hundred and four were over sixty-five years of age.'

'That's a lot more than I expected,' said Caton. 'How many have there been in the past two weeks?'

'I've not done the maths,' Duggie said, 'but I assume about half that number. A hundred and fifty odd?'

'Have you looked at how many were in the Chorlton Wards?'

'Yes, Boss – providing we're only talking about the ones that occurred at home?'

'We are.'

'In that case, there were five in Chorlton, four in Chorlton Park, and a further twelve in the four contiguous wards.'

'Contiguous,' said DC Franklin. 'I like it.'

Caton turned and gave him the death stare. 'Please tell me you haven't taken on the mantle of joker now that DS Hulme has finally mellowed?'

'Sorry, Boss,' said Franklin.

'Go on, Duggie,' Caton said.

'That's as far as I've got,' he said. 'I'm still waiting to hear from the Registrar for the Borough of Trafford.'

'Let's start with the nine in the two Chorlton wards,' Caton told him. 'If we don't get any hits, we can work outwards. Find out which ones were living alone when they died, and prioritise those.'

'Can I ask a question, Boss?' said DS Hulme, who had now taken up position on the far side of the carrel.

'Of course,' Caton said.

'Well, I was wondering how you plan for us to check on each of them, given the circumstances.'

'Circumstances?'

'There won't have been any post-mortems and bodies are being released for fast-track funerals. The odds are that seventy-five per cent of them will already have been cremated.'

'He's right, Boss,' said Wallace. 'There's been a huge increase in demand for direct cremation. No family or friends present, and no proper service. It's cheap and quick, and the family can always plan a memorial service or a proper wake when the lockdown's finally over.'

'Then we'll just have to interview whoever it was that reported finding each of the bodies,' Caton told them. 'Ask them if there was any sign of painkillers, or any other medications when they arrived. We also need to ask whoever it was determined the cause of death, and whoever signed the death certificate – did they view the body? Was the death unexpected at all? And if so, was it referred to the coroner? If not, why not? If there are any flags raised, or if there's any uncertainty or even the slightest hint of doubt, I want that deceased person's home treated as a crime scene.'

'Including fingerprints, DNA and other potential trace evidence?' Jimmy Hulme asked. 'CSI will go ballistic.'

'To begin with, just photos, and a search for painkillers and other meds, or anything that appears suspicious. If anything does crop up, we can raise the ante. And in the meantime, I want a hold on any funerals planned for any of the nine deceased persons in the Chorlton wards that haven't already taken place.'

'That's going to cause a lot of controversy, Boss,' Wallace ventured.

'I don't care,' Caton told him. 'If it gets us any closer to identifying the unsub and saves even just one life, it'll be worth it.'

'Mr Caton!'

He turned towards the voice. Ged was waving her phone at him.

'It's the Assistant Chief Constable.'

'Which one?' Caton asked.

She placed a hand over the speaker and attempted to speak sotto voce. 'ACC Gates.'

'I'll take it in my office,' he told her.

He wove a careful path between the carrels, closed the door and picked up.

'Caton,' he said.

'It's a bloody good job they got the press release out there before the press got wind of this one,' she began. 'Talk about a knife edge. And you swanning off so you wouldn't have to front it.'

Touché, he thought.

'Does attending a suspicious death count as swanning?' he asked.

'You cheeky bugger!' she said, though he could tell her heart wasn't in it. 'The reason I'm ringing you is that while you've been hiding away, the balloon has well and truly gone up. Covid-19 kept Operation Pendle Hill off the front page, but there's no hiding from it now there's been a second one. The Chief Constable intends to hold a virtual press conference from here at Central Park. Comms Branch have scheduled it to coincide with the Government's daily coronavirus briefing at five p.m., in the hope that it'll slip under the radar. You'd better get a move on.'

Chapter 41
GMP Headquarters
Central Park. 1700 hours.

Caton just made it by the skin of his teeth.

He was shown to a chair at the end of the second of three carefully spaced rows. Next to Caton sat Helen Gates, to her right two other members of the Command Team. Gates tutted, and tapped the face of her wristwatch. He smiled back, and turned his attention to the rest of the people in the room.

On the front row, the Mayor of Greater Manchester, the leader of the council, and the Chief Constable each sat facing a laptop perched on a stand in front of them. No one in the room was wearing a mask, but all of the seats were at least three metres apart. He realised that the air-conditioning had been turned off and the windows were all open. He felt a warm draught on the side of his face, and wondered how long it would be before they all started to sweat.

At the front of the room, a large screen had been set up to host the video gallery. The top two rows had already been populated with the GMP team, including Helen Gates. Beneath them, invited members of the press were beginning to pop up one after the other.

Next to the screen, and off camera, Alan Rea, the Acting Head of Communications, was directing operations. He stepped forward and raised his voice.

'As a courtesy to one another, please make sure that you have muted your microphones, and only switch them on when you're addressing the meeting or responding to a question – and please remember to switch them off again as soon as you've finished. Remember Gordon Brown.'

Whether or not the then Prime Minister's 'bigoted woman' gaffe had cost him *and* Labour the 2010 general election, it had endured as a salutary reminder for times like this.

Caton pulled out his mobile phone. The meeting link was there among his most recent emails. He clicked on it, reversed his camera, then looked up at the screen. Ten seconds later, his Adam's apple filled the remaining slot on the second row, alongside ACC Gates. He lifted his phone up and away until he was as satisfied as he was ever going to be with his selfie, and wondered how he was going to manage to hold it steady for the duration of the meeting.

The Acting Head of Communications signalled to a colleague holding a video camera. His image now filled the screen. He began by welcoming the members of the press, and then introduced the five GMP officers, the Mayor and the council leader, neither of whom really needed any introduction.

'Now, before we begin,' he said, 'when it's your turn to speak, you will be invited in turn to ask a question, and allowed one follow-up question. Please remember to otherwise keep your microphone muted at all times. Whoever is speaking will appear on the screen. I will then invite the next person to ask their question, and so on. Please feel free to direct your question to whoever you believe to be the most appropriate person, but I must insist that all questions relating to the current situation, of what is a fast-moving operation, are addressed to the operational lead, Senior Investigating Officer, Detective Chief Inspector Caton.'

Brilliant, thought Caton. *The rest of you may as well go home. And what clown came up with 'fast-moving'? Now I'll be the star of the show, and they'll all be expecting to hear about amazing progress. When in fact the only person right now who appears to be fast-moving is the killer.*

He could feel the sweat in his armpits. A familiar face filled the screen.

'David Grice, BBC North West News. I have a question for Chief Inspector Caton.'

Here we go, Caton thought. His finger hovered over the unmute button.

'We understand,' said the reporter, 'that the first victim was discovered two days ago. Why were the public not immediately alerted to the fact that someone is adding poison to one of the most ubiquitous painkillers on the market?'

The Head of Communications cut in. 'That question should be directed to . . .' he began.

Caton decided to answer anyway. 'We didn't know that was the case until after we had received the results of the post-mortem,' he said, 'nor that pill-tampering had been responsible for that person's death. Once those facts were available, a press release was issued on the same day. Prior to that, all of those organisations that represent first-responders were asked to brief their staff accordingly.'

Alan Rea looked relieved. 'Do you have a follow-up question?' he asked.

'Yes,' said the man from the BBC. 'Why has there been no product recall?'

Caton was relieved to see Helen Gates raise her hand and wave. Her face filled the screen.

'Assistant Chief Constable Helen Gates will take that question,' Alan Rea announced.

'There are three reasons,' she began. 'Firstly, this is

a generic product. There are too many brands and too many different companies and suppliers involved to be able to achieve that overnight. Secondly, there is no evidence at this stage in the operation to suggest that the tablets were tampered with prior to going on sale, or that they had in fact even been purchased by the victims. Thirdly, we have no way of knowing if this particular product is the only one to have been tampered with in this way. In the circumstances, the priority was, and is, to alert the public to the need to examine any tablets or pills they may have been prescribed, bought privately or been given, before taking them.'

She muted her microphone, lowered her mobile so that her image disappeared from the screen, and glanced across at Caton. He gave her a nod of approval and mouthed his thanks. It had been a smart and timely intervention.

'Anthony Ginley,' said the press officer.

Who the hell had invited him? Caton felt his pulse quicken. He was beginning to lose count of the number of investigations Ginley had obstructed in his obsession for exclusive stories. His face filled the screen like a haunting.

'Anthony Ginley, Independent Press Consultants UK Ltd.'

He had turned forty now, Caton guessed. The angular fringe had become unruly in lockdown, and the designer stubble had developed into a beard. He still had the overconfident smile that came across as a smirk.

'I have a question for the Senior Investigating Officer,' he said. 'DCI Caton, can you confirm that the substance used to contaminate the painkillers taken by both victims was potassium cyanide?'

The body language from Caton's colleagues on the row in front of him reflected exactly how he was feeling.

That information was supposed to be confidential. Either a first responder had put two and two together and blabbed, or someone had leaked from inside the operation.

'I am unable to comment on such details while the investigation is still ongoing,' he said. He couldn't resist adding, 'I'm sure you're aware of that.'

The smile faded.

'In which case,' Ginley said. 'Perhaps you could tell us if the deceased were known to one another. And if you have found any connection between them?'

'At this stage,' Caton replied, 'we have no reason to believe that the deceased knew one another. That is something that we're still seeking to clarify.'

'Did they both have the same doctor, for example?' Ginley asked.

The Head of Communications stepped in. 'Thank you for your questions, Mr Ginley,' he said. The screen was returned to the gallery view. 'The next question comes from . . .'

'If they weren't known to each other,' Ginley persisted, leaning close to his camera, 'does that mean there's a serial killer on the loose?'

'Please mute your microphone, Mr Ginley,' Alan Rea ordered, 'or I will have to ask you to leave the meeting!'

Caton felt a touch on his shoulder. A woman was standing in the aisle just behind him with a note in her outstretched hand. He read it, picked up his phone and logged out of the conference, then stood up as quietly as possible.

Helen Gates stared up at him, looking furious. Caton shrugged and held up three fingers. Her expression morphed into something between panic and alarm.

As Caton left the room, he heard a voice saying, 'My question is for DCI Caton . . .'

Chapter 42
Gatley, South Manchester. 18.15 hours.

He turned right immediately opposite Sharston Business Park onto the normally busy B5166. This evening, at the height of the rush hour, it was deserted. Two hundred and fifty yards later, he pulled in where a uniformed officer stood alongside a patrol car blocking the road.

Caton held his ID card against the window for the officer to check his name and enter it on his tablet. The officer then pointed to his left, and directed Caton into a cul-de-sac of 1930s semis, each with a pair of bay windows. Two marked cars and a CIS van were parked outside one of the houses at the far end. Caton found a space and got out of the car. Jack Benson in full Tyvek protective suit, boots, gloves and mask, strode down the garden path towards him.

'Want the good news, Boss, or the bad?'

'Give me the good news,' Caton said. 'I could do with some of that.'

'We've found an identical pack of painkillers, minus two tablets, in a medicine cupboard in the kitchen. And there's no need to view the body because it's been removed.'

'And the bad news?'

'That list of deceased elderly women you wanted? She was one of the nine women on the list. The body was discovered on the twenty-eighth of March. She was cremated the day before yesterday.'

Another figure in a protective suit appeared, and started down the path towards them.

'Who signed the death certificate?' Caton asked.

'DI Carter has the details,' Benson replied. 'He'll fill you in. Is it okay for me to carry on?'

'Of course,' Caton told him.

The CSI stepped deftly two paces to his right, and circled around the approaching figure as he made his way back to the house. The figure took his place and pushed back its hood to reveal a red-faced Nick Carter. His hair was wet and sweat pooled below his hairline.

'It's like a bloody furnace in there,' he said. 'Someone forgot to turn the heating off.'

'Jack said you'd fill me in,' Caton said.

'Oh, right,' Carter responded. He tried to brush the sweat from his forehead with his sleeve.

'I hope you've not sneezed into that particular elbow,' Caton said. 'The team's small enough as it is.'

Carter grimaced. 'Very funny,' he said. 'Do you want to hear about her or not?'

'Fire away,' Caton said.

'Martha Riley, eighty-three years of age, widowed schoolteacher. Discovered ten days ago by a care worker who came in once a week just to check she was okay. She rang 999 and waited outside for the police and ambulance to arrive. The uniformed officers who came on scene could see no evidence of a break-in or injuries of any kind. The ambulance crew, including a paramedic, reckoned she'd been dead for a couple of days, so the police discharged them to carry on with another call and rang her GP.'

'What did the GP say?'

'He said it wasn't entirely unexpected since she had a history of diabetes, a dicky heart, and he'd spoken with her three days earlier when she'd reported having a bad cough. On that basis, and given what the ambulance crew had told the police, he said that under the current guidelines there was no requirement for him to see the deceased, and he'd be happy to complete the certificate of cause of death and send it on to the funeral director, so he could register the death and arrange for the funeral.'

'What did he put on the death certificate?'

'Heart failure, with possible but unconfirmed Covid-19 contributory factors.'

'Why the hell didn't the police officers who attended flag this up as soon as we put out the first appeal for information?' Caton said. 'We could have put a hold on the cremation.'

'Maybe they didn't see the appeal?'

Caton snorted. 'What – or read the newspapers, or watch the news?'

'To be fair, Boss,' Carter said, 'it was before our first victim turned up, and they would just have wanted to get out of there as quickly as possible and move on.'

Caton shook his head. 'That's no excuse for not seeing the connection afterwards.' He paused to put his anger aside and clear his mind. 'So, who was the next of kin?'

'She had one daughter – she agreed to the cremation.'

'Did she attend?'

'She watched on her phone from Milan.'

'Milan?'

'She was working there when the Italians threw a ring of steel around the region. She wasn't able to come home. Still isn't.'

'It's a pity we didn't do the same,' Caton observed. 'Have family liaison call her in the morning and bring her up to date, and find out if any of the other victims' names ring a bell.'

'Will do,' said Carter. 'I asked DS Hulme to set up a team to do the door-to-door enquiries and passive media collection. I'm assuming you want the same procedure as for the first two – interviews with friends and family, and known associates? Same for owners or drivers of any vehicles picked up by the CCTV analysis?'

'Plus, interviews with the ambulance crew,' Caton said. 'We need to know if they saw or disturbed anything. Send me the details for the GP and the care worker that found the body. I'd like to talk to them both myself, and I'll start with the GP. I'd like you to speak with the care worker's line manager. And before you leave, get the contact details for the daughter. Somebody, preferably family support, is going to have to appraise her of the fact that her mother's death was suspicious, before she hears about it on the bloody news. We also need to know if she was aware of anybody befriending or visiting her mother.'

'Is that it, Boss?'

'I'm struggling to see what else we can do,' Caton admitted. 'Do I need to see inside?'

'Not really. I've had a good gander, and we'll have all the video footage and photos by the end of the day. I didn't spot anything out of the ordinary, other than this is remarkably similar to the other two.'

'In what way?'

'Homely, quaint, neat and tidy. Lots of pictures of family members. God's waiting room, if you know what I mean?'

Caton did. His aunt's house had morphed into exactly that after his uncle died. So much so that towards the end it had felt like a mausoleum, with photos of his own parents given pride of place alongside those of her husband. In a way, he was glad she hadn't lived to experience lockdown. He immediately felt a pang of guilt that this was as much about his not having the worry, as about how it might have been for her.

'Boss?' Carter said. 'Are you okay?'

'Sorry, I was miles away.'

Carter rubbed the back of his gloved hand against his chin. 'If only.'

Caton pointed. 'Hand! Face!' he said.

'It's alright,' Carter replied. 'I gave the gloves a spray as I left the house.'

'Remind me,' Caton said, 'what's at the back of the house, behind the garden?'

'Wythenshawe AFC football field and Hollyhedge Park.'

'That stretches down to Hollyhedge Road, and South Wythenshawe?'

'That's right, Boss.'

'Aren't there some allotments round here too?'

'The other side of the football field between the council estate and those new houses.'

Caton remembered chasing a flasher across that allotment when he was starting out as a probationer. The fugitive was so busy trying to get his tackle back inside his pants that he'd run straight into a wheelbarrow, and ended up head first in a heap of steaming horse manure.

'What are you thinking, Boss?' Carter asked.

'I'll let you know when I've checked it out,' Caton told him. 'I'll meet you back at Nexus House.'

Chapter 43

Caton walked back to the main road, and found the entrance to the path that led down beside the empty football pitch and the playing fields. At the end of the pitch, he turned left and headed for a stand of trees, his eyes on the sun-baked grass in the hope of finding something significant, however improbable, twelve days after she died, and God knows how long since she had received the tablets that killed her.

The silver birch and blackthorn trees were only two or three thick at the point where they bordered the victim's property. He had no problem weaving his way between them until he found himself at a wooden slatted fence, beyond which lay her garden. On the way, he checked for footprints, and any strands of fabric that might have snagged on the rough surface of the wood. Finding none, he put on a pair of nitrile gloves, placed one foot on the lowest backing rail, and then hauled himself up.

A CSI in a white protective suit was examining the ground at the foot of the fence. He looked up. Startled by Caton's head staring down at him, he stepped back, caught his heel on an ornamental gnome, and fell, landing in a plastic wheelbarrow that could almost have been placed there for the sole purpose of catching him. The wheelbarrow toppled, pitching the CSI on his back on a compost heap.

Caton jumped down from the fence to avoid adding to the man's embarrassment. When he finally managed to compose himself, he climbed back up and discovered that he needn't have bothered. Two of the CSI's colleagues further down the garden had their arms around one another's shoulders, and were shaking with mirth like a pair of demented phantoms.

Their colleague dragged himself to his feet and proceeded to brush himself down. He glared up at Caton, who could only begin to imagine the full expression beneath the hood and mask.

'I'm so sorry,' Caton said. 'Are you alright?'

Fortunately, the reply was rendered incomprehensible. The CSI went back to examining the ground, while Caton turned his attention to the garden.

Near the end of the cul-de-sac, it was relatively small and oddly shaped, but well maintained. Caton assumed that the owner was either a keen gardener herself, or had had someone tend it for her. Given her age, he thought the latter, and made a note to have someone check that out.

Around a lawn that looked as though it had been regularly mown, edged and watered through the unseasonal drought, were neat borders replete with anemones, forget-me-nots, hyacinths, white narcissi and red and yellow tulips. Caton wondered if the lawn might furnish footprints where the baked soil had not. Though had he been the intruder, he'd have chosen the tarmac path leading from the compost heap via a green-painted shed to the back door.

He examined the house, and the two on either side, for cameras or external lights, and found neither. It would have been easy, he decided, for someone to slip across the fields and between the trees in the dark, climb over the fence and make their way to the house. But was that likely, when your aim was to win the trust of the woman inside, such that she would without hesitation take the poisoned pills you had brought?

He made his way back to the open parkland, where he climbed the grassy bank and crossed a tarmac path. Hoping to gain a vista of the entire park, he scaled the low hill ahead of him. His view was partially blocked by a stand of trees on the next rise, so he took out his mobile phone, switched it to silent mode, set the camera to video and slowly turned through three-hundred-and-sixty degrees. He walked down the slope to the path and began to follow it, videoing as he went.

It was approximately a quarter of a mile to the southernmost end of the park, and took him less than five minutes. In that time, he encountered just two dogwalkers, a jogger and two boys in their teens riding side by side on mountain bikes. As soon as they realised that he was filming, they parted in a belated attempt to demonstrate adherence to the outdoor two-metre rule. Caton was impressed. Nine out of ten wouldn't have bothered even if he'd been in uniform. But the fact they were on bikes reinforced a theory he'd been mulling over since setting foot on the playing fields.

The enclosed basketball court at the end was locked. Behind it stood two cars on the car park. The climbing frame and slide in the empty play area stood like forlorn sentinels waiting for children to return. One of the two bowling greens had been left to go to seed. The other was a beige-bleached carpet. Caton stopped filming and looked back the way he had come.

If he wanted to approach that house at night, on foot or on a bike, then this was the route he would have chosen. By keeping to the perimeter, it was possible to stay within the shadow of trees all the way. He turned, and walked the short distance down to the entrance on Hollyhedge Road. Just short of the gates, where the hedge ended, there was a narrow stretch of old railings, barely three feet in height, lacking the iron spearhead deterrent of their newer neighbours. Caton stepped over them with ease.

He glanced at his watch. It was 4.37 p.m. and the sun was beginning to set. He hurried back the way he'd come, chasing the light.

By the time he reached the allotments, the sun was setting. A pure white orb, surrounded by a golden circle, from which an orange glow leached into a grey apocalyptic sky, casting melancholy shadows from the surrounding trees.

It was near pitch-dark. He switched notifications back on his phone and used the torch to follow the path back to the road. There was a rapid succession of pings as messages began to fill his screen. Most of them from Helen Gates.

Caton sighed and called back. She answered after two rings.

'I'm sorry for leaving you in the lurch like that, Ma'am,' he said, hoping to assuage the torrent of vitriol heading his way.

She surprised him. 'Forget that,' she said. 'There was nothing I couldn't handle. What I want to know is if we really are looking at a third victim?'

'The evidence is circumstantial,' he told her. 'It's highly likely, but we're never going to be able to prove it beyond any doubt.'

'Why not?'

'There'll be no post-mortem.'

'Because?'

'We don't have a body, Helen. She was cremated two days ago.'

'But the MO's the same?'

'Yes.'

'We don't have a body, but we do have a serial killer?'

'Three identical murders become a series,' he said. 'So yes, we do.'

She swore. 'I've just told the press that it was too early to come to that conclusion.'

'It was when you said it. Now it isn't.'

'Why don't I find that reassuring? Tom,' she said, 'what I really need is some good news.'

'Rest assured, Ma'am,' he said, 'that as soon I have some, you'll be the first to hear.'

'Make sure I am. I have a meeting with the Chief Constable, the Mayor, and the leader of the city council in twenty minutes. What am I supposed to tell them?'

'That catching a serial killer is a slow process at the best of times, and this is not the best of times. That if there are any more victims, they're likely to be historical now that members of the public have been warned and are more likely to be on their guard. That if the unsub does try to carry on, the odds will swing in our favour. Then it's only a matter of time before he or she makes a mistake.'

'Time is running out, Tom,' she said.

It was always a hollow threat. At best, it meant there would be an external review, which would waste time and end up making the odd suggestion about how to improve the running of the investigation. Nothing would really change. At worst, someone else would be brought in to take over as SIO, but they'd come up against the same obstacles, and have the additional challenge of winning over and motivating his team. Gates knew that, and she knew that he knew that she knew.

'I'm doing my best, Helen,' he said.

To her credit, she resisted telling him that his best was not good enough. She had trod where he was treading, and cheap shots were not her style. He decided to get his request in before she changed her mind.

'Another five detectives would speed things up,' he said.

'What for?' she asked.

He took comfort from the fact it was not an outright no.

'It isn't only Public Health England that needs more hands for contact track and trace,' he said. 'We need to connect these victims, and we need to follow up every contact they may have had in the past few weeks, including deliveries by post, by courier and by hand. It's really labour-intensive, Helen, and my team is working around the clock. They have families at home in lockdown. I'm already two down. The strain is emotional as well as physical. I'm not sure how long they can keep it up.'

'Enough with the heartstrings,' she said. 'I'll see what I can do, but, and I stress *but*, if I do manage to find you some, where will you put them? As I understand it, your Incident Room is maxed out when it comes to social distancing?'

'Don't worry about that,' he told her. 'I'll have Ged set up some carrels at the back of the conference room.'

'I have to go,' she said, 'and next time, you're coming with me.'

'I understand,' he replied.

'Good. I'll be in touch and when I do, I'll expect some good news.'

Caton was tempted to tell her to leave it a while, but she'd already gone. He reached the B5166 and walked back to the junction, where someone was gesticulating at the uniformed officer whose car still blocked entry to the cul-de-sac. As he approached, he discovered that it was Ginley, the investigative journalist. He stopped, took his mask from his pocket and put it on. Then he turned up the collar of his jacket and hugged the hedges as he made his way towards them.

He turned his head away as he flashed his warrant card at the officer, and then without breaking step, turned right and strode briskly towards his car.

Behind him a familiar voice rang out.

'Detective Chief Inspector Caton, can you confirm this is another victim of the Manchester Lockdown Poisoner? DCI Caton!'

Caton could see the headlines in tomorrow's papers, if not the late-night TV news.

'Another Victim for The Manchester Lockdown Poisoner!'

The Chief, the Mayor, and the leader of the council were sure to go ballistic, and he'd be the one with the target on his back. He got into his Audi, switched on the engine and selected Radio Manchester.

A song was playing from the classic Oasis album, *Standing on the Shoulder of Giants*. There was a time when Caton would have ranked it as one of his favourite Mancunian albums, but tonight, in the middle of a pandemic, with a serial killer on the streets of Manchester and Caton's investigation stalled, it felt disturbingly prophetic. It was almost as though Noel Gallagher had stuck his head over the parapet to perform this number just for him. In a moment of self-flagellation, Caton flicked up the volume and set off.

As he turned onto the main road, he and Noel were belting out the words that gave the song its title: 'Where Did It All Go Wrong?' In the rear-view mirror, he could see the uniformed officer and the reporter standing gobsmacked in the middle of the road, watching as he sped away.

Chapter 44
Nexus House. 1930 hours.

The deceased's GP rang back just as Caton was about to go down and interview the care worker. He decided to get this call out of the way. Without her car, Janice Jackson was going nowhere.

'Thank you for returning my call, Doctor,' he said. 'I take it you've heard about our concerns regarding one of your patients: Martha Riley, eighty-three years of age, living in Sharston?'

'Your colleague told me,' he said. 'It came as a complete surprise. I felt that I needed to go back and check her records before I rang you.'

'And what did the records tell you?'

'Exactly what I told the police officers at the time, and what I put in my report for the coroner. Mrs Riley had been suffering from type 2 diabetes for over twenty years. We struggled to control it, mainly because she failed to take it seriously. As a result, she had a number of long-term complications, including kidney disease, leg ulcers and macrovascular problems. The latter resulted in her having several moderate strokes and angina. She also struggled at times with her breathing, and I had actually spoken with her three days prior to her death following a referral from NHS 111.'

'I understand that she reported having a cough?'

'That's right. We spoke for several minutes, during which time she had several bouts of coughing. They sounded to me more like wet, phlegmy seasonal bronchitis, rather than the dry, coarse barking cough typical of Covid-19. She was often breathless in any case, and Covid symptoms sometimes start with a dry cough that becomes progressively more congested. It makes diagnosis virtually impossible without a test.'

'I can see that,' Caton said.

According to the newspapers and TV pundits, there weren't enough tests available for hospitals, let alone care homes and GP's surgeries.

'I should have gone to see the body myself,' the GP continued, 'but the ambulance crew were adamant that it had all the signs of a standard heart attack. I was in the middle of a practice meeting to plan how we were going to use telephone appointments to service our patients. We're having to share PPE, and there was and is no way we can respond to a tenth of call-outs.'

He sounded mortified and Caton decided to cut him some slack.

'You acted in good faith, Doctor,' he said, 'and, as I understand it, within the current guidelines. Even if you had gone to see her and spotted something amiss, it wouldn't have changed the outcome.'

'That's very generous of you, Detective Chief Inspector.'

Caton didn't have the heart to tell him that he'd have plenty to worry about once the press got their claws into him. And that he'd have to face an inquest somewhere down the line, not to mention the trial. The irony was that if he had made that house call, he'd probably have recommended she take that painkiller, and then felt even more guilty.

'I'll send someone to take a statement,' he said. 'You stay safe, Doctor.'

'You too, Mr Caton.'

Chapter 45

He could tell the second he entered the room that Janice Jackson was not happy. In her early forties, thin, with light-brown hair pinned in a bun, what he could see of her face had the pasty colour and texture of a habitual smoker. Her arms were crossed on the table in front of her. Her eyes, just visible above a blue disposable mask, stared daggers at him.

'At last!' she said, edging her chair back another foot. 'You do know I was just about to see to a client when that police van pulled up?'

Caton sat down. 'Your line manager has taken care of that,' he said, 'along with all of your remaining clients. And there's no need for the mask, Mrs Jackson. You were more than the minimum metres away even before you decided to move back.'

'*Miss Samuels*, thank you very much,' she said. 'We've been separated two years and I'm expecting the decree absolute later this month. I've gone back to my maiden name.'

He could have told her that she'd jumped the gun – that there was no guarantee that GOV.UK or her employer would recognise her maiden name following her divorce; that they might require her to register the reversion by deed poll. He decided it was best to wait and see how the interview progressed.

'And I'll stick with my mask if you don't mind,' she said, 'and I'd appreciate your wearing one too.' She folded her arms across her chest to make it clear that this was more than a request.

'It's my understanding,' he said, 'that when you arrived here, you were offered a completely virtual interview using our two-way CCTV system?'

'I prefer it this way,' she said. 'That doesn't mean I'm prepared to put my health at risk.'

Caton cursed silently. There was nothing in the protocol about being able to require an already identified witness or suspect to remove a mask. He sighed, took his own mask from its protective covering and put it on.

'You're not here under caution, Janice,' he said, 'but as a witness. However, I am obliged to tell you that everything is being videoed on these cameras' – he pointed them out as he spoke – 'so that you won't have to sign a written statement at the end, and we can keep the contact between us to a minimum. Are you happy with that?'

She shrugged, like a sulky teenager. 'I s'pose.'

'I'm sorry I had to ask you to come here today,' he said. 'In the current circumstances, I would have been more than happy to email you a form containing my questions, which you could then have completed and returned. Unfortunately, because there has been a significant time delay since you discovered the body of your client, that was no longer possible.'

'I told the police everything at the time,' she said. 'I don't see why you had to drag me here to say it all over again.'

'At the time that you gave your statement,' he said, keeping his voice calm and steady, despite his frustration and the discomfort of the mask, 'the officers were under the impression that Mrs Riley's death was from natural causes.'

Her pupils dilated. She sat up straight. 'And you're saying it wasn't? So what was it then? An accident?'

'We're treating her death as murder.'

'Murder?!'

Her mask had risen up. She pulled it down so that it was balanced on the tip of her nose. Caton could see her brain was working overtime.

'How was she murdered?' she said at last.

'I'm afraid I can't tell you that,' he said, 'but I do have a few questions for you that I'm hoping will help us find out. Can you tell me how you gained access to the house?'

'With my key. I knocked. When she didn't come to the door, I used the key we have for emergencies.'

'Were you wearing any protective clothing before you entered?'

'A face mask, an apron and a pair of gloves. I put them on in the car before I go in.'

'And when you found Mrs Riley lying there, did you touch anything? Move anything?'

'Like what?'

'Her body, items of furniture, anything on the tables or surfaces . . . her medicines?'

'No. I could see she was dead, so there was no point in touching her, and I knew better than to move her before the police and ambulance got there.'

'Quite right,' he said. 'So what did you do while you were waiting?'

'I went in the kitchen and poured myself a cup of water. For the shock – you know?'

He nodded.

She tugged her mask back down and folded her arms. 'It's not the first time I've found one of my clients dead,' she confided, 'but it is always a shock, even when you're expecting it.'

'When was the other time?' he asked.

She thought about it. 'Henry Crawshaw – that

would have been just before Christmas two years ago. His heart gave way. He was ninety-two, mind. Then there was Alice Rider. That was last July: brain haemorrhage. It's inevitable that it's going to happen with some of those who should really be in a care home.' She smiled thinly. 'Mind you, the way this coronavirus is going, they're a damn sight safer at home.'

'When you were in the kitchen, pouring that glass of water, did you see any other glasses or cups?'

Her forehead creased and she screwed up her eyes. 'I . . . don't remember seeing any.'

'Where did you get your glass from?'

'It was in the rack, on the drainer. I rinsed it out, and then filled it from the tap. I had a drink, then rinsed it and put it back on the rack.'

'Did you see any medicines . . . or painkillers?'

She thought about it. 'Now you mention it, there was a packet of painkillers the window ledge. I put them back in the medicine cabinet.'

She saw the expression in Caton's eyes and rushed to defend herself. 'I know, I know, I shouldn't have, but I was in shock. I didn't think. It was what I always did – tidy up. It was automatic.'

Caton swore silently. Her fingerprints were going to be on the packet that contained the tablets that poisoned Martha Riley, and were almost certainly the only ones they'd find on the glass that the victim had used to wash them down. If, and it was a big if, she was the killer, she had just provided a perfectly innocent explanation as to why they were there.

'Do you know where the painkillersl came from?' he asked.

This time her pupils contracted. She unfolded her arms and rested her hands on her knees. She was suddenly on high alert. He guessed that she had put two

211

and two together and made four. It didn't take a genius.

'How do you mean?'

'Was it prescribed? Would she have bought it herself? Did you buy it for her?'

'I have no idea where she got them from,' she said. 'I can tell you they're not part of her regular prescription. Why would they be? They're not prescription drugs. Did she take painkillers sometimes? Well, doesn't everybody? As for who else might have bought them for her, that's anybody's guess. Maybe one of her neighbours popped in. I don't know.'

There was a pattern building. Too many reverse questions.

'Were her neighbours in the habit of popping in?'

She shrugged. 'Not that I know of.'

'She was living on her own and her daughter's away in Milan. Who did her shopping for her?'

'She was on the Government shielding list, so she got a weekly food parcel with everything she needed – bread, milk, rice and pasta, cooking sauces, loads of fruit and veg, tins of tomatoes, beans, meat, tuna, coffee, teabags, biscuits, shower gel and toilet paper. She ate like a bird, so it was far too much for her.' She paused, and shifted nervously in her chair. 'She didn't have anywhere to store it all, so she insisted I take some of it.'

Caton didn't feel he was in a position to judge. He made a mental note to check if she'd cleared it with her line manager. He was still mulling it over when she launched into another defence.

'It's not like I didn't need it. The council pay my firm £15.20 an hour. I get £8.75 an hour, which is laughingly called the Manchester living wage. I've had to buy my own face masks because the agency was slow off the mark and they're still waiting on their first order to be delivered. I'm allowed a twenty-min unpaid rest break per day, and one day off per week, which often as not I don't get to take because they don't allow enough travel time between visits.' She sat back and folded her arms.

'How do you manage to eat and drink?' he asked, deliberately leading her back into her comfort zone. He saw her relax a little.

'I fill a bag every day with a couple of sarnies I've made up the night before, a packet of crisps, a flask of coffee and a bottle of water. I have them on the go in the car.'

'Do you recognise either of these names?' he said. 'Millie Dyer? Erica Edwards?'

Her hands tightened around her arms. 'No. Should I?'

Caton was surprised by how much the absence of facial clues had sharpened his recognition of those tells in her body language and verbal responses. She was rapidly moving from the status of witness to that of suspect. The only thing that prevented him from cautioning her was the lack of any tangible evidence.

'One of them lived on an estate in Stretford,' he said. 'The other one lived in Chorltonville. Have you had any cause to go there? For work or to meet someone?'

She adjusted her mask again. Her hand obscured his view of her eyes. 'No.'

'You're sure?' he said.

She sat bolt upright, her arms by her side, her fists clenched.

'Hang on! You just said *lived*. They're those women that are on the news? The ones that got poisoned. That's what you think happened to Martha. You're saying you think I had something to do with their deaths!' Her voice was becoming increasingly strident, with an undertone of panic.

Caton didn't buy it. 'I'm not saying anything, Janice,' he said calmly. 'I'm just trying to establish the facts.'

She gripped the sides of her chair, stood up, and stabbed an accusing finger towards him.

'No! No!' she shouted. 'You're not going to fit me up for this. I had nothing to do with it. Any of it!'

Chapter 46
Nexus House. 2040 hours.

Caton was climbing the stairs back up to the Incident Room when his phone rang. It was Carter.

'Boss, Janice Jackson,' he said. 'Is she still in the building?'

Caton stopped on the landing. 'DC Nair is walking her down to the car park to wait for a van to transport her home,' he said. 'I'm not happy with her responses, but there wasn't nearly enough to charge her. I released her on the basis that she's still under investigation. Why?'

'Well, given what her boss just told me, I suggest you pull her back in,' Carter responded. 'We've got a potential connection. Number two, Erica Edwards. Her next-door neighbour was a client of Jackson.'

'Shit!' said Caton. 'I knew it. Nick, get back here as fast as you can.'

He ended the call and ran back down the stairs, two at a time. He caught her about to climb into the back of a marked VW Transporter.

'Hold it there, Mrs Jackson,' he said. 'I need you to come back inside with me.'

She paused, one foot on the bottom step, and stared at him. 'Why?' she said. 'I've told you everything I know. And can you back off, please? You're too close.'

'I'll explain inside,' he told her.

She didn't move. 'You said I was just a witness. Well, I've nothing more to say and now I'm going home.'

She gripped the rail with her left hand, hauled herself up into the van, and plonked herself on one of the benches.

Caton turned to the driver who'd been watching in bemusement. 'Is your body cam on?' he asked.

'No, Sir,' said the officer. 'Would you like me to switch it on?'

'I think that would be a very good idea,' Caton told him. He waited until he'd been given the nod and then turned to the care worker.

'Janice Jackson,' he said, 'I am arresting you on suspicion of perverting the course of justice, by giving false information to the police with a view to frustrating a police murder enquiry. You do not have to say anything, but it may harm your defence if you do not mention, when questioned, something which you later rely on in court. Anything you do say may be given in evidence. Do you understand?'

She sat there in silence, scowling at the pair of them.

'I think she understands,' said Caton. 'What do you reckon, Constable?'

'Ooh, I'm pretty sure she understands, Sir,' said the officer.

'You have a choice, Janice,' Caton said. 'You can step down under your own steam, or we can come up there and get you. What's it to be?'

She made them wait, then slowly stood up and climbed back down. Caton put his mask on, thanked the driver and pointed Janice Jackson towards the entrance to the building.

'Off you go then,' he said.

* * *

They watched on the monitors in the interview suite as Jackson sat fuming in one of the interview rooms. She kept crossing and uncrossing her legs, and stared angrily from time to time into the CCTV cameras high up in the corners of the room.

'Her boss wasn't happy that we'd pulled her off shift to answer questions,' said Carter, 'especially since it meant that she was going to have see to the two remaining clients herself.'

'Never mind that,' Caton said. 'What exactly did she tell you?'

'That Jackson's only been working her current patch in Sharston and Northenden for the past seven weeks. Prior to that, she'd been covering Chorltonville and Northenden for just short of two years.'

'Why the change?'

'The agency had just taken on someone who lived in Chorlton, and it made sense for her to pick up that patch. Jackson didn't fight it because she lives closer to Sharston.'

'And Erica Edwards was definitely one of her clients?'

'Definitely, Boss. Had been for a couple of months, while she was recovering from a minor stroke. By the end of February, Mrs Edwards was sufficiently well to look after herself, and at the same time Jackson was pulled out of Chorltonville to work in Sharston.'

Caton stared at the care worker. 'I specifically asked her if she recognised the name. And if she had ever worked or visited Chorltonville.'

'You said you had your suspicions. Why was that?'

'Her whole demeanour was shifty and her verbal responses were full of classic tells. One minute she was making passive denials, the next she was being aggressive. Some of her answers were over-elaborate, and she kept replying to my questions with ones of her own. She also admitted to washing up a glass she found on the drainer, and putting that packet of painkillersl back in the cupboard.'

'Bloody hell!' Carter exclaimed.

'I know,' Caton said. 'I knew there was at least one or more lies in there, but I couldn't pin them down.'

Carter grinned. 'Until now.'

There was a knock on the door. Ged was outside in the corridor.

'The duty solicitor is insisting on a live video link,' she said. 'She says having to attend in person would be a breach of Article 2 of the Convention on Human Rights with respect to the safety of a public servant, herself that is, and the right to safe working conditions.'

'What about our safety?' Carter grumbled.

'And she says she expects you to send her any disclosure in advance by email.'

'Just do as she asks, Ged,' said Caton. 'I'll send you the disclosure. When the video link is ready, tell her she can have ten minutes with her client. Let me know when they're done.'

Chapter 47

'I have to remind you that you're still under caution,' Caton said. 'Do you understand what that means?'

'Yes,' Jackson replied.

The techies had set it up as a four-way conference call. The duty solicitor was in her office, Carter was in the comms room, and Caton was back in the interview room with Janice Jackson. Whatever the duty solicitor had said had clearly worked its magic. The care worker had shed her confident, pseudo-aggressive manner. If anything, she looked anxious.

'Good,' Caton said. 'In which case, I am going to repeat a question that I asked you in your first interview. Do you recognise the name Erica Edwards?'

'Yes.'

'In what context do you know that name?'

'I was her allocated care worker.'

'How long were you her care worker?'

'From just before Christmas until the twenty-seventh of February.'

'Just over two months?'

'That's right.'

'So how do you account for the fact that when I first asked if you recognised that name, you said you didn't?'

She glanced nervously at the monitor screen on the table between them, placed so that both of them could see. Caton saw the duty solicitor nod her head. Jackson turned her head to look at Caton, and then looked down at the floor.

'I was frightened.' She said it so quietly that he had to ask her to repeat it. She looked up, and her eyes met his. 'I said, I was frightened.'

She had managed to hide that pretty well, he thought. Until now.

'What were you frightened of?'

That triggered another check with her solicitor and another nod of encouragement.

'I'd had a text from the woman who took over my caseload to ask did I know that one of my former ladies had been found dead. And that the police were treating it as murder.'

'And why would that make you frightened?'

For the first time there was a spark of the repressed anger she had displayed in the first interview. 'It's obvious, isn't it? Two women I'd been supporting, both dead. You calling it murder? I was worried you'd put two and two together and make five.'

'But if you had nothing to do with either of these deaths, why would that be a problem?'

'Because I knew this would happen. That you'd have me in here and you'd keep on asking questions. And then I'd lose another half day's pay I can ill afford.'

'If you'd told me the truth straight away,' Caton said, 'it would have saved us both a lot of time. Now, I have a few more questions for you, Mrs Jackson.'

He saw her hands tense and a flash of annoyance in her eyes. He guessed that she had been about to remind him to use her maiden name and had thought better of it.

'When did you last see Mrs Edwards?' he said.

'The day I finished at hers – the twenty-seventh of February.'

'You've never been back to the house?'

'No, why would I?'

She was doing it again – throwing questions back at him. The duty solicitor spotted it too. She leaned towards the camera.

'Janice,' she said, 'remember what we agreed. Just answer DCI Caton's questions.'

'Did you leave her anything when you left?' Caton asked.

'Like what?'

'A farewell gift – anything at all?'

'No.'

'Did you send her anything? By post, or delivered by hand?'

She looked confused. 'No. Why would I?'

'Janice!' said the solicitor.

Jackson ignored her. She leaned forward. 'No, seriously,' she said. 'Why would I?'

It was a fair question, Caton observed, unless you didn't want her or anyone else to know that it was from you.

'I asked you about another name,' he said. 'Millie Dyer. Do you recognise that name?'

She folded her arms and sat back. 'No.'

'Have you ever worked in the Highfield Estate area of Trafford?'

'No. You can check with my agency.'

'Have you ever been there for any other reason?'

'No!'

'Mr Caton,' said the duty solicitor, 'my client has already answered these questions.'

'I am aware of that,' he said, 'but since your client has already lied once, I thought it only fair to give her the opportunity to clarify the situation.'

He turned back to the care worker. 'I have only one more question for you, Janice,' he said. 'Is there anything else that you think that I should know?'

'Like what?'

'Anything that might help us understand how two of your clients came to die in suspicious circumstances within twenty-four hours of each other?'

Her fists clenched. 'I don't know! I told you, I hadn't seen Erica in over six weeks.'

'Very well,' he said. 'Interview terminated at eight thirty-seven p.m.' He clicked the tablet-sized control in front of him and stood up. 'I would like to search your house, Mrs Jenkins,' he said, 'and your car. We will also be examining your mobile phone. And in light of the gravity of the offences that we're currently investigating, I'm going to hold you here until those searches have been completed. If at that time no evidence has emerged that might implicate you in these murders, I propose to release you on bail.'

She looked at the video screen. 'Can he do that?' she said.

'I'm afraid that he can, Janice,' the solicitor told her. 'And he can hold you for up to twenty-four hours before he has to seek an extension. As Mr Caton explained, a search will be the quickest way to get you out of there.'

'If you agree to a voluntary search of your property, it will speed things up even faster,' Caton added. 'And I promise that we will use personal protective equipment so that you have no need to be concerned about any contamination.'

'What if I say no?' she asked.

'Then I will have to apply for a search warrant, which I am sure your solicitor will confirm is likely to be granted. That will only delay the inevitable and mean you will have to stay here much longer, almost certainly overnight.'

She thought about it, sat back in her chair and folded her arms.

'You'd best get on with it then,' she said.

Chapter 48
Wythenshawe. 2155 hours.

All the curtains and blinds were drawn in the white-rendered, two-storey buildings a stone's throw from Baguley Hall. Members of the search team in white protective suits passed ghostlike beneath a single streetlamp emitting spasmodic bursts of sodium light. Caton and Carter stood watching, close to the entrance to the flat.

'It's just as well she agreed,' said Carter. 'Magistrates are getting leery about signing warrants during lockdown. Apparently, they're worried about people's mental health.'

'I have a feeling the threat to people's lives posed by our killer might well have trumped those concerns,' Caton said.

He was conscious of his breath, visible in the cold night air. It reminded him of disturbing media images of coronavirus riding on jets of vapour. He moved another yard away from his deputy.

'What impression did you get from watching her on the monitors?' he asked.

'Good question,' Carter replied. 'All that passive-aggressive stuff? I couldn't make out if she was trying to hide something, was seriously spooked or is just a stroppy mare.'

Caton turned up his collar against the cool breeze. 'Stroppy mare? I hope you don't intend to use that in a witness box any time soon. You sound just like Gordon Holmes.'

Carter laughed. 'I bet you were thinking the same though?'

Caton smiled. 'Maybe, but it's not how I'd have put it.'

'Go on then,' Carter invited. 'How would you put it?'

'An obstreperous, bolshie, obstructive, bloody-minded, bad-tempered person.'

Carter stamped his feet. 'We can't all be a walking, talking thesaurus,' he said.

'Watch out, Nick!' said Caton, stepping back onto the postage stamp lawn. Carter turned, saw Jack Benson walking down the path at the side of the building towards them, and joined Caton on the lawn, careful to maintain his distance.

'Well?' Caton asked, as Benson halted a few yards away.

The CSI shook his head. 'We've done a thorough search of the flat, and the garden at the back, including a small shed. We've found nothing incriminating. I've bagged up an address book and a laptop so we can see if there's anything connecting her to any of the victims or their addresses, either in writing or in her search history, texts or emails. I've also got someone taking photos and prints of her shoes and trainers, just in case.'

Since they had not yet retrieved a single useable footprint from any of the current crime scenes, Caton knew that 'just in case' referred to the fact that it was dependent, just like the rest of the investigation, on there being more crime scenes and more victims.

'Do you know where the search of her car is up to?' Caton asked.

'The last I heard, they'd found nothing suspicious and no evidence of false compartments. Do you want them to strip the car down?'

'Not unless and until we have enough evidence to warrant that,' Caton said. 'What about the analysis of her mobile phone?'

'The techies are onto that,' Carter told him. 'I'll give DS Hulme a ring and see where they're up to.'

He took out his mobile and moved out of earshot. As he did so, he noticed that lights had appeared in two of the neighbouring flats. In one of them, a face was peering through a gap in the curtain. He was back in less than two minutes, by which time the CSI team had departed. He shook his head.

'Her story holds up,' he said. 'There's nothing on her phone that places it anywhere near victim one's address, the Highfield Estate, or even Stretford come to that. Nor has it been anywhere near the Chorltonville address since she stopped working there. Furthermore, as part of the work contract, her employer insisted that she enabled location tracking so they could see where she is at any one time and how long she spends with each client. She's never given them any cause for concern in that regard.' He grinned. 'And there's a bonus.'

'Go on,' Caton said.

'It looks like she couldn't be arsed to turn it off, so they'll have a complete record of her movements around the clock.'

'The movements of the phone, not necessarily *her* movements,' Caton pointed out.

Even so, it meant that they didn't really have enough to justify keeping her in custody.

'We'll have to let her go again,' he said. 'Only this time, it will be under caution. Then we'll see what the diary, address book and laptop throw up, run a check on her friends, and dig deep into her life and background. If she is involved, there has to be a motive, and that's where the answers will lie.'

'Alright if I head home?' Carter said. 'Only this bloody lockdown's sending Angie stir-crazy.'

'Of course,' Caton replied. 'I'll be doing the same just as soon as I've given madam a piece of my mind, and sent her on her way with the usual warnings.'

As he was driving away, he noticed a dark Ford Fiesta forty metres down on the opposite side of the road, with its interior overhead light on. He slowed as he drew level, and glanced across. The male occupant had turned his head and was leaning across the passenger seat as though looking in the glove box. Caton could have sworn it was Ginley, the investigative reporter.

As he reached the end of the road and was preparing to turn right, he checked in the mirror. The Fiesta had moved. It was now close to Janice Jackson's flat.

Chapter 49
Wednesday 8th April
Nexus House. 0759 hours.

'You'd better see this, Boss!' said Carter.

He was standing with DS Hulme, DS Whittle and DCs Nair and Powell in a loose semicircle around the TV screen. Caton finished drying his hands, applied a squirt of hand sanitiser and went to join them.

As the circle shuffled backwards to widen its arc, Jimmy Hulme and Carly Whittle made space for him.

'What's this?' he asked.

'BBC Breakfast,' said Hulme. 'They've announced an upcoming newsflash concerning our investigation.'

On the red sofa, the female presenter, Lana Coretti, addressed the camera.

'We can now bring you the latest news concerning the series of murders in Manchester labelled by some as the work of the Manchester Lockdown Poisoner. Late yesterday evening, developments saw police and crime scene investigators searching a property in the Wythenshawe area of the city that is believed to belong to a person they are questioning in relation to the deaths of three elderly women.'

As she spoke, slightly blurred and shaky video footage appeared on the screen, in which Caton and Carter could be seen standing outside Janice Jackson's property, watching two CSIs entering the flat.

'How the hell?' said Carter.

'Ginley!' Caton told him. 'He must have filmed it from his car.'

'We have with us, by video link, Anthony Ginley, the reporter who captured that footage, and whose account appeared in several papers this morning. Mr Ginley, thank you for joining us. What can you tell us about these developments?'

'Bugger all!' muttered Carter. 'I bet he doesn't even know she's been released.'

The investigative reporter had chosen his background with care. Books on crime and criminology were artfully displayed. Over his left shoulder, one of his own books, *The Hunt for The Falcon Tattooist*, had been given prominence. On the wall beside the bookcase were framed copies of newspaper headlines and an award for investigative journalism. As he leaned forward, his smug smile filled the screen. He had made a poor attempt to trim his fringe and his beard.

'Cocky bastard!' said Carter.

'Shush,' Caton told him. 'We need to hear what he has to say.'

'Lana . . .' His tone was sycophantic and patronising. 'Thank you so much for inviting me onto your programme.' His expression switched seamlessly to one of fierce concern. 'I have been following the police investigation into the sickening murder of these poor defenceless women ever since the first victim was discovered. I have become increasingly concerned about how little progress the police have made in identifying the perpetrator, and about how little information they have been sharing with either the public, or with representatives of the press and media outlets such as the BBC.'

'And?' the presenter pressed.

'And I decided that the only way in which I was going to be able to shine a light on the investigation was to shadow the Senior Investigating Officer . . .'

Ginley paused to take a sip from a metal flask.

Caton swore. 'Shadow!' he said. 'He means stalk.'

228

'At least he hasn't mentioned you by name, Boss,' said DS Hulme.

'. . . *DCI Caton.*'

'Whoops,' DC Powell murmured.

'That led me to a street in the Baguley district of Wythenshawe, where I observed crime scene investigators and what I took to be a search team, removing items from a flat that I later discovered as belonging to a care worker. I then ascertained that the occupant of the flat had been detained by the police for questioning. My sources have confirmed that she was released in the early hours of the morning without charge, but under continuing investigation.'

'Not on police bail then?'

'No. The police often prefer to use "under investigation" as a means of avoiding the time limit on bail, while still being able to seize a person's belongings and search their property for evidence.' He paused, and gave a knowing smile. *'The police have declined to give the name of this person, but I can confirm that she's a care worker in her early forties.'*

'Age, address and occupation! The bastard may as well have told them her name,' Carter observed.

'A care worker?' Coretti said.

'That's right. A care worker. And it does not take a genius to work out that the police are currently pursuing the theory that the killer is what is often termed an "Angel of Mercy" or an "Angel of Death".'

'And is that your belief, Mr Ginley,' Coretti asked, *'or could it be that this is what the killer wants the police to believe? That he or she is in fact very cleverly masquerading as an Angel of Death?'*

The reporter stroked his beard in the manner of a pseudo-intellectual.

'I think that unlikely. You see, Lana, it is something of a myth that every serial killer is a genius. That is a narrative that police forces, home and abroad, have promoted in order to hide

the fact that the reason so few serial killers are caught, is really down to their own incompetence.'

The presenter uncrossed her legs and sat up. *'That is a very serious allegation, Mr Ginley.'*

'I can assure you,' he retorted, *'that I am not alone in holding that view. And I would go further. The perpetrator in this case is very far from being a genius. With the right resources, I am certain that an investigative reporter such as myself could unmask him, or her, before any more women are—'*

Lana Coretti had heard enough. She shifted to the edge of the sofa.

'Thank you for your time, Mr Ginley,' she said, swivelling round to face the camera.

'And so, the hunt continues,' she said. *'If you have any information that you think may assist the police, please call or text one of the following numbers, where your information will be treated in the strictest confidence.'*

The dedicated numbers for Operation Pendle Hill and those of CrimeStoppers scrolled across the bottom of the screen.

'Switch it off,' Caton said.

'That bit at the end,' said DC Powell. 'What on earth did he think he was doing?'

'What he does best,' Caton said. 'Stirring the pot. It's the equivalent of prodding a snake with a stick to see how it's going to react. If this causes our killer to escalate, Ginley will have blood on his hands.'

* * *

It took precisely seven minutes for the balloon to go up. Ged found Caton in his office.

'I have a message from ACC Gates,' she said. 'There's an emergency meeting to discuss Operation Pendle Hill in Room 434 at the Force Headquarters building at oh-nine-thirty hours. She said you're to be there.'

Caton's watch read eight nineteen. It was five point three miles to Central Park. At this time in the morning, under normal conditions, it would have taken him a good half-hour. Courtesy of Covid, he'd do it in less than fifteen. He hurried into the main body of the room and called for order.

'Listen up!' he said. 'In just over an hour, the entire Command Team, the Police and Crime Commissioner, and God knows who else, are going to want to hear from me that we know what we're doing and are making progress. You'll know by now that we have just been accused on the national news of being out of our depth and totally incompetent. You have fifteen minutes in which to prove them wrong.'

Chapter 50

Caton arrived with ten minutes to spare. The car park for the Fujitsu building was empty, as was that of the innovative business and academia hub, One Central Park. He assumed there would be plenty of police vehicles on the other side of the North Division Headquarters, but for now, his was the only vehicle on the road, and there was not a cyclist or pedestrian in sight.

He imagined it would feel pretty much the same if the sirens warning of an impending nuclear missile attack had sounded, and everyone had gone to ground. That, or a scene from *Dawn of The Dead*.

He showed his warrant card at the barrier, parked up, and walked around the impressive six-storey steel and blue glass building that was the Force Headquarters. As he approached the main doors, he looked up at the huge badge high up on the wall: a seven-sided star, topped by a crown. A sudden thought stopped him in his tracks. It could easily have been a symbolic representation of the coronavirus. He shook his head. There were times when his imagination had stood him in good stead. There were others, when it was a bloody curse.

He was crossing the atrium towards the lifts when his phone pinged. It was a text with the information he had been waiting for. He allowed himself a faint smile. Duggie Wallace had thrown him the faintest of lifelines. He sent a reply, saw there were two other people waiting for a lift, and headed for the stairs instead.

232

There were seven people seated at the long table. Three on each side, five empty chairs between each of them. Helen Gates, the Deputy Chief Constable, and all three of the remaining Assistant Chief Constables, apart from the one who had tested positive a week ago and was off sick. The one person that Caton did not recognise, he assumed from the pad in front of her, had been tasked with taking the minutes.

The Deputy Chief and two of the ACCs acknowledged him as he applied sanitiser from the dispenser by the door, and then took a seat at the furthest end of the table. The others, including Helen Gates, studiously ignored him. Not exactly a pariah yet, he concluded, but it wouldn't take much to tip the scales. Caton wondered why they were all here. It was not as though their briefs – with the exception of Helen as Head of Crime – were likely to add anything constructive to the investigation. It was probably a show of force, designed to put pressure on him. Though it might just be that the Chief was hoping that the shared and varied experience of the people in this room might lead to a flash of inspiration.

The door opened and in marched Robert Hampson, the Chief Constable, followed a few seconds later by Charlotte Mason, Mayor of Greater Manchester, and former Police and Crime Commissioner until the post was subsumed into her current role.

Hampson slammed the file he was holding onto the table, pulled back his chair, and sat down. He waited until the Mayor had taken her seat, and then looked around the table, his gaze lingering briefly on Caton before moving on.

'Thank you all for agreeing to be here in person,' he said. 'But in view of the urgency of the situation, and the time it would have taken to arrange an online meeting, I thought it best we do it the old-fashioned way.'

That invoked a few smiles and the odd polite laugh, but Caton had the feeling that it hadn't been intended as a joke. The Chief flipped open his folder.

'Operation Pendle Hill,' he said. 'I take it that you're all aware of what happened on BBC Breakfast News earlier today? In case any of you are not, we were basically accused by an investigative reporter – not a stranger to this force, and who seems to possess more information than I do – of being secretive, complacent and downright incompetent. The Mayor immediately contacted me, and quite rightly asked what the hell is going on? We're here to find out. And then to do something about putting it right.'

Caton was surprised at Hampson's tone and demeanour. He had every right to be angry, although he was disappointed that the Chief's ire appeared to be directed at him rather than at Ginley, and that he had clearly already decided that something was not right. But he had never seen him like this before. He wondered if the additional strain that Covid-19 was placing on the force was getting to him.

The Chief Constable addressed the Mayor.

'Charlotte,' he said, 'is there anything you wish to add before we begin?'

'Yes, thank you, Robert,' she replied.

Caton studied her closely as she tucked a stray lock of hair behind her ear. If the rumours were true, her passionate commitment to the creation of the Northern Powerhouse across the region, and to the homeless in the city, had led her adopt a punishing work routine that was bound to take its toll. Even so, Caton was surprised at how tired she looked. Her face had that sickly pallor that usually came with sickness, shock or emotional stress. When she spoke, her voice had lost the power and confidence of her TV and radio performances.

'There are three things that concern me,' she said. 'Most important of all is that we prevent the deaths of any more women. Secondly, that we are able to reassure all vulnerable elderly women across the city that this investigation has the highest priority for both the police and the Mayor's Office, and everything possible is being done to catch the perpetrator.'

Her voice faltered, and she had to stop to take a sip of water from the bottle she had brought with her.

'And finally,' she said, 'given Manchester is now under a national spotlight, that we ensure that from now on, we are totally honest, timely and transparent in sharing information with members of the public, through whatever means.' She sat back and took another sip from her bottle.

'Very well,' said Richard Hampson. 'I propose that we leave the current state of Operation Pendle Hill until last. Let's start with the media. Helen?'

Without looking in Caton's direction, Gates adroitly batted the question in his court. 'As SIO, DCI Caton is responsible for the media strategy for the investigation,' she said. 'DCI Caton?'

Caton had been here before. He was prepared. 'I would have brought copies with me,' he said, 'but in the interests of minimising multiple contacts with paper versions, as per GMP Covid precautions, I have an email link that I can share with you.'

'That won't be necessary,' said Hampson tersely. 'Just give us the salient points, please.'

Caton opened the file on his tablet. 'The strategy follows exactly the ACPO *Murder Investigation Manual* recommendations,' he began. 'Initial press releases were agreed with ACC Gates and the Press Office, in the form of holding statements. With regard to victim identification, I believe that it would have been imprudent to give more details than were contained in those releases until the next of kin had been contacted, and I was in possession of accurate information regarding both the cause of death and the manner in which the first victim was murdered. Furthermore, I decided there was no point in generating unnecessary panic among the public. At the same time, it was important to elicit as much information from potential witnesses – family, neighbours, friends – without the risk of that information being contaminated by media speculation.'

'I rather think that horse has bolted,' the ACC on the left of Helen Gates muttered.

'It has now,' Caton said, 'but it was essential that it didn't do so during the early stages of the investigation.'

'DCI Caton makes a fair point,' Gates said. 'Can I suggest that we allow him to finish uninterrupted?'

'Agreed,' the Chief said grudgingly. 'Carry on.'

'As soon as we had confirmation from the post-mortem and from forensics as to the circumstances surrounding the death of victim one,' Caton said, 'the matter of appeals and warnings to members of the public was considered. This was a highly sensitive matter, given that it would have been very easy to terrify vulnerable members of the community already struggling with isolation and mental health issues – something which I suspect is part of the perpetrator's intention. I discussed the timing and nature of these matters with ACC Gates, who then liaised directly with the Press Office.'

He was aware of Helen Gates's eyes boring into him, wondering what he might say next. That was fine by him. All he had to do was stick to the truth and try not to appear to be passing the buck. Easier said than done.

'Finally,' he said, 'with regard to information germane to the investigation, I had to decide how much information to release and when. How much to drip-feed, and how much to make front and centre of press releases. I made the judgement call to release as little additional information as possible on the grounds that given the unusual nature of these murders, so much of it would be known only to the perpetrator. To reveal it would be to prejudice our ongoing investigation, even more so once we apprehend and begin to question the perpetrator.'

He sat back, hoping that he had done enough to move the conversation on. When he looked up, they were all staring at him, even the minute-taker. And he had not the foggiest what any of them were thinking.

Chapter 51

'Who would like to start?' said the Chief Constable.

The ACC with the brief covering corporate communication raised a hand. 'DCI Caton,' he began. 'Can you tell us how Ginley came by his information? Is it possible that someone on the inside of Operation Pendle Hill is feeding it to him?'

Caton had anticipated the question. And it was no surprise that it should come from this direction. When the proverbial hit the fan, everyone rushed to cover his or her back.

'It is always a possibility,' he replied. 'However, I have done everything I can to ensure that my syndicate remains watertight, and I am confident that is the case. As with every investigation, there are people on the periphery – first responders, witnesses, neighbours questioned door to door – eager to share what they know. But Anthony Ginley has proved in the past that he's not dependent entirely on sources. He's a ferret. He stated, for example, that having spotted me leaving the press conference, he set out to follow me.'

'How is that possible?' the ACC asked. 'Given that it was a virtual conference, with you here in this building, and Ginley at home?'

'I don't believe that he was at home,' Caton replied. 'He may have followed me here from Nexus House, or more likely, knowing that the conference was being streamed from here, he waited across the way and followed the link on his mobile phone, with the intention of tracking me when I left at the end of the briefing.'

He realised that he was casting himself in a poor light. A senior detective, trained in surveillance, allowing himself to be followed around the city?

'It wouldn't have been difficult for him with the streets this quiet,' he said. 'He would have stayed well back, his headlights dimmed, and once he realised that I was heading into Baguley, he could have afforded to lose me, because a quick tour of the streets would have led him to spot the crime scene vans, if not my car. I glimpsed him sitting in his car as I left. He would have taken note of which flat we were searching, and then when everyone had left, knocked on the door of one of the neighbours we'd disturbed to obtain details of the occupant. The rest of his claim – about us pursuing an Angel of Mercy – was mere supposition.'

He paused to give added weight to what he was about to say. 'As to his being aware that the woman we were questioning had been released under investigation, I think you'll find that the source he referred to was in fact the GMP Facebook page.'

The others looked at the ACC Caton had been responding to. At least he had the grace to look sheepish.

'Anyone else, before we move on to the current state of the investigation?' said Robert Hampson.

The Assistant Chief Constable on his left leaned forward.

'As you know,' he began, 'I am the National Lead for Vulnerable People and, as you have already noted, DCI Caton, there is deep concern about the mental health of the elderly, many of whom felt isolated even before lockdown began, and were already scared witless by the way in which the virus is targeting their cohort, but are now terrified that if Covid doesn't get them, a serial killer will. Firstly, what reassurance can you give them that they are in fact safe? And, secondly, had you issued the warnings earlier, do you believe that lives could have been saved? That is what the media are beginning to ask.'

'As to your second question,' Caton replied, 'I can categorically say that none of the victims of whom we are so far aware could have been saved, even if we *had* issued warnings prior to knowing for certain that the first of the deaths had been caused by poisoning. In fact, I would go further – it would have made no difference if warnings had been issued as soon as we suspected that those tablets had been tampered with.'

'How can you possibly know that?' the ACC demanded.

'Because the post-mortem on the second victim showed that she was already dead *prior* to the first one having been discovered. And the latest victim, Martha Riley, had died and was cremated before either of the other victims was discovered.'

He sensed a wave of relief around the room. For the first time, Robert Hampson appeared to relax.

'Having cleared that up,' he said, 'I propose, DCI Caton, that we move on to the current status of the investigation.'

It took less than five minutes for Caton to set out the salient facts. It was depressingly easy. Three women deceased. All of them poisoned in the same manner. A forensically aware perpetrator, so no trace evidence other than the packets and pills themselves. Nothing to connect the three victims, other than their age, gender, the fact that they lived alone and the manner of their death. No witnesses. No solid suspects. He would have used the phrase 'chasing shadows', except that there weren't even any shadows to chase. But at least he had a couple of bones he could throw them.

'I have officers working twenty-four seven wading their way through a range of passive media covering the vicinity of the victim's homes, including CCTV, fixed traffic cameras, and even footage from dashcams belonging to postal workers, delivery drivers and couriers, ambulances, police cars and key workers who live nearby. That is our best chance of finding a lead.'

What he failed to mention, because it was blindingly obvious, was that none of that would help if the packets of painkillers had arrived by post.

'However,' he added, 'I have just been informed that analysis of the phone records for Millie Dyer and Erica Edwards – victims one and two – have both thrown up, among a number of obvious spam or cold calls, two burner phone calls to each victim, all of them of between two and three minutes' duration. This suggests that on each occasion, the victims took the call and a conversation was held. Interestingly, different phones were used each time: four different phones in total. Two of them were pre-used phones whose owners have been traced and eliminated. I have ordered as a matter of urgency details of the locations of those phones at the time of the calls, and if the phone companies have it, the record of any other traffic from those two phones.'

He glanced at Helen Gates, who raised her eyebrows at him.

'I received this information as I entered the building,' he added, to assuage her unspoken question.

The Chief Constable broke the silence. 'Thank God we have something to go on,' he said. 'Now, as you all know, Jack is the lead on North West Counter Terrorism. I asked him to contact GCHQ, the NCA and MI5 to discover if there is any likelihood, however remote, that these attacks might have a terrorist dimension, if only to head off some of the sensational conspiracy theories circulating on social media, as well as several of the tabloids. Jack?'

'I did as the Chief Constable asked,' the Deputy Chief Constable responded. 'There continue to be many conversations regarding the use of biological, chemical and radiation weapons in various forums among a wide spectrum of terrorist organisations – including far-right terrorists and eco-terrorists, who should not be confused with the legitimate activities of climate activists. The contamination or poisoning of a nation's food supply or water supply features regularly. The most frequently mentioned agents are those that cause botulism, *E. coli*, salmonella and cholera. In other words, biological agents. However, poisons administered by means of injection, or food-tampering, including medicines – and that includes cyanide and its derivatives – are rarely mentioned in these forums, other than as a means of targeted assassination.'

'I don't see any of these women as Russian dissidents or working for our secret services?' one of his colleagues said as an aside.

Nobody laughed.

'I think we can safely put out a statement that we have ruled out terrorism as a line of enquiry,' said the Chief. 'Agreed?'

There were no dissenters.

'Good,' he said. 'Now, DCI Caton, in your opinion is there anything we can do to accelerate this investigation and breathe some life into Pendle Hill?'

It was all the encouragement Caton needed. 'I have three requests, Sir. Firstly, I need far more bodies to assist with the trawl of passive media and to conduct the multiple interviews to which they will inevitably lead. Secondly, I would like the unknown subject of our investigation designated as a serial killer, and on the back of that, permission to engage a geographical profiler to narrow down the area within which the unsub is most likely to live. I believe that with the current restrictions on travel, and the location and proximity of the crime scenes, there is a strong likelihood that the killer is local to the area, if not the city. It would help immeasurably if we could narrow that down.'

'I have no problem with the designation of the murders as serial killings, or the geographical profiling,' Robert Hampson responded. 'As to the additional manpower, I mean *staffing*, the effect of this pandemic coming on top of twelve years of swingeing cuts has stretched GMP to its limits. We cannot, for example, divert resources from either Operation Xcalibre or Operation Talon, nor indeed pressure points such as attempted murder, blackmail, kidnapping and manslaughter.'

He looked around the table. 'Can any of you suggest ways in which we can support this operation without undermining critical strategic policy areas?'

Helen Gates raised her hand. 'If I may,' she said. 'There is one way in which we can meet DCI Caton's need, at least in the short term.'

'Go ahead,' he said.

'Why don't we lend Operation Pendle Hill the Category C Murders team, initially for a two-week period?'

One of the ACCs was about to object when Robert Hampson thrust out his arm.

'Let's hear Helen out?' he said.

'Given that the cases they're dealing with are ones where the offender is already known,' Gates said, 'and that Covid-19 has brought Crown Court proceedings almost to a complete halt, a fortnight helping DCI Caton out would hardly make a dent in their current caseload.'

'That's a brilliant suggestion, Helen,' said Hampson, forestalling all objections. 'However, there is a quid pro quo here. We need a fresh set of eyes on this. In light of public concern and the growing media interest, I don't believe we can wait for the twenty-eight-day review. I propose to initiate one straight away.'

Caton felt his pulse begin to race and his palms grow sweaty. It wasn't that he was afraid of external scrutiny – he had done everything by the book – but he doubted that a review would move the investigation forward. On the contrary, it would waste valuable time and cause a perilous loss of momentum. He was about to object when Helen Gates beat him to it.

'Chief,' she said, 'I absolutely understand where you're coming from, but I really don't believe that a review will add anything at this stage. Furthermore, how will DCI Caton manage to bring the Cat-C team up to speed, and smoothly integrate them into Operation Pendle Hill if he and his deputy are forced to divert their energies to preparing for the review?'

'I take your point, Helen,' said Hampson, 'but I am not prepared to wait another three weeks for a review, and risk God knows how many more victims.'

Caton took a deep breath. 'May I propose a compromise, sir?' he said.

Hampson frowned. 'Go ahead.'

'From the outset, I have been utilising the HOLMES 2 Dynamic Reasoning Engine to support this investigation and to suggest possible lines of enquiry. I will be surprised if a full review at this stage will add anything that it has not. However, rather than a full review, I propose that you arrange for colleagues from neighbouring forces – Cheshire and Lancashire – to join with ACC Gates in an interim review limited to the two aspects of most concern to us here, namely, to seek and identify further investigative leads and intelligence opportunities in support of the enquiry and to improve internal and external communications related to Operation Pendle Hill.'

The Chief Constable and the Mayor held a whispered conversation behind their hands in a manner reminiscent of a Premiership manager and his coach. Hampson nodded and straightened back up.

'Very well,' he said. 'Helen, I'll leave it to you to arrange. The Mayor and I will announce it to the press later today.' He paused. 'DCI Caton?'

'Yes, Sir?'

'We will also be stating that we have absolute confidence in the running of Operation Pendle Hill. Don't make us regret it.'

Chapter 52

Caton's relief was short-lived. He was on his way back to Nexus House when the call came through. It was DS Hulme.

'We have the report on those mobile phones,' he said. 'I thought I'd better let you know in case you were still there.'

'I'm incoming,' Caton told him. 'ETA ten minutes.'

'You don't happen to have a couple of helicopter gunships with you?' Hulme said, with a smile in his voice.

'The phones?' Caton said.

'Sorry,' a chastened Hulme replied. 'The analysis reveals that both phones were used in a different location each time, and always within a five-mile radius of the kill zones. They're going to send over a map showing the location of those calls and the movement of the phones. Each of the four phones was used for a total of three calls, none of which lasted for more than three minutes. All of the phones then appear to have been discarded after the third call. The techies arrived at that assumption based on the fact that there's no record of any subsequent calls from those numbers, and they know the time and location when the phones and SIM cards ceased to be trackable.'

It was not the good news Robert Hampson had been hoping for. Caton took his time thinking it through.

'If those calls did come from our unsub,' he said, 'then it suggests there are three more victims out there?'

'That's about the size of it,' Hulme agreed. 'Of course, he could have been using more burner phones to call other victims.'

They both fell silent. Caton spoke first.

'They must have a record of any numbers called from those phones, other than those belonging to the three known victims?'

'Yes, they do,' said Hulme. 'They're sending them over with the map. Should have them by the time you arrive.'

Finally, there was some good news. If the recipients of those calls had not yet succumbed, there was the slightest chance of saving them.

'Do we know where the phones and SIM cards were purchased?' he asked.

'Gorton Market, a small shop in Levenshulme, and a pop-up shop in Wythenshawe. DI Carter's already sent people to see if they can recover CCTV.' He paused. 'I wouldn't hold your breath though.'

'Why not?' Caton said.

'Because the pop-up shop won't be there any more, and in any case, all of the purchases were made last September. Places like that, they'll have copied over their footage at least three times by now.'

And if the unsub hadn't activated the phones and Sim cards until he began to use them, Caton realised, their historical data, including location data, would be meaningless.

'He's been planning this for some time then,' he said.

'Looks like it. Covering his tracks from the outset. Even before he could have known there was going to be a pandemic.'

'Let's pursue this when I get back. I'm on Droylsden Road. I'll be with you in two minutes.'

A minute later, he was turning right onto the approach road when he had another call. This time it was his deputy.

'Boss,' said Carter. 'Where are you?'

'At the barrier to the car park.'

'I'm afraid it looks as though we might have another one,' Carter said.

Caton nodded to the security guard. The barrier rose and he drove in.

'Where?'

'Heald Green, on the Manchester and Stockport boundary, just off Simonsway. I'm on my way down to the car park. I'll meet you there.'

* * *

Caton's pulse was racing as he parked up. Carter was waiting for him by his own car. His expression said it all.

'How certain are we?' Caton asked.

Carter shook his head. 'Sorry, Boss, it doesn't l ook good.'

Caton swore

'Seventy-year-old widow, living alone,' Carter told him. 'Found this morning by her daughter, who happens to be a nurse. She clocked it straight away as dodgy and called 999. The paramedic confirmed her suspicions. Uniform have preserved the scene. CSI are on their way.'

'Come on then,' Caton said. 'I'll follow you.'

He walked slowly back to his car. Gone was the rush of adrenalin that he normally experienced at times like this. It had been replaced by a sinking feeling in his gut, and bone-sapping weariness. He had never experienced anything quite like it – the sense of impotence and hopelessness. That wasn't entirely true, he realised. This was exactly how he had felt when he was told that he was the only survivor of the crash that had killed his parents. And it was the same sensation he always had just before he woke from those increasingly rare nightmares in which he relived the accident on that stony road in Turkey.

He climbed into the car, and sat there while he fought the rising tide of panic. Deep breath ... Hold it ... Slowly exhale. He was on the fourth repetition when he heard the horn. He looked through the passenger window. Carter had stopped two cars along, and was staring back at him with a look of concern. Caton exhaled, gave him a thumbs up and started the engine.

Chapter 53

Caton followed Carter as he turned right off Simonsway, immediately before the Atlas Business Park.

Two hundred yards later, his deputy stopped at the back of a line of vehicles, including two marked cars and two CSI vans. Caton parked up and took his murder bag from the boot.

He trailed his deputy past several detached 1980s houses, ripe for renovation but with neat gardens and trimmed hedges. Having logged in at the police cordon, they walked to a gate manned by a uniformed officer.

'Good morning, gentlemen,' he said. 'I've been instructed to ask you to suit up over there on the verge, and then wait for the senior crime scene manager. He's currently preparing the common approach path.'

'Do you know who the first responder was?' Caton asked.

'That would be me,' he replied. 'I'm with the Sharston neighbourhood team. This is my patch. I was only two minutes away when the call came in. I knew the minute I saw her, it was sus. The paramedic confirmed it.'

'How did you know?' Caton asked.

'Well, ordinarily I might have just thought a stroke or a heart attack, but there was this packet of painkillers. That might have said suicide, except there were only three tablets missing. So I dug a little deeper.' He noticed a look of unease on both detectives' faces.
'It's okay,' he said. 'I'd got my latex gloves on and the foil strip was just lying there. All I did was flip it over.'

'And?' said Caton.

'There was no branding on the front or the back of the foil strip. That's what we've all been told to look out for.'

'But you still let the paramedic in?' Carter said.

'I thought that was standard,' he replied nervously. 'Preservation of life?'

'She was already dead,' Carter observed drily.

'I'm not a medic,' said the hapless officer. 'She could have been in a coma for all I knew.'

'It's alright,' Caton said before Carter could make any further objection. 'You did well. You say you're part of the neighbourhood team. Did you know the victim by any chance?'

The officer smiled with relief. 'I did, as it happens. I first met her a couple of years ago when we were doing our courtesy visits. I was with one of our PCSOs. She invited us in, insisted we had a cup of tea. I also spoke to her last summer, when she reported youths on trailbikes in the fields at the back of her garden. And she gave me a wave from her window just as the lockdown was starting. We were doing a drive round. I got out and stood at the gate, and she opened her door and we had a chat. I asked her how she was – did she need anything?'

'What did she say?' Caton asked.

'That she was fine. Her daughters were taking it in turns to call her, she had a regular supermarket slot, and one of her daughters was popping round regularly dropping off ready meals.'

'Tell us about her,' Caton said.

'Her name is Patti Dean, just turned seventy. I know because she had birthday cards on the windowsill.' He turned and looked over his right shoulder. 'In fact they're still there, look. She's of African-Caribbean heritage, widowed, has the two daughters and a son who all live locally. Both daughters are nurses working at Manchester Royal and Wythenshawe hospitals respectively. She was a lovely lady – full of life and always cheerful. Always asked how I was. She used to be a nurse and she still had that caring nature, I guess.' He shook his head. 'This is pure evil, what's happened to her.'

Caton wasn't going to disagree. 'One of the daughters found her?' he asked.

'Stella. She rang to check on her. When her mother failed to answer, she came round here, looked through the window and saw her on the couch. She banged on the window but couldn't raise her, so she used her key and went inside. Discovered she was dead, saw the painkillersl, put two and two together, called 999 and asked for us and a senior paramedic.'

'Where is she now?' Caton asked, looking back at the marked cars to see if she might be in one of them.

'She went to the hospital to explain why she'd not be on shift tonight. She said she'd get her sister to meet her there and bring her back here. I told her you'd need to speak to her, so she promised to be back by . . .' He looked at his watch. '. . . any time now.'

Caton saw Jack Benson standing in the doorway, waving.

'When they do get here, make sure they don't leave,' Caton said. 'And again, well done.'

'He shouldn't have let her go,' Carter complained as he followed Caton up the path. 'And he shouldn't have touched anything.'

'Give him a break, Nick,' Caton said. 'Whichever CIS lifts that blister pack is also going to be wearing latex. And the daughter's going nowhere. I assume you clocked the bit about the youths on trailbikes?'

'You're not suggesting they were involved ,Boss?'

'No,' Caton replied, 'but it does show how easy it would have been for our unsub to approach the house under cover of darkness. And the same goes for Martha Riley's place.'

Chapter 54

Patti Dean wore a pink tracksuit top and grey leggings. She had been sitting upright, and had toppled onto her side. Her left arm was trapped beneath her, her right hung over the side of the couch. Both legs dangled in mid-air, her feet six inches or so from the floor. A hardback book was splayed open on the floor. Caton crouched down and read the title at the top of the right-hand page. *Girl, Woman, Other*. He didn't need to check the author's name on the verso page. This was the joint Booker Prize-winning novel by Bernardine Evaristo that he had bought Kate for Christmas.

He shifted his weight and swivelled to study her face. Her eyes stared into the distance, her mouth fixed in a sardonic grin. Caton knew there was no correlation between the expression on the face of a corpse, and the extent to which they had suffered, but he suspected that in this case it would have been a terrifying way to die.

As he stood up, his right knee creaked. Another reminder that he was no longer as young as he thought he was. Next to a lamp on the side table, he saw a glass of water, a packet of painkillers – beside which lay the silver blister pack missing three of its pills – and a half-eaten Hotel Chocolat bar: dark chocolate with chilli.

'Can I have a look, Boss?' Carter asked.

Treading carefully, Caton followed the plastic stepping plates through to the dining room to make way for his deputy. Not that there was likely to be any trace evidence on the floor. The perpetrator had managed to bring death to these women without so much as setting foot over the threshold.

He took stock of his surroundings. Both rooms appeared clean and tidy. All the furniture was teak. Bright cushions, rugs and lampshades, together with a leopard-print throw over one of the armchairs, reflected her cheery personality. There were photo frames on almost every surface, filled with memories charting a life filled with love and happiness. This must have been such a joyful family home in which to grow up, he mused, with a touch of envy. Not that his aunt and uncle hadn't done their best during the long boarding school holidays. But it could never have matched this. Or the one that he had enjoyed before the accident.

'Doctor Tompkins is here.' The crime scene manager's voice was muffled behind his double-layered mask. 'One of you will have to leave.'

'I'll go,' Carter said.

Caton stepped back and waited for the pathologist to appear.

She struck a bland and curious figure against these vibrant surroundings: a diminutive woman in white, toting an aluminium case and a secure-seal shoulder bag. She placed the case down on one of the footplates, stretched, and turned to look at him.

'Morning, Tom,' she said. 'I think it's time you put a stop to all this, don't you?'

It was the first time she had used his given name, something her predecessor had never done. It was a measure, he decided, of just how close these murders were drawing them together.

'Don't you start, Carol,' he replied. 'So far today, I've been pilloried in the press and given a strict warning by the powers that be. I'm not looking for sympathy, but I was hoping for a little understanding.'

'What was it you wanted to understand?' she said. He detected a twinkle behind the mask.

'Who's doing this. Why he's doing this. And where to bloody find him,' he said. 'Although for now, I'll settle for a definitive cause of death and an approximate time of demise.'

'Approximate, I can do. Definitive will have to wait until the post-mortem. Now, why don't you go and find out what everyone else is doing and leave me to get on?'

Caton went off in search of Jack Benson. He was in the front garden talking to one of his team.

'You can start out back now,' he told his colleague. 'You know what you're looking for.'

Caton waited until the CSI had disappeared through the open side gate, and then stepped closer.

'Where are you up to, Jack?' he asked.

'We completed the photos, the videography and the sketches before you arrived,' Benson replied. 'As soon as Dr Tompkins has finished, we'll try to recover fingerprints, fibres, footprints and so on. But I have to say it all feels pretty futile.' He held up a hand before Caton could protest. 'I know we have to do it. And I know there's always a chance he'll have changed his MO, or slipped up in some way. But it's just like all the others. There's no indication that he's been anywhere near the house.'

'Not in person,' Caton said, 'but part of him has. Those pills, the packaging, whatever they were wrapped in. Sooner or later, his DNA or a stray fingerprint is going to turn up. It has to.'

Even as he said it, he knew that wasn't true. If Jack Benson had been behind these killings, he'd have made damn sure he didn't leave a trace. And the unsub appeared to be almost as forensically aware as Jack.

'That's why we're focussing all of our energy into examining those items back at the labs,' said Benson. 'But don't worry. Like I said, we won't leave a stone unturned.'

Caton watched him head back into the house, then sought out Carter. He was briefing two of the door-to-door teams, so Caton decided to head for the end of the row of houses, up ahead.

Chapter 55

Yellow and white narcissi lined the verge on which a row of birch trees was coming into leaf. At the end of the last house, he encountered a stretch of open grassland a hundred yards long that ended where another row of houses began. A line of wooden posts no more than two feet high held the remains of a barbed-wire fence that had been trodden to the ground, leaving nothing but a few brambles and a slight ditch as a barrier. Caton stepped over the ditch and into the field.

It stretched ahead of him for several hundred yards to a boundary of trees, through which he spotted the occasional red-tiled roof. Twenty yards in front of him, a large black crow, perched on a top of a dead oak, regarded Caton with disdain as he walked towards it. Waiting until he was almost upon it, the crow took off with a leisurely flap of its wings, painting the sky with flashes of gunmetal grey and indigo.

On reaching the end of the fence by the last house, Caton saw the fields stretch to north and south in a corridor of meadowland dotted with trees, a green lung in an urban landscape. He concluded that this was farmland of some sort. A deduction made easy by the sight of a line of stables, and a cluster of substantial farm buildings three hundred yards away to his right.

High up in the vast expanse of blue sky was a single white vapour trail, where less than two weeks earlier, there would have been a dozen or more. There were reminders wherever you looked of how far and how deep this pandemic had reached. The sun was hot out here, and Caton had begun to sweat profusely inside his Tyvek suit. He pushed back his hood, lowered the mask so that it hung at his neck, and pulled the zip down to his waist. Then he turned right and followed the backs of the houses, counting as he went.

He stopped at the back of the garden that had belonged to Patti Dean. Some of the neighbouring properties had large trees at their boundary. One neighbour had an ugly berberis that ran the length of her house, its wicked spines the perfect deterrent. Patti Dean had no such protection. Her wooden fence, only four foot high, had begun to rot and sag in places. Caton peered over. There was a bare border running across the back, with the green shoots of spring bulbs beginning to poke through the baked earth. Two CSIs were inching their way towards him on their hands and knees.

He had a strong sense of déjà vu as he examined the back walls of the houses for lights and cameras. A house two down, towards Simonsway, had a security light, but Caton doubted that it would have provided any kind of deterrent, or done little more than light the way for an intruder this far off. There were, in any case, no cameras.

Sweat stung his eyes. He delved deep down inside the protective suit and into his trouser pocket for his handkerchief to wipe them. He retraced his steps, cursing the heat, the killer and this malign coronavirus. Two killers, both silent and relentless. Both targeting the old, the weak and the infirm. Opportunists in a world ill-prepared to stop either of them.

As he came back round to the street, Carol Tompkins was standing by her car, talking to DI Carter. Caton hurried to get there before she drove away.

'You're cutting it short,' she told him. 'I can spare two minutes. After that you'll have to ask DI Carter what

I already told him. And can you either back off or put your mask on? I'm not immune just because I'm a pathologist.'

'Sorry,' he said, opting to step well back. 'I appreciate you waiting. Could you just give me the headlines?'

'If I was relying on the physical evidence alone,' she said, 'I couldn't at this stage say with any certainty that this was poisoning by cyanide. There's no telltale odour, but then she has been dead too long for that to be expected. As for the indications from hypostasis common with the other victims, I'm afraid that's very difficult to discern when the deceased is black, or of a naturally dark skin tone. I'd need to use a tristimulus colorimeter to spot it, let alone distinguish between outwardly visible symptoms of carbon monoxide as opposed to cyanide poisoning. Having said that, all the indications are that she was poisoned not gassed.'

'And the time of death?'

'Again, that's tricky for the same reason, and also because the ambient temperature has been all over the place in this mini-heatwave. However, there is some lipid leakage and other indications suggesting a window of between eighteen and twenty-four hours.'

'Thank you,' Caton said.

She pressed her key to unlock her car. 'I'll do the PM first thing in the morning. And, Tom . . .'

'Yes?' he said.

She raised her eyebrows. 'Be good if this was the last of these.' She ducked inside and pulled the door to.

'All we needed to know was that she'd been poisoned, Boss,' said Carter as they watched her drive away. 'That blister pack is the real clincher.'

'Knowing when she took them doesn't really help us,' Caton said. 'When and how she came by them are the only questions that matter.'

'You do know your hair is ringing wet?' Carter said.

Caton mopped his eyes and forehead with his handkerchief.

'I don't suppose you've got a towel in your car?' he said. 'I need to sort myself out before the daughter gets back.'

'Sorry,' Carter replied, 'but I bet the paramedic can help you out. He's bound to have a few paper ones. Failing that, you could always try a bandage.'

Chapter 56

Caton was finger-combing his hair in the rear-view mirror when he spotted a female PCSO walking towards his car ahead of a woman he assumed to be the victim's daughter.

He got out, opened the rear door, unhooked his linen jacket and shrugged it on. He still smelled like a wet dog and for once was grateful for social distancing.

'This is Mrs Unsworth, Sir,' said the PCSO. 'Stella.'

'Thank you,' he said. 'I'll take it from here.'

The PCSO stepped across the verge and into the road, then walked back the way she'd come, leaving the two of them facing each other an awkward three metres apart.

Stella was the image of how her mother must have looked at fifty. Her eyes were brimming with tears above the surgical mask, like a dam about to burst. The distance between them felt like a chasm. Caton was tempted to step closer and place a comforting hand on her shoulder, but knew he couldn't.

'I am so sorry for your loss, Mrs Unsworth,' he said.

She nodded in response. He saw the mask move but couldn't tell whether she had replied or not. He took out the spare mask he carried in his breast pocket and held it up.

'Why don't I put this on, and the two of us can go and sit in my car?'

She shook her head. 'No, it's safer for you if we don't.' She saw the puzzled expression on his face.

'I work in ICU,' she said, 'on the frontline. Believe me, it's best for the both of us if we stay out here.'

Caton spotted a low stone wall outside a house a little further down the road. He pointed. 'Why don't we sit over there instead?' he said. 'It'll be more comfortable.'

She turned and walked over to the wall, where she sat at one end, Caton at the other. He put his mask on and sensed her relaxing a little.

'I was told your sister would be coming with you?' he said.

'Leah's husband texted me to say she's off sick,' she replied. 'He said he'd get her to call me.'

'I understand that you found your mum,' Caton said. 'That must have been hard?'

'I blame myself,' she said.

He was tempted to tell her that she shouldn't, but could see she needed to let it out.

'I called her yesterday evening,' she said, 'like I always do before I go on shift. I should have followed it up straight away but I was running late. My colleagues depend on me. *And* all my patients. I should at least have called this morning when I came off shift.'

She dabbed her eyes with a balled-up handkerchief. 'I was exhausted. You have no idea what it's like.' She wrapped her arms around herself, her eyes appealing for forgiveness, or at least some understanding. 'That American series on the TV? The field hospital in Vietnam?'

'*MASH*?' he said.

She nodded. 'It's like that but without the jokes.'

'Your mother was already dead when you rang, Stella,' he said. 'Believe me when I tell you that there was nothing you could have done. And nothing for which you need reproach yourself.'

'When did she die?' she asked.

'We don't know yet for sure, but we think somewhere between eleven o'clock yesterday morning and five o'clock yesterday evening.'

Her eyes filled with alarm. 'Oh my God! I rang at a quarter to six. She might still have been alive.' She beat herself with her fists and began to rock backwards and forwards. 'Oh my God! I could have saved her.'

Caton inched closer and held out his arm, stopping short of actually touching her. 'No, Stella,' he said, 'listen to me! She would already have been dead. And even if you had got there shortly before she passed away, you'd not have been able to save her. No one would.'

She looked at him, searching his eyes for the truth. 'You don't know that?'

'I do,' he said, 'and I think you do too.'

The rocking slowly subsided. She pulled her mask down a little with one hand and dabbed her eyes again with the other. She hitched the mask back into position and looked at him. 'Mum was poisoned, wasn't she?'

He nodded. 'I'm afraid so.'

'It's him, isn't it?'

'Him?'

'The man who's been poisoning elderly women across Manchester. The one on the news.'

'We think so.'

'I knew it,' she said, 'when I saw there was no brand marked on the blister pack. I just didn't want to believe it.'

She closed her eyes and her head sank onto her chest. When she finally looked up, he could tell she had composed herself.

'Mrs Unsworth,' he said, 'Stella . . . I'm going to have to ask you some questions. Is that alright?'

She nodded. 'Of course.'

'You called your mum every day?'

'That's right. Before I went to work if I was on the night shift; when I got back if I'd been on days. On my days off, I'd come round and stand in the garden. She'd come to the door and we'd chat.

'And on any of those occasions, do you remember he mentioning having received a packet of pankillers?'

'No, definitely not. I'd have remembered that. And I'd either have made her give them to me, or told her to throw them away.'

'Did she ever mention receiving any unsolicited packages or presents?'

'Not unless you count fundraising charities sending packets of seed, Christmas cards or address labels.'

'Did she mention any unexpected visitors? Or people she seemed to know but had never mentioned before?'

She had to think hard about that one.

'No, I don't think so.'

'Can you think of anyone who might have held a grudge against your mother? Someone who may have wished her harm?'

This time she shook her head vigorously.

'No! Absolutely not. Mum was not the kind of person to make enemies. Everyone loved her.'

'I'm sure,' Caton said. He knew it sounded lame, but he was at a lost to know how else to respond.

'It's not fair,' she said, her voice soft and gentle.

Caton had to strain to hear her. 'What's not fair?' he said, even though he guessed what the answer would be.

'That she should die like this. Terrified and alone.'

She took a deep breath, and let it out with a sigh.

'Mum was one of the last of the Windrush Generation, Mr Caton. She was just twelve when she arrived in Manchester with our grandad. It was 1962, just before the Commonwealth Immigrants Act cut back on the flood of immigration the Government had encouraged themselves. It was a terrible culture shock for her, made worse by the casual racism – and the not so casual. They'd only been here a week when a brick was thrown through their window with a note tied round it telling them to eff off back home. Her father, our grandad, was a dock worker on the Manchester Docks. He was a good worker and a mild man, better educated than most of the others. But he was passed over for promotion again and again. He never complained. But when someone in Mum's class pinned a golliwog to the blackboard, and her teacher brushed it off as a harmless prank, he stormed up there and read the Riot Act.'

He could tell from her eyes and the twitch of her mask that she was smiling.

'Then he told her to be proud, to stand up against racist taunts – that she could be whatever she wanted to be. She just had to work hard, do her best and believe in herself. And she did, Mr Caton. She became a nurse, and rose through the ranks to become a matron. She was our inspiration. She's the reason my sister and me both do what we do.'

She burst into tears and put her head in her hands, rocking back and forth in her grief. Caton sat there, feeling useless, sad and angry, all at once. It was several minutes before the tears subsided. Eventually she sat up, pulled the mask aside so it was left dangling from one ear, and dried her face on the sleeve of her blouse.

'I'm sorry,' she said.

'You have nothing to be sorry for, Stella,' Caton responded.

'When the NHS started asking for retired nurses and doctors to return, to help out with the pandemic,' she said, 'our mum put her name forward. That was the kind of person she was. Leah and I had to fight tooth and nail to persuade her not to. It was a real battle. Even when we told her that our ethnic heritage and her age made her especially vulnerable, she wouldn't have it.'

'What happened to change her mind?'

'I asked one of our consultants with whom she'd worked in the past, to explain how black, Asian and minority ethnic frontline workers were among the first to be infected and end up in ICU. She told him she hated that BAME label, and now he'd caused her to worry about Leah and me. But at least it led her to back down.'

She took another deep breath. As she slowly breathed out, her mask fluttered like a fledgling's wing. She looked up at the clear blue sky.

'It's ironic,' she said, 'if she'd gone ahead and volunteered, she might still be alive.'

'We'll never know the answer to that,' Caton said. 'But if the perpetrator already had her down as a target, I doubt that it would have made any difference.'

She turned to stare at him, her eyes hard and unforgiving.

'She was a target? You think that evil bastard targeted her – that it wasn't a random attack?' She shook her head. 'I can't believe that. Not our mum. I told you, she had no enemies. *Everyone* loved her.'

Caton wondered if that was part of the killer's motivation? He remembered quoting Oscar Wilde at the syndicate. The bit from *The Ballad of Reading Gaol* about each man killing the thing he loved. Was the unsub killing those that *others* loved, in a perverse act of envy? It sounded preposterous, but no more so than Dennis Nilsen killing fifteen men and more out of a sense of loneliness, and the sudden fear of losing them.

'We believe that all of the women who've been killed like your mother were targeted in some way, Stella. We won't know why until we catch the person responsible, which is why I'd like you to look at some photographs. Could you do that for me?'

A change come over her and she sat up straight, balling her hands into fists. Her voice and her stare were steely.

'Of course,' she said. 'I'll do whatever it takes.'

Chapter 57

Caton retrieved his tablet from the passenger seat of his car, and took it back to where Stella Unsworth was waiting.

'Are these pictures of your suspects?' she asked as she waited for him to bring them up.

'I'm afraid not,' he said. 'These are photos of the other women who've been poisoned in the same manner.'

'How's that going to help?'

He heard the disappointment in her voice.

'We believe that something other than their age and gender connects all of these women,' he told her. 'That something might just explain why he chose them, and how he was able to win their confidence enough for them to take those tablets.'

He opened the folder of images and looked up. She was nodding thoughtfully.

'I was wondering that myself,' she said. 'Our mother was a nurse for forty-three years. I couldn't understand how she had come to miss the obvious – the fact that those blister sheets were unbranded?'

'It's easily done,' Caton said. 'So long as you just pop the pills from the sheet without turning it over, you would never know. The fact that they were in a branded box would have been enough. Another thing, all these women were getting on in years – less alert perhaps, more trusting?'

He selected the first of the photos and nudged the tablet along the wall towards her. 'I'd like you to look at each of these photos and see if you recognise any of them, or consider whether your mother may have known any of these women?'

She leaned forward to study the photos.

'Take your time,' he said. 'Just swipe the screen to the left when you're ready for the next one.'

He watched as she studied them intently. Several minutes passed. She went back and forth, digging deep into her memory with the same mix of nerves and determination as Caton had seen on the faces of witnesses at identity parades back in the old days.

Eventually she shook her head and slid the tablet back towards him.

'I'm sorry,' she said. 'I don't recognise any of them.'

Her phone rang.

'It's Ralph, Leah's husband,' she said. 'It's a Facetime call. Can I take it?'

'Of course,' he said.

She accepted the call and put it on speaker.

'Stella,' said the brother-in-law. 'I'm so sorry about your mum. I can't believe it.'

'Me neither. How's Leah?'

There was a long pause.

'She thinks she's got Covid.'

Stella Unsworth gasped, and clung to the wall for support with her free hand.

'No!' she cried. 'Oh, please, no!'

'She started with a fever last night, and now she's coughing . . . like a barking noise. Once or twice an hour.' Another pause. 'I haven't told her about your mum yet. I'm not sure she's well enough to take it.'

'I need to see her . . . speak to her,' she said. 'Take the phone in to her, Ralph.'

There was a long silence, then the sound of muffled voices and someone coughing. Stella's expression changed. She stood up, turned her back on Caton and walked a few metres away. When she spoke, he was unable to hear what she was saying, and from the long silences he guessed that she had muted the sound. After several minutes, she ended the call, shoved the phone in her pocket and walked back. She then ripped her mask off and just stood there, tears streaming down her face, shoulders heaving.

Caton's heart went out to her. It was an almost physical sensation that had him fighting to hold himself back from crying too. He remembered reading somewhere that the state of constant vigilance that came with staying safe from the pandemic and keeping others safe, was causing everyone's emotions to rise to the surface. He cursed the virus for how it made him feel, for what it was doing to people like Stella and her sister, and for preventing him from bloody walking over there and putting a comforting arm around her shoulder. And then he began to curse the killer for adding to their misery.

It was several minutes before her tears ceased to flow. She rummaged in her bag, found a pack of tissues and proceeded to wipe her face and blow her nose. Then with a practised ease, she hooked the mask around one ear, and then the next, and sat down on the wall.

'She was sitting up in bed,' she said. 'She looked awful. I didn't tell her. Ralph was right – now is not the time. And what difference would it have made if I had, other than push her over the edge?' She was desperate for him to agree.

'None at all,' he said. 'You did the right thing. Her health has to come first.'

'She's already struggling to breathe,' she said. 'I told Ralph to call an ambulance, that the sooner she gets to hospital the better. He said she didn't want to go. She's seen what's happening to people like us who end up on ventilators.' She paused. 'That's the downside of doing what we do,' she said. 'We know too much.'

'What are you going to do?' he said.

'If he hasn't called an ambulance, I will.'

'I'm so sorry,' he said. 'This is the last thing you need on top of everything. You do what you have to do. In the meantime, I'll arrange for someone from family liaison to contact you. They'll help in any way they can. They'll also need to walk you through your mother's house as soon as the crime scene officers have given the go-ahead, just to see if there's anything that wasn't there before – anything that's out of place or doesn't look right. Can you do that?'

She nodded her head. 'Of course.'

'We have your phone number,' he said. 'I'll just need your address.'

'I moved out to shield my family until we get on top of the virus,' she told him. 'I'm staying at Hotel Football with other health professionals, courtesy of The Class of '92.'

Caton thanked her, and headed back to check on progress with Nick Carter and Jack Benson. As he did so, he reflected on what she'd said. Here were two more examples of the way in which the virus had brought out the best in people. All of those key workers putting their own lives on the line, not only to save their patients, but also to shield their loved ones. And on the other side, commercial organisations setting profit aside to give shelter and support to the homeless and those very same key workers. His world, it seemed, was full of silver linings and shades of grey.

Except for the killer.

'Will that do, Boss?' DS Hulme asked.

Caton took another step closer to the six-foot by three-foot map. All of the crime scenes were marked by red flags.

'Perfect,' he said. 'Now all we need is one of those full-size maps of the city for the geographical profile when it arrives.'

He looked around for Carter and spotted him scrubbing his hands at the sink. Calling to attract his attention, he waved him over. Carter was still rubbing gel into his palms when he arrived.

'This is the sixth time today,' he said.

'That's self-defeating,' Jimmy Hulme told him.

'What do you mean?' said Carter.

'You're stripping the biome from your skin.'

'What's that when it's at home?'

'Millions of micro-organisms that protect your skin. They're also a vital part of your immune system.'

'Don't tell him that, or anyone else for that matter,' Caton said. 'It's bad enough getting people to follow the guidance as it is.'

'What are we looking for, Boss?' Carter said.

'How those packages were delivered. We still don't know if any of them came by post or a delivery firm, and the only other possibility is that the unsub delivered them himself. When I went for a wander at the two previous crime scenes – Martha Riley's and Patti Dean's – something struck me. Something we should have spotted sooner.'

'I've got it!' Hulme said. 'Every one of the victims' homes either backs onto or is right by a green space.'

'And the two latest victims are connected by a virtually unbroken corridor of parkland,' said Carter, 'with just a short stretch of road between them.'

'Parkland, and then farmland,' Caton said. 'Not that that's relevant. They both have paths and lots of cover. That stretch of road you're talking about, Hollyhedge Road, could be key. That's why I asked for a passive media grab along that stretch.'

'What's the distance between the victims' houses?' Hulme asked. 'About a mile?'

'A mile and a half,' Caton told him.

'He could have used Styal Road instead,' Carter said. 'That would have taken him no more than two minutes. Three, on a bike.'

Caton shook his head. 'There are two ANPR cameras,' he said, 'and several CCTV cameras on houses fronting the road. I checked. Our unsub would have checked too.'

He walked up to the map and placed his index finger by the flag marking Martha Riley's house. He traced a route directly due south across the park, along the short dogleg at Hollyhedge Road, right into Crossacres Road, behind two clusters of school buildings. Then straight down through the farmland, where he stopped at the back of the house belonging to Patti Dean.

'I checked the back of the house,' he said. 'A child could have climbed that fence, and there are no lights or cameras. Then he could have slipped a package through the letterbox, knocked on the side door and handed it over, or simply left it at the back door.'

'Would he have gone back the same way?' Carter wondered.

'He wouldn't want to risk leaving by the street,' Jimmy Hulme pointed out. 'Too much risk of being seen or caught on camera. But he could have carried on down the fields and come out at the bottom.'

'That would mean either going through the farmyard, or over or through this hedge,' Caton said. 'Probably the latter.' He turned to his DS. 'Jimmy,' he said, 'can you open up Google Earth and we'll take a closer look.'

Caton and Carter stood either side of Hulme's desk, staring intently at the screen as he slowly zoomed in on the relevant area.

'There!' Caton said. 'At the corner of the paddock, where the houses start.'

'What are you looking at, Boss?' Carter said.

'That thin dark line you can see between the fence of that first garden and the trees.'

The 3-D image blurred as Hulme zoomed in too close, and cleared again as he zoomed out.

'Stop!' Caton commanded. 'There – just there.'

'It's definitely a path,' Carter observed, 'where people have trampled the grass to get to the road.'

'Let's see where it comes out,' Caton said.

DS Hulme switched to Street View, and placed the little man in the road where there was a wide gap in the pavement.

'Bingo!' he said.

They were looking at a five-bar steel gate, with a small wooden stile on the left.

'Where does he go from here though?' Carter asked.

'Let's have a look,' Caton said.

Hulme switched back to the aerial view and Caton pointed.

'There you go,' he said. 'He's only got a couple of hundred yards along Simonsway, then right past the airport car park, and then once he's crossed Ringway Road, it's all fields and footpaths for miles and miles. If he's on foot, or more likely on a bike, he can use the pavements and cycle tracks and not get picked up by the traffic cameras.'

He straightened up.

'Thanks, Jimmy,' he said. 'Can you brief someone to pick up where you left off? Get them to carry out the same analysis of routes to and from the houses of victims one and two, concentrating on access via open ground, paths and cycle tracks, and then let you have it ASAP.'

He walked back to the wall map, Carter following on behind. Together, they stared at the green corridor that linked Erica Edwards and Martha Riley.

'You're not suggesting we search the whole of this area are you, Boss?' Carter said. 'I mean, this is someone who goes to a hell of a lot of trouble – what kind of evidence is he likely to leave, other than a possible footprint?'

'I'm not sure we have a choice,' Caton responded. 'You're right about the fact that we have no idea when either package was delivered, but it hasn't rained in weeks, so the likelihood is that if he did drop or discard anything at all, even a strand of cloth on a fence or barbed wire, it'll still be there.' He pointed to the photos of the victims. 'But I am certain that there's something else connecting these victims. I want to know what it is.'

He moved along to the next board, headed LINES OF ENQUIRY. There were progress notes attributed to each category, with only one of them was highlighted as a significant lead.

'Are you thinking what I'm thinking?' he asked.

'What's that, Boss?' said Carter.

'When that Review team gets here, they're going to have a bloody field day.'

'If they come up with anything we're not already doing, I'll eat my hat,' Carter said.

'You don't wear one,' Caton observed morosely.

'Boss!'

DC Franklin was standing up at his desk, waving a piece of paper.

Caton walked towards him. 'What is it?'

'We've got a hit on one of the vehicles that was parked outside the latest victim's address the day before yesterday!'

'A hit from where?'

'It was someone already on the system as connected to victims one and two.'

'Who is it?' Caton said.

'That district nurse. Thelma Green.'

Caton's pulse began to race. 'We need to cross-check Patti Dean's name against the list of patients she provided us,' he said.

Franklin grinned. 'I already did. She's not on it. Nor are any of the other addresses on that street.'

Chapter 59

'I'm sorry, what is this in connection with?' said Janet Hardy, line manager for the district nurses. She frowned. 'Your colleague wouldn't say.'

She pushed her designer glasses higher up her nose. Caton couldn't tell if she was anxious or simply on the defensive. That was the problem with these video calls. So much depended on the quality of the lighting, where people chose to sit, and how much they bobbed around. Janet Hardy was doing a lot of bobbing, and consequently moving in and out of focus.

'I need to ask you some questions regarding two of your nurses,' he told her. 'Thelma Green and Angela Malhotra. I'm sure you must be aware from previous enquiries my officers have made, that this is in connection with a series of unexplained deaths. As far as we're aware, none of them were patients of Miss Green or Mrs Malhotra. We're just trying to eliminate from our enquiries anyone whose vehicle has been reported as having been in any of the relevant neighbourhoods.'

Hardy leaned forward, filling the screen with a disconcerting image of her face as though viewed through a goldfish lens.

'I have already vouched for both of these ladies, and I understood that you had already been given a list of their patients and their addresses.'

'I am aware of that,' he told her. 'However, there's a discrepancy between the addresses on one of those lists, and an address that has come to our notice.'

'I see.'

'I'm going to give you an address,' he said, 'and I would like you to tell me if any of your employees have any reason to visit that same address. Can you do that for me?'

Again the same frown. 'Of course, but it'll take a few minutes.'

'I'll wait,' he told her.

She disappeared from the screen. Three minutes later she was back. 'The address you gave does not correspond with any of our patients. However, we do have a patient at the following address.'

Caton wrote it down. 'That must be next door but one to the address I gave you?' he said.

She bobbed back from the screen and became a blur. 'If you say so.'

'Which of your nurses has been seeing this patient?'

'Thelma,' she said.

'Miss Green?'

'That is correct.'

'When did she start seeing this patient?'

'The day before yesterday.'

'Morning or afternoon?'

'According to her schedule, ten a.m.'

Approximately twenty-four hours before Patti Dean died. It was pushing it, Caton decided, but definitely possible.

'How long has Nurse Green been working for you?' he asked.

'Since December 2017.'

'Have you had any concerns regarding her work?'

'None at all' – she paused – 'other than her sick record.'

'Could you be a little more explicit, Mrs Hardy?'

She was suddenly back in focus. Caton guessed

from her expression that she was wondering how much she could, or should, tell him.

'This is potentially a murder investigation,' he reminded her.

It gave her the permission she sought. Her tone and body language changed – less officious, more confiding.

'Well, she has the odd day off every month. She rings in with a migraine or saying she's had a panic attack, but that's only to be expected.'

'Why is that?'

'She previously worked at the Manchester Royal, but was voluntarily redeployed to us after she returned to work following the Manchester Arena bombing.'

The hairs on the back of Caton's neck began to prickle. 'She was caught up in the Arena bombing?'

She shook her head. 'Not directly. As I understand it, she'd been visiting a friend in Prestwich and come back on the tram. She'd just left Victoria Station when the explosion happened. I think she said she was in Cathedral Gardens. She went back to help, but the police clearing the area wouldn't allow her inside. She did her best, triaging some of the walking wounded until the paramedics arrived. Even they weren't allowed inside, so she got a taxi to the Royal and offered her services at A&E. She worked through the night, and then went on to do a late shift on her own ward. The next day, the ward sister sent her home. She was off sick for over six months. She was having panic attacks, flashbacks, migraines. She couldn't come to terms with the fact that she wasn't able to help some of the critically wounded at the scene. She was convinced that she could have saved some of them.'

Caton was thinking about the man a few years back who had haunted and very nearly killed his friend Rob Thornton, the barrister. He'd been suffering from PTSD. Survivor's guilt.

'If she's still having these episodes,' he said, 'are you sure that she's fit to work?'

'Absolutely. We're only talking one or two days more a year than most of her colleagues. She sees an NHS therapist every couple of months. If he had any concerns, he'd be duty-bound to share them with me. For my part, she's proved an exemplary worker. If anything, she's over-conscientious.'

'In what way?'

'Well, her records are meticulous. She spends more than the allotted time with patients. She frequently offers to come in on her rest days. That sort of thing.'

Those alarm bells were getting louder. Here was a highly organised professional, with significant medical knowledge and expertise. Someone who would be readily accepted by the victims. It sounded as though she had ongoing mental health problems, and there was no doubt that her experience at the Arena was just the kind of traumatic life event that might trigger an irrational pattern of behaviour. What he was struggling with was the internal narrative by which she might possibly justify these killings to herself. That was the one thing that didn't make sense. But then, he reminded himself, sense rarely came into it with serial killers.

'Tell me about Angela Malhotra,' he said.

The sudden switch of direction threw Janet Hardy. She bobbed out of focus and back in again.

'Angela? There's nothing to tell. She was originally from Uganda. Her father was a doctor. Her parents brought her over here when she was very young. They were among the eighty thousand or so East African Asians who were forced to leave by Idi Amin.'

Just like the parents of Home Secretary Priti Patel.

'Have you ever had concerns over her work?' he asked.

'Absolutely not. She is first class. The patients all love her, and she's an excellent mentor to the student nurses who spend time with us.'

'You've been really helpful,' Caton told her. 'There's just one last thing you can do. I need a list of any patients to whom Nurses Green and Malhotra have been assigned whilst with you and who've subsequently died. I also need the cause of death in each case.'

Janet Hardy looked horrified. 'I really can't believe that either of them would . . .'

She found it so impossible to countenance that she couldn't even put it into words. It was conceivable that she was also thinking about the implications of something this awful happening on her watch.

'We have no reason at this point to suspect any wrongdoing on either of their parts,' Caton said, 'but we have to investigate every avenue, however implausible it may seem. This is the quickest way in which you can help us eliminate your two colleagues from our investigation.'

He was expecting her to object, but she managed to pull herself together.

'Of course,' she said. 'I'll do it myself.'

'And,' he said, 'I do have to remind you that as this is part of an ongoing police investigation, you must not under any circumstance mention this request to anyone else. Besides, I wouldn't want you to worry either of them unnecessarily.'

Or, more importantly, alert them.

He was sitting in his car completing his notes on his tablet when his phone rang. It was DS Hulme.

'Ginley's just been on the phone, Boss,' he said. 'He was in a right state.'

'Tell him he'll have to wait for the press briefing like everyone else,' Caton replied.

'It's not that. His mother took her dog for a walk at lunchtime. When she got back, someone had pushed a package through her letterbox. It contained two packets of painkillers.'

'Let me guess,' Caton said. 'They're both unbranded?'

'One is, but the other isn't.'

Caton put his tablet down and turned the key in the ignition.

'Give me the address,' he said.

Chapter 60
Prestwich, North Manchester. 1500 hours.

Built in the 1950s, it was a solid red-brick semi-detached on the outskirts of Prestwich. Ginley was standing at the downstairs bay window, waiting for the police to arrive. He went to the door and watched Caton open the gate. His face was red and his manner jittery. It was the first time that Caton had seen him looking flustered.

'You took your time,' Ginley said.

'I hope you didn't touch anything, Mr Ginley?'

'Of course I bloody didn't! What do you take me for?'

Caton was sorely tempted. 'Good,' he said instead. 'Our crime scene investigators are on their way.'

Ginley scowled and turned back into the house. Caton followed him into the through lounge.

Mrs Ginley had a kind face beneath a mop of curly white hair. She was sitting on the sofa. Beside her, a white West Highland terrier observed Caton with interest.

'I'm so sorry to put you to all of this trouble,' she said.

'Don't be silly, Mother,' Ginley said. 'It's his job.'

'Not at all, Mrs Ginley,' Caton told her. 'You did exactly the right thing, and you have no idea how helpful this may prove to be.'

'It had better be,' said Ginley. 'How the hell did he know my mother lives here?'

'I thought you were an *investigative* reporter,' Caton murmured.

'Would you like a cup of tea?' Mrs Ginley asked, levering herself off the sofa into a standing position.

'That's very kind of you,' Caton told her, 'but can we leave that until after I've asked you a few questions?'

'Very well,' she said. 'Where would you like to start?'

'Where do you think, Mother?' said Ginley. 'Show him what came through your letterbox.'

'Do us all a favour, Mr Ginley,' Caton said, 'and leave the questions to me. If you can't do that, perhaps you could go and make us all a drink?'

'I'm not going anywhere,' the reporter told him.

'Look,' Caton said, 'I get that you're angry and worried about your mother. In your place, I'd be exactly the same, but you're not helping. Please, back off and let me do my job.'

Ginley's mother took him by the arm.

'Do as the officer asked, Anthony,' she said. 'There's a good boy. I'm perfectly fine.'

Caton had difficulty hiding his amusement. The hard-boiled reporter treated like an errant schoolboy in short trousers. Ginley's face was suffused with frustration and embarrassment. His mother let go of his arm and walked through to the back of the lounge. The dog jumped off the sofa and padded after her.

'Here they are,' she said. 'I haven't opened the parcel, and I haven't touched anything since I realised what it was.'

A cardboard box lay open on the table. Caton instantly recognised it as a standard Amazon package, just large enough to squeeze through a letterbox. Carefully laid out beside it was a small box of shortbread biscuits, a well-thumbed copy of *Murder At The Vicarage* by Agatha Christie, and two packets of painkillers. Both of them had been opened, and the foil blister sheets exposed.

'I didn't open the packets of painkillers,' Ginley's mother said. 'Anthony did that.'

It sounded as though the mother was more forensically aware than the son.

'I just needed to be sure before I contacted you,' said Ginley.

'I've been following all the news about these dreadful murders,' his mother said. 'I would have known what to do even if Anthony hadn't warned me several times over. When it arrived this morning, I immediately rang him.' She put her hand to her mouth. 'Oh, should I have rung the police first?'

That would have infinitely preferable but Caton wasn't going to say so.

'Don't worry,' he told her, 'I'm here now. When did this parcel actually arrive?'

'Let me see, I don't remember it being there when I took Snowy out for her walk. That would be about a quarter past twelve. The trouble is, I can't be sure because I always use the back door when we go walkies, so I don't end up with paw marks all over the carpet.'

'What time did you get back, Mother?' Ginley asked impatiently.

'That would be about one o'clock,' she replied. 'Then I wiped Snowy's paws, poured some water in her bowl, and warmed some soup in the microwave. I had that in front of the telly, washed up and then got up to go to the toilet. That's when I saw it, on the front doormat.'

'That would about what time, Mrs Ginley?' Caton said.

'Oh, about half past one, I suppose. Then I got a large Dettol wipe from the tub in the kitchen, wiped the parcel down and left it on the mat to dry.'

'What time did you open it?'

'I'm not sure,' she said.

'Was it just before you rang me?' Ginley said.

Her eyes lit up. 'That's right. I rang you straight away, as soon as I saw those painkillers.'

'That was around two o'clock,' Ginley informed Caton. 'I got here as soon as I could, and rang you when I'd inspected those packets.'

Time lost and evidence contaminated, Caton reflected.

'Do you sleep upstairs, Mrs Ginley?' he asked.

'Oh yes,' she replied. 'My knees are a lot stronger than you might think.'

'And what time did you get up this morning?'

'Eight o'clock on the dot.'

'The parcel wasn't there when you came downstairs?'

She shook her head. 'Definitely not.'

Which meant that it was pushed through that letterbox sometime between eight in the morning and half-past one in the afternoon. In broad daylight. The unsub was either becoming increasingly reckless or Ginley's taunts had really touched a nerve.

'Actually, Mrs Ginley,' he said, 'I'll take you up on your offer now. I'd appreciate a mug of boiled water if that's possible?'

'Of course,' she said.

'Coffee for me, Mother,' her son said.

'It's all he drinks,' she said, as she headed for the kitchen, 'but he still has to say it.'

'It's obvious he targeted her because she's my mother,' said Ginley, 'but how the hell did he know that?'

'Perhaps he followed you here?' Caton suggested. 'When were you last here?'

'Two days ago. I popped in at lunchtime to make sure she was okay.'

'Before you gave that interview on BBC Breakfast, and told the world he wasn't exactly a genius?' Caton said. 'And before you almost got thrown out of the press conference. He wouldn't have had a reason to follow you before that. He must have found out some other way. Not the census, obviously. Not unless you were living in 1942?'

'Very droll,' said Ginley.

'When were you last living here? Caton asked.

'I left home twenty years ago.'

'You're an investigator. How would *you* find out where someone's mother lived?'

'The electoral registers. I'd start with 192.com or the local library archives, plus, there's a load of commercially available data sets out there that companies have compiled. There are even ones you can buy on the Dark Web. I'd keep going back through the years until I found a hit that included both mother and son. Then I'd check she was still shown as living at the address.'

'That may explain it,' Caton observed, 'but it doesn't help us, does it?'

'Here you are.'

Ginley's mother put the tray down on the table. It held a cup of coffee, a mug of steaming water, and two freshly baked scones. Caton didn't have the heart to tell her that under Covid regulations he wasn't allowed to eat anything in another person's home. He wasn't even supposed to accept a drink, but he'd reasoned that boiled water must be safe. Besides which, he preferred it to tea or coffee, and it had given him a chance to speak to her son alone.

'I'd like you to take a look at some photographs, Mrs Ginley,' he said, 'and let me know if you remember any of people they depict.'

'Of course,' she said. 'Just let me fetch my glasses.'

She went off into the kitchen and came back wearing a pair of tortoiseshell spectacles attached to a chain around her neck. Caton placed the tablet on the table and stepped back. Ginley stepped closer so that he could see for himself. Caton moved quickly out of range of the two of them, and surreptitiously wiped the rim of his mug with his clean handkerchief.

'Swipe to the left when you're ready for the next one,' he told them.

'Ooh, it's just like *Crimewatch*,' Ginley's mother said as her son swiped slowly through the photos, twice. When they'd finished, she turned to Caton.

'They could easily be members of our book group,' she said. 'We've agreed to try and keep it going through this dreadful lockdown. Mildred is good on computers and she's going to send us what she calls a link, so we can do it by video – live. I'm really looking forward to it.'

'But you don't you recognise any of them, Mother, do you?' Ginley said impatiently.

'No,' she said.

'That last photo,' said the reporter, 'is that the latest victim?'

'I can't tell you either way,' Caton said, 'but you'll find out soon enough.'

The doorbell rang. Ginley went to investigate and returned with Jack Benson in tow. Benson was already suited up. Caton took him back into the hall so Ginley wouldn't overhear their conversation.

'There's a package on the dining-room table,' he said. 'This is the first time we've had the whole caboodle. I want you to work your magic on it – it could just provide us with the breakthrough we're looking for. It was posted through the letterbox, but the approach could have been from the front or the rear.'

'Leave it with us, Boss,' Benson said. 'We'll do our best. By the way, he's getting careless. We have two strong footprints from the Patti Dean crime scene. One from the border at the back, one from the path.'

'You just said *he*,' Caton observed. 'Was that intended?'

'Yes, Boss. Although it's possible it could be a woman wearing men's shoes.'

'That's a start,' Caton said. 'Now all we need is the feet that wore them.'

He was not going to get too excited. The border beneath the fence sounded promising, but those prints could have been left by a gardener or handyman. He went back into the lounge.

'Could I have a quick word with you outside, Mr Ginley?' he said.

They stood in the rear garden with their backs to the house. Behind the low boundary fence stood large deciduous trees in both directions.

'What is that back there?' Caton asked.

'Prestwich Clough,' Ginley told him. 'It's an ancient wooded valley. I used to play there all the time when I was a kid. I jogged and cycled along it when I was a teen. There are paths everywhere. The National Route 6 Cycle Path runs straight through it. Over to the left, you've got more woods. Dams Head Lodge, Bradley Brook, a canal towpath.'

'And beyond the woods?'

'A wide expanse of hilly pasture, and the Limewood Centre.'

The name rang a bell with Caton.

'The Limewood Centre?'

'It's the NHS Secure Services mental health unit – a purpose-built facility for medium and low secure services.' His eyes lit up. 'You don't think . . .'

'I don't think anything, Mr Ginley,' Caton said. 'I prefer to find out instead.' It was a cheap shot, but he couldn't help himself. 'Is there somewhere you could take your mother for an hour or so while my team carry out a forensic search of the gardens?'

For a moment he thought Ginley was going to protest, but for some reason he relented.

'There's a cafe she likes in Prestwich village,' he said reluctantly.

Chapter 61

The Limewood Centre was surrounded by woods. It consisted of an anomalous combination of two-storey buildings that could easily have been an early twentieth-century replacement for a Victorian mental hospital, along with three self-contained modern single-storey buildings with blue slate roofs.

'I've been here a couple of times before,' Carly Whittle confided.

Caton had asked her to come up to Prestwich and make sure Mrs Ginley was alright, but both she and her son had insisted that was unnecessary. So Caton had invited her to join him. They were sitting in a reception area, waiting for someone to come and talk to them.

'Both times it was girls who'd gone missing,' she said. 'They both turned up unharmed. I got the impression it was a decent place to be if you were really struggling with your mental health.'

'Here we go,' said Caton.

A tall elegant woman in her late forties was walking towards them. She had ash-grey hair cut in a long bob and was wearing a stylish grey suit, with a pink floral-print mask over her nose and mouth. Mildly embarrassed, the two detectives stood up, fished their masks from their pockets and hooked them in place. The woman stopped on one of the yellow circles on the floor, three metres apart.

'Thank you,' she said. 'My name is Hannah Yellin. I'm one of the senior administrators here.'

Caton and Carly introduced themselves.

'Is there somewhere private we can go?' Caton asked.

Hannah Yellin looked pointedly around the large empty open space. 'This is private enough, surely?'

Caton had to concede that it was.

'Very well,' she said. 'How may I help you?'

'We're investigating an incident that took place earlier today less half a mile from here,' Caton said. 'There's nothing to suggest that it had anything to do with your facility, but we're conducting door-to-door enquiries as a matter of routine and this visit is a part of that.'

Even from this distance, he could tell she was far from convinced and was weighing up her options.

'Very well,' she said at last. 'What do you wish to know?'

'Could you start by briefly telling us about the work you do here and how it's staffed?' he said. 'Just to provide context.'

'We provide secure treatment,' she began, 'for people of all genders who have long-term mental health needs. They come to us from across the whole of Greater Manchester. Our focus is on intensive rehabilitation for people who cannot be safely treated in traditional hospital in-patient settings. We use a wide range of treatments depending on the individual needs of each patient. Consequently, we employ a number of clinicians, therapeutic staff and support staff across the full spectrum of care and intervention. To assist in this process, we have a sports hall, gymnasium, swimming and hydrotherapy pools, study rooms and workshops.'

'How many patients do you treat here?' Caton asked.

She stared at him and frowned. 'We prefer "service users",' she said.

'I'm sorry, how many service users do you support?'

'Fifty in our low secure service, in three single-sex, purpose-built wards, and a further one hundred and fifty in our medium secure facility in the main buildings.'

'Can you tell us a little about your service users? In particular, why this is a secure unit?'

She looked from one detective to the other. 'I should have thought that officers of your experience would not need to ask that question? After all, quite a number of our service users are referred to us via the justice system.'

'Neither I nor my colleague have been directly involved with such referrals in recent years,' he said. 'And the guidelines seem to change with each new Home Secretary.'

Strictly speaking, it wasn't even a white lie. Any referrals from convictions that FMIT were involved with tended to be to a high security setting. Fortunately, it didn't matter either way. She had decided to humour him.

'Put simply,' she said, 'they are deemed to present a serious risk to others, and often to themselves. A physically secure setting is required to prevent them from leaving until it's safe for them to do so.'

'Are they ever allowed out – for a home visit, for example?' Carly asked.

'Of course,' she said. 'Carefully planned opportunities to leave the unit for a short period of time are an essential part of the rehabilitation process. It also informs our risk assessments on individual service users, and helps us evaluate their progress and the efficacy of our treatment programmes.'

'When they do have leave, am I right in assuming that they're accompanied at all times?' Caton asked.

She raised her eyebrows. 'No, Detective Chief Inspector, you are not right in assuming that at all. There comes a point in a service user's rehabilitation where the presence of an escort would simply reinforce their own insecurity about being able to cope independently beyond this unit, and also reinforce their dependence on us at the very point at which we need to wean them off that.'

'Have any of your patients . . .?'

'Service users,' she said brusquely.

'. . . service users, been on unaccompanied leave in the past twenty-four hours?'

'Definitely not.'

'You're absolutely certain?'

'I am. Firstly, because all leave has to be approved by me, and secondly, because ever since the lockdown began, we have cancelled all admissions, all discharges and all leave.'

'Thank you,' said Caton. 'That's all I needed to know.'

* * *

'I should have asked her at the very beginning,' Caton said as they walked back to their cars. 'It would have saved us a whole heap of time.'

'When we do catch him or her, is this the kind of place they'll end up in?' Carly wondered.

'I hope not. It's going to be a high-security unit wherever it is, hopefully Rampton. But even that's going to be a damn sight more comfortable than prison. A lot more comfortable than the unsub deserves.'

'That doesn't sound like you, Boss? What happened to mental illness being different from cold-blooded rational motives?'

Caton stopped walking, forcing her to do the same.

'The thing about serial killers,' he said, 'is that they supposedly manage to walk undetected among us by clothing themselves in a mask of sanity. By copying the behaviours and responses they observe in others that signal empathy, wisdom and rationality – traits that they don't in fact possess. I've come to believe, however, that this isn't always the case.'

'No?'

'No. Occasionally you come across individuals like this who know exactly what the impact of their actions will be on both the victims and those that love them, but they don't care. Not because they lack empathy, but because those are exactly the outcomes they're after. They have the ability to empathise, but are devoid of sympathy.'

'Not mad then, just bad?'

'Neither, Carly. In my book, such people are simply evil. If they are aware of the impact of their actions yet show no remorse, then I believe they should be treated as sane.'

'The general public would consider that pretty radical,' she said. 'Serial killers being sane?'

'I know,' he replied, 'so keep it to yourself. Everyone else out there finds comfort in the belief that only a madman would behave in such a way. That way, the likelihood that anyone with whom they're acquainted and whom they regard as perfectly sane, being or becoming a serial killer, would freak them out. It would be like living with coronavirus twenty-four seven for the rest of your life.'

He bleeped the car, walked round to his side and paused with the door half open. 'And we wouldn't want that now, would we?'

Chapter 62
East Didsbury. 1630 hours.

'Number eight! The man with the bat is number eight.'

Kate had popped out to the Tesco supermarket on Kingsway, leaving the two of them playing Emily's favourite game, *Stare!*

'Well done, Emily,' Larissa said.

She was about to reveal the next card when her phone pinged. She had a text.

We have just delivered your package. We have left it outside the back door as per instructions.

Larissa was surprised. She was expecting a box of pastel crayons for the artwork she'd started doing during lockdown, but she'd only ordered it yesterday and didn't remember leaving any instructions, because she assumed it would fit through the letterbox. Besides, these days there was always someone at home.

'I'm just going to go and fetch something, Emily,' she said. 'When I get back, I want you to tell me which creature on that card is the smallest.'

There was an ordinary cardboard parcel on the step. Larissa looked up and down the path to check if anyone was there, took a sheet of Sani-Cloth from the tub on the shelf by the door, and used it to pick up the parcel. She carried it inside and used another sheet to wipe the parcel all over. While she waited for it to dry, she checked the name and address. The parcel was definitely for her.

'It's a frog!' Emily announced.

Larissa turned and found her standing there, the card in her hand and a triumphant look on her face. Emily spied the parcel.

'Ooh, it's a present,' she said. 'What is it?'

'I don't know,' said Larissa. 'I hope it's those crayons I sent for. Shall we take a look?'

She took the parcel over to the kitchen table and snipped the wrapping away with scissors from the cutlery drawer.

'Ooh . . .' Emily squealed. 'Chocolates!'

* * *

Back at Ginley's mother's house, Caton and the reporter were engaged in a heated conversation.

'I'm not asking you,' Caton said, 'I'm telling you. If you reveal any details relating to what happened here that may be known only to the perpetrator and us, you will be jeopardising the investigation.'

'I could also be saving lives,' Ginley retorted.

Caton's phone rang.

'You'd better take that,' Ginley said. 'It could be the killer rubbing your nose in it.'

It wasn't, it was Kate. He could tell she was trying hard not to panic.

'I've just got home from Tesco,' she said, 'to find Larissa and Emily examining a box of chocolates and a used paperback that appeared mysteriously on our back doorstep. They were addressed to Larissa but there was no note. And, Tom . . . there was no cellophane around the box.'

'Stay there,' he said. 'Make sure the doors are locked. And don't touch anything. I'm on my way.'

Caton shoved his phone back in his pocket, waved Carly over to her car and started off down the drive.

'Has there been another one?' Ginley called after him.

'Remember what I told you,' Caton shouted back. 'And don't try to follow me or I'll have you arrested.'

'What for?' Ginley responded.

'I'll think of something,' Caton muttered.

He called Benson from the car.

'Are you done there?' he asked.

'More or less, Boss,' the crime scene manager replied. 'We've got everything we need. Why?'

'Because I need you somewhere else,' Caton told him. 'It just got personal.'

Chapter 63
East Didsbury. 1740 hours.

'I'm sorry, Mr Caton,' Larissa said. 'I shouldn't have opened it.'

She was still pale with shock at the thought of what might have happened. He was still wrestling with his own emotions. Anger and disbelief that his own family had been targeted. Relief that no one had come to harm.

They were sitting in the garden room. Kate was in the lounge playing *Stare!* with Emily, to distract her from the comings and goings. Benson was in the kitchen with one of his team, examining the suspect package, while another member of the team examined Larissa's mobile phone.

'Don't worry,' Caton told her. 'No harm has been done. And we don't know for certain that it's not some secret admirer of yours. That wouldn't be so surprising, would it?'

She managed the beginnings of a smile.

'That's better,' he said. 'Now, I need to ask you a few questions. First of all, are you sure you don't recognise the number from which that text was sent?'

She shook her head. 'No, definitely not. I checked all my contacts. I have never had a call or text from that number before. I also Googled how to do a reverse phone lookup. There was no record of the number.'

From a burner phone then, just like the other calls. Though there was still an outside chance that she did have a secret admirer – the kind who sends anonymous valentine cards and never plucks up courage to come out from the shadows. Or a stalker.

'Is it maybe possible that someone holds a candle for you?' he asked.

She looked confused. 'Holds a candle?'

'Has a crush on you – fancies you. Someone you know or who might know you?'

'No,' she said, 'there's no one.'

'Have you noticed anyone following you at all? Or regularly appearing in places that you frequent?'

Again she shook her head. 'No, I have not.'

Benson appeared in the doorway. 'Can I have a word, Boss?' he said.

Caton stood up. 'One last question, Larissa?' he said. 'Have you ever registered to vote here in the UK since you've been living with us?'

'I cannot,' she said. 'Thanks to you, I have my refugee status, but until I have been granted citizenship, I am not eligible to vote.'

That had been Caton's understanding, but he had to be sure. Check everything.

'Mr Caton?' she said.

He turned back. 'Yes?'

'What I don't understand is how this person knew that I'm a massive fan of Amanda Prowse?'

Carly Whittle and Jack Benson were standing on opposite sides of the kitchen table. She was wearing her mask.

'DCs Powell and Nair are doing a door to door with your neighbours,' she said, 'asking them to check their CCTV. With it being so recent, none of them will have written over their recordings.'

'Good,' Caton said. 'But they won't find anything. My hunch is that the unsub will have followed the

Mersey Path onto Stenner Lane, then cut through Fletcher Moss, hopped over the fence into Millgate Lane, then into our garden. We need to widen the door to door accordingly, but only when we know for sure that this is him.'

'It's looking that way,' said Benson. 'We've seen this cardboard packaging before. The printing of the name and address looks identical to that recovered from all the other crime scenes, including Mrs Ginley's. As for your hunch, although the ground is dry, it looks like we're going to be able to lift a number of footprints from your garden, the path and the verge beyond the garden fence.'

He pointed to the book that had accompanied the chocolates. It was lying on the table in an evidence bag.

'An eagle-eyed member of my team noticed something odd about this,' he said. 'Someone has done a good job at trying to disguise it, but if you look closely, you'll see that a page has been neatly removed with something like a razor blade or a scalpel. It was only the missing page number that gave it away.'

'There must have been something on there he didn't want us to see,' Caton said. 'Maybe the original owner wrote their name in there? Maybe it was his, and he'd written his own name in there when he bought it.' He paused. 'Mind you, Amanda Prowse? It's unlikely unless the unsub is a woman.'

'If it's any consolation,' Benson said, 'there's no evidence that the chocolates have been tampered with, though we can't be sure until we've taken a good look in the lab.'

It wasn't much comfort to Caton that instead of attempting to poison his daughter and au pair, the unsub had merely proved that he could – that he knew where he and his family lived. This was both a threat and a warning. He turned to Carly Whittle.

'Can you stay here until I send someone to replace you?' he said. 'I don't want my family to be on their own.'

'Of course, Boss,' she said. 'What are you going to do?'

'I'm going to arrange for a dog team to come and see if they can track whoever left that parcel. Say hello to my wife, kiss my daughter goodnight, and then I'm heading back to base. I'll make sure there's a patrol car out front too, though I'm sure he's long gone.'

Chapter 64
Nexus House. 1857 hours.

The whole team were assembled. Those about to leave for the night had been asked to stay. There was a buzz about the room and a renewed sense of purpose. An attack on the Boss was an attack on every one of them. Caton pointed to the map.

'There is one feature common to all four of the crime scenes relating to our victims. Each one of these houses is adjacent to green spaces accessible on foot or by bicycle, powered or otherwise. All of them are also crossed by or close to a national cycle path. In addition, crime scenes one and two – Stretford and Chorltonville – are more or less connected by such routes, requiring only minimal road crossings. The same is even more evident of the third and fourth crime scenes in Gatley and Heald Green.'

DC Nair raised his hand. 'The same is true of Ginley's mother's home and your home, Boss, except they're not connected 'cos they're miles apart.'

'Eight and a half miles, to be precise,' Caton replied. 'But if he's using a bike of some kind, that's not a distance that would trouble him. However, it does tell us that he's riled, and that has made him careless.'

Jimmy Hulme raised his hand. 'This is similar to a case some of us were involved with while you were away, Boss.'

'Away?' Caton said. 'You make it sound as though I was in HMP Manchester. Good point though – remind us.'

'The subject in that case was a rapist. He used canal towpaths and cycle paths as a means of escape, which made trying to trace road vehicles fruitless.'

'That is exactly why I am going to request that officers on mountain bikes patrol these routes, out of uniform and dressed like any other cyclist, around the clock, in shifts, until he's caught. But we also need to work out what it is that connects these women, how he obtained their addresses, Ginley's mother's and mine. And how did he know about my au pair, unless he's followed me and been watching my house?'

'To be fair, Boss,' Carter said, 'there was a hell of a lot of publicity last year around the case, and around your au pair getting settled status. That still doesn't give him an address though.'

'Phone directory?' DC Powell suggested.

Caton shook his head. 'We're ex-directory and so is she. So were two of the victims.'

'Census?' DS Hulme suggested.

'I wasn't living at this address for the most recent census.'

'Electoral roll?' someone called out.

'My au pair is not eligible to vote, and my wife and I applied to register anonymously. That reminds me: all of you should make sure you've opted out of the "Open" register on account of the work we do.'

He turned to look at the crime scene photos on the whiteboards. 'What, apart from the pills, is the one thing that was present at all six crime scenes, including Mrs Ginley's and mine?'

They stared in silence.

'Books!' he said. 'They must have come with the packets of painkillers with which he'd tampered. I didn't make that connection until he made the mistake of leaving one for Mrs Ginley, as well as my au pair. Which is why I said that making it personal for Ginley and me has made him careless. This is our connection. The question is – what does it tell us? What significance do these books have for our unsub?'

Caton could almost feel the intensity with which they were all racking their brains. A new DC at the back of the room raised a tentative hand.

'Go ahead,' Caton said.

'I was asked to check out the registered owners of a couple of the vehicles passive media picked up in and around the Trafford crime scene . . .' He faltered.

'Carry on,' Caton told him.

'There was one guy I interviewed on the list, a Nathan Germaine?'

'And?'

'I asked what he was doing on that estate and he said he was a gardener? He showed me the tools in the back of his van – a lawnmower, pruners, hoes, a spade, a fork, refuse bags, the lot. He said he was scouting for business. He showed me a stack of business cards. I asked for one and attached it to my report.'

'In the middle of lockdown?' It didn't sound plausible to Caton. 'Did you ask to see a list of his clients?' he said.

'He gave me a couple to check out. I rang them, and they confirmed he did work for them. Fortnightly visits in summer, monthly in winter.'

'What has this got to do with books?' Caton asked.

'I asked him how long he'd been a jobbing gardener. A year, he said. Before that he was at a garden centre. And before that' – he paused – 'he'd worked for years with the city council as a librarian.'

There was an instant change of mood. People were suddenly sitting up, muttering comments and stage-whispering with colleagues. Everyone in the room was looking at the DC now. His face reddened. He looked like a rabbit caught in the headlights.

'I handed the report in,' he said, 'but I didn't realise at that point that it might be relevant. I'm sorry, Boss.'

Caton turned to Jimmy Hulme.

'It's in the system,' Hulme said, without waiting to be asked, 'but because it seemed to have checked out, and there were no multiple incidences or links to any of the other crime scenes, and there's no record of him on HOLMES 2, it won't have been reviewed yet.' He shrugged. 'With the manpower we've got, there are over three hundred yellow flags awaiting review.'

'Well, he goes right to the top of the pile,' Caton said. 'These clusters are all women of a certain age, all of them readers and all of them likely to welcome a good book, especially if they know the person who sent or delivered it. This wasn't random. It's odds-on that he worked in the libraries that served these two areas. DC Nair, get onto the city council. See if you can find out where and when he worked when he was with the library service. DC Franklin, get onto ANPR and let's see if we establish where that van is right now.'

He turned back to the DC who had set this hare running. 'Where did you interview Germaine?'

'At the address the car was registered to. It's in Whalley Range.'

'Send me the address and a copy of your report,' Caton told him, 'and copy it to DI Carter.'

'Yes, Boss.'

'And don't beat yourself up. You were right. There was no way you could have made that link until now. None of us could. You did well to raise it.'

The room was buzzing now. Caton spotted a Manchester Bee paperweight on top of DS Hulme's in tray. He used it to hammer on the desk to get their attention.

'This may or may not prove to be a breakthrough,' he said. 'If it is, we may need everyone to help track him down. Until such time as we know for sure, I want all of you to focus on the tasks you've already been given. Is that clear?'

'Yes, Boss!' they chorused.

He beckoned to DI Carter and DS Hulme.

'Jimmy,' he said, 'task someone to contact that garden centre. Let's see what they know about him. If it's too late tonight, first thing in the morning. Nick,' he added, 'I'm taking Carly and Henry with me to Whalley Range. As soon as you have his address, I'd like you to prepare a search warrant for those premises, including garages and outbuildings, his van and any other vehicles we find there. Hold back from getting it signed off until you hear from me. With any luck, he'll be there to invite us in.'

Chapter 65
Whalley Range. 2015 hours.

They gathered on the pavement outside the large bay-fronted Edwardian semi-detached. There were no vehicles in the drive or parked outside.

'We're looking for a white Ford Transit Courier van, 1.5-litre diesel,' Caton told them. 'Remember, we don't yet have a search warrant. Henry, you stay here, and if Nathan Germaine turns up, don't let him leave. Carly, you and I are going to knock on.'

They walked up to the front of the house.

'All the curtains are drawn,' Carly observed.

Caton rang the bell and knocked on the door. They waited. He rang the bell again, and this time hammered on the door. When there was still no response, he went round and hauled himself up to the top of the side gate.

'I can see a back door, kitchen window and three windows on the first floor,' he told her. 'There's also at least one large shed. No lights on.'

He jumped down and rubbed his gloved hands together to clear some of the green slime that had accumulated on the wooden surface.

'Let's see if the neighbours are in,' he said.

They rejoined Henry Powell out on the pavement.

'We're going to see what next door can tell us about Germaine,' Caton told him.

'You're in luck,' Powell said. 'The downstairs net curtains have been twitching ever since we got here.'

They had hardly set foot on the drive when the front door opened. A woman stood on the threshold. Caton judged her to be in her early eighties, despite her youthful appearance. Tall and elegant, with a shock of snow-white hair, and a long face tapering down to a prominent chin, she seemed pleased to see them. They stopped far enough away not to need their masks.

'I take it that you're police officers?' she said, with a faint trace of an Irish lilt that reminded Caton of his maternal grandmother. He showed her his warrant card.

'I am Detective Chief Inspector Caton,' he said, 'and this is Detective Sergeant Whittle. How did you know?'

'You have the look,' she replied. 'Three well-dressed, intelligent-seeming people. No briefcases, clipboards or copies of the *Watchtower* or *Awake!* What else could you possibly be?'

Caton smiled. It was always best to build a rapport. 'It's a shame we have an age limit,' he said. 'We're short of good detectives, Mrs . . .?'

'O'Donnell,' she replied. 'Maureen O'Donnell.' She paused while she made her mind up. 'Maggie,' she said.

'Who's that?' a man's voice demanded from within the bowels of the house.

'Nothing to trouble you, Michael,' she shouted back. 'Get back to your programme.' She smiled apologetically. 'He's a little hard of hearing these days and he'd only confuse matters.'

Caton swiftly dismissed an image from *Mrs Brown's Boys* that had popped into his head.

'Your neighbour, Mr Germaine, appears to be out, Maggie,' he said. 'We were wondering if you might know when we might expect him back?'

'Ah,' she said, 'that's a good question. I've not seen him or his van these past three weeks.'

'Have you any idea where he might be?'

'I do not. Sure, it's anybody's guess. He's always been a bit of a closed book has Nathan.'

'You've known him a while then?'

'It's really Bernadette, his grandmother on his mother's side, I've known well. For over fifty years, in fact.'

She moved onto the top step and pulled the door to behind her. Her tone became conspiratorial.

'Bernadette's daughter and son-in-law divorced when Nathan was only twelve. His father, a worthless being by all accounts, though I never met him, took off and was never heard from again. His mother remarried four years later and moved to somewhere in Cheshire. Nathan chose to stay in Manchester with his maternal grandmother and grandfather, and went to school in Chorlton. I watched him grow up, but from a distance – you know what teenagers are like. But I still had the odd chat with Bernadette.'

'Do you know what he did when he left school?'

'I believe he finished his A Levels at Xaverian College, started work as a library assistant at Chorlton Library, and worked his way up to become a proper librarian.' She smiled. 'That was no surprise. He always had his head in a book, according to Bernadette.'

'We understand he now works as a gardener?' said Carly Whittle.

'That's right. Bernadette told me he'd accepted voluntary redundancy when the city council closed the mobile library service he was with as part of cutbacks. That would be about two years back. That's when he started working at the garden centre in Chorlton. But when his grandmother began with rapid-onset dementia, he bought a van and started out on his own. Poor Bernadette, she went downhill very fast. She was in a care home within a year. Nathan went to visit her every evening around teatime, as soon as he got home from work. I'd see his van arrive in the drive next door, and within twenty minutes he'd be out again and not back till gone eight.'

'Do you happen to know the name of the care home?' Caton asked.

'Sunset Mews,' she said, 'in Withington, not that I ever visit. Bernadette and I were never really all that close, like, and to be honest, she wouldn't know me now if I did. But I like to send her a card on her birthday and at Christmas.'

'What is Mr Germaine like?' Caton asked.

She raised her eyebrows. 'Like? How do you mean, Mr Caton? To look at?'

'I was thinking more of his personality – how he comes across to you.'

'Much now as he did when he was a boy,' she said. 'Very serious, polite, unassuming. He loves his books though.'

'How do you know?' Carly asked.

'Over the years, I've seen him taking armfuls of them out to his shed behind the garage. I remarked on it earlier this year. I was putting some spring bulbs in and he was just coming out of the shed with a couple of paperbacks in his hand. I said it was nice to see a young man with an interest in books.'

'What did he say?'

'He looked a bit surprised. Then he asked who my favourite author was. I said Jo Jo Moyes. I told him I'd read all of hers. He asked if I'd read her latest – *The Giver Of Stars*? I told him I'd just finished reading it, that my son gave it to me as a Christmas present. He asked if I'd read any books by Kate Morton? I said no. The next day he brought me a copy of *The Secret Keeper*. Wasn't that nice of him? Now I'm hooked. I'm on my fourth one of hers.'

'When did you last see Mr Germaine?' Caton asked.

Her face screwed up with concentration. 'Ah now, that would be a couple of weeks after he gave me that book. I remember because I'd been waiting to catch him so I could thank him again and tell him how much I'd enjoyed reading it.'

'When exactly would that be?'

'The beginning of February, I believe.'

Caton glanced at Carly. She shrugged.

'I think that's all, Maggie,' Caton said. 'You've been most helpful.'

The two detectives set off down the drive.

'I don't suppose you can tell me what this is all about?' Mrs O'Donnell called after them.

Caton stopped and turned. 'I'd rather not,' he said, 'because there may be nothing to tell. We'd just like a word with Mr Germaine, that's all.'

'If I see him, I'll tell him.'

'I'd prefer that you didn't,' he told her firmly.

She smiled. 'You can count on me, Mr Caton.'

'I forgot to ask,' Caton said, 'Nathan's grandfather – what happened to him?'

Her face creased into a smile. 'Albert? Oh, he was a lovely man. Had a jeweller's shop on Shude Hill. He had a heart attack shortly after he retired. Bernadette never really got over it. If it hadn't been for Nathan, I think she might have taken the devil's way out.'

'One last thing,' Caton said. 'How old is Nathan?'

'Let me think,' she said. 'I remember Bernadette telling me he was ten years older than my own grandson Patrick, which would now make him . . . thirty-eight.'

'Thank you,' Caton said.

She stood there on the doorstep, watching them all the way down the drive and onto the pavement. Neither of them spoke until they were back with Henry Powell, and out of earshot.

'Sunset Mews,' Carly observed. 'Is that supposed to be ironic?'

Caton wasn't listening. 'Germaine was with the mobile library service,' he said. 'That would have given him access to the names and addresses of anyone with a library card. And there's a good chance that he's worked across different areas of the city. That may well be how he came to know the victims *and* their reading preferences. It would be relatively easy to persuade them he was dropping off a lockdown goody bag from the council, including a book, a treat and some emergency meds.'

'That's not what happened with Ginley's mother or your nanny,' she pointed out.

'That's because he's begun to escalate. It's no longer just about carefully chosen victims, creating panic while keeping a low profile. He's angry and getting rattled.'

'Because we're getting too close?'

'Or the reverse.'

'How do you mean, Boss?' asked Henry Powell.

'What if he's telling us we've got it all wrong? Thanks to Ginley, the perpetrator believes we're following the narrative that he or she is a health worker. He's telling us otherwise.'

'Or warning you off.'

'I don't think so, but he may be redirecting us. It's more likely that he's demonstrating how clever he is, and at the same time taking back credit for these deaths. Either way, I'm going to get DI Carter have that search warrant signed off so we can see if there's any evidence that he's been making those pills, anything that connects him with the victims or anything that'll tell us where he's gone. And did you hear what she said about the grandfather?'

'Him dying of a heart attack?'

'No, the fact that he had a jeweller's shop on Shude Hill. What do we know about jewellers and cyanide, Carly?'

Her eyes widened. 'They use it to extract gold from old pieces of jewellery, and when they're silversmithing!'

Caton smiled grimly. 'I wonder what happened to his old stock when he retired?' he said.

'Reckon we've got enough for a warrant?' Carly asked.

'There won't be a problem,' he told her, 'because there's no way consent to enter the premises is forthcoming from the owner or the occupier. One is deceased and the other one is missing. You pay the care home a visit. Find out when he was last there and when they expect him next. Also, if they have any idea where he might be if he's not staying here, and if they have a contact number for him. Find out everything you can. Henry, you stay here and keep watch on the house. If he turns up, let me know and don't let him leave. Arrest him if you have to.'

'What for, Boss?'

'I don't know,' Caton replied. 'Find some defects on his van. Failing that, on suspicion of nicking books from Manchester City Council!'

Chapter 66
Whalley Range. 2200 hours.

It was pitch-black, with a stale smell of abandonment and something else Caton could not place.

'That was a stroke of luck,' Carter said. 'Her next door still having the spare key the grandmother gave her?'

A tiny red light blinked where the wall at the end of the hall met the ceiling. Caton's torch probed the inky darkness like a laser.

'We need to find the alarm,' he said. 'You take a look under the stairs; I'll check in here.'

He opened the door into a cloakroom. A beige box on the wall began to beep. Caton held up the grey fob attached to the key ring. The beeping ceased, and the day's date appeared on a small glass panel. Caton found a light switch in the hall.

Carter re-emerged. 'There's a cellar down there,' he said.

'Let's leave it till last,' Caton decided. 'Remember, everyone, don't move a thing until CSI have finished taking their photographs. And watch out for booby traps. We have no idea what we may be dealing with.'

Rather than join in the search himself, Caton went from room to room, looking to gain an impression of the house. It struck him as homely and quaint – exactly what you'd expect from an elderly lady. The rooms were all neat and tidy, but the layer of dust appeared to confirm

Maggie O'Donnell's belief that Germaine had been absent for the past three weeks.

Downstairs, there was a kitchen and then two reception rooms, one of which contained a round mahogany dining table and chairs. Crude sheets of transparent plastic had been taped over the windows, making it impossible to open them. Caton had seen something like this before in a house where the occupier had been suffering from Alzheimer's. The family had wanted to prevent her from opening the windows and leaving them like that all night – a gift to burglars and the gas company. Over time, the condensation had caused the beautiful parquet flooring to lift and begin to rot. He wondered if in this house there might be a rather more sinister explanation.

Upstairs, there were five bedrooms and a family bathroom. The master bedroom at the front had been left as a shrine to the grandmother. A short-sleeved jersey nightdress printed with flowering primroses lay on the pillow. Photos in ornate silver frames adorned the dressing table. Caton searched, but found no images other than those he assumed to be of Germaine's grandmother and grandfather, and a photo of a young man with a grave expression, wearing what looked like his first suit.

The second largest bedroom appeared to belong to Germaine himself, but the only signs of that were the clothes in the fitted wardrobe. The three remaining bedrooms – a double and two singles, one of which had been used as a study – were fitted out, floor to ceiling, with wooden shelves stacked full of books. In one of the rooms there was even a stepladder of the type one might find in a library.

In the study, the only remaining sign of the past presence of a computer or laptop, phone and chargers were leads routed down behind the desk into an extension lead, and a Wi-Fi connector plugged into a wall socket.

In here, the books were exclusively reference titles. The range of subjects was vast. Caton's attention was drawn to three sections in particular: medicine and poisons, criminal law and justice, forensic science and true-life crime, including two whole shelves on the psychology of mass murderers and serial killers.

The latter section would not have looked out of place in a university criminology department. Caton had read many of these books himself.

In the remaining rooms, the stock included general biographies and fiction. In the main, they were all second-hand or ex-library books, the latter complete with stickers recording them as having been withdrawn from stock. Caton was surprised to discover that some of these looked almost brand new. He went off to inspect the cellar.

There were two light switches at the top of the stairs, one to light his way and the other, he assumed, to illuminate the cellar itself. Well-trod, smooth stone stairs led down to a space the length of the two reception rooms above, and with a comfortable ceiling height. The air was dry down here, and he supposed that the walls had been tanked to keep out the damp. In the centre of the room was a table, beside which stood a humidifier, its plug detached from the nearby socket. The reason for these precautions was self-evident: these walls too were covered by bookshelves, seven shelves high.

On closer inspection, he saw that the books down here were displayed by classification and then by author. It was, in effect, a mini-library separate to the collection upstairs. When he turned, he saw another pair of library steps in the corner behind him. Caton sniffed the air.

There was an unpleasant fusion of second-hand bookshop and stale sweat.

The muted slap of feet on the stone steps told him that someone else was descending. The ghostlike figure of a crime scene investigator in full hazmat suit materialised. Caton clocked the disapproving look behind the PVC and Teflon visor took the hint and went in search of his crime scene manager.

Jack Benson was in the garage. He came outside and stood on the drive a respectful distance away from his boss, before pushing his hood back and removing his goggles.

'Where are you up to?' Caton asked.

'We've done an initial search of the house, the cellar, two sheds, the garden, and I've just finished in here. And we've taken photos and video.'

'Found anything?'

'Let's start with what we haven't found,' Benson said. 'The fridge and the freezers are completely empty but they're still switched on. And we've found no spare keys to his van or any other vehicle – or indeed anything at all to suggest that he even owns a motorised means of transportation. Plus, there's no sign of any pill-making equipment or suspect packaging. As to what we have found, it's not a lot, I'm afraid. Just inside the garage, to your right, we do have a strong footprint in the cement dust surface that we're about to lift. So, if you're intending to have a look in there, please stay on the plates. We also have several pairs of shoes from upstairs that we'll compare with the prints we've recovered from the crime scenes. Oh, and don't touch the bench. We haven't vacuumed it yet for traces of chemicals and powders. And by the way, the bins are all empty.'

'What was in the sheds?'

'One was full of gardening equipment. The other was full of boxes of books.'

'You get on,' Caton told him. 'I'll have a look in here.'

The garage doubled as a utility room. A long workbench ran along the length of the back wall, with beneath it, a washing machine, spin dryer and a front-opening freezer. Caton checked the freezer first. It held four drawers, all of them empty.

On the right-hand wall, a lawnmower, strimmer, car-cleaning kits and coiled cables hung from a collection of metal hooks covered in red plastic. Shelves along the opposite wall were meticulously stacked with plastic boxes containing various items by category. Paints, glues and fillers, screws, nails, bolts, hammers, an axe, ropes and string, heavy tools and a car jump starter.

On the left-hand side, beneath a layer of plastic sacks, sat a triangular metal frame with an irregular partially elliptical centrepiece. He crouched down to see if he could make out what it was. Someone behind him gave a muffled whistle. Caton looked over his shoulder. It was Henry Powell.

'Very nice,' the DC said.

'I thought you were watching out for Germaine's van?' Caton said.

'DI Carter reckons Germaine's going to hightail it as soon as he sees all the police vehicles, so he's stationed unmarked cars at either end of the street.'

Caton nodded. 'Smart move,' he said. He pointed to the contraption. 'I gather you know what this is?'

'A direct-drive turbo trainer for a road bike. I wouldn't mind one of those myself. I've got a cheap magnetic resistance turbo back home, but this one would set you back close to a thousand pounds.'

Caton stood up and turned to look at the boxes on the shelves. There were a number that were clearly empty. He wondered what they might have held. He pulled one out, and examined it. On the back was a white label: DRILL BITS – WOOD, METAL, BRICK, STONE. He put it back, and chose another: DRILL CHARGER/SPARE BATTERY. On the other side of the garage, Powell reached up to the only empty container on the top shelf, lifted it down and turned it to read what was missing.

'Puncture repair kit, spare inner tubes, tyre levers,' he announced, before putting it back.

Beneath the bottom shelf was a small wooden chest.

Caton knelt again and slid it out. He flipped the latch to open the box. Inside sat a wooden tray covered in faded purple velvet. On the tray lay a set of tools, including tiny awls, small pairs of pliers, a miniature ball-peen hammer, a wooden clothes peg, a hacksaw, what looked like a small tapered rolling pin and a wooden mallet.

'What's that, Boss?' Powell asked.

'I'm guessing it's a silversmith's tools,' Caton replied.

Next to the chest was a four-drawer unit. The top drawer held some neatly folded dust sheets. Caton removed the others in turn and read the label on the back of each: GOGGLES AND EAR DEFENDERS; MASKS; COVERALLS. From the shelf above, he pulled out a box which was full of cans of paint, and turned it around. PAINTS: WATER-BASED, INTERIOR. He replaced it and checked several more at random on the other shelves. They all had labels.

'Who puts the labels facing the wall?' Caton wondered out loud.

It was clearly meant to be rhetorical, but DC Powell answered anyway.

'Someone with something to hide?'

Caton had left Benson and his team to get on with the job, and brought his core team back to the Incident Room to take stock.

'The sighting of his van close to a crime scene, together with those library books, and all that kit, give us reasonable cause to bring him in,' he said, 'but it's not enough to charge him. We need something concrete.'

'Speaking of which,' Jimmy Hulme said, pointing to his computer screen, 'the footprint in the cement dust on the floor of Germaine's garage is a perfect match for the one recovered from Patti Dean's house.'

'That'll do,' Caton said. 'Jimmy, put out an all-ports warning.' His mobile rang. It was Carly Whittle.

'I'm at the care home,' she told him.

'And?'

'The grandmother is dead.'

'When did she die?'

'She passed away on the tenth of March.'

'Covid-19?'

'They don't know, Boss. The death certificate said she died of pneumonia. They only began to suspect that some of the deaths in care homes were from coronavirus from the seventeenth of March onwards, and the Care Quality Commission didn't begin recording them as such until the tenth of April.'

'When was the funeral?'

'Wednesday eighteenth of March. It was a burial. Alongside her husband in the Southern Cemetery.'

'Did Germaine attend the funeral?'

'Yes, Boss. He organised it, apparently. There was only him, two of the carers from the home, and the celebrant the funeral director arranged. There was a short service in the chapel, and no wake afterwards.'

'Did you ask them how he seemed?'

'Of course.' She sounded mildly offended. 'Give me a second while I check my notes. Here we are. They got the impression that he was deeply affected. There were no tears, nothing like that, but he was unnaturally stiff, and hardly spoke a word. "Self-absorbed" was how one of them described him. "When we told him how sorry we were, he just grunted," said the other one. "I'd have thought him downright rude if it hadn't been obvious he was really upset. I just think he didn't know how to handle it." He left immediately afterwards and they haven't seen him since. He still hasn't been to pick up his grandmother's effects from the care home.'

'Well done,' Caton said. 'Get back here as soon as you can.'

He shared her news with the rest of the team.

'The neighbour said she hadn't seen Germaine since about the middle of March,' he said, 'so it's safe to assume that he disappeared immediately after his grandmother was laid to rest.'

He pointed to the whiteboard listing the questions raised by the unsub profile. 'I think we have our trigger.'

'You're thinking revenge for his grandmother's death?' Carter asked.

'I'm not sure it's that simple. Let's put ourselves in his position. What kind of narrative might he have constructed for himself? It's going to involve making a number of assumptions, but let's see where it takes us.

So, his parents divorced when he's . . .?'

'Twelve,' Carter supplied.

'Father moves away – or least doesn't have any further contact with the boy. He's effectively been abandoned. No father figure, until mother gets married four years later and moves away to Cheshire. Abandonment number two.'

'Strictly speaking, Boss,' DC Powell said, 'he wasn't abandoned. He chose to stay with his grandmother.'

'True,' Caton said, 'but his mother chose to move away from where his roots were, and I think it's reasonable to assume that the boy didn't get on with her new choice of partner.'

He paused to take stock, before continuing. 'Thus far he's been dealt a poor hand. He probably feels bitter, unloved and undervalued. Life is so unfair . . . But he still has his grandmother. But she's forty years or more older than him. We know from his employers and colleagues that he's a bit of a loner. Must be lonely at home too – watching his grandmother getting older, frailer, more dependent. Is this all he has to look forward to? His one consolation is her dependence on him. This is the one area of his existence where he is in control. This is classic co-dependency. Through his work, he comes into contact with quite a few women his grandmother's age. They're all lonely too. He knows how to relate to them. He learns a little about their lives, and an awful lot about their reading habits. Then coronavirus raises its ugly head.

'Covid-19 has a predisposition for the elderly. It puts an end to their loneliness, and saves them from a sad decline into dementia. Then his grandmother dies. He's been abandoned again. His world implodes. Bitterness is replaced by anger. These other women – why should they live and his grandmother die? They become the vehicles for his power and control, and their deaths an outlet for his rage. The question is, had he been planning it for some time, or only when his grandmother died?'

'Martha Riley's body was discovered on the twenty-eighth of March,' Henry Powell said. 'Okay, she'd died some time prior to that. But at best, he'd have had only ten days in which to get hold of a supply of potassium cyanide salts and a capsule-making machine.'

'And those packets of pain-relief tablets,' Carter added. 'People had already started stockpiling them along with loo rolls and hand sanitiser long before the lockdown started.'

'Remind me,' said Caton, 'when was that exactly?'

'It was announced on the evening of Monday twenty-third of March,' said Jimmy Hulme, 'and started officially the following day.'

Caton nodded. 'Which suggests that it wasn't so much his grandmother's death that was the trigger, but her going into that home?'

'He'd been on his own in that house,' Duggie Wallace offered, 'with all those thoughts going around and around in his head.'

'A carrel from hell,' said Jimmy Hulme

'A whirlpool of wretchedness,' suggested Henry Powell.

Carter stared at them. 'What is this?' he said. 'Who's got the crappiest simile?'

'Let's put his state of mind aside for the moment,' Caton said, 'and have a look at what we've actually got.'

He listed them off on his fingers. 'All those library books; items missing that could theoretically be used to produce those pills; evidence that he has a bike of some kind; that he didn't want anyone to know those things *were* missing; several latent footprints lifted from two crime scenes; and the shoes we've bagged up that look like they may well match those prints for size and shape, if not the precise tread.' He paused. 'Question: is there anything that might tell us where he's staying?'

'Not yet,' said Carter, 'but Jack Benson reckons there's a load of paperwork from his study to go through. He said he couldn't remove it all because there's stuff that belonged to the grandmother, like deeds and other legal documents, that we can't claim is likely to be of substantial value to the investigation, especially since it's currently subject to probate. But there's a chance that among the rest he may find orders, receipts or invoices relating to the purchase of the pill-making equipment, etcetera.'

For himself, Caton doubted that someone as forensically aware and borderline obsessive-compulsive as Germaine would make such a schoolboy error. Jimmy Hulme's phone began to ring. He turned away to take the call.

'Boss,' he said, holding out his mobile, 'it's the control room. They've had a call from one of the mountain-bike patrols who think they may have had a sighting. D'you want to take it?'

Caton popped the lid of a tub of antiseptic wipes on the nearest desk, rubbed the palms of his hands and took the phone.

'DCI Caton,' he said. 'What have you got for me?'

'My colleague and I spotted someone coming towards us without any lights on his bike. We decided to wait for him to come to us, but he must've clocked us somehow, because when he was about fifty yards away, he suddenly turned tail and sped away. We gave chase but we lost him after less than a mile.'

'Where was this?'

'Sale. We spotted him where the National Cycle Network N62 meets the Mersey Path, right by junction seven of the M60.'

That was within spitting distance of the first of the crime scenes. Caton felt a surge of adrenalin. The Chester Road interchange.

'Where did you lose him?'

'About a mile due west, where the Mersey Path goes under the A6144 bridge.' The officer faltered. '. . . I'm sorry, Sir.'

'Don't be,' Caton told him. 'You did right to ring it in straight away. Where are you now?'

'Right where we lost him.'

'Good. Stay there, preferably out of sight. If he comes back, arrest whoever it is.'

'Er . . . for what?'

'Riding a bike on a shared cycle and pedestrian path, without lights, in the dark.'

'It's not exactly a public highway, Sir . . .'

'Failing that, use your imagination!'

Caton handed the phone back.

'Get me NPAS,' he said. 'I want eyes in the sky.'

The three cars, along with a Land Rover Defender Caton had blagged from South Division, were parked up on the A6144 bridge, overlooking the River Mersey. Henry Powell and Carly Whittle were in the Land Rover. DCs Franklin and Nair were in the next two cars. Caton himself and Nick Carter were in the BMW X3 Command vehicle. Carter had his window down, and was wearing a mask. Due to Covid-19, there was no observer in the back to log the thinking behind Caton's every decision. Instead, all channels had to remain open at all times so that every word could be recorded in the control room.

NPAS 22 circled somewhere above them, its engines churning like some deranged washing machine. The *whup-whup* of the rotor blades and the downdraught thrumming against the roof told them it was directly overhead. The powerful NightSun searchlight scythed through the night sky, briefly captured the waves on the ink-black surface of the river, danced across the Meccano-like footbridge, and homed in on the pair of officers standing beside their mountain bikes, before banking away along the Mersey Path where it suddenly disappeared.

'They've switched to thermal imaging,' Carter observed.

'NPAS 22,' said Caton, 'this is Bronze Command. Can we have visual, please?'

'Roger, Bronze Command,' came the reply, 'sending now.'

In the BMW, the blank touchscreen on the dashboard console on the passenger side sprang into life. Now they had a bird's-eye view from the forward-pointing infrared camera up on the chopper. They could see the loops and twists of the River Mersey as it snaked its way like an ugly varicose vein across the Lancashire plain. The banks on either side alternated between ribbons of woodland or meadow that came down to the path alongside the canal.

The camera zoomed out, revealing neat squares of arable land, a golf course, the peat beds of Carrington Moss, and random incursions of housing where Urmston edged its way greedily into the green belt. To the south-west, Caton spotted 'Fortress Carrington', Man United's state-of-the-art training facility.

'No wonder they lost him,' Carter said. 'He could be anywhere by now.'

He was right, Caton reflected. And for all they knew, the cycle patrol had disturbed someone unconnected to Operation Pendle Hill – a casual burglar, a petty criminal, someone riding a stolen bike. And ACC Gates, who because of the potentially hazardous nature of this operation, had been called from her nice warm bed to take on Gold Command at the Central Park Command Room, had initiated the major incident protocols, informed the fire service, NHS, Public Health England. There was a hazmat team, an ambulance, a dog unit and a custody van on the way, as well as an Armed Response team on standby. With all that and the helicopter, if this turned out to be a false alarm, the fallout was going to be massive. In that event, he would not be looking forward to the debrief.

The camera zoomed in again, narrowing the search area to cover five separate farms, each with a number of outbuildings.

'Bronze Command to NPAS 22,' Caton said. 'Can you take a closer look at those buildings, please?'

'Roger that, Bronze Command,' said the tactical flight officer.

They watched as the camera homed in on each of the clusters of buildings in turn. There were telltale borders of white around several of the windows of the first farmhouse, where heat from a fire or central heating leached from inadequate glazing. The second of the farmhouses had lights on in one of the rooms on the upper storey.

'Someone's awake,' Carter observed. 'Probably woken by the helicopter.'

'Keep your eyes peeled for that van,' Caton said.

There were assorted trucks and vans that had seen better times in the courtyard, and several caravans behind a barn. The camera took a closer look, before moving on to the next farm.

Powell's voice came over the radio. 'What the hell is that, Boss?' he said. 'The roof and windows of one of the outbuildings – that long single-storey building – all lit up like Blackpool Illuminations.'

'At a guess,' said the TFO, 'it's either a farm with battery chickens, or someone's growing cannabis.'

'Can you take a look at those vehicles in the yard behind that building?' Caton asked.

There were two trucks, a Ford Transit van and a Land Rover. Nothing that resembled the one belonging to Germaine. As the helicopter slowly moved away from the outbuildings, a light came on in the porch of the farmhouse and the door opened. NPAS 22 hovered overhead. Someone stepped out into the yard and stared up at the sky – a white blob caught in the centre of the thermal image, reminiscent of Neil Armstrong on the surface of the moon.

'If that *is* a cannabis farm, he'll be pissing his pants,' Carter muttered, just loud enough for them all to hear.

'This is Gold Command. Let's stick to the protocol,' Helen Gates said testily.

'Sorry, Ma'am,' Carter responded, pulling a face.

The image on the screen changed as the helicopter travelled westwards. The next cluster of buildings was more compact. Main house, stables, three barns and a small field containing five caravans. Without waiting to be asked, the TFO zoomed in, one by one, on the vehicles parked in the various yards.

'Negative. Negative. Negative,' he said. 'What do you want us to do, Bronze Command?' Caton stared at the coloured satnav map on his main console. It bore little relation to the bleak shades of black and grey captured by the thermal camera. The eerie silence as they waited for his reply bore down on him. He knew that each one of them was waiting on a flash of inspiration. Expecting him to read the mind of a man he'd never met – to magic him out of this jumble of woods and fields and tree-lined boundaries. The helicopter was almost back overhead now, forcing him to raise his voice.

'Can you make one more sweep, starting due south of my position,' Caton said, 'and then directly north, towards the B5213. There's all those woods between Banky Lane, the bend in the river and the start of the housing estate.'

'Roger that.'

A new voice hit the airways. 'Kilo 97, now on station.'

'Copy that, Kilo 97,' Carter responded. He turned to Caton. 'The dog's arrived,' he said.

The sound of the engines and rotors slowly receded. Caton switched his gaze to the laptop. The camera lingered over a wooded area beside a sewage farm, and suddenly the screen was filled with a dazzling chequerboard of bright white light.

'Sorry!' exclaimed the TFO, as the camera panned swiftly away. 'That was a solar-panel farm that powers the treatment works.'

The helicopter now crossed the ink-black oxbow of the river, scanning the woods below, before tracking north to cross the Mersey again. It then hovered over an object in the field below as the camera zoomed in for a closer look. It was a motorhome.

'What's that doing there?' Carter wondered.

'This is Bronze Command,' Caton said. 'Is there any possibility you get the registration of that vehicle?'

'We can pick out a registration at two thousand feet and feed it straight to ANPR and the national database,' the TFO responded.

The helicopter swooped to the right and descended. The camera display showed it hovering at one thousand feet, facing the rear of the motorhome. Carter pointed to the bike clamped to the rack on the back of the vehicle.

'Well, well!' he said.

The licence plate was clear enough for them to make out the details for themselves. Carter fed them into the database on his tablet and the result came back a fraction earlier than for NPAS 22.

'Registered keeper, Bernadette S O'Regan.' He looked across at Caton. 'That's . . .'

'Nathan Germaine's grandmother,' Caton said.

Chapter 69
Urmston. 0130 hours.

The door of the motorhome flew open and a figure emerged. The shape and the way it moved told them it was a male. It ran to the rear of the vehicle, and began to unhook one of the two bikes suspended there.

Caton checked the satnav and cursed under his breath. The suspect was less than a third of a mile away across the river and the fields, but three and a bit by road.

'Bravo Papa Two,' he said. 'The suspect is less than a third of a mile ahead of you along the Mersey Path, currently mounting a pedal bike. NPAS 22 have eyes on. Follow their directions. Proceed with caution at all times. We know he's dangerous, but we have no idea if or how he may be armed. We also have reason to suspect that he may be in possession of a dangerous substance. Do *not* attempt to arrest him until support arrives. Do you understand?'

'Roger that,' responded one of the officers on the bike patrol. 'Proceeding as instructed.'

Caton started the engine. 'Bronze Command, requesting permission for blues and twos,' he said.

'Lights only,' came the swift reply, 'unless circumstances dictate otherwise.'

He understood the reasoning. Most people were spooked enough by the lockdown without five vehicles and their two-tone sirens wailing at this time of night.

'Roger that,' he said. 'Golf Mike One Zero, Hotel Oscar Papa, Victor X-ray Golf, and Kilo Nine Seven, with me. Blues only, no siren. The rest of you, remain on station and await instruction.'

Helen Gates's voice burst onto the air waves. 'All contact with the suspect and that vehicle as per the Risk Assessment, please!'

'Roger that, Gold Command,' Carter replied. 'We have it right here.'

He read it out from his tablet as Caton sped over the bridge and hurtled down the slipway onto the M60, heading west. In his wing mirror, he could see the rest of his team and the Vauxhall Astra van belonging to the dog unit in close order behind him.

'"Possible substances, potassium cyanide or sodium cyanide, in liquid solution, or salt crystals,' Carter read out. 'Potential hazards – poisoning from skin contact or inhalation. Minimum personnel protective equipment essential as follows: CSI barrier suit, including close-toed shoe coverings and mask; disposable gloves – nitrile rather than latex. On discovery of suspect chemicals, all handling and removal to be conducted using hazmat protection . . ."'

He was interrupted by the voice of the tactical flight officer.

'Suspect is cycling east towards the Mersey Path,' he said. 'Bravo Papa 2 and Bravo Papa 3, you should have eyes on in less than two minutes.'

'Maybe we should've stayed where we were?' Carter said.

'Too late now,' Caton told him.

The BMW was touching eighty as they approached Junction 9. Ahead of them, the motorway lay empty. Caton took the first slip road, then slowed as he turned left onto the B5158.

'The suspect has stopped . . . The suspect has stopped. Suspect is turning around . . . Turning around.

He's now heading due west. Bravo Papa 2, do you have eyes on?'

'Negative. That's a negative . . . Hang on – we have eyes on! We *do* have eyes on!'

'NPAS 22. Where is he heading?' Caton asked.

'He's on a path across fields, south of the motorhome. The path leads into a large wood, beyond which is . . . what looks like . . . stabling, and then Urmston Cemetery. Papa Bravo 2 and 3 are approximately ninety yards behind, but the gap is widening.'

'That's because it's black as sin out here, and we can't see where we're going,' said one of the officers on the bike patrol. 'The path is up and down and rutted . . . We no longer have eyes on. Can you spotlight him for us, please, NPAS 22?'

'That's a negative, Papa Bravo' said the FTO. 'We can't use our thermal imager and the NightSun at the same time. The suspect is now in the trees, and we would only have glimpses of him with the searchlight. Just keep heading for the northernmost corner of the woods.'

Caton consulted the satnav. There were nine hundred yards to go to the Davyhulme Circle, then it was virtually a straight mile, down Crofts Bank Road and Queens Road, to the point where the suspect would likely emerge from the woods.

'The suspect is among the trees. One hundred and twenty yards ahead of Papa Bravo. He'll know we're here, but he won't be able to see us,' said the FTO.

'Just don't lose him,' Carter said.

'There's no fear of that,' came the reply. 'Not unless he enters a building.'

'That's probably what he's hoping for,' Carter said. 'Once he clears those trees, he'll have a choice of trying to lose himself in the estate, or those farm buildings straight ahead of him.'

'That's why we've got the dog unit,' Caton said.

'Suspect clear of the trees, close to the river . . . following the path north, slowing at a bridge, dismounting . . . There's some kind of obstacle.'

The camera zoomed in. There was a large, light grey blob in the centre of the bridge. They could see the suspect slowing as he approached.

'Looks like someone's put a rock on there to deter joyriders and illegal dumpers,' Carter said.

'The suspect is remounting,' said the FTO. 'Papa Bravo about to exit the woods.'

'We have eyes on . . .' said Papa Bravo One. '. . . Eyes on!'

'That rock's going to slow them down and all,' Carter observed.

The lights were on as the convoy approached the four-way junction with the B5213. Caton gave it a blast of siren as he prepared to go straight through.

'Woah!' shouted Carter.

Two young women were stepping into the road outside the Istanbul Grill.

Carter clung on to the grab handle as Caton stabbed at the brake and swerved around them.

The two females stood in stunned amazement, clinging to each other for protection, as the procession of vehicles sped past, their blue lights strobing the night sky.

'They'd got their earbuds in,' Carter declared.

'Where is he now?' Caton asked.

'Suspect has emerged onto the path beside the cemetery,' NPAS 22 informed them, 'heading north towards Queens Road . . . No . . . he's stopped . . . turned, is now crossing open ground . . . possibly a turning-circle, or car park. He has dismounted . . . and entered the trees. Suspect is now on foot. Papa Bravo 1 and 2 are seventy yards behind and closing.'

Carter pointed to his screen. 'He's heading for the cemetery.'

Caton checked the satnav.

'Victor X-Ray Golf and Hotel Oscar Papa, go left, left, left, and then right, right, right into Eeasbrook,' he ordered, 'then wait in that turning circle NPAS 22 mentioned. Golf-Mike One Zero, and Kilo Nine Seven, stay with me.'

'Suspect has entered the cemetery,' the FTO announced. 'Suspect is running.'

'He's heading our way,' Carter said. 'If he's hoping to lose the helicopter among these houses, he's in for a big surprise.'

Caton slowed as he approached the sandstone pillars marking the entrance to Urmston Cemetery, and stopped. He thumped the steering wheel with his fist.

The BMW's headlights had picked out the large steel padlock hanging from the heavy wrought-iron gates. The gates were closed.

'That side gate,' Caton said, 'if it's not unlocked, you should be able to vault it. Take Carly and the K9 team with you. Tell DC Powell to knock up the cemetery keeper and get these gates open.'

'On my way,' Carter responded, flinging the door open.

'And don't get up close and personal,' Caton shouted after him.

'No need to shout,' Helen Gates reminded him calmly. 'Not if they've got their radios on.'

'Sorry, Gold Command,' Caton said. 'Heat of the moment.'

Caton watched as Carter, Whittle and the dog handler clambered over the narrow side gate. The German shepherd cleared it in a single bound. The three of them then set off down the central driveway. In his peripheral vision, Caton glimpsed DC Powell running up the path of the imposing Victorian house beside the gates. He turned off the ignition and switched his attention to the feed from NPAS 22.

It irked him that as Bronze Commander, he could only sit there and watch it unfold on a screen, but consoled himself with the knowledge that he wasn't entirely divorced from the action. They all danced to his tune . . . in theory.

The TFO was no longer providing a commentary.

There was no need. The pictures spoke for themselves. The suspect had almost reached the neo-Gothic chapel. The two patrol officers were less than fifty yards behind on their mountain bikes and closing in fast. Carter, Whittle, the dog and her handler converged on the chapel from the opposite direction. The suspect looked over his shoulder and upped his pace as he ran up to the central arch between the two side chapels, where he disappeared. Caton waited for him to reappear on the opposite side, where he would come face to face with the rest of his team, less than twenty-odd yards away.

He waited in vain, and instead had to watch as both teams arrived simultaneously and slowed to walking pace. The dog strained at its leash. Caton lowered the windows, and listened to its furious barking.

'This is Bronze Command,' he said. 'Do you have eyes on? Over.'

There was a long pause. He watched as Carter stepped closer. The infrared camera captured the bright spear of light from his torch as he probed the dark maw beneath the arch.

Caton changed the display to show split screens, one of them now revealing the live stream from Carter's body cam. The suspect was crouching on a step in the entrance to one of the side chapels, pinned like a moth by the beam of light. His back pressed against the wooden door, he had drawn his knees up to his chest, with his arms folded over his face.

'Eyes on, Bronze Control,' Carter said. 'We have eyes on.'

'Do not approach,' Caton told them. 'I repeat … do not approach. Make him come to you. I'm on my way. Out.'

The cemetery keeper was already opening the gates. DC Powell hovered expectantly by the passenger window of the BMW.

'Got your mask with you, Henry?' Caton asked.

Powell shook his head. 'It's in the glove compartment of the Astra,' he said. 'I didn't need it with Carly and me being a bubble.'

'Shame we're not,' Caton said, starting up the engine, 'But it won't hurt to stretch your legs.'

'Nothing!' Carter exclaimed. 'After all that, he's completely bloody clean.'

They watched as Nathan Germaine, clad in a white CSI Tyvek coverall, climbed into the back of the custody van with a little encouragement from the German shepherd.

'What did you expect?' Caton responded. 'That he was going to cycle over all that rough ground in the dark, with a vial of cyanide in his back pocket?'

They had made him stand apart on the chapel approach, in the centre of the circle of light from their headlights, empty his pockets, and remove the jeans and chunky knit pullover he had hastily donned before fleeing the motorhome. Then he had been cuffed and patted down by a member of the hazmat team, before being led away.

It had made an eerie tableau, in the middle of a graveyard at the dead of night. With the helicopter long gone, it was silent but for the shuffling of feet and the muted instructions. Their breaths out had formed wispy clouds that rippled in the halo where light met night.

'Well, at least we've got the right person,' Carter said. 'Not that he helped us with that. Couldn't even bring himself to say *No comment*.'

According to Duggie Wallace, there was not the slightest trace of Nathan Germaine on the web. No social media sites or even the whisker of a mention. They had only been able to identify him thanks to a photo taken from his grandmother's dressing table.

They watched as the custody van set off, followed closely by Detective Constables Nair and Franklin.

'The clock is ticking,' Caton said, opening the driver's door of the BMW. 'Let's start with that motorhome.'

* * *

It took less than five minutes for the hazmat team to declare it safe to enter. Another ten for Jack Benson's team to take their photos, and mark out areas for further investigation.

'You're good to go,' Benson said, 'but there's not a lot for you to see.'

'That wasn't what we wanted to hear,' Carter said, stating the obvious.

'And it's probably best if you go in one at a time. There's barely room to swing a cat.'

The interior was spotlessly clean and obsessively tidy. The only sign that anyone had been staying here was the bed with its crumpled pillows and the duvet thrown back.

A book lay on the floor beside the bed. Caton picked it up and read the front cover. *Gateway To Hell* by Dennis Wheatley. Caton recalled reading the entire Duke de Richelieu series in his third year at Manchester Grammar. They had scared and excited him in equal measure. He opened it to see if this was another former library book. On the second page he found an inscription.

To Nathan. Xmas 1992. Love Grandma X

How old had the neighbour said Germaine was? Thirty-eight. That made him all of ten years old when his grandmother presented him with this book. Had she unwittingly fed the malleable imagination of an already vulnerable child?

He remembered reading an account of the favourite books of some of the world's most notorious serial killers. The Unabomber had been into Joseph Conrad. Bizarrely, Charles Manson's favourite book was reportedly *How to Win Friends and Influence People*. John Lennon's killer had been sitting on the kerb, reading *The Catcher in the Rye* when arrested; he even borrowed the name of the central character when asked to identify himself. And Ted Bundy claimed to have read *Papillon* over and over again while languishing in prison. There was, Caton decided, no accounting for taste. He put the book back where he had found it.

A narrow door opened into a Tardis-like wet room, with a toilet, shower and single vanity unit. Over the basin, an electric toothbrush and an electric razor sat in tubs on a shelf. Two towels hung neatly folded from a rail. Caton closed the door and opened the fridge. It was neatly stacked with enough essentials to last a week. He assumed that the hazmat team had replaced them just as they had found them. He pulled out the three drawers of the freezer mounted below. They were stocked with meat, fish, oven chips and frozen vegetables. No body parts. No dead cats. Nothing that screamed serial killer.

He next turned his attention to the cupboards, and found jackets and jeans on hangers, and sweaters and T-shirts rolled and stacked by colour. Footwear sat in the bottom of the wardrobe, with gaps where the CSI had removed a pair for potential matching. Beneath the bed, in a drawer covered in CSI evidence tape, Caton discovered a laptop, a modem, three mobile phones, a disk drive, and boxes containing recordable disks, data cards and USB flash drives. He itched to know what treasures they might reveal. But what he needed most was something that would tie Germaine directly to the demise of the four victims. He closed the drawer, had a last look around and left. Carter was awaiting at the foot of the steps.

'Any surprises?' he asked.

'Not really. Just confirmation that he's been living here. And that he's obsessively fastidious.'

'He's a neatnik,' Carter said, his foot on the first step.

'Is that even a word?'

'Look it up, Boss,' Carter said as he disappeared.

'Boss!' Carly Whittle jogged towards him, came to a stop several yards away and pulled up her face mask.

'What's the panic, Carly?' he said. 'The suspect's already in custody.'

'DC Powell and I have been visiting the stables and farms around here,' she said. Her breath escaped in intermittent puffs of steam from the top and sides of her mask. 'DC Powell has tracked down the farmer who rented Germaine this land for his motorhome. You need to speak to him.'

'You could have used the radio?'

She shook her head. 'You'd never have found your own way there.'

'Fair enough,' he said. 'Lead on.'

Chapter 72

They crossed three fields, climbing stiles as they went, and passed through an open metal gate, before arriving in a farmyard surrounded by buildings.

DC Powell was standing beside a thick-set, middle-aged man wearing a Burberry overcoat over tracksuit bottoms. He had training shoes on his feet, and a grim expression on his face. In the backlit open doorway of the farmhouse stood a woman wearing a raspberry-coloured velour robe and slippers. Across the yard, a Rhodesian ridgeback strained at the chain around its neck. Powell was the only one wearing a mask.

'This is Mr Jacobs,' he said. 'He owns the field where Nathan Germaine has his motorhome.'

'How long has he been living there, Mr Jacobs?' Caton asked.

Jacobs scowled.

'He asked me four years ago if he could park it up on that field. We don't use it for anything else, so I said yes. But him living there was never part of the deal. I'm not sure when he started to do that because we've no cause to go down there much, but he's been working in the old stables more regular, like, for the past five weeks, so I should imagine that's when he started using it to sleep in.'

'What do you mean by "working in the old stables?"' Caton said.

'That was part of the deal. He asked if I had an outbuilding where he could park his work van and store his tools, so I rented him the old stables as well. We don't have any use for them. This isn't a working farm any more, and neither of us can ride a horse.' He glanced over his shoulder to check on his wife, gave her a reassuring smile and turned back. 'And we won't be interested in learning to neither, not at our age.'

'Could you show us the old stables, Mr Jacobs?' Caton asked.

'I can, but you won't be able to get inside. Mr Germaine put new padlocks on it.'

'You can leave that to us,' Caton said. 'If there's any damage, we'll make it good.'

They followed him around the back of the main house to where six padlocked windows with internal shutters and galvanised steel bars across them were set in a substantial brick building.

'Used to be a riding school,' Jacobs said. 'The main doors are down here.'

At the end of the building were full-height wooden doors secured by heavy-duty brass padlocks. A sliding bar ran between the handles.

'Looks like we need a pair of cutters or the twenty-four-hour locksmith, Boss,' DC Powell observed.

'Maybe not,' Caton said.

He pressed the number of the designated channel for the crime scene team on his Airwave radio.

'Mr Benson, this DCI Caton,' he said, and waited.

'This is Jack Benson,' came the response. 'How can I help? Over.'

'Have you come across any sets of keys in the suspect vehicle?' Caton asked. 'Over.'

'Say again?' said Benson.

Caton adjusted his mask and raised his voice. 'Have you come across any sets of keys? Over.'

'Received. Give me a moment, please.'

Twenty seconds later he was back.

'We have three sets, bagged up. Over.'

'Can you describe them, please? Over.'

'One set looks like a car key, a house key and the key for this motorhome. The second set has duplicates of the house key and the car key, and five others that look as though they might be for other external doors, garages or sheds. The final set has two large brass keys and a specialist key for a cabinet or safe. Over.'

'Do any of them look as though they're for large padlocks? Over.'

'The two brass ones.'

Caton smiled. 'I'm sending someone to collect them.'

'They've already been sealed away,' Benson said. 'You'll need to complete the chain of custody documentation and reseal the packaging. I'll give your courier some tape.'

'Received,' said Caton. 'Out.'

He smiled at Carly Whittle and raised his eyebrows.

'Oh, come on, Boss,' she protested. 'That's twice I've been there and back.'

Caton turned to her Covid bubble buddy.

'Looks like it's your turn for a little more exercise then, DC Powell,' he said. 'I'll time you.'

* * *

The bolts slid back without a squeak.

'He's been busy with the lubricant,' Jacobs joked. There was an underlying tension in his voice as he wondered what the hell his tenant had been up to. He pulled back one of the doors, Henry Powell the other. Then he stepped inside, and flicked a switch on the wall beside the door. The vast space was flooded with light from LED strips along the central beams, and above every stable.

'Solar panels,' Jacobs explained proudly. 'Cheap as chips.'

'We'll take it from here, Mr Jacobs,' Caton said. 'I'll give you a shout if I need you. And you've no need to concern yourself. For our record and your peace of mind, DS Whittle here will be recording everything we see and do on her body camera.

'Right,' he continued, 'let's take a look.'

A white Ford Transit Courier van stood less than five metres away. On the side was emblazoned:

PEMBERLEY GARDENING SERVICES
garden maintenance • lawn care
grass & hedge cutting
planting, shrub & tree pruning
REGULAR SERVICE AGREEMENTS AVAILABLE

'Pemberley?' said Henry Powell.

'*Pride and Prejudice*,' Carly Whittle responded. 'It was in Darcy's gardens at Pemberley that Elizabeth Bennett fell in love with him. His coming out of the woods in his undershirt was the clinching touch.'

Caton tried the doors. They were locked.

'Damn!' he said. 'I should have him asked him to give us the car keys as well.'

'I can open it,' Powell offered.

'No, it can wait,' Caton told him. 'Let's see what else there is.'

The first of the stalls held two lawnmowers, a scarifier and a seed-spreader. The next two were full of gardening equipment: strimmers, spades and forks, and hoes, loppers, pruners and trowels, all arranged by length and suspended from plastic hooks screwed into the woodwork.

The third stall held a wheelbarrow, a lawn roller, plastic bins and sacks. It was the fourth stall that lifted

Caton's hopes. Stacked along the side were tea chests, containing layer after layer of books. A metal chair and table stood against one wall with an outward-facing window. On the table were two small piles of books, and in a plastic tray beside them lay a pair of scissors, a biro and a scalpel.

Caton walked over to the table and examined the book on top of the righthand pile. It was a Manchester Libraries book: *Flower Arranging*, by Joyce Rogers, first published in 1972. He leafed through it and placed it back as he'd found it. He picked up the book on top of the left-hand pile: *Mary Berry's Ultimate Cake Book.* It looked well thumbed. He checked the date: first edition, 1994. He squinted at it, then held it up to the light. The folio page had been neatly excised.

He gestured for Carly Whittle to join him. 'I want a close up of this,' he said, holding the book open towards her.

Having replaced the book, he now crouched to look under the table. There, in a plastic waste basket was page after page listing the record of loans and returns from a succession of books. He placed the waste basket on the table, and stood back as she captured it on her body cam.

They moved on to the next stall. Under the window, they could see the metal legs of a table emerging from beneath a blue tarpaulin. Caton carefully removed the tarp and set it aside. On the melamine surface of the table stood a white metal box, twice the size of a microwave oven. A long handle protruded from one side, while on the front face were two screens and a row of dials.

'What's that?' Powell asked, as Carly leaned her body cam towards it.

'My guess,' Caton said, 'is that this is a pill blister-packing machine.'

He crouched down. Beneath the table was a metal

four-drawer cabinet. Caton tried the top drawer but it was locked, along with the others. He took the bunch of keys from his pocket, and tried the small steel key with a black cover. It clicked and turned smoothly in the lock at the side of the cabinet.

The top drawer was half-full of packets of painkillers. The second contained sheet after sheet of foil. The third held nitrile gloves and several face masks with filter inserts.

Caton had to squat on his haunches to reach the final drawer and slide it open. He held his breath, stood up, exhaled and moved back so the others could see

In the centre of the deep drawer was a single plastic tub with a screw top. It was approximately ten centimetres high and three centimetres in diameter.

On the front was a label printed with a red skull and crossbones.

'You both ready?' Caton asked.

'I reckon we're good to go, aren't we, Carly?' Carter replied.

'I can't wait,' Carly said.

'Off you go then,' Caton told them. 'Remember, don't let him rile you. Just stick to the interview strategy we've agreed.'

'Yes, Boss!' they chorused.

As the door closed behind them, he turned his attention to the bank of video screens. Three of them showed Nathan Germaine sitting alone in the interview room. Two tables had been placed two metres apart, with a large Perspex screen set up between them. Germaine lounged in his chair with his legs thrust out in front of him, his hands cupped behind his head. A face mask lay abandoned on the table in front of him. Occasionally, he glanced up at the video cameras in the angles where the walls met the ceilings. He was staring into one of them right now, challenging whoever was watching to look away.

'I can see now why he refused both to allow you to interview him remotely under the Coronavirus Amendment Act, or to have a solicitor advise him,' said Indra Laghari, the Chief Crown Prosecutor for the North West, via the video link from her office in Sunlight

House. 'This is his show and he has no intention of sharing the stage with anyone. Besides, I have no doubt that he would regard the taking of advice of any form as a sign of weakness.'

Caton agreed. 'Let's hope that extends to barristers too,' he said. 'That way there'd be no likelihood of a plea for mitigation by reason of insanity. It's not as though someone with this attitude is going to declare himself insane.'

'I wouldn't be too sure,' she responded. 'You said yourself you think he's a game-player. In a high secure hospital like Rampton, he could see out his days in a never-ending battle of wits with the psychiatrists, not to mention they'd probably make use of his expertise in the hospital library.'

Caton shook his head. It was a depressing thought. 'Here they come,' he said.

They watched on screen as DI Carter and DS Whittle entered the room. Each of them carried a thick Perspex folder, and wore clear, anti-static, anti-smog and splash-proof face-shield visors. Carly Whittle also carried a box file. Germaine observed them with studied indifference.

'At least this way, the court will be able to draw an adverse inference from his silence, and he won't be able to claim that we didn't give him proper opportunity to provide a full account,' Caton said.

In the interview room, the two detectives glanced at each other. Carter nodded his head, and Carly Whittle made the introductions.

'I am Detective Sergeant Carly Whittle and my colleague is Detective Inspector Nick Carter,' she said. 'This interview is being audio-recorded, together with simultaneous visual recording by the cameras positioned here and here.' She pointed to them. 'Can you confirm, Nathan, that you have been given and have declined the right to have a solicitor advise you in person, by video or telephone?'

They waited for a response. When none was forthcoming, she pressed on.

'Can you confirm, Nathan, that you have been given personal protective equipment, but have declined to use it?'

Again, there was no response. Instead, he regarded her with something like amusement.

'Finally,' she said, 'I am obliged to remind you that you are still under caution, and that your failure or refusal to account for objects, substances and marks, including footwear, found at the place of your arrest, in your possession, or at a scene of crime, may result in inferences being drawn by the jury that may harm your defence in court. Do you understand, Nathan?'

This time when Germaine stared back at Carly, his face was devoid of expression, but there was a look of contempt in his eyes.

Carly sat back. Carter opened the folder in front of him.

'Why, earlier this morning, when you were ordered to stop by a police helicopter, did you fail to do so and, instead, hide in Urmston Cemetery in an attempt to evade the police?'

'No comment.'

His voice was deep and cultured, with a hint of a Manchester accent, the vowels slightly exaggerated. His tone was disdainful.

Carter selected the first of a series of photographs. 'How do you account for a van registered in your name, and for which you are the registered keeper, appearing in the vicinity of a crime scene in Trafford, on Thursday the first of April this year, just three days before a woman was found murdered there?'

'No comment.'

'How do you account for the fact that a print made from the shoe you were wearing early this morning when arrested, and a print lifted from the floor of the garage in the house belonging to your deceased grandmother, and where you have been living since 1996, match footprints recovered at the site of two murders?'

'No comment.'

'How do you account for the fact that cycle tyre tracks found at the back of a house belonging to DCI Caton match those of a bike found in your possession?'

'No comment.'

Carter leaned back in his seat, turned to Carly Whittle and nodded. She opened the box file, selected an evidence bag and laid it on the table in front of him.

'Nathan, how do you account for this CD, found in the same property that you're renting at Siegrith Farm, which contains the private names and addresses of Manchester residents?'

He sighed. 'No comment.'

'Can you explain the purpose to which you have put or intend to put this information?'

'No comment.'

She selected another evidence bag. 'How do you account, Nathan, for this USB drive, found in the same property, that contains a comprehensive list of Manchester library cardholders?'

'No comment.'

'Can you explain the purpose to which you *have* put or *intend* to put this information?'

Germaine yawned. 'No comment.'

Carly put the evidence bags back in the box file, opened her folder and produced a new image.

'Nathan,' she said, 'we have forensically examined

this laptop recovered from the motorhome in which we believe you to have been living. How do you account for the fact that this laptop has been used to access the Manchester Libraries database by means of a password belonging to one of your former colleagues who is still employed in that service?'

'No comment.'

She showed him another picture. 'Nathan, this is a photograph of a page that was found in a waste basket in the property that you are renting at Siegrith Farm. How do you account for the fact that this page matches one removed from a former library-stock book found at the scene of a murder in Heald Green?'

'No comment.'

She placed the photos back in her folder, and sat back.

'Mr Germaine,' Carter said, holding up another photo, 'how do you account for this jar of potassium cyanide salt, which was discovered in a building rented by you at Siegrith Farm on Urmston Meadows?'

His lips barely moved. They had to strain to hear him. 'No comment.'

Carter produced the next photograph. 'How do you account for these foil blister packs found in the same building rented by you at Siegrith Farm, which are from an identical batch to ones containing a mixture of painkillers and cyanide that were found in the homes of four deceased women?'

'No comment.'

Carter folded his arms on the table and stared at Germaine. 'I put it to you, Nathan,' he said, 'that what my colleague and I have just presented to you is overwhelming evidence that you meticulously planned, over a considerable period of time, to murder at least four elderly women, by poisoning them with potassium cyanide, which you mixed with a common painkiller and manufactured into a form that would deceive them into believing it to be said painkiller. That you used previous contact with these women through your work as an employee of the Manchester Library Service and intimate knowledge of their reading habits to gain their confidence, such that they would accept from you a book and sundry other items as presents, together with the painkillers adulterated with poison by you.'

He paused to let this sink in, and took a sip of water. 'Nathan,' he said, 'this is your final opportunity to provide a full and proper account of your involvement in this matter, including an explanation of your motives, and also to inform us of any other person or persons to whom you may have sent or delivered these pills?'

The three detectives and the officer of the CPS watched and waited, but without any great expectation.

Nathan Germaine stared up at the camera to his right. For the first time, he actually smiled. 'No comment,' he said.

As if they had been practising, Nick Carter and Carly Whittle closed their folders with a simultaneous snap.

'Interview concluded at twelve hundred hours,' Carter announced.

Nathan Germaine watched as the two of them pushed back their chairs, stood up and left the room. He transferred his attention to one of the cameras, with the same inexplicable expression of triumph on his face. The red light on the camera blinked once and disappeared. Deprived of an audience, his smile dissolved. He folded his arms, bowed his head and closed his eyes.

In the observation suite, Caton turned his attention to the screen where the North West Director of Public Prosecutions had been watching via the video link.

'Well?' he said.

'You can him charge him,' Indra Laghari replied, 'with five offences under the Poisons Act 1972, along with the murder of all five victims.'

'Including Martha Riley?'

'Absolutely,' she said. 'I don't need to remind you that the absence of a body or physical remains of any kind has not been an impediment to a charge of murder since a case in 1954 involving the disappearance of a Polish farmer in Wales. All that is needed is circumstantial evidence pointing to only one possible conclusion – that the victim was murdered by the accused. I think we can safely say you have that, don't you?'

Caton did, although he took little pleasure in it. Professional satisfaction was one thing, but it was not going to bring those four women back, nor diminish the grief and guilt felt by Sally Buller or Stella and Leah Unsworth. He made a mental note to ring Stella and find out how her sister was doing in hospital.

'How do you think he came by his former colleague's password four years after he'd left?' she said. 'My understanding is that the city council requires its employees to change their passwords on a regular basis. Is there any possibility of collusion?'

'I doubt it,' Caton replied, 'although we will be looking into that. My guess is that each time, she will have simply added a one to the last or first digit of her password, or something like that. Whatever her practice was, he must have known it and exploited it.'

'Tom,' she said, 'do you think there are any more women still out there with a packet of painkillers sitting in their medicine cabinet like a ticking time bomb?'

'I hope to God there aren't,' he replied. 'With the amount of publicity there's been, there can't be many people who aren't aware of the threat. I'm just worried that there may be someone out there with dementia, or who neither watches TV nor listens to the radio, that we haven't reached. The IT team have been going through his computer to see if there's anyone else he's taken a special interest in.'

'And . . .?'

'So far, so good,' he said.

Chapter 74
Friday 10th April
Nexus House. 1345 hours.

'What do you think, Boss?' said Carly Whittle. 'Mad or bad?'

'What do you reckon?' he said.

'Bit of both?'

'That's a cop-out. No pun intended. Is he fit to plead or not?'

'Definitely.'

'Definitely what?'

'Fit to plead.'

'Then you're saying he's sane?'

She shook her head. 'I'm not sure what I'm saying. Okay, I get that his parents' divorce, his mother abandoning him, it messed him up. His grandma dying like that finally pushed him over the edge. But what makes him different from the tens of thousands of others who've experienced exactly that, and much, much worse? The ones that pulled themselves together and got on with it?'

'Not all of them,' he pointed out. 'You're forgetting the ones who developed chronic depression; the ones who became abusers or abused; the ones who left home one day and never returned; the addicts; the ones who took their own lives.'

'When you put it like that,' she said, 'it's like he's at the extreme end of a continuum of human wretchedness.'

'Does he seem to wretched to you?' Caton asked.

She shook her head again. 'Far from it – that's what makes him different. But I have no idea why.'

'Unless he's prepared to tell us, we'll never know. And I don't believe he will.'

'Why not, Boss?'

'Because silence is the one remaining hold he has over us. I predict that he's going to plead not guilty, and then insist on taking the stand in that courtroom, with the eyes of the world on him, and refuse to answer a single question. That way he'll become an enigma. Theories will abound as to his motivation. Books will be written about him – books that will take their place on the shelves in the very libraries that were so much a part of his life. His place in history will be secure. He'll know that long after his death he will have achieved something he never managed in life. He will be deemed a remarkable man, albeit a notorious one.'

'He's shown no remorse whatsoever,' she observed. 'On the contrary, I get the impression he's enjoying it.'

'Of course he is. My guess is that he's been waiting for this all his adult life.'

'And then the pandemic came along and gave him the opportunity he needed.'

'Exactly.'

'That's truly evil,' she said.

Caton smiled. 'You got there in the end.'

'Let's hope the jury does the same,' Jimmy Hulme chipped in.

'What do you mean?' Henry Powell asked. 'They're bound to find him guilty.'

'But of what?' Hulme responded. 'Of murder or of manslaughter? What if the defence go with diminished responsibility? Then he's put in a secure psychiatric unit, and maybe fifteen, twenty years down the line, he tells the doctors how sorry he is, how he understands the error of his ways and he'll never do it again. Next minute, he's out on licence, planning his next escapade.'

'Is that even possible, Boss?' said Powell.

'I have a hunch that Germaine would resist such a move,' Caton said. 'Any suggestion that he was not responsible for his actions would diminish the magnitude of what he sees as his achievement. But in the unlikely event that his defence team do manage to persuade him to go for it, their argument will fail. Having a warped sense of right and wrong is not the same as having your mental functions impaired.' He turned to DS Hulme. 'Stop winding him up,' he said. 'Just tell him.'

Hulme grinned. 'There are four tests for diminished responsibility,' he said, ticking them off on his fingers. 'Is he suffering from mental instability or some mental abnormality? Does he have a recognised medical condition that might explain his actions? If so, does it impair his ability to make rational decisions, exercise self-control, and understand the nature of his conduct? And finally, does any of that explain his actions?'

'Not bad,' Caton said. 'Almost word-perfect. And you, Powell, take note. You'll be able to do that when you've passed your sergeant's exams. The question is, where does that leave us in this case? Whilst Germaine's decision to kill those women was irrational, the manner in which he did so was not. There were no mysterious voices guiding him through every stage of the process. There was no spontaneous outburst of rage. He planned these murders meticulously over months if not years, and executed that plan in a completely logical and highly rational manner.'

He paused and looked over at the photo of Nathan Germaine in the centre of the whiteboard, surrounded by his victims.

'That is what disturbs the rest of us most about serial killers,' he said. 'Their actions may be profoundly immoral and wicked, but many of them are as sane as you and me.'

He glanced towards his office briefly. 'Time to go home, everyone,' he said, 'before your families forget what you look like.'

He stopped and turned to face them. 'I know it feels like an eternity, but it's actually only six days since Millie Dyer's body was found. This is probably the fastest successful investigation of a serial killer in history. You should all be really proud of yourselves.' He had another thought. 'That book he left at my back door – the title was *Will You Remember Me?* I promise you this, Germaine will only ever be remembered as an evil, malevolent aberration. You, on the other hand, will be remembered as heroes.'

'Boss!' Josh Nair was standing at his desk, with his hand in the air clutching a landline phone.

'What is it?' Caton asked.

'CrimeStoppers are on,' Nair said. 'They've got a guy on hold who says he's just discovered that his mother received a package a couple of weeks ago containing a book, some chocolates and a packet of painkillers that he reckons fits the description he saw on the television.'

'Put him through to my office,' Caton said.

Chapter 75

'Where is it your mother lives?' Caton asked. He had put it on speakerphone so that Carter, standing in the doorway, could hear.

'Barlow Moor,' came the reply.

Caton nodded. Between Chorltonville and Sharston. Right in the middle of the kill zone.

'May I speak with her?' Caton asked.

'I'm sorry,' the son said, 'but Mum's in no state to speak to anyone. I'm afraid I panicked when I saw those painkillers and realised they were exactly the same as the ones everyone was warned about on the telly and in the papers. I told her they were stuffed full of poison. What was she thinking, taking them from a stranger? I shouted at her and called her stupid.' His voice was full of remorse. 'She's in the early stages of Alzheimer's and it's the worst thing you can do – calling them stupid or drawing attention to their short-term memory loss. She's in shock and won't even speak to me.'

This wasn't what Caton had been hoping to hear. 'That's a shame,' he said. 'I don't suppose you know how she came by them?'

The man's voice brightened. 'As a matter of fact, I do. It was the book I saw first – she'd already eaten the chocolates. I asked her where she got it from. She said the nice young man who used to work on the mobile library van called her a few weeks back and said he'd like to send her a little something to help her through the lockdown.'

'Did she mention his name?'

'I'm not sure he gave it or that she would even have remembered it if he had. It's the names they lose first. But she remembered his voice and was able to describe him. She said he was about my age – I'm late thirties – blondish hair, a bit curly, very quiet, but always polite and charming. He always asked her what she'd thought about the book she was returning, and then often recommended another. She was very sad when the mobile library stopped coming.'

'Did she say how he got the book to her?'

'Apparently, he rang her up and told her where he'd left the package. I think she said it was outside her back door.' He paused. 'There was one thing though . . .'

'Go on,' Caton said.

'He told her she mustn't tell anyone about their conversation or the gift. It was to be their secret. Because if anyone found out, he'd get into trouble with his bosses, on account of they weren't supposed to have favourites.'

'Thank you so much for calling CrimeStoppers,' Caton said. 'You have no idea how much this means. Can you do us another favour and hang onto those pills until I've sent someone to collect them?'

'Of course,' the son said. 'And don't worry, I won't be taking any in the meantime.'

He was trying to sound upbeat, but Caton wasn't fooled.

'I hope your mother recovers soon,' he said.

'With any luck, she'll have forgotten all about it by tomorrow.' The man paused. 'As for the dementia, that's only going to get worse, but at least she's still alive.'

Caton ended the call.

'The cunning bastard!' Carter said. 'So that's how he got away with it.'

'He didn't,' Caton reminded him. 'Not completely.

But this tells us there could still be some of his little trick-or-treat parcels out there, so we need to get the press office to renew their efforts to push that message that people need to remain vigilant.'

'I'm on it, Boss,' Carter said. 'You've got an investigation to write up.'

It was surreal. The streets were lined with people clapping the key workers. Banging saucepans, blowing kazoos and vuvuzelas. There was even someone waving a wooden football rattle.

Given the circumstances, Caton could have been forgiven for accepting it as a personal accolade for himself and his syndicate. But he was too busy remembering the nurses, Thelma Green and Angela Malhotra, and Janice Jackson – the care worker – all of whom he'd had no option but to regard as potential suspects. Their job was tough enough under normal circumstances, and the nation's lack of preparedness had left them exposed as they went into battle to protect their patients from Covid-19.

In his experience, the term hero was too easily applied to the instinctive reactions people made when faced with a sudden emergency. What these men and women on the frontline were doing was of a totally different order. Returning day after day, ill-prepared and under-resourced, staring death in the face. Seeing their colleagues struck down one after another, and wondering if it was going to be their turn next. Forced to say goodbye to the dying on behalf of their families, and then, when it was all over, having to find some words of consolation to share with those who had been left behind. And finally, going home to their own children and partners, physically and emotionally exhausted, terrified and riven with guilt that they might well be bringing the virus with them. *Hero* barely did justice to these Covid warriors.

Caton turned into his driveway, stopped the car and lowered his window. It was a cool dry evening, the air scented with drifting cherry blossom and hyacinth. He took a deep breath and let it out slowly. Spirits raised, he set the alarm on the car, and let himself into the house.

'Daddy!'

Emily hurtled down the hall to hug him. Caton held his hands out to fend her off.

'Not yet, Ems,' he said. 'You know the rule: Daddy has to shower and change before hugs and cuddles.'

Closing his ears to her protestations, he slipped into the downstairs loo, and closed the door.

* * *

Caton stared down at his daughter as she slept the sleep of the innocent. Her hair fanned like a halo around her head, and her lips moved soundlessly as she sucked on her thumb.

He had delivered the promised hug-fest and started to read her a story, in the middle of which she had fallen asleep. Tucking her in, he had sworn, as he did after every investigation, that he would shield her from everything that was nasty and cruel in this world, and watch out for her for as long as he lived. He gave her one last kiss and closed the door.

Kate was waiting at the bottom of the stairs, sitting on the second step. He sat down beside her.

'You did it then, Tom?' she said. 'It's just been on the news.'

'*We* did it,' he replied, 'and your profile was spot-on.'

'I knew I should have charged you,' she grinned. 'It's not too late though, is it?'

'There is one thing I don't understand?' he said. 'How can someone who visited his grandmother every day in her care home go ahead and kill all those women, any one of whom could have been his grandmother?'

'It's a fallacy,' she said, 'that serial killers don't possess emotion. You do know that, don't you?'

'Even so . . .'

'Well, they do,' she said, interrupting him, 'but they're wholly selfish. These are the emotions that drive them to kill – ones arising from the need for sexual release, control over others and over their own lives, hatred and revenge, along with often misplaced feelings of personal injustice. In the case of this Nathan Germaine, feeling a selfish loss himself is not the same as feeling empathy or remorse for his victims. He can empathise at a cognitive level with his victims and their families, but not at an emotional or compassionate level. Put simply, he understands their pain, he just doesn't care.'

'I see that,' Caton said.

'Then why are you looking so miserable?'

'Because four women are dead. Because we should have found him sooner. Those books were staring me in the face and I didn't see it.'

'What books?'

'I'll explain later,' he said.

'Even if you had? How many deaths would you have actually prevented?'

He thought about it. 'Maybe the last one. Patti Dean. It would all have depended on when she received the pills that killed her, and if he'd have told us about her.'

'He wouldn't have,' she said. 'Like he didn't about

the one in Barlow Moor. Besides, you're forgetting all the other women he'd have gone on to kill if you hadn't tracked him down so fast. Do you have any idea how many serial killers have never been caught? Some of them with hundreds of known victims, and God knows how many more undiscovered?'

She gave him a hug. 'Don't be so hard on yourself, Tom. That way madness lies. I'm proud of you and you should be proud of yourself. Let it go.'

She kissed him on the cheek, and stood up. 'Your son has stayed up in the hope of a catch-up on Zoom. You'd better do it now, before he goes to bed. He's worried that his beloved Wigan are going to fall out of the football league.'

Caton stood up and headed for the hall.

'Try to keep it brief,' she called after him. 'Dinner's in the oven. I ordered a meal from Côte at Home.'

'Poulet Breton?'

'Of course.'

He stopped and turned. 'Doesn't that come with the chocolate mousse?'

She grinned. 'I persuaded them to substitute the crème caramel. You've got ten minutes.'

Caton smiled to himself as he opened the door to the study. Sometimes it was the little things that mattered most in life.

Especially in the middle of a pandemic.

Afterword

The first lockdown was announced on 28 February 2020, just as I was about to begin writing *The Opportunist*. In common with many writers, I found it a struggle to work creatively with all that was going on, but at times it proved a welcome distraction. I completed it on 28 September 2020. Here in Greater Manchester, we were still in full lockdown.

Because all of my novels are written in real time, it was inevitable that Caton and his team, and I as their puppet master, would have the unique challenge of having to carry out an investigation in the middle of a pandemic, with all that that entailed. One of the by-products of writing novels in this way is that in terms of the setting and the context, they stand as a form of historical record.

For that reason, I have decided to include below a poem that I felt impelled to write in the early days of the first lockdown, when those of us of a certain age were told that we had to isolate ourselves and shield others, simply because we were 'old'. My wife and I, and our friends, discovered that this simple statement had irrevocably changed the way we thought about ourselves. For someone who was told twelve years ago that I was too old to stand a chance of becoming a published author, there was also a strong sense of déja vu. But I'm through it now, and back to believing that I'm really thirty and have another fifty books in me.

We'll see . . .

When They Told Us We Were Old
Reflections on Covid-19, May 2020

They called us 'lucky'
'The Lucky Few
Between the Greatest Generation
And the Baby Boom'
The Silent Generation
Emerging from the shelters
And the aftermath of war
To a world of smog and rationing
And atom bombs for sure

Heads down we soldiered on
Rebuilding from the rubble
We took no risks
We played it safe
We saved and scrimped
And kept our peace
And we *were* lucky
In so many ways

Free orange juice, cod liver oil
A council house
And jobs for all
The Welfare State
To keep us safe
Tripartite schools
In which to learn
The facts and gain the skills
With which to thrive at such a pace
But also learn . . .
To know our place

We conquered mumps and whooping cough
Measles, not once but twice
Chicken pox and polio
And none of them were nice
We saw off Asian Flu in '58
When a million people died
And Hong Flu in '68
That took four million more beside

We married young
Amidst the rise
Of Flower Power
And Rock and Roll
And wished our kids
A better life
With peace, prosperity
And health their goal

We bought our council houses
Though we weren't sure that was right
And we took the kids on holiday
While money was still tight
In tents and caravans
At home and then abroad
We watched them grow and learn to fly
And smiled when they soared

And then when we retired
With our pensions all secure
Our health intact, our homes, new wealth
Our lives some way to go
We told ourselves that we *were* lucky
And we were really young
That 60 felt like 40

70 little more
That 80 was just a number
We'd keep going
That's for sure . . .

Then came coronavirus
And it made our blood run cold
Not because we were a target
But when they told us
We were old

It didn't help that Number 10
Had got it in their heads
That we were all expendable
Or so the papers said
They'd wait for herd immunity
To sort the wheat out from the chaff
Save jobs and public spending
And it wouldn't be much faff

Then sanity prevailed
And we were all reprieved
They said we'd lockdown early
But be the last to leave
There'd be no Barnard Castle trips
Or outings to the sea
The rest would have to shield us
While we stayed in and watched TV

Well, we've managed
Cos we've been through worse
When there was no such thing as toilet paper
And you cleared ice from the windows
With a wooden scraper

When your hankie was a mask you wore
To go out in the smog
Television was a luxury
And instead you had a dog

We've played it safe
We took no risks
And we know that if we're lucky
We'll all come out of this unscathed
And tell ourselves we're plucky
So to paraphrase the words
We all heard Sir Tom Moore say
Tomorrow without doubt
Will be a better day

But . . . we won't forget coronavirus
That it made our blood run cold
Not because we were a target
But when they told us
We were old

About the Author

Photo: Paul Whur, 2015

Bill Rogers has written sixteen crime novels to date, all of them based in and around the City of Manchester. Twelve feature DCI Tom Caton and his team, set in and around Manchester, while four novels in a spin-off series feature SI Joanne Stuart on secondment to the Behavioural Sciences Unit at the National Crime Agency, located in Salford Quays. Formerly a teacher, schools inspector, and Head of the Manchester Schools Improvement Service, Bill worked for the National College for School Leadership before retiring to begin his writing career. Born in London, Bill has four generations of Metropolitan Police behind him. He is married with two adult children, and lives close to the City of Manchester.

For more information, and to contact Bill, visit his Amazon Author page, or send him an email:

Email: billrogers@billrogers.co.uk.
Author Page: amazon.co.uk/-/e/B0034NWVC0

Acknowledgements

It is an understatement to say that this has been a strange year in which to write a novel. In some ways doing so has provided a distraction for me. I am therefore more conscious than ever of the debt that I owe to my wife, Joan, for her support, wisdom, and encouragement.

As ever, I also owe a huge debt to my copy-editor, Monica Byles, who, as always, has gone that extra mile to ensure that *The Opportunist* is the best that it could possibly be - given what I gave her to work with.

I would also like to acknowledge Suzie Tatnell, at commercialcampaigns.co.uk, for whom this was the fifteenth book that she has typeset for me.

Joseph Mills, at blacksheep-uk.com, for the stunning array of custom covers that he sent me, and the speed and professionalism with which they were produced.

And, finally, my thanks to Brian and Mariella Wilde, of J&B Wilde Fish merchants, for their advice and permission for me to include them in what is otherwise a completely fictional account.

Stay safe everyone!

Bill

Lightning Source UK Ltd.
Milton Keynes UK
UKHW041445161222
414042UK00004B/314